D1005774

EAGLE VALLEY LIBRARY DISTRICT
06 0004998248

The Long Hitch

OTHER FIVE STAR WESTERN TITLES BY MICHAEL ZIMMER:

Johnny Montana (2010)
Wild Side of the River (2011)

The Long Hitch

A Western Story

Michael Zimmer

FIVE STAR
A part of Gale, Cengage Learning

Detroit • New York • San Francisco • New Haven, Conn • Waterville, Maine • London

Five Star Publishing, a part of Gale, Cengage Learning.

Set in 11 pt. Plantin.

LIBRARY OF CONGRESS CATALOGING-IN-PUBLICATION DATA

Zimmer, Michael.
The long hitch : a western story / by Michael Zimmer. — 1st ed.
p. cm.
ISBN-13: 978-1-4328-2524-9 (hardcover)
ISBN-10: 1-4328-2524-0 (hardcover)
1. Murder—Investigation—Fiction. I. Title.
PS3576.I467L66 2011
813′.54—dc22 2011013162

First Edition. First Printing: July 2011.
Published in 2011 in conjunction with Golden West Literary Agency.

Printed in the United States of America
1 2 3 4 5 6 7 15 14 13 12 11

For Betty Lou, who would have made a
fine muleskinner in her own right.

PROLOGUE

The dog looked half starved and possibly rabid as it padded around the outside corner of the deserted Central Pacific depot. Thinking at first that it was a wolf, Arlen Fleck slammed back into the shadowy alcove where he'd been nervously lurking for the last hour. The yelp came from Arlen, not the dog, but the dog jumped too, its lips peeling back in a snarl, hackles rising. Slipping a hand inside his green plaid jacket, Arlen wrapped his fingers around the grips of a rusty Manhattan revolver tucked into the waistband of his trousers. With his shoulders pressed solidly against the V-ed plank walls of the depot, he knew flight would be impossible if the dog decided to attack. His only recourse would be the revolver. He only wished that he'd taken time before the sun went down to check the caps on the Manhattan's chambers. The gun was old, its nipples misshapen from wear and abuse, and its percussion caps had a tendency to fall off if they weren't seated properly.

"Nice dog," Arlen mumbled. He figured Nick Kelso would have his scalp if he drew attention to himself by shooting a dog, but the husky mongrel scared him. Truth was, just about everything he was up to tonight was making his blood run cold, and he'd been ruing his involvement with the flint-eyed killer—Kelso—when the dog showed up.

It hadn't been more than a few hours ago that Arlen had drawn a sleeve across his sweaty brow and thought longingly of cold beers, shady parks, and going home. He had no stake in this affair save for the $50 Nick had promised him, and that was starting to seem like poor compensation for what was about to happen. A man was going to die tonight, and, in his own small way, Arlen was going to help kill him. That should've been worth a lot more than $50.

If Arlen had been hot that afternoon, he was damned near freezing now. His nose was dripping steadily and his toes ached inside his cheap, thin-soled shoes. The icy wind that blew in off the vast Western desert was pungent with the odors of greasewood and alkali, tinged with the briny scent of the Great Salt Lake, which lay to the south like a slumbering giant.

It was that largeness, that empty desolation of land and water and sky that surrounded him, threatened to swallow him, that Arlen blamed for the sense of foreboding clung to him like a bad smell. He was a city boy at heart, more at home within the cobblestoned cañons of a thriving metropolis than he was out here. Fate had brought him West. Well, fate and a $100 bounty for his head that still circulated through the back alleys and gambling dens of the Eastern seaboard.

Ironically his future wasn't going to be any brighter out here if he failed to do his part tonight. One man was already going to die. He doubted if Kelso would have much compunction about killing another.

And now, as if his life weren't complicated enough, this yellow-fanged menace had stepped into his life. Arlen was afraid to pull his pistol for fear of setting off the tick-infested beast. Besides, if he did haul it out and it wasn't capped, and the hulking creature did attack. . . .

Arlen shivered, maybe from the chilling breeze, maybe not. With as much authority as he could muster, he ordered the dog: "Git!"

A growl rumbled low in the canine's chest; saliva hung in glistening threads from its exposed teeth. Arlen glanced across the street at the International Saloon, but the crowd of revelers that had swarmed its boardwalk earlier had gone inside at sundown. He was alone, save for the dog.

"Damn' cur," Arlen muttered, returning his eyes to the unblinking stare of this newest nemesis. Nick's instructions had been blunt but clear. Arlen was to wait here for a hard-headed wagon boss named Mason Campbell to tire of his carousing and head for home. When Campbell exited the International and started down the street toward the boarding house where he kept a room, Arlen was going to walk out into the open and, in the light of a quarter moon and whatever lamp shine drifted his way from the saloon, take off his hat and slap it hard against his leg, as if beating dust from the porkpie's cheap felt.

That was the signal Nick waited for. When he saw it, he would abandon his post in the second-story corner room of the Promontory Hotel and hurry down the back stairs to intercept Campbell on the boardwalk. After that, Arlen wanted no part of whatever happened. The trouble was, right now he wasn't going anywhere. Not with this drooling monster standing in front of him.

Arlen's eyes suddenly widened. Across the street, Mason Campbell was standing on the boardwalk in front of the International, the batwing doors behind him swinging in ever decreasing arcs. Campbell glanced casually up and down the street, then turned in the direction of the boarding house. His stride was even, his carriage erect, and Arlen felt a moment's admiration for the man's ability to handle liquor. He'd been inside the International earlier and watched Campbell down three straight whiskeys in a row, before settling in on a poker game with a fourth drink in hand, an uncorked bottle at his elbow. That much booze would've put Arlen in a blind stagger.

Arlen felt a sinking sensation in the pit of his stomach. Keeping his eyes on the stiff-necked mongrel, he attempted a sideways escape that the dog's lowering head brought to a sharp halt. Across the street, Campbell had already passed out of the lamplight from the International's big front windows. Arlen knew he had to do something quickly. The dog might bite. Nick Kelso surely would if Campbell escaped his ambush.

Sliding his right foot forward a couple of tentative inches brought a deep, intimidating rumble from the dog's chest. Arlen's pulse loped madly, but his fear of Nick was proving to be greater than his fear of the dog, and he grimly edged forward another experimental step. Surprising him, the dog gave up an equal amount of the Central Pacific's deck. Risking a third miniature stride, Arlen's hopes began to rise. The dog backed off several paces, its head lowering more in a skulk than a threat. A sickly grin toyed with the muscles of Arlen's cheeks, then quickly disappeared when he realized Campbell was no longer in sight. Panicking, Arlen whipped off his hat and swung it in the dog's face. The brute snapped at the ratty porkpie but jumped back enough for Arlen to dodge past. He raced into the street, too desperate to consider the possibility of a rear attack.

Skidding to a halt in the middle of the broad thoroughfare, Arlen heaved a loud sigh. Campbell had paused near the mouth of the alley beside the International. Arlen started to lift his hat to signal Nick, then stopped with his arm half raised when a tall, lean stranger emerged from the alley. Glancing at the hotel's corner window, where he knew Nick was watching, Arlen contemplated his next move. Nick's plan depended on timing, and with Campbell stopped, Arlen was afraid to send the gunman scurrying down the back stairs too soon. Yet lingering on the street too long only invited unwanted attention.

Campbell had stiffened at the stranger's approach, but now he seemed to relax. He reached inside a pocket, and a moment later a match flared in his cupped hands. The stranger leaned forward and the match ebbed down to almost nothing as the stranger drew on a stubby cigarette. Then both men straightened and Campbell tossed the spent match into the street. For a moment, Arlen wasn't sure where the muffled report of a gunshot came from. Then Campbell stumbled backward, the front of his coat flaming yellow from a muzzle flash at close range. The stranger ducked into the alley as if he'd never existed even as Campbell crumbled to the ground.

Arlen stood numbly in the middle of the street with his hat half raised until it occurred to him to get the hell out of there. Get away before someone came outside to investigate, or before the law showed up. Or worse, before Nick Kelso learned that his plan had been ruined by a stranger's unexpected appearance and he started looking around for someone to blame. . . .

Chapter One

Corinne, Utah Territory
1874

Ashes to ashes. Dust to dust. It didn't seem like much, Buck McCready thought as he lifted his eyes from the cold, damp walls of the grave to stare across the alkali flats to the south. The sum of a man like Mason Campbell ought to have amounted to more than ashes and dust and a small granite marker, not yet ordered. More than six feet of poor soil waiting to be stomped down on top of a plain pine casket, too, although Buck knew Mase had never wanted anything more than what he had—his job, the respect of the men he worked with, a reputation few would ever equal. Mase would've been satisfied with the hastily arranged funeral, but Buck wasn't.

He was aware of the others watching him, waiting. The minister, a pudgy, dough-cheeked man dressed in black, stood at the head of the grave. He carried a leather-bound Bible clasped in both arms but had recited the service from memory, occasionally inserting little tidbits of information from Mase's past that he must have culled from others, Mase never having been the kind to seek out the company of men of the cloth.

To Buck, the minister's words had seemed coldly insipid—an easy $5 in the pocket rather than any genuine concern for a man's soul—although Buck knew that would have humored Mase, too. Far more comforting had been the presence of Dulce

Kavanaugh, standing firmly at his side. The clean scent of her soap and the gentle touch of her hair, lifted on the gusting breeze, had been a needed reassurance to Buck that he still had a place in this world. That he still belonged.

At Dulce's other shoulder stood her father, who was also Buck's employer, Jock Kavanaugh. Jock had been fidgeting quietly throughout the service, and Buck figured he was hurting badly. Jock's hip had been crushed last fall when a wagon jack collapsed, pinning him between a heavy freight wagon and the wall of his repair shop. He could remain on his feet for only so long before the pain became unbearable.

"Mister McCready," the minister said quietly.

"Buck." Dulce gave his hand a squeeze.

Reluctantly he pulled his gaze away from the distant horizon. Staring at the plain pine casket, he noticed for the first time the amber bead of sap that oozed like a single tear from the corner of a small knot in the coffin's side. The minister was watching him expectantly. So were the fifty or so other men and women who had accompanied the funeral procession from Corinne to pay their final respects. Dulce slipped her fingers from his and Buck stooped to pick up a handful of dirt that he crumbled over the foot of the coffin, careful to avoid the neatly coiled bullwhip that lay centered on top of the flat lid. Then he walked swiftly away, only peripherally aware of Dulce hurrying to catch up.

Away from the crowd, Buck unbuttoned his suit coat and loosened his tie. The air that had felt so smothering beside the grave seemed fresher here, easier to draw into his lungs. Stopping beside Jock's polished black carriage, he reached for Dulce's elbow to help her inside, but she pulled back with a puzzled expression, and, when Jock limped up, Buck lowered his hand.

"Buck, I'd like for you to ride back to Corinne with Dulce

and me," Jock said quietly.

"I'd like that, too," Dulce quickly added.

Buck hesitated. He'd intended to ride back with the crew in the company mud wagon, but supposed that was no longer an option. "Sure, if there's room," he said.

"There'll be room," Jock replied brusquely. He glanced at the dispersing crowd, where a pair of middle-aged men in dark suits and black, narrow-brimmed Homburgs were trying to break away, and motioned for them to hurry.

Buck eyed the two men as they made their graveside farewells. The shorter of the pair was Hank Miller, Jock's yard master. Hank was in charge of the day-to-day operations that kept Kavanaugh Freight, known in the mountains as the Box K—its trademark being a bright green K butted up hard against a square of the same color—running efficiently.

The second man, taller, slimmer, bespectacled, was Walt Jepson, the Box K's chief accountant. Although their presence at Mase's funeral wasn't unexpected, Buck detected something more in their guarded expressions as they approached the carriage. A Box K caravan had been scheduled to pull out in two days for the gold fields of Montana. Mase was to be its captain, Buck its ramrod, and Jock would expect that train to leave on schedule, whether hell froze over or heaven burned.

"Buck," Dulce murmured, stretching her leg for the carriage's iron step. He quickly took her arm and helped her in. Leaning close as she arranged her skirts around her ankles, she whispered: "You'll still come to supper tonight, won't you?"

He delayed only briefly. "Wild horses couldn't keep me away."

Dulce smiled and touched his hand, then settled back against the gleaming leather upholstery.

Arriving together, Hank and Walt shook Buck's hand, Jepson adding: "I'm sure sorry, Buck. I know you and Mase were close."

"He was a good friend," Buck acknowledged calmly, but he

seethed inside at the inadequateness of his words. Yet how much could a man say? Could he remind Walt that Mase had risked his neck to rescue a frightened ten-year-old from the Sioux, then fed and clothed and taught that boy everything he knew, treated him like a son when he had no reason to, when it would have been easier to send him East to an orphanage? Was that the response he was supposed to give, without choking up or sounding like an idiot?

"Buck," Jock said gently.

He looked up, swallowing hard.

"Ready?"

"Sure," Buck croaked, climbing in after Hank and Walt and seating himself next to Dulce. Jock hauled himself into the driver's seat and shook out the lines to his team of matching sorrels. Although Buck didn't look back, he knew the boys would be watching, wondering what was going to happen next. No doubt a lot of townspeople were asking themselves the same question. With Mason Campbell dead, what would Buck McCready do now? He didn't have much of an answer for them, but he did have a vow, made two nights before at the head of a littered alley beside the International Saloon.

I'm going to find your killer, Mase. I'm going to find him and bring him to justice. Either that or bury the son-of-a-bitch.

Buck expected Jock to take them past his home first, to drop off Dulce. Instead, he skirted their Cove Street residence by several blocks to reach the Box K's office on Montana Street.

It was late morning in late April, and with the mountain passes to the north just coming open, traffic was congested along Corinne's two main arteries, Front and Montana Streets. Bull trains and jerkline outfits clogged the broad thoroughfares, and pack strings of up to a hundred head of horses or mules wound sinuously through the stalled vehicles, bound for the more remote regions where roads had yet to be built. Smaller farm and delivery wagons, buckboards, and men on horseback competed for what space remained.

Jock avoided the traffic by looping expertly through the town's back streets and alleys, swinging onto Montana less than half a block from the Kavanaugh Freight office. He stopped on the street out front, rather than driving around back as he normally did. Buck helped Dulce to the ground while Hank and Walt exited on the far side, then the little troop mounted the steps to the boardwalk to wait for Jock.

Standing slightly apart from the others, Buck caught a glimpse of his reflection in the freight-office window. It always gave him a start to see himself among others, to realize how he stacked up, as Mase used to say. He was taller by several inches than either Walt or Hank, slimmer through the waist but broader in the chest and shoulders; years of hard work in freight yards across the West had done that. He was wearing a new suit of blue serge for the funeral, with a red tie and a new, medium-brimmed hat. He'd kept his dark brown hair long enough to cover his collar in back, the way he figured a man of the mountains and plains was meant to wear it, but had slicked it down with tonic water that morning. His face was lean and tan, his eyes gray. He was twenty-four, but feeling quite a bit older today.

The image at his side was easier to look at. Dulce Kavanaugh stood just a shade over five feet tall, although with her thick, coppery hair piled high, she looked, in silhouette, about the same height as Walt. She had an oval face that was fair of complexion and freckles on her nose and cheeks. Her eyes were the exact same shade of green as an emerald Buck had once seen in a Denver jewelry shop, right down to the sparkle when she laughed, and her heavy black dress did little to hide the full, compact figure beneath it.

Jock claimed Dulce took after her mother, who had passed away several years ago, leaving Dulce an only child.

After securing his horses to a street-side post, Jock climbed the steps in his gimping hitch and they all went inside. They walked single file through the big front room where clerks labored over invoices and order forms, and into his private office in back. With the door firmly latched behind them, the mood seemed to change abruptly.

Buck moved to a window overlooking the wagon yard and leaned against the sill, folding his arms almost defiantly across his chest. Hank and Walt staked their claims to a pair of ladder-back chairs in front of Jock's desk, and Dulce headed for the sideboard where her father was pouring drinks from a decanter of bourbon. "I'll do that," she said, stepping between him and an engraved silver tray filled with matching shot glasses.

Jock acquiesced without argument and limped over to the cushioned chair behind his desk. He looked tired, and Buck knew from Dulce that his injured hip had been paining him more than usual recently. Dulce passed out the drinks, and no one looked surprised when she included one for herself.

"Gentlemen, Dulce," Jock said solemnly. "I won't stand, but I will offer a toast." He lifted his glass. "To Mason Campbell, one of the best wagon masters to ever captain a train."

"Here, here," Hank and Walt echoed in unison. Dulce glanced at Buck, but he kept his eyes averted. After an obligatory sip, he set his drink on the sill beside him. Looking up, he met Jock's gaze across the room.

"I knew Mase a good many years," Jock said, his voice roughened by either the bourbon or emotion. "He thought highly of you, Buck."

"I felt the same way about him," Buck replied, but he was thinking: *Uhn-uh, let's not do this. Let's just get on with why I'm here.*

Jock nodded as if reading his thoughts and set his glass on the desk. "What are your plans?" he asked the younger man.

"I intend to find Mase's killer."

"The law is attempting to do that even as we speak," Walt reminded him.

"The law around here is a fat-bellied old fart who couldn't find an egg in a hen house," Buck shot back.

Jock's brows twitched in surprise. "I wouldn't be too quick to dismiss Sam Dunbar," he said, then, after a pause, added almost warily: "You realize there's more involved here than a disagreement over cards, don't you?"

Buck nodded. He knew. He just hadn't been sure anyone else did. "Tom Ashley's a liar," he stated flatly, causing both Walt and Hank to look up. Tom Ashley was one of the two bartenders who had been working at the International the night of Mase's murder, but Buck didn't believe the story he'd told Dunbar, especially the part about Mase showing up drunk and looking for trouble.

"How much did Mase tell you about our next run to Montana?" Jock asked tentatively.

"He told me about a cargo you'd have to get through in a hurry, once it got here, but most of Corinne knows that much."

Jock smiled. "You're probably right. Nevertheless, I'd asked Mase to keep the details under his hat, and it sounds as if he did."

"What are you driving at, Mister Kavanaugh?"

"I'm attempting to explain a deal that I've been working on since last summer, but I'm not sure where to start. Let me tell you the whole story, so you'll understand why I'm going to ask you to give up your search for Mase's killer. . . ." He quickly held up a hand to stave off Buck's objection. "Hear me out. Maybe I can shed some light on this for you."

Buck leaned back against the sill and refolded his arms, his muscles thrumming like telegraph wires.

Jock sighed, as if sensing an uphill battle. "Bannock Mining Corporation is a subsidiary of a larger combine out of Philadelphia," he began. "I'm told it has interests around the world . . . mining in Africa and Brazil, sugar in the Caribbean, tea and silk from the Orient. Nothing of any real consequence to us, other than that it underscores how, even though the Bannock company itself is relatively small, it has powerful backing.

"BMC has committed itself to building a stamp mill near Virginia City, and they've hired the Box K to transport part of their machinery north from Corinne. We've hauled for BMC before and never had any complaints, but there's a catch this time. Several, in fact. There's also a carrot at the end of the stick. BMC wants to affiliate itself with a reputable freighting firm, and the outfit that meets their demands will be awarded an exclusive three-year contract to handle all of their mountain freight, with an option for renewal at the end of that time."

Buck remained silent, but he knew what a deal like that could mean to the Box K.

"It could wipe away every debt I have," Jock said. "It could solidify the Box K for years to come and double its size. And it goes without saying that it would also benefit several key employees in this firm. I'll make no bones about it, gentlemen, I want that contract. Unfortunately, so do others, and they may be wanting it more than I'd anticipated, if Mase's death is connected to it in the way I think it might be."

Buck stiffened. "Are you saying another outfit killed Mase for the Bannock contract?"

"I'm not saying anything," Jock replied evenly. "I have no proof, just a gut feeling that I've learned to trust over the years." After a pause, he added: "I want Mase's killer as much as you do, but I won't let my desire for revenge cloud my judgment or threaten the future of this company."

"I'm still listening," Buck replied tautly.

"Good. I mentioned several catches, but the largest by far is that we'll be competing for this contract with another firm."

"Crowley and Luce," Walt Jepson supplied, his scowl clearly expressing his opinion of the company and its founders. He glanced at Jock as if for permission to elaborate, then went on at his employer's nod. "Bannock Mining, like most Eastern companies with interests in southwestern Montana, is being deluged with false information from the Utah Northern about its new terminus in Franklin."

He meant the Utah Northern Railroad and the town of Franklin, in southeast Idaho Territory, Buck knew. The Utah Northern had finished laying track that far just last fall, and was attempting to lure freighters and businesses alike away from Corinne by emphasizing its more northerly location.

"What Crowley and Luce's agents in Philadelphia aren't saying is that the Utah Northern is a narrow-gauge railroad," Hank Miller contributed. "It has to be if it's going to negotiate the narrow cañons and mountain passes they claim they eventually will."

"But a narrow-gauge track can't handle the larger boxcars of the Union Pacific and Central Pacific lines," Walt continued. "That means cargo shipped through Franklin has to be off-loaded at the Utah Northern's depot in Ogden, then reloaded onto narrow-gauge cars before they can even begin their journey to Franklin. That's additional handling, which translates into additional charges, plus two more days in transit for most orders." He sniffed self-righteously. "Any sane man can see that such a delay completely negates Franklin's advantage in location."

"Not to mention that road north of Franklin." Hank said. "That Marsh Valley route will bury a freighter in wet weather. Some years, it's almost June before it's dry enough to support heavy traffic."

"I'm sure Buck is already aware of Franklin's drawbacks and advantages," Jock interrupted, "and the Marsh Valley route can be overcome with the right financial backing. The question BMC has to be asking itself is whether that more northerly location will compensate for the loss of time in switching their shipments onto narrow-gauge cars. In my opinion, it won't, but that's something only a season of freighting will tell us for sure."

He looked at Buck. "On the other hand, we could have an idea of what that answer might be within the next few weeks, depending on how well the Box K performs." After a pause: "Mase was supposed to captain that train."

"I know."

"I was counting on him to get it through ahead of Crowley and Luce."

"They're shipping at the same time?"

Jock nodded. "I mentioned that we're carrying only part of the components BMC will need for its mill. C and L will handle the rest . . . a similar shipment of nearly equal tonnage . . . and I've been assured, as fair a split of the larger pieces as the Bannock Corporation could manage. Everything is to come west on the same train, and the clock will start ticking for both companies as soon as the U.P.'s locomotive crosses the Utah line." He grimaced. "A race between the Box K and C and L, but not, as I said, without catches."

"There's more?"

"A few. Rules of the contest, so to speak. In an attempt to evaluate each firm fairly, neither party will be allowed to take any unusual advantages. That means no double teaming, no driving an extra remuda along to switch teams along the way, no extra wagons to lighten loads, no additional hands. In addition, we'll be required to fulfill any outstanding contracts at the same time. That means, day after tomorrow, thirteen outfits totaling twenty-six wagons will roll north for Montana. Eight of those wagons will be hauling BMC's equipment. The other eighteen will carry merchandise already contracted for from our usual customers in Virginia City. I don't have twenty-six wagons in Corinne right now, but since I've hired independents in the past, BMC has given me the go-ahead to do so again. But in order to assure compliance with the rest of their rules, they're sending a representative along with each train . . . one with us, one with Crowley and Luce."

Buck frowned. "With how much authority?"

"Absolutely none," Jock returned bluntly. "As much as I want this contract, I won't jeopardize either my reputation or the company's by assigning jurisdiction to anyone outside of the firm. Whoever they send will come along strictly as an observer."

Buck nodded. He understood Jock's position and respected it, but there was another matter they had yet to discuss. "Why are you telling me this, Mister Kavanaugh?"

"I suspect you already know the answer to that. I trusted Mase implicitly. He and I spoke on more than one occasion about you someday captaining a Box K train, when the business grew large enough to support three caravans. He was convinced you were up to the task and I agreed."

Buck looked away, staring out the wavy glass panes in the rear door to the wagon yard. Right now, Kavanaugh Freight kept two mule trains on the road throughout the freighting season. The second unit was commanded by Lew Walker, an old Santa Fe Trail wagon boss who had worked with both Jock and Mase on the plains, before following Jock over the mountains to Utah. Lew was on his way to Montana with an outfit now and, barring bad weather or some other calamity, should be somewhere along the Snake River in Idaho Territory.

"There's no one else who can do it, Buck," Jock said quietly. "Drivers can be found, but a competent wagon boss, someone who knows the road, who's been over it as many times as you have, *who I trust,* that would be impossible to find on such short notice. Plus, you've got a history with the company. You know the drivers, and they know and respect you. You've been up and down that trail with the majority of them the last four years."

"They'll follow you, Buck," Hank added confidently. "I've already talked to some of them and they all agreed, no hesitation."

"I can't do it," Jock said, without having to remind them of his maimed hip, "and Hank and Walt don't have the trail experience. If you don't do it, I'm afraid Crowley and Luce will win this race, and I'd hate to see that happen."

"I appreciate the offer, Mister Kavanaugh, and that you think I'm capable of the job, but you haven't said yet why I should ignore Mase's killer."

"Buck, right now we don't have a clue who his killer is. What did Ashley say? That Mase got into an argument with a big man with long, greasy hair? That describes a hundred men walking Corinne's streets right now, and there's no guarantee that even if we did find him, that he was the one who pulled the trigger. It could have been anyone. I will say this. I'm don't know if Crowley and Luce are behind Mase's death, but I think they're capable of it. For the kind of money we're talking about, I think they could hire a man to pull the trigger."

Buck remained silent, contemplating Jock's offer as well the possibility that Herb Crowley and Anton Luce might be involved in murder. The ticking of the wall clock above Jock's desk seemed to grow abnormally loud.

After a while, Jock steepled his fingers above his watch fob. "I've said all I'm going to, Buck. Think about it, and if you want the job. . . ."

"I'll do it."

Jock blinked rapidly, taken aback by the swiftness of Buck's decision. Walt and Hank exchanged elated glances. But there was no joy in Buck's expression, no pride of promotion, just the same grim determination to see his promise to Mase fulfilled.

"If you're right about Crowley and Luce, then maybe the reason Mase's killer hasn't been found is that he's already somewhere up the trail, waiting for us. If that's the case and it starts looking like the Box K might beat C and L, maybe that'll flush him out."

A look of concern crossed Jock's face. "This train isn't bait, Buck. Our future depends on you getting it through to Montana in one piece, ahead of the competition."

"That's what I intend to do," Buck said, but, even as he uttered the words, he was thinking that, whether Jock wanted it or not, the Box K could very well turn out to be bait for a killer, or any number of killers. And with nearly half a mile of mules and wagons stretched out along the road, it would be a hard target to miss.

Chapter Two

The sudden whirring of pigeons in the rafters brought Nick Kelso surging to his feet. Wrapping his fingers around the walnut grips of his revolver, he moved cautiously to the front of the stall. After waiting in the abandoned Ogden livery for more than an hour, his attention had started to wander; it came snapping back now keen as a razor.

In the vertical bars of twilight that slanted between the boards of the livery's front wall, he could see a cloud of barn dust littered with small, downy feathers floating toward the floor. The birds were little more than chunky silhouettes, cooing nervously as they treaded the rafter closest to the front wall. Nick couldn't tell what had disturbed them. It could have been a snake or a rat or. . . .

There was a sharp, metallic *pop* as the iron latch on the front door was knocked free of its rusty catch. With a drawn-out creak, the door swung open. Nick's fingers tightened on his revolver. At first he couldn't make out anything, but, as the figure moved closer, he caught the distinctive odor of licorice, and recalled it from his last meeting with this man—the little chunks of black candy kept in a paper bag in his coat pocket, his teeth stained as if from rot.

"That's far enough!" Nick barked, stepping into the center aisle.

"Sacre bleu!" the man with the licorice exclaimed. "Nicholas, that is you?"

"Did you bring the gold?"

"Yes . . . two hundred dollars."

"In coin?"

"*Oui,* in coin." The stocky, well-dressed Frenchman pulled a leather poke from his coat pocket and held it away from his body so that Nick could see it.

"Put it on the floor, then back away," Nick instructed.

"You do not trust me?"

"Do what you're told, LeBry."

Baptiste LeBry opened his fingers and the poke dropped heavily, striking the hard-packed dirt floor with a dull ching. "Three hundred dollars you have now been paid. Our deal is completed, no?"

Nick didn't even try to suppress the grin that warped the lower portion of his face. What did he care who'd actually killed Mason Campbell, as long as the wagon master was dead and Nick Kelso was the one paid for it? "Yep, our dealing's done. Now back away."

He waited until LeBry had moved off about ten paces, then went forward to pick up the sack of coins. He hefted it in his left hand a few times, as if gauging its weight, then cast LeBry a suspicious glance. "You ain't holding out on me, are you, Frenchy?"

"*Non, monsieur,* it is there. All of it."

"It'd better be."

"There could be more." LeBry spoke in the manner of a parent, encouraging a child to finish his spinach with the promise of rock candy afterward. "You are interested?"

Nick hesitated, wary of a double-cross. Had he underestimated this stubby Frenchman with the oily smile? No, he decided, LeBry couldn't know what had happened that night in Corinne. Only Arlen Fleck and the whore, Sally Hayes, knew what actually occurred at the alley's mouth, and they wouldn't talk. Slipping the coins into his pocket, he said: "Who do you want killed?"

"*Sacre,* no one! We did not want Campbell killed."

"You wanted him stopped," Nick said harshly. "Well, he's stopped. Don't go hollering innocent now."

"Stopped, *oui,* but not murdered. Too much killing makes men nervous, Nicholas. They wonder why. The law wonders. Eastern investors wonder. Even my own people ask why."

"That's your problem, LeBry, not mine."

"*Non,* Nicholas, it becomes our problem. The law, especially, becomes our problem. Too curious, the law."

"I've got my own way of doing things. Think about that before you make any new offers." Nick chuckled at the cornered look on the Frenchman's face. "Why don't you tell me what you want done, LeBry, then we'll figure out how much damage it's going to do that fat wallet of yours."

Sighing, Baptiste said: "There is to be a train of wagons, a caravan, to Montana."

"Kavanaugh's outfit?"

"*Oui,* the Box K. It must not reach its destination before, shall we say, certain other parties arrive."

"You mean Crowley and Luce?"

LeBry nodded. "You can arrange this?"

"I can arrange just about anything you want arranged, providing you've got the cash to back it up."

"I have been authorized to pay you one thousand dollars to see that the Box K does not reach Montana before C and L."

Nick had to struggle to keep his surprise from showing. $1,000 was twice what he'd intended to charge. "How do you want it done?" he asked.

"The details I leave to you. The Box K must be slowed, but not obviously so. If anyone is to die, it must look like an accident. You understand, *monsieur?* An accident. That is most imperative."

"All right," Nick agreed, still somewhat chary of the offer.

"Then we have a deal?"

After a long pause, Nick chuckled loudly. "For a thousand dollars, LeBry, I'd wipe the Box K off the face of the Earth."

Chapter Three

They moved from the kitchen to the parlor, leaving the supper dishes to be dealt with later. Taking possession of a comfortable chair next to the fireplace, Jock gingerly lifted his aching leg onto a padded footstool. Standing in the open archway to the kitchen, Dulce said: "Your hip is worse, isn't it, Papa?"

"My hip is fine," Jock replied dismissingly.

Dulce looked at Buck. "Don't you think he's limping more?"

"I reckon I'll stay out of it," Buck said, taking a nearby chair.

"You shouldn't be worrying about your old man so much," Jock chided his daughter. "You don't need to be staying home tonight, either. Why don't you two take a walk somewhere and let me enjoy my paper in peace?"

"You mean your cigar."

Jock grinned. "Now that's a fine idea. Why don't you fetch me one so I won't have to get up?"

Shaking her head in vexation, Dulce said: "You are incorrigible. Mama used to warn me of your shenanigans, but I didn't believe her. I do now."

"I suspect my incorrigibility is one of the traits your mother liked best about me," Jock retorted.

"What she loved about you was your gentleness. I'm not sure where your impish nature fit into the picture." She placed a box of matches on the table beside his chair, then headed for the twin bedrooms at the rear of the house. "I'll bring your cigar."

Jock's expression was warm as his daughter left the room. It changed completely when he turned to Buck. "Did you see Hank this afternoon?"

"Uhn-huh. Everything's loaded except for BMC's machinery."

"That's on its way. I received a telegraph from Evanston, Wyoming, just before I left the office tonight. The train carrying BMC's equipment is scheduled to pull into Ogden around two A.M. Give them a couple of hours to switch engines and complete the paperwork with the Central Pacific, and it ought to be here by five tomorrow morning. You'll load directly off the cars at Central's siding."

"I'll be there," Buck promised. He already felt guilty about not being on hand that afternoon—cargo was the wagon master's responsibility from the moment it left the warehouse until it was off-loaded at its destination—but he'd had other obligations. He'd settled all of Mase's accounts around town that he could find, then made arrangements for a granite headstone out of Salt Lake City to be placed on the grave. It had been late by the time he finished squaring things away at the boarding house where Mase kept a room, and he hadn't been able to make it to the Box K warehouse, or to the International to talk to Tom Ashley about the events leading up to Mase's death. Sheriff Sam Dunbar was investigating the murder, but Buck still didn't trust him to see it through.

Shifting restlessly in his chair, Buck said: "Do you know what BMC is sending us?"

"The bigger pieces. There'll be eight iron stampers at a ton apiece, four boilers, a pair of hundred horsepower steam engines, and four twelve-foot sections of smokestacks."

"Smokestacks?"

"Specially designed to be hauled one inside the other, like a telescope. Hank's already built a cradle for them out of two-by-fours. We'll strap them down solid as a pack on a pinto.

Everything else should be small enough to fit inside crates. Forty-eight tons for BMC alone, more than one hundred and fifty tons all together." A smile cracked the businessman's normally stoic countenance. "This will be the biggest caravan I've ever run."

"Can't the two of you discuss anything other than business?" Dulce asked, coming into the room with a long Virginia cigar in one hand.

Jock chuckled good-naturedly. "I'm afraid the opera would be beyond the scope of either of us," he confessed, then glanced at Buck with an uplifted brow. "Unless your young friend here has been holding out on us."

Laughing and getting to his feet, Buck said: "Nope, you were right the first whack."

"There are more pertinent issues than the opera, which is deplorable in this community anyway," Dulce countered, placing her father's cigar on the table next to the matches and the latest edition of the *Corinne Reporter.* "Buck and I are going for a walk," she informed him. "We shall discuss tonnage and axle weight."

"A splendid idea," Jock replied solemnly. "Concepts any young lady should understand if she ever aspires to become a muleskinner."

"I give up," Dulce said, pulling her coat and a shawl off a peg in the adobe wall beside the front door. "Will you accompany me, Mister McCready, or shall I solicit Peewee Trapp as my escort?"

Buck wondered what the men of the Box K, especially Peewee Trapp, would say if they could see this unarmored side of their boss. Dulce had praised her father for his gentleness, but the only reference to Jock's personality Buck had ever heard from the crew was that he was a fair but hard-assed son-of-a-bitch. Buck understood that Jock's openness in his own home was a private matter, something he had been exposed to only because of Dulce's feelings for him.

He helped Dulce into her coat, then brought down the new hat he'd purchased for Mase's funeral and put it on. "We'll be back in an hour," he told Jock.

"Don't fall in the river," Jock replied absently, already reaching for his cigar.

Buck and Dulce moved to the edge of the porch, then paused as Dulce pulled on a pair of kidskin gloves. "It's chilly tonight," she said, her breath puffing visibly in the moonlight. "Will you be warm enough?"

"I'll be fine." He had on only the suit coat he'd worn to Mase's funeral that morning, not having taken time to go back to his room above Chin Lo's laundry to retrieve something warmer; the tie was in his jacket pocket.

Dulce stared at him as she worked the tight gloves down between her fingers. Speaking softly, so that her father wouldn't overhear, she said: "We could go to your place first, for a heavier coat."

Buck's pulse quickened. He knew Dulce could have volunteered one of her father's coats. Although the offer was exciting, a sense of urgency had been nagging at him all evening, and he said reluctantly: "We'd better not."

"No?" She gave him an engaging smile. "If I remember correctly, Mister McCready, a heavier coat was the song you sang the first time we visited your room."

He grinned. "That's true, but I've got other business to take care of. . . ." There was a sharp smack, and Buck's head rocked back in surprise.

"I wouldn't be so presumptuous in the future," she said coolly, stepping around him and heading for the street.

Buck hurried to catch up. "Dangit, why'd you slap me?"

Slowing down but not stopping, Dulce said: "I just don't

want you assuming too much, Buchanan. I don't want you thinking I've ever done anything like that with anyone else, or even considered it." She stopped abruptly, facing him. "Oh, Buck, I know you're grieving for Mase, yet you never even mentioned his name tonight. You're as stubborn as Papa, when he refuses to speak of Mama's passing. I swear I despise this silly society that won't allow a man to mourn openly or a woman to tread even a single step into the male world. It just makes me so angry."

Buck lowered his hand from his stinging cheek, smiling in spite of her stormy mood.

"You mock me!" she accused.

"I guess I just never thought of you as being afraid to step into a man's world. It seems like you do it pretty regularly."

"When?" Her doubt seemed genuine.

"Today, when you had a glass of bourbon with the rest of us in your dad's office, or when you ride Beau clothespin style."

Beau was Dulce's claybank dun, a gentle gelding kept in the family pasture behind the house. Although Dulce owned a side-saddle, she usually preferred a man's rig and a lady's range clothes—lace-up boots, baggy canvas trousers, and a flat-brimmed, flat-crowned Spanish hat. She only tolerated the side-saddle for more decorous occasions—the 4th of July parade or church picnics. She owned an elaborate English riding dress of black-trimmed green satin for those events, complete with heavy skirts designed to cover her ankles and a cloth hat topped with a black ostrich plume.

"I suppose you'd prefer a more proper young lady to squire about," Dulce charged. "Most men would."

"I don't believe that," Buck said, laughing. "I think that's just a rumor started by a bunch of old crones with warts on their noses."

"You!" She grabbed his chin between her thumb and

forefinger and pinched gently. "You exasperate me. Sometimes I fear you're picking up all of Papa's worst traits." Slipping her arm through his, she said: "Come along, but don't think for one minute that I don't know what you're doing."

"What am I doing?" he asked.

"Avoiding the subject."

Maybe, Buck thought, but his feelings about Mase weren't something he wanted to share. Not yet.

It wasn't far to the banks of the Bear River, on the town's east side. They stopped on top of the flat plain to watch its flowing waters. In the waxy moonlight the current looked swift and angry, fueled by the melting snows of the high country, and it made Buck wonder what the road to Montana would be like. Was the Snake River still in its banks? What about the sandy soil north of Camus Creek? Was it solid enough yet to support the heavy Murphy and Schuttler wagons he would soon be guiding over it? How deep was the snow over Monida Pass, and how quickly was it melting?

"What are you thinking?" Dulce asked. "You look so serious."

"I was wondering what it must've been like around here before the railroad came, before they built Corinne."

"The land is so flat," Dulce mused. "Papa says there aren't a dozen trees between here and the Malad Divide."

"There aren't many," Buck allowed. "Some small groves along the Bear and Malad Rivers, then junipers and scrub pine on the mountains that run along each side of the road." He started to tell her about the taller pines near the Malad Summit, but a sound from behind, like a small, metallic chink, distracted him. He turned but there was no one there, nothing to see except clumps of sage and patches of grass.

"What was that?" Dulce asked.

"Just the wind, I guess," he replied, but subtly eased a hand inside his suit coat to touch the butt of a stubby .31-caliber pocket pistol he carried concealed when he didn't want to wear his heavier Colt on his hip.

"Maybe it was a dog, pulling on its chain," Dulce suggested.

"Maybe," Buck said dubiously.

They began to walk upstream toward the Central Pacific bridge, barely visible in the distance. Under different circumstances, Buck might have led Dulce down off the plain to the river's edge, where there would be shelter from the wind and enough privacy for him to steal a kiss or two. Instead, he remained alert as they followed the river, glancing frequently over his shoulder until Dulce finally forced a halt.

"What is it?" she demanded.

"What's what?"

"Why are you acting so furtive? Did you see something?"

"No. . . ." He shut up abruptly and pulled his arm free of hers. A flat-roofed stock shed occupied the rear corner of a long house pasture about sixty yards away. An abandoned buggy was parked beside it. There was a shadow behind the buggy. There hadn't been a moment ago.

"Buck, you're frightening me."

He cut her off with a low shush, drawing his revolver just as the shadow darted into the sage toward them. "Watch out!" Buck cried, pushing Dulce to the ground and stepping in front of her. A round flashed from the sage, the bullet passing close on Buck's left. He dropped to one knee to steady his right wrist with his left hand, silently cursing the little cap-and-ball pistol's inherent inaccuracy at such distances. He wished he had his Colt, or, better yet, his rifle. He squeezed off two quick rounds that wrung a startled yelp from the sage. A moment later the shadow was up and running in the opposite direction, tall and lean in silhouette, like a telegraph pole retreating from the grimy window of a speeding train.

"Buck?"

He pivoted on his knees. Dulce lay on her stomach in the new grass, her eyes as big as saucers.

"Who was it?"

"I don't know. It was too dark to make him out."

She got to her knees and wrapped her arms around his neck and began to cry.

"Hey, it's all right," he said gently.

"I don't think so, Buck. I don't think it's a bit all right when someone tries to kill you."

"We don't know if that's what he was trying to do. He was probably just drunk and sleeping it off in that shed, then we came along and scared. . . ."

"Don't treat me like a child, Buck. I won't stand for it. I know what happened to Mase. Now they want to kill you, too."

"You don't know that, Dulce."

"Don't I? Can you honestly say you believe Mase's death wasn't somehow connected to this . . . this damn' race to Montana?"

He wanted to allay her fear, but couldn't without lying. "I don't know," he said finally. "Maybe it is. Herb Crowley and Anton Luce are determined men. They'll be tough competition. But murder? I just don't know if they'd go that far."

"Well," she said, her voice suddenly brittle, "I suspect you soon will. I suspect we all will." After a pause, she asked: "Will you tell Papa about this?"

"I ought to."

"You most certainly should. He has every right to know." After a pause, she added: "But you don't want to, do you?"

"No."

"Then don't, and I won't, either. I'll respect your wishes, Buck, and stand behind you, but you have to promise that you'll do the same for me, and trust me when I ask you to."

"You know I will."

"Promise me, Buck. No matter what."

He stared into her eyes, puzzled by the seriousness he saw there. "All right, I promise," he said.

Dulce smiled. "Then that's good enough for me, Buck McCready, because I know you're a man of your word." They stood and she linked her arm through his once more. "Now, sir, walk me home. Walk me home so that I can tend to my supper dishes and you can do whatever it is you've been itching to do ever since you knocked on my door tonight."

Chapter Four

In his room above Chin Lo's laundry, Buck skinned into more suitable attire—sturdy wool trousers, low-heeled mule-ear boots, a cotton shirt, and a sack coat of the same dark color as his pants to ward off the early spring chill. His trail hat was wide-brimmed and round-crowned, dented and sweat-stained above a frayed horsehair hatband.

Leaving the pocket pistol on the table beside his bed to be cleaned and reloaded later, he buckled on his everyday pistol, a converted Army Colt. He was almost out the door when he remembered to grab a block of matches off the top of the chest of drawers.

He went back to the stock shed where his attacker had lain in wait. He thought it unlikely the man would return, but he remained cautious as he checked out the shed, then moved on to the buggy. Dropping to one knee, he began a more thorough search of the ground where he'd first spied the crouching shadow. He used his matches sparingly, but still managed to go through most of the block before he made his first discovery—a solitary heel print in the moist soil next to the buggy's rear wheel.

Buck bent closer as he passed a second sputtering lucifer over the shallow imprint. He was a muleskinner, not a tracker, but he would have bet a month's wages that the print had been made by a drover's boot, the kind with the deep arch and stacked heel favored by men who made their living pushing cattle from range to market. On the plains of Texas and even into Kansas, such a track wouldn't have amounted to much as a clue, but out here in Utah, where the cattle industry was still in its infancy, Buck considered his find significant.

He spotted a dull glint in the sage a couple of feet away and leaned over to pick up an empty copper cartridge, the rotten-egg odor of burnt gunpowder still strong at its mouth. His excitement waned as he twirled the stubby case in his fingers. It was a standard .44 Rimfire, the kind that could be purchased off the shelf of any grocery or hardware store in town. He plucked a loaded round from his own cartridge belt and held it alongside the empty. There was no appreciable difference between the two pieces of copper. Even the head stamps—the letter H, referring to the Henry rifle and the man who'd developed the cartridge for it—were identical.

Buck was almost certain that whoever had taken a shot at him had done so with a rifle, although that didn't mean as much now as it once did. It was becoming more popular all the time to have a rifle and revolver chambered for the same cartridge. Even Buck's Colt, originally a cap-and-ball model, had been converted to .44 Rimfire.

Dropping the empty copper in his pocket, Buck made his way back to town, stopping in front of the International Saloon. The International was a two-storied frame structure with a balcony that overlooked the main thoroughfare. It sat across the street from the Central Pacific depot and attracted a lot of its clientele from the railroad. Buck had never cared much for the International, not even in the days before he'd met Dulce. The saloon's scantily clad hostesses had always seemed a little too desperate to him, and its music, produced by an ever-changing orchestra of transients scratching out tunes for meals and drinks, had seemed jarring even on its best nights.

Mase had been different, though. He'd seemed to crave the

noise and hustle of rowdy establishments like the International. He liked to play cards and drink whiskey, to laugh loud and long, and tell stories only the rawest greenhorn would swallow whole. And once or twice a week, Mase would go upstairs with one of the International's whores, usually paying for the entire night so that he wouldn't have to get up afterward and go home.

Although Mase had never claimed a favorite among the dozen or so hookers who worked at the International, Buck had heard from some of the Box K muleskinners that he'd recently become attached to an older prostitute named Sally Hayes, who'd drifted in from San Francisco the preceding fall. In addition to the barkeep, Buck wanted to talk to Sally.

There must have been close to two hundred men crammed inside the saloon's big main room that night. The press at the bar reminded Buck of a freshly opened tin of sardines. He recognized a few of the patrons—muleskinners and bullwhackers from other freighting companies, warehouse men and clerks—but the majority were strangers, bound for the northern gold fields—miners, adventurers, speculators in everything from horses to timber. Many of them would buy passage on one of the stagecoaches that started out daily for Idaho and Montana; others would hold over only long enough to procure their own transportation. A few, too broke to afford better, would walk the entire distance, carrying their possessions in backpacks or wheelbarrows.

At first, Buck was startled to recognize a few Box K teamsters in the crowd. He spotted Joe Perry at the chuck-a-luck cage and Lou Kitledge and Andy LeMay sitting at a table jawing with a couple of Gilmer and Salisbury hostlers. Ray Jones stood at the bar with another Gilmer and Salisbury man, a slim, black jehu—or stagecoach driver—called Hoots.

Kitledge and LeMay motioned for Buck to join them, but he declined with a curt shake of his head. He found a gap at the bar and wedged in. At this time of the year, with the hordes just starting north after the long winter, the International kept two bartenders working the evening shift.

Tom Ashley had the near end, and Buck caught his eye.

"What'll it be?" Ashley asked, perspiration beading his forehead.

"Beer."

Ashley drew a full mug and set it in front of Buck, then scooped up the two-bit piece Buck tossed onto the counter. "I heard you had some excitement in here the other night," Buck said, before the bartender could walk away.

Ashley grunted in recognition. "I thought I recognized you. You're Mase Campbell's pard, the one that's takin' over his job."

"Buck McCready."

"Sure." A sneer curled Ashley's lips. "Sparkin' Kavanaugh's little gal, too, ain't cha?"

Buck's face went dangerously flat. "Easy, friend. She's not the kind to be talked about in a place like this."

"Aw, I didn't besmirch your little darlin's honor," the barkeep snarled, then stalked off.

The man on Buck's right chuckled softly. "Slimy bastard, ain't he?"

"Ashley?"

"Yeah."

"You know him?"

"Just from buying beers from him." He put out his hand. "I'm Milo Newton, of Kansas."

"Buck McCready." Buck shook the man's hand, liking the firmness of the Kansan's grip, the steady return of his gaze.

"I heard," Milo said. "Did Ashley say you were skinning mules for the Box K?"

"I was Mason Campbell's ramrod until he was killed a couple

of nights ago. They offered me his job this morning."

"Tough way to get a promotion," Milo said. "I knew Campbell when he was still captaining for Majors, Russell, and Waddell. Not well, but by reputation. I was working at a relay station along the Platte River Road outside of Fort Kearney, just a kid, and Mase . . . hell, Mase was a legend even then. Was never a train Mason Campbell didn't get through, never a cargo he lost." He smiled. "At least that's what they said."

Buck turned for a second look. Milo Newton was an inch or two shorter than he was, but broader through the chest and shoulders. He had wavy brown hair and brown eyes, and sported a mustache that curved down on either side of his mouth. His clothes were trail-worn but reasonably clean, and he carried what looked like a Navy Colt on his left hip, its butt canted forward in a manner even then falling out of vogue. He looked to be about thirty, which would have made him several years older than Buck.

"That was Mase, all right," Buck said after a pause. "There aren't many as good, and none better."

"Time's running out for it, that's for sure. The damn' railroads." He lifted his glass. "Here's to the long hitches, and the fools who drive them."

"To the long hitches," Buck murmured, clinking glasses.

They talked like old friends for another hour, and Buck learned that Milo's story was similar to his own. Orphaned at seventeen, Milo had gone to work for the giant freighting firm of Majors, Russell, and Waddell as a roustabout. When that company went out of business in the early 1860s, he'd taken a job skinning mules out of Leavenworth for the Army. Later, he'd hauled between end of track on the Kansas Pacific railroad and various military posts throughout eastern Colorado and New Mexico, until economic depression in the East forced the lay-off of several hundred employees. It was the rumor of good-paying jobs for muleskinners in Utah that had brought him over the mountains.

"You ought to talk to Jock, down at the Box K, if you're looking for work," Buck told him.

"Jock?" Milo's brows furrowed. "Kavanaugh's little. . . ." He looked up in surprise. "The same Jock Kavanaugh who used to run freight out of Arrow Rock, Missouri?"

Buck's smile faded. "That was a long time ago."

"Before I was born," Milo acknowledged. "Still. . . ."

"I wouldn't believe everything I heard about that incident," Buck said, stiffening defensively. "I've known Jock a long time, and he's a good man."

Milo nodded absently, staring at the damp surface of the bar. "I reckon it wouldn't hurt to talk to him."

"No one's forcing you to," Buck replied coolly, then picked up his beer and walked away. He'd almost felt good there for a while, talking about Mase and the old days, but Milo had wrecked that brief peace.

Damn those old stories, Buck thought. They clung to Jock and those around him like ticks on a deer. Even if there was some truth in them, they didn't change the kind of man Jock had become or diminish the things he'd accomplished since then. Chihuahua was a long time ago, and Buck had always taken comfort in the fact that no two tales he'd heard of that affair were ever alike. It gave him hope that most of what was said was nothing more than the rants of men jealous of Jock's success, and that those who had died out there on the blazing plains of Mexico—the mutineers—had deserved their fate.

Buck pushed his niggling doubts aside. He'd come here for a reason, then allowed himself to be sidetracked by a chance to forget. It was time he got back to business.

He took up a position near the end of the bar, within sight of the storeroom door behind it. Within twenty minutes, Ashley yanked an empty beer keg from its rack under the bar, hoisted it onto his shoulder, then disappeared into the back room. Buck waited until the second bartender turned away, then slipped behind the counter and through the door.

Ashley was in the far corner, wrestling a full twenty-gallon keg onto a steel-wheeled dolly. He looked up when Buck walked in. "Hey, you can't come in here."

"I want to talk to you," Buck said, making his way down a narrow aisle of whiskey crates stacked shoulder-high.

"The hell with you, McCready. I got nothing to say."

The only light in the room came from a single lamp fixed to the wall beside the door, but its chimney was blackened with soot, and, in the shadows, Buck couldn't see Ashley's hands. Stopping several paces away, Buck put his own hand over his Colt. "I want to talk to you about Mase."

"I already talked to Dunbar about him. I don't hafta talk to you, too."

"Sure you do," Buck said, sliding his revolver part way out of its holster. "Who killed him?"

"How should I know? It could 'a' been anybody. Hell, it could 'a' been you. You got his job, didn't cha?"

"Tell me, Ashley, or I'll ram your head through that beer keg."

"By God, you're a snooty son-of-a-bitch. Why should I tell you anything?"

"Because I'm quick running out of patience," Buck replied, his fingers tightening on the Colt.

Ashley looked disgruntled for a moment, then swore and said: "All right, keep that hogleg sheathed." He paused briefly as if to collect his thoughts. "Campbell came stumblin' in here 'bout ten o'clock that night and bullied his way into a card game. Was seven or eight of 'em playin', all of 'em strangers and ever' damn' one drunk as skunks. After an hour or so a fracas got up between Campbell and some big fella with a beard. Big fella started callin' Campbell a cheat and threatenin' to cut off his ears with a Bowie knife, but Campbell called his bluff. Pulled his own sticker and told that big bastard to come ahead and try, but the big fella wouldn't do it. He tried to pull in his horns, but Campbell wouldn't let him. He kept badgerin' that big fella till he finally quit the game and left. He was makin' some dark promises when he went that night, lookin' meaner'n a treed cougar. That's it, that's all I can tell ya."

"What about Mase?"

"Threw his cards in 'bout midnight, had hisself a last drink, then wobbled out the front door to go home."

"Wobbled?"

"Barely standin'." Ashley smirked brightly. "Ya might 'a' thought the moon rose and set on Mason Campbell, sonny, but most of the boys 'round here figured he was a. . . ."

"Keep it to yourself," Buck warned.

Ashley's grin broadened. "Why, sure, boss. Hell, it wasn't me all the time kissin' Campbell's ass. I reckon. . . ."

Buck's right hand came up smoothly, the Colt leveling down on Ashley as if it had a mind of its own. "Don't push your luck, brother."

The bartender swallowed hard, his grin disappearing. "All right, what else ya wanna know?"

"I want to know about the big guy with the beard."

Ashley considered the question a few seconds, then said: "Had him a pitted face, like he'd one time or another had the pox. Kinda greasy-lookin', his clothes all worn out and dirty. Mostly he was just big, real big. Six foot, three or four and maybe weighed two-fifty. Not fat, just solid, like an ox."

"You told Dunbar he had a partner."

"Naw, I didn't say he had a partner. I said there was a skinny little fella following him out the door like he had a purpose in doin' so, but I didn't get a good look at 'im. He wore a green plaid jacket and an old porkpie hat and was pretty scroungy-lookin' himself, come to think on it."

"You'd never seen either one before?"

"Not before nor since."

A shadow loomed at the door, and the second bartender shouted: "Gawd dammit, Tom, what are you doing back there? I need some help."

Ashley met Buck's gaze. "Anything else?" he asked, his sarcasm returned.

Buck holstered his Colt. "No, I guess not."

Laughing, Ashley said: "I been listenin' to some of the boys talkin', and they been sayin' ol' Buck McCready's ridin' straight into the jaws of hell, like a mule with blinders on. Might not come back is what they're sayin'."

Buck eyes narrowed. "Just who is it that's saying that?"

"Oh, just some of the boys, McCready. Just some of the boys."

Chapter Five

Buck was at the C.P. siding before dawn the next morning to supervise the loading of BMC's freight onto Box K wagons. It was gut-busting labor to make the transfer. The eight big iron stampers weighed just under a ton apiece, and the boilers took up the bulk of two wagons all by themselves. The collapsible smokestack, two steam engines, an assortment of parts needed to assemble everything once it reached Montana, plus tools and furnishings for a new regional office, filled the rest of the wagons.

Each Box K muleskinner would handle one wagon loaded with BMC freight, while their second, or trail wagon, carried lighter goods for Jock's regular customers in Virginia City. The five independent drivers Jock had hired for the journey would haul smaller orders for long-standing customers—merchandise that wouldn't be as expensive to replace as BMC's specialized equipment, in the event of an accident.

Around midafternoon, Buck started to worry that Jock had underestimated the amount of space they'd need for such a motley collection of machinery, but by 5:00 P.M. he was breathing easier again. By 7:00 P.M., they were lashing down the last of the twin osnaburg covers that would protect the cargo against blowing rain or a late-season snowstorm.

"By God, Bucky," Peewee said when they'd finished, "one more box of pencils and we'd've had to beg another wagon from the old man."

"It was tight," Buck agreed.

Peewee chuckled as he rolled down his sleeves. He was a short-legged man in his early forties, his face and hands weathered to a leathery toughness, his arms ropy with muscle. Although he lacked an official title with Kavanaugh Freight, it was generally understood that, on the trail, he ranked behind only the wagon boss and ramrod in authority.

"You coming over to the camp tonight?" Peewee asked, referring to the spot across the Bear River where the Box K's Montana train was waiting to pull out.

Retrieving his coat and gun belt from where he'd laid them that morning, Buck said: "Probably not."

Peewee's smile revealed a row of perfectly carved ivories—elephant, the dentist had assured him. "You tellin' me Dulce can't do without your company for one night?" he demanded.

"It ain't that. I've got some other business to take care of."

Peewee's expression sobered. "Mase?"

Buck nodded and glanced across the street to where Ray Jones, Joe Perry, Nate Evans, and Nate's son, Rossy, were standing beside Nate's lead wagon, killing time. Buck knew he should at least drop by the camp long enough to share a cup of coffee with the crew, but time was growing short and it still bothered him that they hadn't discovered Mase's killer. He was afraid that, if they didn't find him soon, they never would. "Is everything all right over there?" he asked Peewee.

"At camp? Sure."

Buck gave him a gauging look, and Peewee shrugged.

"You know how it is with new men. It'll shake out as soon as we get rolling."

"You're in charge," Buck reminded him.

"The old hands think that way. The new ones don't."

"Tell 'em."

"It ain't my job to tell 'em," Peewee reminded him gently.

Buck flinched inwardly, but he wasn't going to give up his

last chance to look for Mase's killer. "I'll talk to Jock. Maybe he can drive over before he goes home tonight."

Hesitantly Peewee said: "We've got something for you, Buck. If you was comin' over tonight, we'd wait so that all the boys could be there, but since you ain't, and since we're putting out first thing tomorrow. . . ."

"What is it?"

Peewee waved for the muleskinners across the street to join them. "Come on over!" he shouted. "Let's do it now."

"Let's do what now?" Buck asked suspiciously.

"Now, don't go gettin' wall-eyed on us. It's just something me 'n' the boys talked about yesterday at Mase's funeral, and we all agreed it was the thing to do. The others would've been here, too, if they wasn't watchin' over the wagons and stock."

Buck glanced across the street. Rossy had stayed back with the wagons and mules, but Ray, Nate, and Joe were already stepping over the iron rails of the C.P. siding like a trio of grim-faced hangmen.

"It ain't nothing horrible," Peewee assured him. "We ain't gonna ask you to ride a horse instead of a mule. It's just something we figured ought to be."

Buck eyed the approaching men skeptically. Ray was carrying a parcel wrapped in gunny sacking under one arm. He was one of the older hands on Jock's payroll, an ex-Missourian with sandy-colored hair that was thinning rapidly under a gray felt hat he seldom removed. His faded blue eyes were set into a deeply-tanned face, and his shoulders were endlessly slumped as if from exhaustion, although Buck knew that, even at fifty, Ray could outwork most men half his age.

Nate was on Ray's right. He was Jock's newest muleskinner, having shown up in Corinne barely a year ago with a wife, two young daughters, and a fourteen-year-old son named Roscoe, who everyone called Rossy. Nate was tall and well-proportioned, with skin the color of stained mahogany; his short, kinky hair was starting to gray at the temples, but he still carried himself with a younger man's confidence.

Rossy Evans was even darker-skinned than his father, and already as broad through the shoulders, although he still lacked several inches of Nate's six feet. Rossy swamped for his father on the trail when he wasn't riding night hawk on the remuda. He was the youngest man in the outfit by quite a few years, a good, dependable hand, though shy around the evening mess. The Evanses hailed from Ohio, where Nate had been working with mules since he was old enough to hang onto a lead rope.

Joe Perry, on Ray's left, was a Kentuckian by birth, maybe twenty-eight or thirty, lean and muscular. He had coal-black hair, a thick beard, a quick smile, and a temper that was just as swift. He'd learned the mule trade during the war, hauling freight for the Confederacy, and had stayed with it afterward. It was rumored that Joe's father owned a sizable chunk of farmland along the Rolling Fork River below Louisville, and that Joe stood to inherit about five hundred acres of it if he would give up his wayward life as a muleskinner and return home. Those who knew him best doubted if he ever would. They said Joe liked his freedom too much to settle down where the horizons never changed.

The muleskinners stopped beside Peewee, facing Buck in a semicircle. Looking almost embarrassed, Ray shoved the parcel he was carrying into Buck's hands. "Here," he said gruffly. "This is yours."

"We all decided, Buck," Peewee added quickly. "It ought to belong to you."

Buck unwrapped the bundle slowly, but he already knew what he would find inside. He could feel its coils through the coarse sacking like a resting snake. Peeling back the last fold, he stared numbly at Mase's twelve-foot bullwhip, purchased so many years ago from H.K. Knight, out of Chicago. The last place he'd seen it had been on top of Mase's casket, where he'd assumed it had been interred with the body.

Buck turned the whip over in his hands. The black, tightly woven lash slid smoothly through his fingers, cool and alive to the touch, leaving the slightly oily trace of well-cared-for leather on his fingers. Twin poppers of soft lead, encased in slim leather pouches at the tip, added weight and crack to the whip's snap, and a basket-weave design on the hickory handle ensured a firm grip. The hard knob of woven leather on the butt was crowned with a silver concho, and on that had been engraved the image of a span of mules, their knees bent, heads low as they leaned into their collars. The initials M and C had been added on either side of the team.

Buck took a deep, wrenching breath, then looked up to meet the muleskinners' eyes. Joe and Nate were grinning broadly. Ray looked half peeved, as if he expected rejection. Peewee's demeanor was more optimistic, although he was clearly aware of the emotions the gift had dredged up.

"You don't have to use it," Peewee said. "It was just an idea me 'n' the boys had."

"What!" Joe exclaimed. "Sure he's gotta use it. That's why we grabbed it off Mase's casket. We sure as hell ain't gonna go back and bury it with him now."

"No," Buck agreed, "it's too late for that. Besides, I'm . . . I'm glad you kept it. I appreciate it." He twisted part way around to fasten the whip to a leather thong on his gun belt, just in front of the knife he wore on his left hip and where, on the trail, he normally carried his own plain but sturdy ten-footer. Dropping the hem of his coat over the coiled lash, he said: "Tell the boys thanks. Tell them I'll talk to them about it tomorrow."

Ray grinned as if in relief, and Nate and Joe laughed, slapping Buck good naturedly on the shoulder before turning away.

Ray and Peewee followed them across the tracks, but Buck took a moment to collar the sudden stab of anguish within himself, before heading into town to see Jock.

It had been a pleasantly warm day after what had turned out to be a long, damp spring, but, with the sun already down, the desert's chill was creeping into town like a banished thief. Buck pulled his coat tighter around his shoulders as he trod the familiar path to the Box K office. A lantern hanging from an iron hook above the main door partially illuminated the bright green lettering of *Kavanaugh Freight,* arched boldly across the front of the building. Inside, a clerk was working late, wrapped in a cocoon of yellow lamplight. He looked up when Buck entered, then nodded to the rear door, where a small brass plaque read: *PRIVATE.* At his knock, Jock called for him to enter.

There were three men inside the office. Jock sat behind his desk with a tumbler of bourbon on the leather pad in front of him. Walt Jepson stood beside the desk with a sheaf of papers in one hand. And in a chair in front of the desk, filling out even more paperwork, was the Kansas muleskinner, Milo Newton.

Milo gave Buck a guarded nod, then returned his attention to the form in front of him. From its heading, Buck recognized a standard Box K contract. Jock lifted his chin in question and Buck closed the door. "It's done," he said. "It was tight, but it's all on board and buckled down. We'll be ready to pull out at first light with your say-so."

"You'll have it," Jock promised, then indicated the new man with a tip of his head. "I believe you've met Mister Newton."

"Uhn-huh, last night."

"I hired him in part because he says you recommended he come here. I had in mind to either assign him to you as your ramrod, or have him carry express to some of the Sawtooth camps. I still need a packer for that contract."

"I'll take him," Buck said, crossing the room to shake the Kansan's hand. He hadn't forgotten the feelings Milo had stirred in him last night over the Chihuahua tales, but he'd decided later that Newton had made no accusations, and Buck couldn't fault a man for curiosity. "Besides," he added, "he's got too much experience to tote second-class mail over the mountains on a jackass."

Milo smiled in gratitude. "I was hoping for a job handling a jerkline. I hardly expected to be made a ramrod."

"None of the old hands wanted the job," Jock informed him. "I wouldn't have offered it to you if they had."

"Well, just the same, I'm glad for the opportunity."

Nodding to the papers in Walt's hands, Jock said: "Are those Buck's?"

"Yes, sir, but I haven't finished them yet."

"Go ahead and get 'em done. Buck and I have some business to discuss." He glanced at Milo. "Questions?"

"No, sir." Milo handed the signed contract to Walt, then stood and shook Jock's hand. "Thank you for the job. You won't regret it."

Jock's expression was inscrutable. "I hope not." He nodded to the back door that led to the wagon yard. "I've got a team of sorrels in the stable . . . horses. Hitch them to my carriage and we'll drive out to the camp in a few minutes. I'll introduce you to the men."

Milo nodded and flashed Buck a grin as he made his way to the rear door. Buck stiffened as he passed, his gaze drawn to the cuff of the Kansan's tan trousers, where the hard heels of a pair of drover's boots rapped hollowly against the wooden floor.

Buck walked to the door to watch Milo cross the wagon yard to the stables, recalling the solitary heel print he'd found behind the flat-roofed stock shed the night before.

"Something wrong?" Jock asked.

"You don't see a lot of muleskinners wearing drover's boots."

Jock shrugged without interest. "Let's get down to business," he said. "Walt, leave the contracts for the independents with me, and when you're done with the invoices, leave the ones Buck will need on your desk. I'll find them when I want them."

"Yes, sir," Walt replied, hurrying out of the room.

Buck dropped into one of the ladder-back chairs in front of the desk, and Jock said in a suddenly annoyed tone: "I won't make a habit of this, but, under the circumstances, I'll honor the request." He fixed Buck with an unblinking stare. "Dulce asked that you not come by to see her tonight."

Buck's head came up in surprise. "Why not?"

"I delivered her message," Jock replied brusquely. "I won't speculate upon hidden meanings." His expression softened then. "It's not as bad as you imagine. If it were up to me, I'd tell you, but I promised Dulce I wouldn't." He picked up the contracts for the independents that Walt had left behind. "You're probably familiar with some of these men. . . ."

Jock's voice faded as Buck mulled over Dulce's message. He couldn't help wondering if he'd done something wrong, maybe hurt her feelings somehow.

". . . Kroll will probably try to wrestle some kind of leadership with the drivers. It'll be your job to. . . ."

"Kroll!" Buck exclaimed, straightening in his chair. "Mitchell Kroll?"

Jock hesitated and his lips thinned irritably. "If I hadn't once courted her mother. . . ." he started, then sighed. "What didn't you hear?"

"I guess I didn't pick up that Mitch Kroll was one of the independents," Buck admitted self-consciously. "Who else is signed on?"

Independents owned their own rigs and hired out to whoever offered the best contract. They were a varied lot, nearly all of them tough as nails. Most were good, hard-working men, but the freedom of the road attracted a rougher element, too, teamsters who weren't opposed to doing whatever they felt was necessary to guarantee a profitable load. Mitch Kroll fell into that category—a large-framed man of incredible strength, cruel and dark. A rumor some years ago claimed Kroll had once taunted a competitor along the Denver Trail into a fist fight, then deliberately broke the man's spine. Two days later, when no one else could be found—or were too afraid to attempt it—Kroll had contracted to haul the crippled teamster's load of perishables into Denver at triple the going rate.

Shuffling through the contracts on his desk, Jack said: "I hired Keho Kona. You know Big Kona, don't you?"

Buck nodded. Keho Kona was a Sandwich Islander, from the big island called Hawaii. He was a large man, too, although on a different scale than Kroll, who was all muscle, thick hide, and bone. Big Kona was shorter and fleshier, with jet-black hair and a dusky complexion. He had legs as solid as oak stumps, but so short they stuck out on either side of his big nigh wheeler's barrel at an almost comical angle, rather than hanging naturally along the mule's side. He was a good man, though, and well thought of in the business.

"Lyle Mead?"

"I know who he is. Peewee says he's new to the territory."

"Claims he's from back East," Jock said distractedly, a frown creasing his forehead. "He's a strange one. I can't help thinking. . . ." He shook his head, letting whatever he was about to say trail off. "I know even less about these last two. Little Ed Womack's got that Mexican swamper, Manuel Varga, that some say is jinxed."

"Does that worry you, hiring a Jonah?"

Jock snorted dismissingly. "Then there's Garth Lang, who says he just came up the trail from San Diego with a load of oranges, lemons, and avocados for the Salt Lake City market. I hadn't heard of either him or Mead before a couple of days ago." He tossed the contracts on his desk. "I admit it bothers me to hire men I don't know."

"What about swampers?" Buck asked, meaning the second man, hired out of the teamster's own wages, who helped with the stock and manned the brakes on downgrades. Not many teamsters used them any more. Among the Box K drivers, only Nate kept his son on, at least when Rossy wasn't night hawking the remuda. The rest manned their own brakes with long cotton ropes strung between the brake levers and the saddle horn of their near-wheelers.

"Mitch Kroll has a man called Bigfoot Payne, who's supposed to be a simpleton," Jock said. "Womack has Varga."

"Are they all already across the river?"

"The independents were there as of sunset yesterday. You sent the last Box K wagon over tonight." He gave Buck a wry look. "As I was saying, Mitch Kroll will probably challenge Peewee for leadership among the drivers, especially the independents. He's not to get it, under any circumstances."

Buck nodded, although he wasn't worried. "Peewee'll put him in his place if he tries," he said.

Jock grunted, then smiled grudgingly. "You may be right. For a small man, Peewee carries an extraordinary amount of authority. Still, if it looks like Kroll is up to something, stop him . . . any way you have to. I don't care for his reputation. I wouldn't have hired him at all if my back wasn't against the wall with Bannock Mining."

"What about Bannock's representative? Has he shown up yet?"

Jock hesitated. "There's some confusion right now as to who BMC's representative will be, but I'll have it sorted out by tomorrow." He drummed his fingertips thoughtfully atop his desk. "Walt will have your bills of lading ready within the hour, but there's no point in you waiting around for them. Come by the office in the morning, before you head out to camp. You can pick up your paperwork then and . . . there may be some kinks we'll need to work out at the last minute."

"What kind of kinks?"

"Just stop by the office in the morning. It might not be anything."

"All right," Buck said, heading for the door.

"Buck," Jock called, stopping him. "Don't worry about Dulce. You'll see her tomorrow, too. I guarantee it."

Chapter Six

The soft tread of footfalls in the hall outside Arlen's door caused the flesh across the back of his neck to crawl as if his collar had suddenly become infested with fleas. With the rusty Manhattan clutched tightly in hand, he moved swiftly to the far corner of the room he was renting above 25th Street, in Ogden, and ducked behind a rickety pine highboy.

From a lumpy chair across the room, the whore known as Mousetooth Millie cackled loudly. "Wasamatter, honey?" she quizzed. "You 'fraid of that ol' bogeyman?"

"Shut up!" Arlen hissed as the footsteps came to a stop outside his room. A single, heavy rap seemed to rattle the door on its hinges, and Arlen's Adam's apple bobbed violently.

"Open up, Fleck."

Recognition didn't ease Arlen's fears one bit. "It's open, Nick," he returned. "Come on in."

"Open this god-damn' door, you half-witted son-of-a-bitch!"

Slouched loosely in her chair, fat Millie brayed laughter and spittle with equal abandon.

Arlen's face grew warm as he stepped clear of the highboy. Sheepishly returning the Manhattan to an inside pocket of his coat, he crossed the room and opened the door.

Nick Kelso stood across the hall and to one side, out of the line of fire from a bullet blasted through the door. Ignoring the gunman's obvious gesture of distrust, Arlen said: "Hello, Nick."

Nick stepped inside, his gaze drawn immediately to the ratty whore in the ratty chair. Then he looked at a slowly writhing figure wrapped in a vomit-encrusted quilt and grimaced.

"What?" Arlen asked nervously.

"It stinks to high heaven in here is what. You got some kind of aversion to water?"

"Hell, you get used to the smell. Besides, it'd be a waste of water to soak him down. That boy's pukin' every couple of hours."

Nick's gaze shifted back to the whore. "What's she doing here?"

"Honey, I'm the pacification for when the opium don't work," Millie informed him haughtily.

"The kid likes her," Arlen added in an apologetic tone. "He's pretty doped up most of the time."

"Hey," Millie protested. "I ain't that over-the-hill."

But even Arlen, whose standards had never been especially high, had to admit that Mousetooth Millie looked fairly used up. She claimed to be twenty-nine, but he'd guess her closer to fifty. She was vastly overweight, with massive breasts and jowls that shook obscenely whenever she laughed. Her two upper front teeth, slanted sharply inward, were the inspiration for her name. Arlen didn't like her, but he hadn't been able to get rid of her since she'd lured the kid upstairs a couple of nights ago.

Nick didn't seem interested in her reason for being there, and said flatly: "Get out."

Millie's eyes narrowed dangerously. "Honey, I don't abide that kind of talk from no one. If you. . . ."

Nick's Colt slid from its holster like butter off a hot blade, the hammer snicking back coldly. "If you're not out of here in two seconds, I'm going to blow that ugly head of yours off your shoulders," he snarled.

Millie blanched visibly under her war paint. Arlen almost laughed, then thought better of it. Two seconds later the only part of her that remained was her odor, a kind of fetid, rose-like aroma created out of cheap perfume and sweaty flesh that hadn't seen a bar of soap in weeks.

"Damn," Arlen said, staring through the open door until Nick kicked it shut.

Nick crossed to where the kid was lying on the floor and pulled the quilt back, wrinkling his nose in disgust. "How much dope have you been feeding him?"

"Just what you said . . . about every six hours."

"Cut it back a little," Nick said uncertainly. "I don't want him to die." He glanced at the small, teakwood box on top of the highboy. "You got enough tar there to keep him out of sight for another couple of days?"

"Sure, that won't be a problem."

"You ain't been leaving him alone, have you?"

"Well, I got to fetch grub and such. I been lettin' Millie sit with him while I was gone, but. . . ."

Dropping the quilt back over the kid's shoulders, Nick said: "I have to go up to Corinne for a few days, maybe a week."

"A week! That much opium'll kill him."

"You won't have to keep him doped up that long. Just feed him what's left, then you're free to go. Hang around Ogden until I get back. I'll find you."

"Ah. . . ."

Nick's expression hardened. "You worried I'm not comin' back?"

"Naw, it ain't that, it's just that a man like me's got to keep movin' if he ain't got no money. You know what the law's like. If they think you're a bum, they run you out of town on a rail."

"Don't let 'em think you're a bum," was Nick's curt reply. He walked to the door, then paused and muttered a curse. Pulling a handful of coins from his pocket, he tossed them onto the rumpled bed. Arlen eyes widened as he counted the silver. There was at least $40 there, twice what Nick had promised him for keeping the kid out of sight. "This is important, Fleck." Nick's gaze bore into his like hardened steel. "Don't muck it up."

"I won't."

"Don't." Nick stepped through the door and started to pull it shut.

"Nick, wait!"

The door stopped.

Arlen nodded at the kid. "You know he's got a sister?"

"So?"

"Well, ah . . . she came to town with him on what they call a vacation. Got herself a chaperon and everything, but now she's. . . ."

"Take care of it."

"Huh?"

"God dammit, take care of it. Just make sure the kid's not found for a few more days." Nick slammed the door shut, the musical jingle of his spurs quickly fading down the hall.

Arlen sucked in a deep breath, then moved to the window. He stared down at the street until Nick appeared and turned west toward the Union Pacific depot. Lifting his eyes to the early spring night, Arlen smiled to himself and whispered: "You cocky son-of-a-bitch. I hope they hang you." Then he pulled the curtains closed and turned away.

Chapter Seven

Buck's hopes flagged at the International's front doors as he peered in over the top. The crowd looked even larger than the night before, and he knew his chances of finding Mase's killer were growing slim. He would be leaving for Montana before sunup tomorrow. That left only tonight to sort out a riddle not even the town's sheriff had been able to unravel.

Buck pushed through the swinging doors. The press at the bar was so tight he didn't even try to find a spot, settling instead for a warm beer purchased from a sweating waiter who wove through the crowd with a tray of drinks held above his head. He took the mug to the east wall, where there were no games of chance and where the crowd was thinner and not nearly as raucous. Propping his shoulders against the gaudily flocked wallpaper, he let his eyes roam the big main room, looking for Sally Hayes. Tom Ashley was working the near end of the bar. Buck couldn't see him, but he could hear him above the din of the crowd, loudly impatient as he tried to keep up with the demand for liquor. Nearly an hour passed before Buck spied Sally coming down the stairs with a young dandy in a checked suit and a narrow-brimmed bowler.

Buck had always considered Sally coarse and unattractive, but those who knew her said she had her charms. Several of them stopped to watch her descent from the second-floor cribs, the upper shelf of her breasts jiggling above the scooped neckline of her dress with every downward step. Sally's dusty blonde hair was gray at the roots, done up in tight curls that added width to a narrow face and a too-sharp chin. Rouge gave her cheeks a ruddy glow; mixed with theater grease, it also added a full, sensual cupid's bow to her lips. Her figure was full and fleshy in a way most men appreciated, and most women didn't.

Leaving his empty mug on the floor, Buck moved to intercept her. She was standing on tiptoe in a vain attempt to catch the bartender's eye when he caught up. Stepping close, he said: "Miss Hayes."

She graced him with a dismissing look until his greeting registered in her mind. "*Miss* Hayes? Honey, where the hell have you been?" Then she recognized him and her smile quickly deflated. "What do you want?"

"I want to talk to you. I'm a friend of Mason Campbell."

"I know who you are, and, if you don't leave me alone, I'll scream."

She didn't have to. She'd spoken loudly enough to draw the attention of several nearby men. One of them, maybe four or five inches taller than Buck and at least sixty pounds heavier, lurched around drunkenly. "This pissant botherin' you, Sally?"

"Oh, Christ," Sally groaned, rolling her eyes. She looked at Buck. "I'll tell you what, honey . . . you slip in there and buy me a whiskey and I'll talk with you until it's gone. How's that?"

"I'll buy you a bottle if we can talk right now. But not here. Some place quiet."

"Uhn-uh. I ain't goin' nowhere with you without I get paid."

"All right." Fishing a $2 note from his pocket, Buck slipped it unobtrusively into her hand. "Let's at least go over by the wall where it's quieter."

Sally followed warily, leaving the larger man who had been willing to gallop to her rescue looking confused and angry. "What do you want?" she asked when they'd stopped.

"I want to know who killed Mase."

"So does Sam Dunbar, but, like I told him, Mase didn't come upstairs that night."

"But you saw him?"

She hesitated, then shrugged. "Mebbe, but I didn't talk to him. I didn't recognize any of the men he was playing cards with, either."

"What did they look like?"

"Like men. Ain't much difference between 'em after a while." Her gaze flitted away briefly, then came back. "Look, Mase was just another customer, and none too gentle, if you catch my drift." When Buck frowned and said he didn't, Sally laughed harshly. "You ain't much smarter than one of them mules you stare into the ass of all day, are you, honey? Your friend liked it rough, liked to use his fists when he was upstairs with one of the girls. Liked to use his fists on me, too, but I charged him extra for it, which only made him meaner. Now, if you can't figure that out, you're too young to be in here."

"I don't believe that," Buck said sharply. "Mase treated women with respect."

"Honey, why don't you go back to the tit for a while? You ain't growed up enough for this crowd." She started to slip away but Buck grabbed her elbow. Jerking free, Sally blazed: "You keep your shitty paws off me, muleskinner!"

Around her, men turned to look. Among them was the tall, gut-heavy man who'd offered his assistance earlier. Pushing forward, he said: "You want me to haul this little pissant outside and teach him some manners, Sally?"

"I don't care what you do with him," she replied coldly, turning her back on both of them.

Buck started after her but the big man stepped in his path. "Hold on, short stuff," he snarled. "You 'n' me. . . ."

Buck hit him—hard. Bringing his fist up from the waist, he put everything he had into the swing. The larger man took the blow solidly on the chin and his head snapped back, teeth clicking shut with a sound like breaking glass. Blood spurted from his lower lip and his eyes seemed to cross briefly, before rolling up under his lids. Then he toppled over backward, knees and spine as rigid as tree trunks.

"Timmmber!" someone yelled, and the crowd broke into laughter. When it died, they turned away, their interest gone.

Buck stepped over the fallen man to follow Sally, then decided she'd told him everything she was going to. He wasn't sure what to do then. He was on the verge of going off in search of Sheriff Dunbar when he felt a tug on his sleeve and turned. "Lotty!" he exclaimed.

Lotty Beals smiled up shyly. She was a small woman with short dark hair and doe-like eyes, and for a while, before Buck had been introduced to Dulce, she had been his favorite from among the whores who worked at The Muleskinner's Retreat. He hadn't known she'd shifted her business to the International, although he supposed that, in the world of prostitution, the larger saloon just across the street from the Central Pacific Depot made more sense than a teamsters' hang-out on a gloomy side avenue.

"Hi, Buck," Lotty said, acting genuinely glad to see him. "I wasn't sure you'd remember me."

"Of course I remember you. I. . . ." He stopped, lifting his hands in a vaguely embarrassed manner.

"It's all right, really. Mase told me you'd started seeing a respectable girl. It's nice you remembered me, though." Then her smile vanished and she cast a nervous glance into the crowd. "I know what you're looking for, and I think I can help."

"How?"

"I heard some things that night, when Mase was killed. Buck, Sally was there, in the alley but out of sight. There was another man there, too, but I don't know who he was or why he wanted to kill your friend. At first I thought it was robbery, and that Sally was part of it, but everyone says Mase wasn't robbed, and Sally's been acting awfully scared lately."

"Scared of what?"

"I don't know."

"Did you see who shot Mase?"

"No, but I've seen some things since then. I've just been . . ."—that look into the crowd again, like a frightened child—"afraid to talk to anyone. Even Sheriff Dunbar. I don't trust him, Buck, but I trust you." She hesitated, then blurted: "We can't talk here."

"Then where?"

"Upstairs." Her eyes looked suddenly large and solemn. "You don't have to do anything . . . upstairs I mean. Unless you want to."

"I'll come upstairs, but just to talk."

After another quick peek over her shoulder, Lotty said: "I'll go up first, then you come up in a couple minutes, so that it won't look like we're together." She touched his hand lightly, smiled, then hurried away.

Buck watched her climb the stairs. She held her skirt away from her knees, and in the smoky light, her creamy white stockings shone dully. When he turned away, he saw the waiter he'd bought his beer from coming toward him. Pointing at the big man sprawled unconscious on the floor, the waiter said—"Did you do that?"—as if scolding a dog.

Buck laughed. "He asked me what a mule kicked like. I showed him."

"Next time, take it outside," the waiter ordered, then tucked the empty tray under his arm, grabbed the big man by his ankles, and dragged him into a corner where nobody would trip over him.

Buck waited a few minutes, then pushed through the crowd

to the stairs. He was almost to the top when he heard a woman scream. Taking the rest of the steps three at a time, he rounded the corner into the large central room at the head of the stairs where the whores conducted the financial end of their business, before taking their clients to a crib down the hall. He saw Sally lunging at Lotty with a polished stiletto in her hand. Lotty screamed again as the blade pierced her breast. She staggered back against a piano where an elderly piano player with a shiny baldhead scrambled to get out of the way. Sally followed closely, her face ugly with rage as she forced the slim blade all the way in. Then she yanked it free and plunged it in once more.

A choked cry was ripped from Buck's throat as he rushed forward. He didn't see the International's upstairs bouncer, a big black man with arms and legs as thick as newel posts, charging into the fray like a maddened bull. The bouncer crashed into Buck from the side and sent him stumbling. As Buck struggled to keep his balance, a shot roared from the door to the balcony that extended over the International's verandah. The bullet slammed into the wall a few inches above Buck's head, gouging a hole in the plaster.

Buck threw himself to the floor just as a second shot rang out. He figured the bullet was meant for him, but it was Sally whose strangled grunt rose painfully on the heels of the pistol's blast. Buck rolled onto his side, palming his Colt. A third bullet tore into the carpet in front of him, just before he snapped a round at a lean, shadowy figure crouched at the balcony door, but the Colt's report was drowned out by the deafening bellow of a double-barreled shotgun, wielded by the bald piano player.

Powder smoke filled the room; at the balcony door, buckshot had ripped away a large section of the jamb. The opening itself was empty, though—Sally's assassin having already fled.

Buck scrambled to his feet. The bouncer was down on one knee in the middle of the room, a snub-nosed .44 cap-and-ball revolver gripped tightly in one huge paw. The piano player stood with his back to the wall, looking pale and shaken; both barrels of his shotgun trickled smoke. Sally lay on the floor near the bouncer, a bullet hole above her right eye. Lotty lay a few feet away, Sally's stiletto hilt-deep in her chest.

"God damn," the bouncer hissed, staggering to his feet.

Buck holstered his Colt, then raised both hands shoulder high to show that he wasn't a threat.

Turning to the piano player, the bouncer said: "Sweet Jesus, Gene, what happened?"

Leaving the two saloon employees to sort out the details, Buck moved to the balcony door. He drew his Colt before poking his head past the splintered jamb, but the deck was empty. Keeping his thumb over the hammer, he slipped outside.

The balcony spanned the breadth of the saloon facing Front Street. It was sixty feet long but barely eight wide. A low white railing surrounded the outer edge. There was a single window on Buck's right, several more on his left, but no other doors and no outside stairs.

Buck edged over to the solitary window on his right. It was closed, but a lamp burned inside. When he tapped lightly on the glass with the muzzle of his pistol, the bedsprings squeaked noisily. A man wearing only his hat lifted the sash. "Whazz all th' shootin'?"

"Did you see someone run past here?" Buck asked.

"Yeah, coup'la seconds 'go. Whazz all th' shootin'?"

"Go back to bed," Buck advised, moving on. He sidled up to the railing on the west end of the balcony and peered around the corner, into the alley—the same alley where Mase had been gunned down only a few days before. He didn't see anyone, but there wasn't much light to see by; at ground level, it was dark enough to hide a dozen gunmen. Still, Buck knew he couldn't wait there forever. The odds were that whoever had shot Sally was still running.

Holstering his Colt, Buck stepped gingerly over the railing. There was a rain barrel below him, fastened to the saloon by a twist of wire. Grasping the bottom crosspiece of the railing, Buck carefully lowered himself until he could feel the barrel's rim under his feet. Then, releasing his hold on the railing, he stepped away from the barrel and dropped to the ground, drawing his Colt as he straightened.

His breathing was shallow as he made his way down the alley. At the far end he came to a large, weedy lot, littered with empty tins and broken bottles. Beyond that was a pasture where several yearling Holsteins grazed. The rear of the Oxbow Billiards Hall, a bullwhackers' joint, blocked escape to the east. To the west was another empty lot behind the general store, then an abandoned wagon yard, given up the year before for a larger facility across town. Several small, dilapidated vehicles sat behind the stables, waiting to be sold or parted out. Surrounding them was a network of corrals and runways—a jungle of shadows, rife with hiding places.

Buck moved instinctively in that direction, but hadn't gone more than a dozen paces when he heard the sharp, metallic chatter of a pistol being cocked behind him. He froze, not even sneaking a peek over his shoulder.

"That's real smart, sonny," a man said. "Now go ahead and drop that hogleg, or I swear I'll blow a hole in you big enough to run a wagon tongue through."

Buck let the Colt drop, then eased around as the figure of a stocky man with a drawn revolver emerged from the shadows of the International's rear door. At first Buck didn't recognize him. Then a piece of moonlight glinted off the nickel-plated star pinned to his chest and Buck exhaled loudly. He started to lower his hands, but Sam Dunbar barked for him to keep them high.

"I'm Buck McCready," Buck said. "I'm not the one you're after."

"You just keep reaching for them stars till I tell you not to."

"You're letting whoever shot Sally Hayes get away."

"You've got an active mouth for someone staring into the business end of a Forty-Five. You ought to rein it in a bit, before it gets you in more trouble than you already are."

Buck glanced once more at the sheriff's pistol. It was one of the new Army Colt models that had been introduced the year before, and still somewhat of a rarity outside of military circles. But it was pointed at his belly, the hammer eared back and the muzzle yawning big as a water spout, and Buck reached silently higher.

"That's better," Dunbar said, pleased. "I like a man who knows when to shut his trap. Kick that hogleg over here where I can reach it."

Buck placed the toe of his boot behind his .44 and scooted it across the grass. Dunbar picked it up, held the muzzle to his nose, and sniffed loudly. "This don't bode in your favor," the sheriff said, tucking Buck's Colt behind his belt. "It's been fired."

"It wasn't me who shot her."

"Shot who?"

"Sally Hayes. Haven't you heard?"

"You just answer the questions, sonny. I'll ask them."

At the lawman's prodding, Buck related the events he'd witnessed upstairs, omitting only his own involvement that evening with Sally and Lotty.

Finally Dunbar said: "That's enough. Let's go back and talk to the bouncer and piano player." He jerked a thumb over his shoulder. "Come on, McCready. You ride point."

They returned to the saloon, climbing the back stairs to the central foyer where the two women had been killed. Buck expected the place to be filled with gawkers, but there was only the bouncer, the piano player, Tom Ashley, and a couple of working girls. The bodies of Sally and Lotty had been taken away, although the carpet was still stained where they had bled. Everyone looked at Buck when he stepped through the door, but only Ashley continued to stare at him after Dunbar entered the room.

"What's been going on up here, Tom?" the sheriff asked mildly.

"Nothin' to get worked up over. Couple gals got into a brawl."

"McCready thinks they're dead."

"What's he doin' here, anyway?" Ashley demanded.

"He's here because I told him to be here. When I want him somewhere else, I'll tell him to go there."

"Just seems like he's always pokin' around, askin' too damn' many questions."

"About what?" Dunbar inquired, but Ashley abruptly changed the subject.

"Yeah, there was a fight. That god-damn' Sally knifed Lotty over some argument been brewin' between 'em a couple days now, then someone shot Sally." He glared at Buck. "Might 'a' been him."

Dunbar looked at the piano player. "What about it, Gene? Did young McCready here shoot Sally?"

"No, sir. Whoever shot Sally did so from over there." He indicated the door to the balcony, its frame riddled and torn. "This fella"—he nodded at Buck, then to the door leading to the main room downstairs—"was standing right about there when the shooting started."

Dunbar glanced at the bouncer. "That true, Josiah?"

The black man shrugged. "I don't know where he was standing when Sally got shot, but I saw him take off after the shooter.

It wasn't him that killed her. It was some skinny fella out on the balcony."

Dunbar handed Buck his pistol. "Get out of here, McCready."

Buck hesitated only a moment, then holstered the Colt and slipped out the back door. He paused at the bottom of the stairs. He felt as though he'd stepped square into the middle of a muddy bog, without any notion where solid ground lay. Glumly he tramped back through the narrow alley to Front Street, merging with the crowd that had spilled off the saloon's boardwalk in the wake of the shootings. Forty or more individuals stood in the street, their necks cranked back to ogle the International's buckshot-torn upper doorway, as if the killer might still be lurking there among the splinters. Most of the crowd was speculating that a man was involved, maybe a gambler or some slick-haired money man from back East.

"Emotions outta control," one man kept saying. "There's a woman for ya, emotions outta control."

Buck turned away. He finally began to understand what Jock had meant the other day when he said there was more involved here than a simple disagreement over cards. Buck had known that, but he hadn't really comprehended the depth of what he was getting himself into, the magnitude of what he'd been asked to accomplish, until tonight. It began to sink in now with the disquieting sensation of a slug of whiskey on an empty stomach. Three were dead, and two attempts had already been made on his own life. If he wasn't careful, he could end up the same as Mase and Lotty and Sally. And if he failed, he could destroy the lives of quite a few others, people he cared about, perhaps even loved.

His hands trembling, Buck walked across the street to the Central Pacific depot and lost his supper in the weeds.

Chapter Eight

It was after midnight before Buck made it back to his apartment above Chin Lo's laundry, but he couldn't sleep. He gathered the few belongings he would take with him—extra clothes in a valise, and his rifle a .50-70 single-shot Remington. His bedroll was already bundled and ready to go, wrapped inside a double layer of oilcloth for protection against the elements. His regular bullwhip lay on top of the bedroll like a coiled snake, while Mase's fancy whip resided on top of the dresser. Buck eyed the two tightly-woven coils thoughtfully, then hung his old bullwhip on a wall coat rack and dropped Mase's long blacksnake onto his bedroll.

It was still dark when Buck walked up to the Box K the next morning. He'd thought everything was under control when he left last night, but he'd barely stepped through the door to Jock's office the next morning when it all started to come apart. Everyone looked up when he entered—Jock from behind his desk, Walt and Dulce from where they stood next to the sideboard, and a trio of strangers huddled like refugees in the middle of the room, one of them a woman.

"You're here," Jock said brusquely.

Buck glanced deliberately at a wall clock above Jock's desk, registering a quarter of four. "Early, too," he replied.

Jock accepted the rebuttal without comment. Indicating the woman and her companions, he said: "This is Miss Gwendolyn Haywood. Thaddeus Collins is on her left, Paddy O'Rourke on her right. Miss Haywood is the daughter of Robert Haywood, a senior vice-president with Weber, Forsyth, and McGowan."

"Weber, Forsyth, and McGowan, Incorporated, of Philadelphia," Walt emphasized, tipping his head conspiringly. "The parent company of Bannock Mining." He gave Gwendolyn a guarded look. "Mister Haywood is the executive officer of BMC."

"In other words," Miss Haywood interjected, "Daddy is the man"—she glanced deliberately at Jock—"whom other men have to please if they hope to continue a relationship with Bannock Mining." She stepped briskly forward to offer Buck the back of her gloved hand. "You must be our captain, Buchanan McCready."

Buck accepted the proffered hand uncertainly. Protocol demanded a kiss, or at least a quick brush of his lips across her slim fingers, but he'd already deduced from Dulce's taut demeanor that rudeness might be a more prudent option. "Ma'am," he said, pumping her hand vigorously.

"You may call me Gwen," she informed him, not bothering to mask her amusement. Then something she'd said exploded in Buck's mind, and he dropped her hand.

"You said, *our* captain?"

"Miss Haywood may accompany the caravan as Bannock Mining's representative," Jock informed Buck in a strained tone. "I've wired their home office twice, but as of this morning I haven't received anything to either confirm or deny what she's telling me."

"I'm afraid Mister Kavanaugh is uncomfortable with the rôle of the modern woman," Gwen stated. "I believe he considers the female form too delicate for such an arduous adventure. He's forgetting the deeds of the Molly Pitchers and the Joans of Arc throughout history."

"Women travel the Montana Road all the time," Jock replied

flatly. "My own wife bullwhacked an outfit all the way from Leavenworth, Kansas, to Salt Lake City in 'Fifty-Nine, and did a fine job, too. What I find difficult to believe is that a senior vice president with a firm as prestigious as Weber, Forsyth, and McGowan would assign his own daughter to this kind of a task. There are dangers along the trail that even an executive officer must have heard of, not to mention the fact that his daughter would be traveling alone with a crew of muleskinners."

Gwen laughed cheerfully. "I appreciate your concern, Mister Kavanaugh, but my father has learned to accept the headstrong nature of his only daughter. I'm sure you will, too, in time."

Jock's expression turned to granite. "Whether or not I accept anyone's nature will be my decision, Miss Haywood. Make no mistake, this is a Kavanaugh train you're asking permission to travel with. Whether you go or stay will be at my discretion. I don't care who your father is."

Gwen looked momentarily startled, but quickly recovered her composure. "*Touché,* Mister Kavanaugh. I acknowledge your authority and bow to your judgment . . . but not without a reminder that, lacking a representative, no matter what the reason, your prospects for a long-term contract with Bannock Mining will be seriously jeopardized."

"But my authority won't be, not for anyone's contract."

Gwen curtsied almost demurely, then slid back to stand with her two companions, although careful, Buck noted, to keep herself slightly in front of both men.

Buck studied Gwen curiously, as puzzled by her bravado as he was the incongruity of her claims. She was tall for a woman, slender and lithe. Locks of yellow-gold hair tumbled loosely about her shoulders, and a pale winter's complexion vied with what was obviously a recently acquired ruddiness for control of her complexion. She had a sharp, narrow nose, ice-blue eyes, and carried herself with a regality born of privileged upbringing. Buck guessed she was a year or two younger than he was, but no more than that.

Her two companions were clearly of a lesser caste. Paddy O'Rourke looked more Mexican than Irish. He was small-boned and dark-featured, with sloping shoulders and piercing black eyes under woolly brows. He wore the rough clothing of a range man—corduroy trousers worn slick at the knees, low-heeled boots, a dark shirt under a soiled canvas vest, and a broad-brimmed hat that looked as if it had seen many a smoky campfire. A large-framed pistol resided on his right hip; a sturdy butcher knife in a buckskin sheath was carried on his left.

Standing behind Gwen's other shoulder, Thaddeus Collins presented the almost haughty air of someone who viewed himself as several cuts above everyone else in the room, with the exception of the woman at his side. Like a bodyguard, Buck mused—or loyal dog. He was probably in his early thirties, which made him considerably older than Gwen but at least a decade younger than O'Rourke. He was as tall as she was, but not as slim. His dark hair was cut short, and he sported a wafer-thin mustache across his upper lip that looked more like soot than facial hair. His dress—a worn brown suit, wrinkled white shirt, narrow tie, cheap shoes, and a medium-brimmed brown hat—reminded Buck of a man with more ambition than money. Buck couldn't detect a sidearm, but figured he would have something lethal concealed about his person. Thaddeus Collins didn't look like the kind of man who would leave his personal defense to the whims of fate.

"This puts Kavanaugh Freight in a delicate position," Jock told Buck. "I won't hold the train up waiting for a reply, no matter how much I'd like to have this issue with Miss Haywood resolved, but, at the same time, I'm loathe to send an inexperienced person on such an important assignment."

"Is this the kink you mentioned last night?" Buck asked.

Jock nodded grimly. "I'd hoped to have my reply from Philadelphia by now, but, since I don't, here's how the situation stands . . . if Miss Haywood does accompany the caravan, she'll furnish her own wagon, which I understand she's already rented from Gilmer and Salisbury."

"A *mud* wagon, I believe it's called," Gwen confirmed. "A quaint term for an even quainter vehicle. Sort of like a stripped-down stagecoach."

That wasn't a bad description, Buck thought. With its hard bench seats and full-length canvas sides that rolled up for ventilation, instead of wooden side panels, the mud wagon was the poorer cousin of the brightly painted, gild-trimmed Concord coaches of the East. It was a popular staging vehicle in the West, though, where practicality almost always won out over the fanciful, and where the high desert sun and blowing sand could strip gold trim to bare wood in a matter of days.

"It'll be a well-maintained vehicle if it's from Gilmer and Salisbury," Jock said. "You're lucky they're letting you have it. Most of their coaches are on the road around the clock this time of year."

Gwen smiled prettily. "Money has its charms, Mister Kavanaugh, but a letter of credit can buy you the world."

Jock didn't bother to hide his disgust. "Paddy O'Rourke is her driver," he told Buck, leaning back in his chair. "Thad Collins is her bodyguard. BMC will foot the bill for their food and gear, and Miss Haywood has purchased a pair of saddle horses for herself and Collins. Consider the lot of them a part of your cargo. I want them delivered safely to Montana, then returned here in the same condition.

"And you"—he gave the BMC trio a sweeping glance—"will conduct yourselves accordingly. I don't know how you were raised in Philadelphia, Miss Haywood, but personal freedom has its limits on a wagon train. The wagon master's word is law.

You obey it without question." His gaze shifted to Dulce. "That goes for you, too, young lady. On the road, Buck's word is final."

"Wait a minute," Buck said. "Dulce ain't going."

"Dulce is going," Jock returned flatly. "I don't like it any more than you do, but I won't have Miss Haywood, an unmarried woman and an executive's daughter, traveling unchaperoned. Dulce will fill that position, and vice versa."

"It's too dangerous," Buck said.

"It's no more dangerous than following a wagon across the plains, like Mama did," Dulce piped up. "Besides, Papa's already said women travel the Montana Road all the time."

"This is different," Buck replied stubbornly.

Dulce's expression softened. "I'm asking for your trust, Buck, as you asked for mine the other night. Do you remember?"

Buck glanced helplessly at Jock.

"You're in charge, Buck," Jock said quietly. "I've said they can go, but if you want to countermand that, I'll honor your position. To tell you the truth, I've enough qualms about this whole fiasco to wonder at my own motives."

Buck sighed, then shook his head. "Naw, let 'em come, as long as they remember who's boss."

Dulce smiled, and Gwen mocked a sloppy salute. Buck glanced at Paddy and Thad. The sulky-looking Irishman shrugged as if he didn't care one way or the other, but Collins's spine seemed to stiffen under Buck's gaze.

"My charge is Miss Haywood," he said stonily. "No one else."

"Mister Collins will do as you bid, Mister McCready," Gwen hastily intervened, then gave her companion an imploring look. "You will do as you're told, won't you, dear Thaddeus?"

Without any apparent loss of dignity, Collins bowed to Buck. "It would appear that I am at your service, after all."

"Lord God," Buck muttered.

"Mister Jepson has your paperwork at his desk," Jock told

Buck. "Why don't you get it, then head on out to camp? Dulce will be along later with Miss Haywood and her *quaint* little mud wagon. I've got a man putting her stuff on board now."

Buck nodded and shook Jock's hand, and Jock mouthed: *Take care of her, Buck.*

"I won't let you down, Mister Kavanaugh," Buck promised, but in his gut he couldn't help wondering if that was an oath he would be able to keep.

It was still dark when Buck exited the Box K office twenty minutes later, a leather folder tucked under one arm. Inside the folder were bills of lading, a letter of introduction from Jock, and a power-of-attorney contract between Buck and the Box K that allowed him to represent the company on the trail.

Pausing on the rear porch, he stared across the wagon yard to the lantern-lit entrance of the main stable, where a hostler was currying a long-legged black mule. Seeing the animal under someone else's care caused Buck a twinge of guilt. Readying his mount was his responsibility, not the hostler's. It was just one more mark of neglect, accrued while he'd stumbled around town looking for an elusive killer.

The rear door to Jock's office opened and closed softly behind him, but Buck didn't turn around. "Did you know about this the other night, when you asked me to trust you?" he asked Dulce.

"I knew it was a possibility."

"So you lied to me?"

She put a hand on his arm. "Don't think like that. I wasn't sure, and I was afraid you'd stop it before the opportunity arose if I spoke too soon."

"A lie's a lie," Buck insisted.

"Is it any more of a lie than what you've already withheld from Papa?"

"That's different," he said, but he knew she was right; he'd betrayed the truth with his silence. Yet he couldn't summon up any remorse for his deception. There was more going on here than met the eye. Until he discovered exactly what it was, he wasn't sure who he could trust.

"Mama and Papa came to Utah in Eighteen Fifty-Nine," Dulce said quietly. "They were attacked by Indians along the North Platte River in Wyoming, and she stood at Papa's side, loading and firing her own rifle. Before that, she chased off border ruffians in Missouri by refusing to allow them into her home to ransack it for food and ammunition. She once fished a water moccasin out from under her bed, killed it with a hoe, then cooked it for supper.

"Mama *lived,* Buck, and she had wonderful stories to tell because of it. She climbed mountains and forded rivers. She shot a buffalo. I still use its robe in winter. But I was so young when we came out here that I barely remember what a buffalo looks like. I've never climbed anything taller than Little Mountain, and that's hardly a hill. It doesn't even have trees. Do you realize there's not one tree in Corinne? Not one!

"But I'm Papa's daughter, you see? His precious survivor . . . all he has left of Mama. Since her death, he's become so protective of me it feels as if I'm being smothered, and it's only been recently, with you, that he's relented enough to allow me some measure of freedom for courtship. But they're such small measures, Buck, they only make me yearn for more."

She smiled. "Montana! What images that conjures for the imagination! Grizzly bears and wild Indians, road agents and wicked, wicked mining camps. Why, just think. . . ."

"My God," Buck interrupted, laughing. "Are you listening to yourself?"

For a moment, Dulce looked puzzled, then her expression changed to hurt. "Is it that funny, that you'd laugh, or is it just offensive to your sense of propriety?"

"It's not offensive, but . . . Dulce, there's no mining camp in Montana wilder than Corinne is right now, and Shoshones and Utes both range within sight of the city regularly. You have your own rifle and your own horse that you can ride at will, within certain limits set by your father. Sensible limits, I ought to add, considering the nature of this town. Surely you have more freedom than most women. Look at Peewee's wife, or Nate's wife and daughters? I know you've got more freedom than they do."

The injured expression remained. "Then you think I'm a spoiled child?"

He would have denied that even without his recent encounter with Gwen Haywood. "No, and I don't blame you for wanting to see something new. After a winter holed up in Corinne, waiting for the roads to open, I'm half wild to get away myself. All right, Dulce, I'll respect your wishes, and I'll trust you, too."

She leaned in to kiss him. "Thank you, Buck," she said, her voice oddly choked.

He put an arm around her shoulders, strangely affected by the depth of her emotion. Then, stepping back, he said: "You need to get ready. We'll be moving out in less than an hour."

"I'll be there," she promised, then flashed him a brilliant smile. "You won't regret this, Buck. I promise! It'll be wonderful!"

Chapter Nine

Night was waning as Buck jogged his black mule over the rattling planks of the Bear River bridge. To the southeast, beyond the griddle-flat plain separating Corinne from the small Mormon farming community of Brigham City, the prickling of lantern light signified the stirring of life after a night's repose. Directly east, thrusting up sharp as daggers into the pearled belly of the sky, the snow-mantled peaks of the Wellsville Mountains were already tinged with the glow of the coming sun. Another half hour and it would be light enough to roll, Buck thought, and suddenly he was grinning like a kid with a mouthful of taffy. Damn but it was going to feel good to be on the move again.

The black picked up its pace as the column of huge freight wagons took shape about three hundred yards away. Buck let the mule have its head. On the books, the leggy john with the soft, rust-colored muzzle and keen eye, was listed as Ezekiel, but everyone called him Zeke. He was Buck's favorite among the dozen or so saddle mules kept by the Box K. Zeke had an easy stride in all three gaits and a level-headed disposition that made him dependable in the tightest situation, but to Buck the mule's greatest attribute was its withers, that narrow, muscular taper at the base of the neck that was so vital in keeping a saddle firmly in place, rather than slipping to one side or the other.

High withers were so uncommon on mules that few people would judge that they even had any. Normally low withers and a reputation for orneriness was what kept most men astride horses, although Buck considered a good mule the equal of any six horses for sure-footedness and mountain smarts.

Buck had intended to transfer his bedroll and valise to the mess wagon as soon as he reached camp, but as he guided Zeke between a pair of high-sided freighters, he spotted trouble brewing ahead and knew his gear would have to wait.

Near the north end of camp, Peewee Trapp was standing in front of his morning breakfast fire, short legs spread wide as if to brace a strong wind. Ray Jones, Joe Perry, Nate Evans, and several others from the Box K crew were bunched solidly behind him.

Facing them was a smaller group of men, although no less grim-looking. Mitch Kroll stood at its forefront, reminding Buck of an ox reared up on its hind legs, wearing pants and boots and a narrow-brimmed hat. Mitch's fists hung at his side like tooth-scarred hams, and his massive shoulders were hunched forward as if contemplating a charge.

Buck rode in their direction without hurry, taking time to assess the situation before planting himself squarely in the middle of it. No one spoke as he came up, or even looked around until he stopped about ten feet out. "What's the trouble?" he asked.

"Who the hell are you?" Mitch snarled, throwing him a quick, irreverent glance.

"I'm Buck McCready."

Mitch snorted, and Peewee said: "Ain't no trouble, Buck. We was just hammerin' out some details."

But Ray wouldn't let it drop that easily. "Kroll thinks he's gonna take the lead-dog position, Buck," he said. "Thinks the rest of us is gonna chew on his dust all the way to Montana."

"It ain't been decided yet who's takin' the lead position," Mitch countered, glaring at Peewee, "but I sure as hell ain't takin' no orders from runts."

Buck's hand slid unconsciously to the bullwhip fastened snugly to his gun belt. In his mind's eye he saw Mase standing tall and firm, taking guff from no man. Taking a deep breath, he said: "Well, that's not entirely true. You'll take orders from me first, then from Milo Newton if I'm not around. Peewee has the point position and he'll keep it until I decide differently. Ray brings up the rear with the mess wagon. It'll be his job to see that nobody falls behind. I ain't decided yet where I'm going to put you."

Mitch's eyes narrowed. "I ain't used to playin' second fiddle, bub, especially to kids and runts and blow-hards like Ray Jones."

"It won't be hard to get used to," Buck replied firmly. "The Box K has been running its trains this way for a long time."

"I ain't a Box K man," Mitch returned, his smirk broad enough to reveal a pair of yellowed incisors peeking through the shaggy curtain of his mustache. "Maybe us independents ought to make our own way north. We could wait for you Box K boys in Virginia City, if you don't take too long gettin' there."

Glancing at the men standing behind Kroll, Buck thought their alliance seemed oddly placed. He recognized the blocky Sandwich Islander called Big Kona, and Little Ed Womack, whose swamper was thought to harbor bad luck. Neither seemed particularly comfortable with the way things were shaping up. Speaking to Womack, Buck said: "Is that the way you feel, Ed?"

Little Ed quickly shook his head. "No, it ain't."

"How about you, Big Kona?"

Keho Kona's voice rumbled from deep within his broad chest. "Mitchell Kroll does not speak for me. I sign the paper to haul for Jock Kavanaugh. That is whose company I drive for."

Buck glanced at the last two men—Garth Lang and Lyle Mead. Garth looked worried, but Buck couldn't read anything from Lyle's expression; he stood silently to one side with a stubby cigarette stuck in one corner of his mouth, his left hand thrust into the pocket of his coat. "What about you two?" Buck asked.

Garth shrugged and said: "I contracted with Jock."

Lyle hesitated, but, after an uncertain glance at Kroll, he allowed that he was hauling for Kavanaugh, too.

"Spineless pieces of shit," Mitch grumbled. "I ought to bust all your balls with a hammer."

"That'll be enough of that," Buck said sternly. "Mitch, you've got a contract with the Box K. Breach it and Jock'll see you in court before you get your mules stabled." The burly teamster stared back darkly, and Buck squared his shoulders, suddenly angry. "It's a long haul to Montana, Kroll. I want this settled before we pull out."

For a minute, Mitch's glare was like a steel shaft welded between the two men. Then the crazy gleam abruptly left his eyes and his broad shoulders came down. Looking Buck up and down, he said: "You're that kid Mase Campbell pulled outta a Sioux camp some years back, ain't cha'?"

"I am," Buck acknowledged.

"And now you're takin' his place."

"Nobody'll ever take Mase's place."

Mitch laughed jeeringly, but Buck understood that, in his own way, the big man was backing down. Breathing a silent sigh of relief, Buck said: "There's one more thing. A couple of women will be traveling with us. One of them's the representative for Bannock Mining. Her name is Gwendolyn Haywood. The other is Jock's daughter, Dulce. Miss Haywood is traveling with a couple of male associates, a camp tender and a bodyguard. You'll meet them tonight, although I expect they'll keep to themselves as much as possible. Mind your manners when they're around."

Mitch scowled. "This is a muleskinners' outfit, McCready. If them ladies want to cozy up to polite company, leave 'em ride the president's car on the U.P."

"God dammit, I ain't gonna argue with you all day," Buck told Kroll irritably. "You mind your manners when those women are near."

A yell from the sage-covered flat to the north thankfully severed any further argument. Buck turned his eyes to where Milo and Rossy Evans were bringing the remuda in off its night pasture. Bigfoot Payne, Mitch's dull-witted helper, and Little Ed Womack's Mexican swamper, Manuel Varga, stood outside the wagons with long ropes stretched between them and the wheels of the nearest freighters, creating wings by which to funnel the mules inside the loosely circled wagons.

The drumming of shod hoofs grew thunderous as the racing herd swept toward the wagons. The feisty snorting and squealing of well-kept animals that hadn't been worked hard since last fall added to the cacophony. Soon, the camp would be engulfed in braying mules and cursing men, swinging bullwhips and halter chains with a vengeance as they sorted out their teams. As the leading edge of the remuda slowed to a trot down the rope funnel, Buck quickly reined Zeke out of the way. "Here they are, boys!" he hollered. "Get 'em hitched and ready to roll. We pull out in twenty minutes."

Buck jogged his mule down the line of double-hitched outfits to where the mess wagon was already secured behind Ray Jones's two big Schuttlers. Dismounting, Buck pulled his gear from the back of his saddle and hefted it into the low-wheeled Studebaker, packing it securely so that it wouldn't bounce out. Then he moved around to the front of the wagon and stepped up on the tongue. Bolted to the Studebaker's left sideboard, just inside the front pucker of canvas, was an oblong oak box reinforced with iron strapping, called the office. A sturdy padlock to which only Buck carried a key hung from the latch.

Buck popped the lock and lifted the lid. Inside were several narrow slots, like a roll-top desk turned on its back. Within these slim compartments was the paperwork that would keep the train running—permits, company vouchers, a tin box with enough cash to cover unexpected expenses, and a small, leather-bound journal the wagon master was expected to keep up daily, noting the outfit's problems and progress.

Buck added the leather folder Walt had given him, then closed and locked the lid. Standing on the tongue, he ran a rough inventory on the remainder of the load. The bedrolls and personal gear of the muleskinners were stacked near the front, where it would be easy to find in the dark. Foodstuff—potatoes, dried fruits, beans, flour, coffee, and a few cases of canned items—was stowed toward the rear, buffered on either side by casks of side-pork and hams.

Extra parts for the wagons—a spare tongue; a pair of rough-hewn axles; a carton of big, square lug nuts; wrenches, hammers, wood-working tools to shave and fit the parts; copper wire to patch cracked spokes; kegs of Mica Axle Grease, buckles and coils of leather for harness repair; shovels, picks, axes; several hundred feet of rope for makeshift corrals; farrier's equipment and a box of iron shoes for the mules—were stacked toward the middle and bottom of the load.

Stepping off the tongue, Buck saw Milo loping a spotted molly toward him. There was a lever gun booted under the ramrod's right leg, and Buck muttered to Zeke: "I'd give a twenty-dollar gold piece to know if that's a Forty-Four Rimfire."

Pulling his mule to a stop, Milo said: "*Que pasa,* boss?"

" 'Morning," Buck replied, but his attention was drawn now to the southwest, where the sounds of a four-mule hitch pulling a Gilmer and Salisbury mud wagon over the Bear River bridge came to him like the rumble of distant thunder. Behind the coach came a trio on horseback, and he shook his head ruefully. "This ain't gonna be a normal wagon train at all, is it?"

"Aw, it'll shake out in a few days," Milo predicted.

"Let's hope so," Buck said, but, as his gaze settled on Gwen and her entourage, he thought: *There's trouble in that brew.*

The riders—Dulce on her claybank, Beau, Gwen on a lively-looking chestnut, and Thad atop a well-put-together bay—spotted Buck and galloped ahead through the sage. Milo perked up noticeably when he spotted Gwen. "Who's the gal riding that copper horse?"

"That's Miss Haywood," Buck said, stepping into his saddle.

Milo whistled appreciatively. "She'll be a thing to study on, won't she?"

"She's BMC's rep," Buck replied. "I'd watch myself around her if I was you. Women like that generally have sharp claws. Besides, her daddy's the head of Bannock Mining, and I doubt if he'd think too highly of a muleskinner randying after his daughter."

But Milo was only half listening. "Who's that stiff-looking hoss riding beside her?"

"That's Thad Collins, her bodyguard. I'm not sure what he thinks his relationship is with her, but I'm pretty sure Miss Haywood sees it differently."

As the riders approached, Dulce called: "Are we on time?"

"Two minutes to spare," Buck said, forcing a smile. He introduced Milo to the others, then added, for Gwen and Thad's sake: "Milo's second in command. He'll give the orders when I'm not around."

"Miss Haywood," Milo said, removing his hat with a flourish. "If I'd have known Bannock Mining had such pretty representatives, I'd have sought employment there, instead of with the Box K."

Gwen's face lit up with delight. "Perhaps we could induce

you to switch sides."

"It's a definite possibility," Milo acknowledged cheerfully.

Scowling, Thad said: "Jock Kavanaugh tells us you're new to this territory, Mister Newton. What experience do you have as a guide?"

Milo looked briefly annoyed, then returned his full attention to Gwen. "Miss Haywood, I need to get this rowdy bunch of muleskinners on the road, but maybe later I could escort you in the direction of those mountains yonder." He nodded toward the Wellsville range. "I haven't visited them yet myself, but I've something of a knack for locating suitable glades for picnics."

"That sounds like a splendid idea," Gwen enthused. "Toward noon, shall we say?"

"Well, now, Milo's gonna be busy around noon," Buck chimed in. "Fact is, he's gonna be busy for the next few weeks."

"Why, boss, it's a fact I've got a heap of responsibility riding on my shoulders, being more or less the heart and soul of this here operation, but I expect I'll be able to wiggle free from time to time to squire Miss Haywood around. So long as she's agreeable to it, that is."

"Miss Haywood won't be in need of a squire," Thad tautly interjected. "I've been retained to see to that duty myself."

Thad Collins was looking mighty put out, Buck thought with more amusement than he would have expected. The bodyguard's thin face was flushed, and his little mustache was twitching like bait on a hook, but his ire seemed only to fuel Milo's impudence.

"That's quite all right, old man," Milo said, mimicking Collins's stiff, Northeastern dialect. "I doubt if Miss Haywood will require your services much longer, anyway. Perhaps Mister McCready will have a position for you. Tell me, what experience do you have worming mules?"

Buck tried to cover his laughter with a strained cough, but, as he watched Collins's reaction, he was startled by something so subtle, so swiftly there and gone, that he wasn't sure he'd seen it at all. "Milo," Buck said curtly, "why don't you go see if anyone needs help?"

"Yes," Dulce said, sounding peeved by the ramrod's behavior. "You shouldn't make light of others, Mister Newton."

"Aw, Collins knows I'm just funning him, Miss Kavanaugh. Don't cha, ol' boy?"

Collins refused an answer, but Buck noticed that there was no back-down in him, either. It was something to remember, he thought.

"Go on," Buck said to Milo, the humor gone from his voice. "Collins, tell O'Rourke to fall in behind the mess wagon."

Collins nodded mechanically. "All right, but I'll remind you that I'm not your message boy, McCready. My responsibility is to Miss Haywood's protection. I won't be distracted from that."

"You just put O'Rourke where I told you to put him, after that I don't care what you do." As Buck pulled Zeke around, he caught Dulce's eye and motioned for her to ride with him.

"Well, that was interesting," Dulce said when they were out of earshot. "I met Mister Newton briefly yesterday and found him charming. I had no idea he could be so . . . maddening."

"That's a fair way of putting it," Buck agreed. He glanced over his shoulder. Gwen and Milo were sitting their mounts close together, talking earnestly, while Collins rode off to confer with O'Rourke.

"Mister Newton's arrogance doesn't concern you?" Dulce asked.

"What concerns me more is the look Collins gave him."

"Well, do you blame him? I'd be upset, too."

"Collins didn't look upset to me," Buck said. "He looked more like a man getting ready to squash a bug, and not questioning his ability to do it, either."

"Thad?"

"Uhn-huh."

Dulce looked doubtful. "He didn't strike me as a . . . a particularly dangerous fellow," she said hesitantly.

"No, he didn't strike me that way, either. Now I'm not so sure." He looked behind him once more. Milo and Gwen had broken apart and Gwen was walking her chestnut toward the mud wagon, where Collins waited for her. Milo had disappeared, probably somewhere along the outside of the caravan, and Buck faced forward again with an odd sense of relief. "Will you be all right on your own for a while?" he asked.

"Of course."

He smiled and said—"Good."—then lifted Zeke into a lope.

As Buck cantered down the long line of wagons, he was pleased to see that the men were hitched and ready to roll. Thirteen outfits, each comprised of two big freight wagons pulled in tandem, except for the small mess wagon behind Ray's two Schuttlers. Each outfit was drawn by either a twelve- or fourteen-mule jerkline hitch—six to seven spans apiece, depending on the teamster's preference. Nearly one hundred feet of wagons and mules stretched along a taut chain, called a fifth chain, that ran from the pull rod under the front wagon to the doubletree behind each span of mules, before terminating at the heels of the leaders.

The squat, canvas-covered bows on the tall Murphy, Schuttler, and Bain wagons crested at nearly twelve feet above the ground. Some of the wheels stood seven feet or better, the iron-rim tires as much as eight inches wide. The larger lead wagons could carry over three tons of freight when packed tightly, the trail wagons, or trailers, somewhat less, but each outfit would haul close to six tons of freight apiece.

Watching the train prepare to pull out was enough to stir the blood of even the most jaded muleskinner, and Buck was hardly that. His excitement flared as he approached the head of the column. Peewee was already mounted on his brawny roan nigh-wheeler—the left- or near-side mule—harnessed just in front of his flatbed lead wagon. He carried a coiled bullwhip in his right hand; in his left he held the free end of a sturdy cotton jerkline that ran up the left side of his hitch to the lead team; the line was strung through brass rings fastened to the shoulder harness of each nigh-mule, before being clipped to the bit of his left-side leader.

Only the nigh-wheeler, at the rear of the long hitch, and the leader, at the front, were fitted with bridles and bits. The rest wore only halters, fastened to nothing, although Buck knew they would all pull with the hearts of troopers.

That slim, half-inch cotton line would be Peewee's only control over his seven teams, other than a ten-foot bullwhip, a leather sack of fist-sized stones for throwing, and a reputation among his mules for tolerating no mischief without just cause. Barring a green team or an unskilled driver, all that was usually required to set an outfit into motion was a short tug on the jerkline to alert the mules that a command was imminent, then a tap to the ribs of his riding mule and a yell to "get up" or "hup."

Reining to a stop at the head of the column, Buck stared back down the line of wagons. All eyes were upon him, silent, expectant—awaiting his word. Buck's fingers tightened on Zeke's reins, his pulse quickened. Taking a deep breath, he waved his hat above his head and bellowed loud enough to be heard at the farthest reaches of the train: "Streeetch out! Stretch out! Come on, boys! We're going to Montana!"

Chapter Ten

Sitting alone in a dark rear corner of the Hanover Saloon in Franklin, Idaho Territory, Nick Kelso had to struggle against the urge to have another shot of whiskey from the bottle sitting on the table in front of him. Although he still felt clear-headed, he knew he'd had enough. Maybe too much, he reflected, glancing at the bar where Arlen Fleck stood with one heel balanced atop the brass footrail, his elbows flopped over the counter like a pair of half-empty flour sacks.

"Worthless little turd," Nick murmured, staring at Fleck's hunched shoulders and sloping spine. He wondered if the scrawny dunce had any idea how close he'd come to dying last night. Nick's jaws tightened as he recalled Arlen's trepid approach in the lobby of the Utah Northern's Ogden depot, the worn brim of his porkpie hat crushed in a white-knuckled grip, his voice high and quavery the way it got when he knew he was in trouble. . . .

". . . he's gone, Nick, just flat gone."

"Who's gone?" Nick had demanded, but in his heart he already knew.

"The kid." Arlen had swallowed hard in the stony silence, then added: "There wasn't nothin' I could do. Hell, a man's gotta visit the privy once in a while, don't he?"

Only a station filled with witnesses had prevented Nick from wringing the little shitheel's neck right then and there. Keeping his voice low, his temper delicately in check, he'd said: "Did you look for him?"

Arlen had nodded vigorously. "I sure did. Everywhere, but he's just gone. Flat gone."

Nick had exhaled slowly, but, after a moment's reflection, he'd decided it probably didn't matter any more. Still, he didn't let Fleck off the hook too easily. "Go get yourself a ticket to Franklin," he'd instructed the smaller man.

Arlen had looked suddenly wary. "Franklin? W—. . . why?"

"Just go get a ticket," Nick had grated in a low voice. "When we're in the car, I'll sit up front and you sit in back. Stay close when we get to Franklin, but don't come near me or try to talk to me. Keep your mouth shut until I tell you otherwise. Understand?"

Arlen's head had bobbed rapidly. "You afraid someone'll see us together?"

"No," Nick had explained carefully. "I'm afraid I'll cut your throat if I have to listen to any more of your mindless crap."

That had shut him up, Nick remembered grimly, and kept him quiet until they'd reached Franklin shortly after 3:00 A.M. It was only then that Arlen had approached him once more, hat again humbly in hand.

"I know you're mad at me, but there's somethin' else I gotta tell you, and you ain't gonna like it."

He hadn't, either, but a wire to Baptiste LeBry, in Corinne, had confirmed the worst. The Box K was pulling out at first light, a BMC representative firmly in place. . . .

And who in hell, Nick thought angrily, *would have ever considered the sister?*

His gaze swung back to Fleck, draped over the bar as if he intended to homestead the spot. Hadn't Fleck mentioned a sister, and hadn't Nick told him to take care of her? He should have known better, he berated himself. Give Arlen Fleck a chore to do and he might pull it off. Give him two, and he was sure to bungle both.

The puzzling part was that Arlen still insisted there was no way the girl could have known the shape her brother was in when she left Ogden. Apparently little Eddie Haywood, BMC's official agent, had a reputation for indulgences of the flesh, including a penchant for opium he'd developed while still in Philadelphia. It was because of that, Arlen claimed, along with a past history of disappearing for days at a time, that the sister hadn't been overly alarmed by her brother's absence.

Well, she'd thrown a hell of a wrench into his plans, Nick acknowledged bitterly, but there was nothing for it now but to continue on.

His eyes shifted to the Hanover's front door, where the first rays of the morning sun were just starting to creep inside the sour-smelling saloon. Baptiste LeBry had insisted on subtlety to slow the Box K, but that obviously wasn't going to work now. Nick smiled coldly. If LeBry's way wasn't getting the job done, he had his own methods to fall back on—harsher, true, but indisputably effective. And this time, there weren't going to be any mistakes.

Chapter Eleven

The Box K reached Hampton's Crossing shortly before 10:00 A.M. the next day. Buck settled the toll bridge fees with a company voucher, then crossed the Bear River for the last time until their return in another six to eight weeks.

The bridge company's buildings and a stagecoach relay station sat on a narrow shelf of fertile bottom land along the Bear's east bank. On the far side, the flat widened to almost half a mile, before the road scaled a steep dirt bluff that would lift the caravan out of the bottoms in a long, S-shaped curve. Buck kicked Zeke into a lope to get ahead of the train, then slowed when he saw Dulce cantering after him.

"Do you mind if I join you?" she called, reining her horse alongside Buck's mule.

"Not a bit," he replied. "How are you faring?"

"Splendidly. Did you know Miss Haywood has a collapsible cot that she sleeps on?"

Buck laughed. "No, but I can't say I'm surprised. Does she snore?"

"Like a muleskinner," Dulce returned blithely. Among the equipment the two women shared was an eight-by-twelve-foot wall tent, with an oriental rug to throw down over the wiregrass and sandburs. "I missed you at supper last night," she added. "Do the drivers always eat separately?"

"Generally. Me and Peewee, Ray, Joe Perry, and sometimes Nate and Rossy, will share one fire. Chris Hobson, Andy LeMay,

Lou Kitledge, and Charlie Bigelow share another, although we visit back and forth a lot. It's easier to fix supper if you're not elbow to elbow with everyone else."

Dulce nodded thoughtfully. "I'd hoped you and I could dine together in the evenings, alone," she ventured. "I understand that your responsibilities don't end at sundown, but . . . is Peewee's fire any warmer than mine?"

"You know it's not. It's just that things are always a little hectic the first few days on the road. Plus, we've got all these new drivers, then Gwen Haywood and her people." Glancing back at Peewee's leaders, he said: "Come on, I want to show you something."

Dulce kept Beau close as they galloped across what remained of the flat. They slowed to a trot at the first tight bend of the long S curve, then a walk. The grade steepened as it climbed toward the second bend, nearly three hundred yards away. On their left the dirt wall towered high above them; on their right it fell almost straight down, but, near the top, a little jut of land offered an unobstructed view of the bottoms. Buck reined in there and Dulce followed, catching her breath at the vista that opened before her.

"This is one of the best places I know of to watch a team at work," Buck said. "You can see the whole process from up here. It's like riding on the back of an eagle."

But Dulce's eyes had been drawn to the river. "What a lovely sight!" she exclaimed, staring at the hotel and way station on the far side of the Bear.

Buck gave the scene a cursory glance, enough to take in the horses standing in the corrals behind the barn—relay teams for the stagecoaches that rattled north and south between Corinne and the mining camps of Montana and Idaho—and the half dozen or so milk cows grazing in a small green pasture to the south.

"It's like paintings I've seen of Eastern farmlands," she said. "So perfectly tranquil." Then the crack of a bullwhip cleaved the cool morning air, and Dulce jumped.

"Watch," Buck said excitedly. From their vantage point they had a clear view of Peewee's leaders entering the first turn.

Recognizing what was about to unfold, Dulce's voice deepened with concern. "Shouldn't you be down there helping?"

"Not yet. I want to see how Milo handles himself."

At the bottom of the bluff, Milo was hugging the inside of the curve, crowding Peewee's eights—the fourth team from the rear—with his spotted molly, while the leaders and twelves were already swinging into the turn. In another minute the forward teams would be climbing in the opposite direction, their hoofs level with the tops of the wagons as they leaned into the grade.

A good teamster could make just about any kind of corner on his own, but Buck knew even an old hand like Peewee—especially an old hand like Peewee, with nothing to prove—appreciated help in situations like this, where the margin for error was so small. In any turn, but especially in tight ones along steep, narrow grades, it was critical that each individual team within the larger hitch did its part fluidly and without hesitation. It was just as important that whoever was assisting the muleskinner knew what he was doing. Give a team the wrong command, or confuse it with directions that ran counter to their own instincts or what they were receiving from the jerkline, and the whole hitch could crumble into pandemonium, threatening not only the wagons and its cargo, but the lives of the driver and his mules.

Although everything seemed to be going smoothly, Buck could feel himself tensing up. Even from here, he could see the fifth chain, running from the wagon to the doubletree behind the leaders, stretched tight along the legs of the offside twelves and tens, those teams directly behind the leaders.

"Dammit, Milo, get off those eights and move back on the pointers," Buck rasped. It was vital now, right now, that the wheelers and pointers keep the wagons running straight, moving toward the outside of the curve. Otherwise, they'd pull the massive vehicles off the inside of the curve, straight into the bluff.

"He can't hear you, Buck," Dulce hissed sharply. "Milo can't hear you."

"He shouldn't have to hear me," Buck snapped, gathering his reins, but Dulce stopped him before he could wheel away.

"No, he's doing it. See? Peewee's calling him back, too."

Buck lowered his reins as Milo whirled back down the line of mules, cracking his whip expertly alongside the pointers. "Jump 'em," Buck urged. "Ease 'em over."

Milo and Peewee were both popping their whips alongside the pointers, turning the air blue with threats and curses, and, with angry tossing of their heads, the off pointer and the off number six mule turned abruptly to face the fifth chain.

The fifth chain didn't curve with the road. It remained in as straight a line as the body of mules would allow. It was up to the middle teams—five spans in a fourteen mule hitch—to jump the chain at the proper moment so that they continued to pull away from the curve until the wagons were in a position to begin turning without being dragged off the road.

Buck's heart was pounding. Peewee's rear mules were facing the chain, already pulled well above their knees because of the road's steep, upward grade. But mules were born jumpers. Any farm boy knew that. Despite its height, the mules cleared the tightly drawn fifth chain easily, their long ears laid back, front hoofs tucked neatly beneath their chests, as if leaping a hedge.

Buck's breath escaped with lusty exhalation. With those four extra mules now pulling straight with the wheelers, even as the leaders, eights, tens, and twelves were already well into the turn, he knew everything would be all right.

"They were beautiful," Dulce exalted, "so exact in their precision."

"It's a sight to see, all right," Buck acknowledged with a broad, happy grin.

"I never would have imagined it. From ground level it's always seemed so chaotic."

"From the ground, fourteen mules can look like they're heading in fifteen different directions," Buck agreed. "A bird's-eye view gives it perspective. That's why I wanted you to see it from up here."

Dulce smiled her gratitude. "I'm glad you did. Thank you."

Pulling Zeke around, Buck said: "I'd better get down there. It's good to know Milo can handle the job, but it'll be easier with another man."

"I think I'll stay up here and enjoy the view for a few more minutes."

Buck nodded absently, his attention shifting back to Peewee's wagons, just coming into the long straightaway up the side of the bluff. Peewee's mules were back in position along either side of the fifth chain, but it was obvious something was wrong. Then a startled shout from Peewee was nearly drowned out by the shrill ripping of seasoned oak ringing across the bottoms like the scream of a dying woman, and Buck swore and slammed his heels into Zeke's ribs, racing back down the long grade.

Buck pulled up when he realized the load on Peewee's lead wagon—the huge, two-ton telescoping smokestack—had broken free of its moorings and swung out with enough force to wrench the big Murphy violently to one side, even as it yanked a number of mules off their feet. The wagon had come to a shaky stop at the edge of the road, the front end of the smokestack hovering perilously over the rim of the bluff. Directly beneath it, Nate

Evans was staring helplessly up at the looming mass, its shadow like a funeral shroud covering not only Nate and his wheelers, but the wagon where Rossy innocently slept.

"Sweet Jesus," Buck breathed, dropping from his saddle. Peewee's nigh-leader tossed its head in fright as Buck sidled past. "Easy, boy," Buck murmured. "Take it easy."

Peewee was still sitting his nigh-wheeler, his feet braced rigidly in the stirrups, the jerkline drawn tight in both hands. His mules were straining into their collars, hoofs dug into the hard-packed road like fence posts. Although only the front of the smokestack had broken loose, its weight was enough to twist the flatbed wagon sharply at its center, lifting the left front wheel several inches off the ground.

"She's gonna go, Buck!" Peewee called softly. "Don't come any closer."

"Like hell," Buck replied grimly, making his way down the narrow aisle between Peewee's long hitch and the inside of the bluff. He stopped beside the nigh-wheeler, looking into the eyes of his old friend. They were wide with fear, unblemished by any need to appear tough.

"What're we gonna do, Buck? If that damn' smokestack busts another strap, the whole outfit's gonna go over the side."

"If it starts to go, you bail out of that saddle like your butt's on fire." He glanced under the necks of the wheelers, relieved to see that the caravan had ground to a halt, its crew rushing forward to lend a hand. Most of the men were with Nate's rig, helping him get it out from under the bluff, and that was a relief, too. Buck wanted Nate and Rossy safely out of the way before they tackled Peewee's outfit.

"Let's give 'em a minute," Buck said, gently patting the nigh-wheeler's shoulder. Then one of the pointers jumped and snorted as if stung, and the whole line lurched backward nearly a foot.

"Aw, God," Peewee moaned as the wagon's left front wheel rose even higher. He looked at Buck as if he wanted to cry. "You tell Hannah that I love her, Buck! The kids, too. You tell 'em. . . ."

"Shut up," Buck said raggedly. "Tell her yourself when you get home."

"I might not. . . ."

"I said to shut up, and I meant it. Now hang onto that jerkline and don't let it go slack again."

"It didn't go slack."

"You just hang onto it. Start acting like you've handled mules before. You're scaring your hitch."

Peewee glanced at his mount. The mule's agitation was obvious in the sharp, backward slope of its long ears, the trembling muscles in its shoulders. Taking a deep breath, he said: "All right." Then, calmer: "All right, what's your plan?"

"As soon as Nate's out of the way and we've got some help, we'll tie this load down enough to get you off this bluff. We can wait until we're on top before we worry about sliding it back in place." He glanced at the muleskinner. "Can you handle things here for a couple of minutes?"

"Sure, I've got it."

"I'm going to take a look at that smokestack. I want to see how bad it is."

A strained smile appeared on Peewee's face. "I'll wait for you here," he said, and Buck grinned and tapped the teamster's knee affectionately with his fist before he walked away.

They'd strapped the smokestack down in four places after cradling it in a frame made of two-by-fours. It was the first two straps that had given away, allowing the bottom of the smokestack, the heaviest end, to swing out over the bluff. Buck's throat went dry as he examined the last two straps, both of them taut enough to hum. Returning to the front of the wagon, he knelt to study the front wheel, floating about three inches off the ground. Putting both hands on the hub, he pressed down with all his strength, causing the wagon to dip tenuously toward the road.

"Hey, what's going on back there?" Peewee demanded.

"Nothing!" Buck called, allowing the wheel to rise slowly back to its original position.

The drumming of hoofs drew Buck's attention to the lower curve, where Milo was cantering his molly up the steep grade. Ray Jones was hanging onto the saddle horn and running alongside, taking ten-foot strides with the molly's assistance. Just coming into the bend behind them was Joe Perry, Charlie Bigelow, Lou Kitledge, Andy LeMay, Chris Hobson, Little Ed Womack, and Manuel Varga, all of them on foot. Keho Kona came last, his broad, swarthy face as imperturbable as ever, although he was making good time for his bulk.

Milo whistled when he saw the cant of the wagon and the two remaining straps, pulled so tightly they looked like they could be twanged like banjo strings. Stepping down from his saddle, he said: "Lord A'mighty."

"Ray, get up front and take the bits on Peewee's leaders," Buck ordered the puffing muleskinner. He glanced down the road to where Nate and Rossy were just coming around the bend behind Big Kona. No one else was in sight. "Where the hell are the rest of them?" he asked.

"Staying close to their rigs, I guess," Milo replied, down on one knee to study the flatbed's undercarriage.

"Sons-of-bitches," Buck murmured, and walked to the edge of the bluff. Lyle Mead and Garth Lang were standing with Mitch Kroll and Bigfoot Payne, at Kroll's lead wagon. Thad Collins sat his mount next to Gwen, close beside the mud wagon where Paddy O'Rourke was leaning back in his seat, smoking a cigarette.

"I want every one of you lazy misfits up here on the double!" Buck bellowed, anger adding strength to his voice. "Collins, that includes you and O'Rourke. Right now!" He glanced up the road to where Dulce had ridden part way down on Beau. "Get Zeke out of the way!" he hollered, and Dulce nodded and leaned from her saddle to collect the black's reins. Buck tramped back to where the others had gathered around the left front wheel, all of them breathing hard from their run up from the lower flat. His mood lightened somewhat when he saw Milo and Joe up on the wagon bed, looping a rope around the forward end of the smokestack.

"Milo figures we can tie the rope to the front wheel and lever the stack back that way," Andy explained to Buck.

"Then let's get it done."

Andy nodded and reached for the loose end of the rope. Milo and Joe were fashioning a slipknot that could be drawn tight to the smokestack, yet quickly loosened in the event they needed to let it go in a hurry.

Buck pulled Chris Hobson aside. "How sharp's your knife?"

"Sharp enough. What do you want done?"

"I want you up on the wagon, and, if I holler for you to cut those straps, you do it quick as you can, then get the hell out of there. Cut 'em both if you have time, but don't let it take you over the edge. Jump if you have to."

Chris stared at him for a moment, then said—"All right."—and walked away.

Buck knew what he was asking of the muleskinner. If the load started to go, only Peewee's seat atop his tall nigh-wheeler would be more perilous. But cutting the straps in time could mean the difference between life and death for Peewee and his mules, and Chris understood that, too.

Buck's expression was dark as he helped Andy secure the rope to the top two spokes of the front wheel. While they did that, Charlie, Lou, Little Ed, and Big Kona were busy unhitching Peewee's trail wagon and chocking its wheels so that it wouldn't roll backward. By the time they finished, the rest of the independents had come up. Buck quickly assigned them their tasks, putting the largest and strongest—Kroll, Big Kona, Bigfoot Payne—at the front of the wagon to help hold the wheel to the ground, then spread the rest of the men out along the line of mules to help keep them calm and pulling. Lyle Mead, protective of an injured left hand, was placed alongside Peewee with instructions to yank the muleskinner from his saddle if the wagon started to go.

With everyone in place, Buck walked over to Peewee's side. "You gonna be all right?" he asked.

Peewee smiled bravely. "It's crazy, but I was just thinking of Mase. He would've been proud of you, Bucky."

Buck's throat tightened unexpectedly. "Mase ain't here," he said. "It's just you and me this time."

Peewee nodded calmly. "That'll be enough."

There was a drawn-out groan from under the flatbed, and Milo said: "We'd better get moving, boss. This wagon won't hold together forever."

Buck and Peewee shook hands, then Buck turned away. "All right," he called sharply, "let's get this done!" He climbed onto the wagon with Milo. Chris was crouched at the rear end, his knife pressed lightly to the third strap. The two exchanged a long look, then Chris nodded and Buck said: "Slow and easy, Peewee, a few inches at a time."

"Hup!" Peewee shouted to his team, and the flatbed jolted as the mules pushed into their collars. The wagon swayed ominously, the front wheel rising, then settling back under pressure from the men crowded around it. There was a loud pop from beneath the wagon, a moment's wide-eyed paralysis among the men, then another forward surge that drew the rope to the

smokestack tight.

"Easy," Buck cautioned as the hemp line began to stretch and thin. The wagon rolled forward another few inches and the rope bit into the hub, but the smokestack refused to budge.

"Buck," Milo whispered.

"Not yet," Buck said quietly, the words thrumming his vocal cords. The wagon creaked forward another couple of inches. The rope moaned as if in pain.

"It's gonna break," Milo whispered.

"No, it's not," Buck said, as if he could prevent the strained fibers from parting by sheer will. His chest was tight and his ears roared, but he didn't take his eyes off the thinning line or lose faith in the skills of his men. Just when he thought they could go no farther, when he was convinced the rope surely had to separate, sending the rig tumbling over the edge of the bluff, the smokestack shifted, scraping back toward the wagon a single, triumphant inch.

"Easy!" Buck called hoarsely. "Easy now. It's coming. Just keep those mules moving slow and steady."

Milo's breath hissed loudly. They both knew the battle was far from won. The wagon crept forward, the iron rim of the front wheel only loosely gripping the hard-packed roadbed. Buck could hear the low squeal of stretching leather as the mules dug into the grade, their clopping shoes loud on the hardpan as they hauled the wagon forward another precious foot. The smokestack shifted again, then abruptly slid toward the wagon, the pressure lessening everywhere at once.

The was a muted cheer from some of the men, and Peewee shouted: "We're doin' it, boys! By God, we're doin' it!"

Buck glanced at Milo, sweat dripping off the end of his nose. "I believe the man's right," he said faintly.

It was pretty easy after that. When they finished securing the stack, Buck ordered the rest of the crew back to their wagons, keeping only Rossy, Manuel, and Milo with him. "Soon as we get up top, we'll come back for the trailer," he told the men. "When that's out of the way, bring your own rigs up. We'll lever that smokestack back into its cradle then."

It took less than twenty minutes to get the big Murphy wagon on top and unhitched. While Peewee went back with Rossy and Manuel to collect his trailer, Buck climbed onto the flatbed to check the damage. He was expecting to find some flaw in the cradle's workmanship that could be traced back to Jock's yard master, Hank Miller, who had overseen its construction, but after several minutes of inspection, he found nothing incriminating. The cradle had been minorly damaged when the smokestack slipped, but there was no evidence there of what had caused the accident. It was Milo who discovered that.

"Take a look at this, boss!" the Kansan called from the other side of the wagon.

Buck walked around to where Milo was standing beside the right front wheel, stopping short when he saw the loose end of the strap clutched in the ramrod's hand.

"This was no accident," Milo said hollowly. "It's been cut."

CHAPTER TWELVE

"But who would do such a thing?" Dulce asked in dismay. She was still in her saddle, holding Zeke's reins.

"Maybe someone has a grudge against Peewee?" Milo suggested.

Buck turned the strap over in his hand. The flat, two-inch-wide woven hemp had been severed cleanly for more than three-quarters of the way across, leaving only a few thin strands to keep the heavy smokestack in place until the wagon started up the side of the bluff. Gravity had done the rest.

"Against Peewee or the Box K," Buck mused aloud.

"The same people who killed Mase?" Milo asked.

"To someone determined enough to commit murder, I reckon cutting a strap on a wagon would seem like a pretty small risk," Buck said.

"Two straps," Milo corrected, holding up the loose end of the second tie-down. It had also been sliced nearly in two, both cuts made close to the turnbuckle, where the damage wouldn't be easily spotted. "The question is, who did it?" Milo continued. "Someone with the train, or someone who slipped into camp last night while we were asleep?"

"It'd be pretty risky to sneak into a freighter's camp," Buck said. "A mule's better than hounds for sniffing out strangers." He glanced at Milo, the unavoidable conclusion lodging roughly in his brain. "We've got a traitor in our ranks."

There was a distant shout from below the bluff, and Dulce

said: "That's Peewee. He's got his trailer hitched."

Buck nodded, coming to a quick decision. "Let's get these straps off," he told Milo. "Dulce can ride 'em out and dump them where no one will find them."

"You aren't going to tell the men?" Milo asked.

"Not yet." Buck freed the hook from the wagon's side bracket and began coiling the longer section along his forearm. "I don't think anyone knows about this except for the three of us and whoever did it. That could be to our advantage if someone slips up and says something."

It took only moments to free the two straps and hand them to Dulce, who loped out onto the plain and tossed them into a coulée. She was back before Peewee's leaders topped the bluff.

It took an hour to repair the cradle, drag the smokestack back in place, then lash it down with new straps. Several of the muleskinners were curious about the accident, but Buck brushed it off as a faulty strap, and no one questioned him further or thought it odd when he told them to check their own tie-downs every morning from here on.

They left the Bear River for good after that, the land to the north stretching away flat as an ironing board. There were no farms or settlements in sight. Although still within the borders of Utah Territory, they'd left most of its population behind. From here on they would pass only relay stations for the stagecoach companies and an occasional trading post—some with tiny, rough-barked communities grown up around them—all separated by long, lonely stretches of high, wind-scoured deserts and snowy mountain passes.

Buck maintained a position about a hundred yards in advance of Peewee's leaders, matching Zeke's pace to that of the wagons. Dulce rode next to Peewee, the two of them chatting amiably like the old friends they were. Milo was in the sage off to their right where he could keep an eye on the entire length of the train. Gwen and Thad rode opposite him, also in the sage but paying no attention to the long line of wagons.

To Buck's mind, the scene appeared as idyllic as that which Dulce had viewed from the jut of land above Hampton's Crossing, but he knew the image was a lie that hid an undercurrent of malevolence. Perhaps even a killer. His hand strayed to the fancy bullwhip at his waist, and he wondered what Mase would do in such a situation, then shook the question away. This wasn't Mase's problem, it was his.

It was late enough in the afternoon for Buck to start looking for a suitable camping spot when he heard the drum of approaching hoofs. He glanced over his shoulder, expecting Dulce, but it was Gwen he saw galloping her tall chestnut after him. He nodded a cautious greeting as she pulled alongside. "Miss Haywood."

"Might I join you for a while, Mister McCready, or does that privilege belong solely to Miss Kavanaugh?"

"You're more than welcome to ride up here," Buck said, his gaze straying to where Collins now rode alone through the sage. "I'm surprised your bodyguard didn't come along."

"Thad is quite serious in his commitment to my safety, but he is in my employ, Mister McCready, not my father's. Thad does as I tell him."

Buck gave her an appraising look. "You hired him? That wasn't what I was led to believe yesterday, in Jock's office."

"Words do have a tendency to be misinterpreted in times of stress, don't they?" she replied glibly. "Nevertheless, all that's really important is that he does his job, wouldn't you say? The purpose is the same, regardless of who pays his wages."

"I'm afraid not, Miss Haywood. I need to know what's going on in my train, anything and everything that might affect its safety. Knowing a man's loyalty is imperative."

"Oh, please, we are hardly in a state of war. I would venture to say that we are little more than highly paid delivery boys, no different than those lads who bring us our weekly groceries. And can't we drop this silly formality of Mister This and Miss That, at least on the trail? It's stifling and it creates barriers that"—she smiled sweetly, adding a tilt to her head that allowed the late afternoon sun to highlight the richness of her blonde hair—"to be perfectly honest, I'm not at all sure I desire to be there."

Buck's expression remained unchanged. "Are you always so bold in your conversations, Miss Haywood?"

"Gwen, please."

"All right, Gwen, although I'm not sure a first name basis is going to change anything."

"It's a grand start though, don't you agree?" Before he could respond, she quickly changed the subject. "I am simply staggered by the greenness of your desert landscape. I had been led to believe that we would be journeying through a wasteland of blowing sands filled with ferocious beasts."

"It's spring, Miss . . . Gwen. The dust will come soon enough, and we're still too close to the settlements to see much wildlife. That'll change the farther north we go. We ought to see elk, antelope, even grizzly bears, before we reach Montana. It wasn't too many years ago that you'd find buffalo around here."

"We saw bison as we crossed the plains. That's their proper name, you know. They were so thick at one point they nearly darkened the prairies. They are ugly, though, don't you think? I had thought oxen boring, but only a bloodhound casts a stronger shadow of homeliness than a bison."

She was as full of herself as anyone Buck had ever met, filled with naïve self-confidence, yet he had to admit she held a certain fascination; he found her off-putting and shallow, yet strangely exciting in her directness.

"I reckon beauty is in the eye of the beholder, as far as buffalo are concerned," he said finally. "I saw plenty of them when I was freighting across the plains, and I always thought. . . ."

But Gwen apparently wasn't interested in what he thought of bison. Gasping in fake astonishment, she exclaimed: "Why, Captain McCready, you quoted Plato! And to think I expected only fringed leather garments and flowing beards from the male population out here."

"Gwen, you are a hard woman to hold a conversation with. You got more twists in you than a green-broke mule."

"I have not. I am a delightful conversationalist, and I've been told so by more than one suitor. I'll have you know I've taken classes on the subject. Now, tell me how you became a student of Plato's teachings."

"If I was quoting him, I didn't know it."

"Ahhh," she said with a knowing smile. "Then my original assumption was correct."

"More'n likely."

"Tell me about your mule. I would have expected a wagon master to ride a blooded steed, a stallion with a silver-studded bridle and saddle."

He chuckled and shook his head. "You've got an active imagination."

"So I've been told," she replied throatily, giving him a sidelong glance, "but I was talking about your mule."

Buck knew he should put an end to her tawdry flirtations. He'd worked hard to earn not only Dulce's and Jock's trust, but the respect of the Box K crew. He'd be risking all of that if he fell victim to Gwen's little games of amour. But there was a challenge in her words and in the deep, penetrating looks she'd given him that spoke to the maleness within, an invitation as old as life itself; it taunted, daring him to follow.

"Father would be livid if he saw me riding astride," she continued, once more abruptly changing the subject. "And

Mother would be convinced I've ruined myself forever for children. She's so old-fashioned, my mother."

"Most are, I reckon. I didn't know mine very well."

"Oh, no. She died?"

"When I was ten."

"How horrible, but I'm sure she wasn't as fuddy as my mother. She couldn't have been." Gwen smiled and shifted aim yet again. "What's your mule's name?"

"Zeke," Buck replied, aggravated with himself for bringing up his past, vowing not to do it again.

"Is he fast?"

"He's sure-footed, which is better out here."

"I prefer speed," Gwen pronounced. "There is nothing quite so exhilarating as a fleet mount."

"I reckon," Buck answered distractedly, glancing over his shoulder at the sound of hoofs.

"It's Mister Newton," Gwen said unnecessarily.

"So it is." Buck reined off the road, waiting for Milo to catch up.

"Howdy, boss," Milo said, then tipped his hat to Gwen, sporting a grin broad enough to span a small stream. "Miss Haywood."

"What's up?" Buck asked irritably.

"It's more like what's back." Milo nodded toward the rear of the train, where Paddy O'Rourke had fallen nearly a quarter of a mile behind Ray's trailer, the mud wagon looking almost like a child's toy at this distance.

"What the hell's he doing 'way back there?" Buck asked, his brows furrowing.

"Whatever it is, he was doing it yesterday, too. I kept telling him to catch up, but he just gives me a dirty look and doesn't say anything. He'll stay close for a while, then next thing you know, he's fallen behind again. There's sure no need for it. He's got a good four-mule hitch and pulling just that light coach." He gave Buck a sheepish look. "I'm getting tired of telling him. I thought maybe he'd listen to you."

"Naw, go on and take care of it. Tell him that from here on, I don't want any more than fifty feet between him and Ray."

Milo shrugged but turned away without argument.

"Is my driver causing you problems?" Gwen asked in concern.

"Nothing we can't handle," Buck said, tapping Zeke's ribs with his heels. "Where'd you hire him?"

"In Ogden. I'm told he came highly recommended."

"From who?"

"Thad was introduced to him by the superintendent of the Wall Street Livery."

Buck's eyes narrowed.

"You don't approve?"

"I've heard some stories about the Wall Street Livery," he replied vaguely. "I couldn't say if they're true."

"I could speak to him," she volunteered without enthusiasm.

"You don't sound like you want to."

"Frankly, Mister O'Rourke frightens me. An air of violence surrounds him, more so than even Thad, who I consider qualified for the job of bodyguard but wholly manageable. Thad obeys. I am not as confident of O'Rourke."

Buck twisted in his saddle to stare back down the long line of wagons. From here, he could barely make out the man handling the mud wagon's lines, but, as he recalled the Irishman's surly expression every time Buck came near him, he thought Gwen was probably right. Paddy O'Rourke would not be an easy man to handle. But was that reason enough to suspect him of murder or sabotage?

They'd barely crossed into Idaho Territory when they met their first southbound caravan, a Leavitt Brothers train out of Ogden, returning from its first run of the season. The two outfits passed without stopping, although Buck reined to one side to talk with the Leavitt captain, a grizzled Mormon named Hans Schutz. Buck was eager to hear about the condition of the road to the north, and the progress of the first Box K train, led by Lew Walker.

Schutz's report on the road was about what Buck expected—hard and dry for the most part, with a few lingering bogs in the low places along the rivers. The higher elevations over Monida Pass, going into Montana Territory, would be the worst, the old German predicted.

"Over Monida dere is still snow," Hans warned. "You take care in dat places, you hear? A spot or two, to the axles you vill sink if you are not vatchful. Make you a base vit sapling poles if you have to. Dat's vhat ve did."

Snow-packed roads could be either a blessing or a curse at this time of year, Buck knew. It all depended on how warm it was in the high country, how firm the trail.

Lew Walker, Hans added, was already north of Camus Creek and approaching the mouth of Monida Cañon when the two trains had passed. "Yah, by now in Virginia City he vill be, contracting for a load of ore or lumber for to bring back vit him south."

"He's making good time," Buck observed.

"Sure, dere's one vhat knows his business, dat Lew Valker. Prob'ly around Monida you vill meet him, coming south vit full vagons, sure."

Buck thanked Hans for the information and the two wagon masters parted company. The Box K camped that night in a grassy oval in the middle of a waist-high forest of sage. Buck ate with the first mess again, discussing the day's events with Peewee, Ray, and Joe. None of them expressed any real concern over Schutz's opinion of the road, and only Ray pointed out the gloomily obvious consequence of a lingering storm.

"We get a week-long rain and the bottom'll drop outta all these roads," he stated morosely.

"Naw, these roads are too hard-packed," Joe replied, fiddling with a briar-root pipe. "They've been haulin' freight over 'em since the early 'Sixties."

"Don't go tellin' me what can happen to a road when it rains, Joe Perry," Ray said churlishly. "I was haulin' freight over these mountains when you was still a sucklin' pup."

"Well, hell, pard, that's right," Joe said with a puckish grin. "I'd forgotten it was you 'n' God who laid out these roads. You just go ahead and forget I said anything."

"You're a damn' fool, Perry," Ray growled.

"Likely that's the problem," Joe agreed solemnly. "The Lord's work again, no doubt."

"Don't go mockin' the Lord, boy. I won't stand for it."

Laughing, Peewee said: "Hey, Ray, remember the time we got bogged down on top of Malad?" He was watching Ray closely, a little anxiously, Buck thought. "You remember that?"

Slowly Ray pulled his eyes away from Joe. "Well, I'll say. Ol' Lew was captainin' that train, mebbe a year or two before Mase showed up." His eyes brightened in the dancing light; he looked excited now, retelling an incident Buck knew had probably caused him to boil with rage at the time. But that was Ray, and, as far as it went, that was Peewee and Joe, too, each as predictable in their own ways as blue skies in summer. Steadfast, loyal, resolute.

Boring. The word popped unexpectedly into Buck's mind, surprising him even if the voice didn't. The voice belonged to Gwen. He remembered her using it that afternoon to describe buffalo. Or, properly, bison.

He glanced around the fire at the faces of the men sitting with him, the word echoing in his skull. They were boring, all of them. Among the Box K teamsters, the subjects changed constantly but the conversations never did. There was a sameness about every tale as they were told and retold, embellished with age, sometimes festooned with half lies for humor. Like the time Ray's jerkline broke making the turn onto Montana Street in Corinne, and how his mules had instinctively continued on without guidance until they came to a stop in the middle of the Box K wagon yard. Or how Rossy had gotten turned around one night while 'hawking the remuda and drove the entire herd into a sleeping Shoshone village, up on the Blackfoot River. Laughing at the same jokes, ribbing one another for past mistakes, they were like a bunch of old married couples. It was the way their evenings passed, the way the miles passed, and ultimately, Buck supposed, it would be the way the years would pass, too.

He lowered his eyes to the fire. Until that evening it had never occurred to him that there might be more to life than freighting, a goal loftier than skinning mules. The idea that there could be had been planted in his brain that afternoon by a slip of a girl he didn't really respect or care for. He was a wagon boss at twenty-four, a full decade younger than most men who achieved that rank. Some didn't reach it until they were closer to forty, and many never reached it at all. Soon he would be a husband, too, and with that, a son-in-law, his future laid out like a Sunday suit before church. Marriage was expected of him. Peewee, Ray, Nate—they all teased him about it, and probably wondered why it hadn't come to pass yet.

Sometimes, Buck wondered about that, too, his reluctance to take the final step. He thought Dulce would say yes if he asked her, but he never had. Pushing to his feet, he left the fire, the conversation behind him continuing uninterrupted.

The night air was chilly, and his breath created a thin fog of the same translucent hue as the dusty starlight. The big, double-hitched freighters weren't corralled in the traditional circular pattern made famous on the plains. There was less need of protection against marauding Indians here, and no buffalo herds to stampede the stock in the middle of the night. For convenience's sake, Buck had ordered the train separated into two units, then brought the rear half up even with the front, forming a thirty-foot-wide corridor that served no purpose other than to make communication between the front and rear of the caravan easier.

Stepping over a wagon tongue, Buck made his way onto the plain west of camp. He didn't consciously try to be quiet, it was just an old habit acquired early in life. Tonight it allowed him to approach within twenty feet of a couple of men standing together in the sage in front of him. Although too dark to make out individual features, he recognized both of them by their silhouettes—Mitch Kroll, tall, beefy, arrogant even in profile, and the small-boned, furtive Paddy O'Rourke, his narrow shoulders sloping like the sharp pitch of a barn roof.

The pairing surprised Buck and he stopped. Although he didn't call out, O'Rourke immediately spotted him. Cursing, the jehu spun, making for the rear of the train.

"Hold up!" Buck called, but O'Rourke kept going, his short legs paddling rapidly.

Mitch's reaction was just the opposite. He came deliberately through the sage, keeping as straight a line as the brush would allow. Recalling his earlier encounter with the teamster, Buck planted his feet wide for balance and let Mitch come to him.

"What're you up to now, bub? Spying on your own people?"

"I was taking a walk. I didn't expect to find you two out here."

"What did you expect to find?" Mitch stopped half a dozen feet away and casually slid a heavy-bladed butcher knife from his belt. Buck tensed but kept his hand away from his pistol.

Grinning, Mitch fingered a plug of tobacco from his vest pocket.

"What were you two doing out here?" Buck asked, feigning a calmness he didn't feel.

"How do you figure that's any of your business?"

"Anything that might affect the safety and progress of this train is my business, Mitch. You know that."

"Was I you, I'd come up with a better excuse," Mitch replied, using his knife to pare a wedge of tobacco from the end of his plug. "That one's weak."

Buck's anger stirred, overriding caution. "What were you and O'Rourke talking about?"

"None of your business."

"Suppose I make it my business?"

Mitch returned the tobacco to his pocket but kept the big knife in his hand. "Don't push it, McCready. I got a short fuse where idjits is concerned, I don't care what title they're sportin' or whose daughter they're sparkin'."

Buck let his breath out slowly. He sensed Mitch was trying to goad him into a fight, and feared that, sooner or later, they would have to have it out, just to see who was the better man. At least according to Mitch Kroll's standards.

But not here, Buck thought. *Not in the dark, with Kroll holding a butcher knife.* Keeping his voice level, he said: "How long have you known O'Rourke?"

"Long enough."

"I'm asking you a question, Kroll."

"You're askin' too damn' many questions."

"How long?"

Mitch hesitated, his stubbled jaw working furiously. He looked like a bull ready to charge, then all of a sudden the wind went out of him, as it had that first time outside of Corinne—abruptly, without warning. Twisting at the waist, Mitch spat into the sage, then wiped his mouth with his sleeve. "I met him in Arizona in 'Sixty-Eight."

"You two haven't been acting like friends," Buck observed.

"Never said we was friends. Said I knew him in Arizona, in Prescott."

He could have been telling the truth, Buck knew, but something about the way he said it didn't wash. Buck had been keeping an eye on the new men ever since they'd started for Montana, and neither Kroll nor O'Rourke had acted as if they'd ever seen one another before. "Something's going on here, Kroll. What is it?"

"Ain't nothin' goin' on, bub. You're just too jumpy." He started forward and Buck closed his right hand into a fist, but Mitch walked past him as if he didn't exist, continuing on to the wagons.

Buck's hand rose to the coils of Mase's bullwhip as if seeking his old friend's reassurance through the whip's leather weaves. He was glad his conversation with Kroll had come to an end without violence. He wouldn't have backed down if the burly teamster had pushed it, but he hadn't been looking forward to a fight. The fact was, with or without a knife, he wasn't sure he could whip Kroll.

Although Buck had thought they were alone, he wasn't all that surprised when a shadow detached itself from the side of a wagon and glided toward him. He peered into the darkness, then smiled.

"He's a sparky one, ol' Kroll is," Nate said.

"Some," Buck agreed.

"You got to watch yourself around him, boss," Nate added seriously. "He's about as mean as they come, and I've seen some mean ones in my day."

"I won't let him walk all over me like a headstrong mule."

"I've heard a lot of stories about Mitchell Kroll, and not in any of them did I ever hear of him backin' away from a fight the way he's backed away from you twice now."

"I know."

"It don't make sense."

"I know."

"He might not do it a third time. Third time, he might just kill you."

"He might."

"He easy could, Buck. It's just that simple. Mitchell Kroll's a killer."

"Maybe he ain't as bad as the stories make him out to be," Buck suggested.

"You want to count your life on that?"

Buck gave the older man a curious look. "What were you doing out here, anyway?"

The tall man's teeth shone whitely in his black face. "Why, just keepin' an eye on things."

"Watching my back?"

"Kinda worked out that way, didn't it?" Nate started to turn away, then hesitated. "You got to watch out for yourself, Buck, closer than you ever done before. Whoever killed Mase is still out there."

"You think Kroll could be involved?"

"I don't know what Mitchell Kroll is or ain't involved in, but we've all heard stories about him. If he can push you into a fight, ain't a jury west of the Mississippi gonna put him in jail for breakin' your neck. Not that it'd matter to you, but it'd sure matter to little Dulce. Matter to the rest of us, too."

Buck was touched by the sincerity of the muleskinner's words. "Thanks, Nate."

"Shoo, don't be thankin' me. You just get this train through in one piece, so we can go back to bein' a normal crew again. This high-stakes gamblin' is for younger men, not us old geezers."

Buck smiled as Nate made his way toward the wagons. After a moment, forgetting why he'd come out here in the first place, he followed the muleskinner back to camp.

Chapter Thirteen

They passed Malad City on their third day out, fifty-odd miles north of Corinne and the only real town they would come to between the borders of Utah and Montana Territories. There wasn't much to the place, just a ramshackle collection of small adobe and log buildings surrounding a relay station, the town's single street pounded to a fine powder by passing traffic.

Buck led the train through town without stopping and kept it rolling for several more miles before he ordered a camp made near the base of the Malad Mountains. He was pulling the saddle from Zeke's back when Gwen rode up on her chestnut. Flashing a saucy smile, she said: "It's still light, let's take a ride."

Buck dumped his gear in the grass, then pulled a brush from his saddlebags and set to work on the mule's sweaty back. "Not tonight. Maybe when we reach the end of the trail in Montana."

"Why, Mister McCready, are you intimidated by the thought of being alone with me?"

"Not so much intimidated as concerned about the evening chores. The reason we stopped early tonight is because we've got a long climb ahead of us tomorrow. We'll. . . ."

He shut up when he realized she was no longer listening. The rapid drumming of hoofs came to him from the south, and he stepped away from Zeke's side for a better view. A stagecoach was coming up the road at a good clip, its driver perched on top of the high box with his boots braced firmly against the footboard. Buck thought for a moment that it might be a runaway team, then recognized it as one of Gilmer and Salisbury's express coaches, bound for Montana. Gilmer and Salisbury kept their express rigs running day and night, switching hitches every ten to fifteen miles, depending on the lay of the land. It was a hard run on drivers and horses alike, and even the passengers came out at the other end looking quite a bit worse for wear, but, if a man was determined to reach Montana in a hurry, an express was the way to go.

As the stage rattled past, Gwen's mouth parted in surprise, her eyes widened. Following the direction of her gaze, Buck saw a man's face framed in the coach's forward window—wide and square-jawed, his gray hair clamped down under an expensive hat. Muttonchops whiskers gave him the look of a full-maned African lion, but his expression remained inscrutable as he stared at the tableau of wagons parked in the tall sage, the beautiful woman sitting her red horse beside it in the late afternoon light. Then he was gone, leaning back from the window as the coach rolled swiftly onward.

"Something wrong, Miss Haywood?" Buck asked gently.

She looked at him numbly for a second. "Why, no, I was . . . just watching." Then something snapped in her eyes and the numbness vanished; a smile spread across her face like slim wings. "And what is this *miss* business? I thought we'd agreed it was Gwen."

"All right, but if there's something I should know about. . . ."

"If anything arises that I think you should know about, I shall rush to your side with the information." She lifted her reins. "Now, if I can't interest you in an evening's excursion, perhaps I can talk Thad into one."

"Don't be gone too long."

"I sha'n't," she replied, her smile undiminished.

"I mean it," Buck said. "Be back before dark."

She saluted him in the same sloppily patronizing manner she'd used in Jock's office, then wheeled her horse and trotted toward the road. Collins caught up with her without being summoned and the two of them kicked their mounts into easy canters.

Buck finished caring for Zeke, then turned him loose with the remuda. While Rossy and Manuel watched over the mules, the teamsters inspected their rigs. Even the independents who had never been this way before could see what they faced on the morrow. Buck pitched in where he could, helping go over wagon tongues and undercarriages, looking for splits that could snap under stress. He was especially careful to check the hemp straps that secured the oddly shaped pieces from BMC—the smokestack, the boilers, the steam engines. Everyone checked their brakes. With the climb and descent that awaited them, that was a given.

Most wagons had two sets of brakes, the first a wooden pad that worked off a standard lever on the side of the wagon, set or released by means of a rope that was handled by the teamster from the saddle. The second brake was called a drag. It was a shoe-like device that rode up under the wagon's bed for most of a journey, and was only lowered for the steepest grades. A heavy chain bolted to the wagon's frame was just long enough to allow the rear wheel to roll up onto the iron cradle of the shoe, creating a sort of skid that prevented the wheel from touching the ground or rolling. Of course that meant the mules were forced to pull the wagon as if one, and sometimes both of its rear wheels were locked, but that was never much of a problem on a downgrade steep enough to warrant the use of drags in the first place.

It was after dark before they finished putting things in shape. Knuckling the small of his back, Buck arched the kinks from his spine as Nate lowered a jack under the rear axle of his trail wagon.

"Lordy," Nate said, mopping sweat from his brow with a wadded bandanna. "This kinda work'll make a man old."

"It'll give you fresh appreciation for supper tonight," Buck replied, smiling.

"I dunno. Side-pork, beans, biscuits. I'd sure fancy sinkin' my teeth into something different for a change."

"Don't say that too loud or you'll have half the crew hoofing it back to Malad City for their suppers."

Nate chuckled. "Tell you what, boss-man, I might just lead that mutiny myself." His expression changed then, and he turned away guiltily.

Buck didn't say anything, but he was remembering the look on Milo's face the night he'd learned that the Box K was owned by Jock Kavanaugh. The word *mutiny* held a special meaning to the men of the K, and not a pleasant one.

Buck lowered his arms. A lantern was gliding swiftly toward them; he'd already identified the sturdy canvas riding skirt at its side.

"You go on and see what she wants," Nate said. "I'll put this away."

Buck nodded absently. He could tell from Dulce's long stride, captured in the lantern's yellow light, that something was wrong. Leaving Nate to return the jack and chocks to the mess wagon, he walked out to meet her.

"Buck, it's Gwen," Dulce said when they met. "She hasn't come back yet."

"Are you sure?"

"I can't find her, and her horse isn't on its picket line. Neither is Thad's."

"Have you talked to O'Rourke?"

"No. Mister O'Rourke isn't very . . . approachable."

"Let's go talk to him now," Buck said curtly.

They found Paddy O'Rourke hovering over a small fire in front of the women's tent, tending to a skillet of sizzling bacon and frying potatoes. He looked up as Buck and Dulce approached, but didn't rise or offer a greeting. In the pulsating light, his face looked like a rough-hewn walnut plank left too close to the hearth, and his black eyes glinted like slivers of polished coal.

"Miss Kavanaugh tells me Miss Haywood hasn't returned," Buck said, coming to a stop across the fire. "Do you know where she is?"

Paddy shrugged. "The lady don't tell me what she's gonna do."

"What about Collins?"

"That pig . . ."—it came out peeg—"don't tell me nothing, either."

"Did you see which way they went?"

"I see the woman with you at the head of the train. I am back here." His eyes narrowed to slits. "Like a good little *peón,* eh?"

Buck's dislike for the man ratcheted up another notch. "It's late, O'Rourke, and your boss isn't back. Doesn't that worry you?"

The dark-skinned Irishman's teeth flashed briefly through the veil of his mustache. "No, it don't worry me, but that's one very rich lady, very important." He stood fluidly, like a waterfall in reverse, and hooked his thumbs in his belt. "Maybe it worries you, eh?"

"Buck," Dulce said softly. "Let's go."

"Not yet." Buck's eyes had narrowed with a barely contained anger. "How long have you known Mitch Kroll?" he pressed O'Rourke.

"Kroll?" O'Rourke shrugged. "I don't know Kroll."

"I saw you talking to him last night, outside of camp."

"Is that against your rules, too, that a *peón* like me talks to one of the great Box K drivers?"

"Kroll says he knew you from Arizona. Are you saying you don't remember him?"

Again that expansive shrug, almost in mockery. "I meet so many. Who knows?"

Buck was getting nowhere, and running out of patience. He said: "We're going to have to talk one of these days. I'm real curious about where you learned to handle a coach the way you do."

"Sure," Paddy replied with a crooked grin. "I be right here, eh? Where you put me."

Buck turned away, Dulce staying close to his side. When they'd put some distance between themselves and O'Rourke, she shivered and clutched her arms under her breasts. "I don't like him," she said. "He frightens me."

A shout from the upper end of the camp announced the arrival of riders, and Buck lengthened his stride. By the time he got there, Gwen and Thad were guiding their horses between the wagons. Collins's hat was crumbled on one side, coated with dust, and Gwen's hair was in disarray. She was subdued, more cowed than frightened, a demeanor that seemed unnatural on her.

Grabbing the chestnut's reins, Buck said: "What happened?"

"Nothing happened," Gwen replied snappishly. She tried to pull away, but Buck held tightly to the reins.

"Dammit, I'm getting tired of people telling me nothing happened when I know something did."

Gwen's voice turned icy. "I can assure you, Mister McCready, nothing occurred that is of any concern to you."

"You should've been back two hours ago."

"When I return anywhere is my business, not yours."

"The hell," Buck spat. "I told you to be back here before

dark. If you've got a reason for disobeying that, you'd best spill it now."

Collins nudged his horse forward. "Curb your tone, McCready. I'll not let you speak to Miss Haywood that way."

"Hush, sonny," Ray Jones said, coming up on one side of Collins while Joe Perry came up on the other. "The wagon master's talkin'."

"Maybe we all ought to cool off a little," Peewee suggested. Sidling close to Buck, he added: "She's back and she's safe, that's all that matters, ain't it?"

Buck drew a ragged breath, but he knew Peewee was right. Pushing Gwen now would only worsen matters. Letting go of the chestnut's reins, he said: "Take care of your horse, Miss Haywood, then go have your supper. We'll talk about this later."

Gwen's expression was taut with fury as she drove her slim heels into the chestnut's ribs. Collins followed her. Glancing at the others who had been drawn by the sounds of confrontation, Buck said wearily: "Go on, all of you. Grab yourselves something to eat and get some rest. Tomorrow's going to be a long day."

They wandered off, all except for Peewee and Dulce, and, when Buck shook his head at Dulce, she retreated, too, taking the lantern with her.

"How're you doin', Bucky?" Peewee asked gently.

"I'm all right. Just wound a little tight right now."

"You're doing good, boy. We're making good time, and under conditions Mase never had to face."

"What do you mean?"

"Look at what you're saddled with. A ramrod no one's ever heard of, that Haywood gal and them two jaspers she's got workin' for her, muleskinners you don't know from Adam . . . not to mention how important this cargo is to Jock."

Buck nodded thoughtfully.

"You notice her hair?" Peewee asked.

"Thad's hat was bunged up, too."

"Makes a man wonder."

"About Thad and Gwen?"

"Stranger things have happened, and that Haywood gal is a wild one. Ain't no doubt about that."

"She's wild, but I can't see her hooking up with Collins. She'd consider him too far beneath her."

"Something sure as hell happened out there."

"I agree," Buck said. "I'll talk to her tomorrow."

"She won't tell you anything. That gal's as stubborn as my off pointer, Betsy."

Buck wanted to tell him about the straps that had been cut on the smokestacks, to query his old friend about motives and suspects, but he knew that, if he said anything, Ray would know about it before the evening passed, and the rest of the crew would hear of it before dawn.

"I keep telling myself it's because of Mase and . . . some other things that've happened."

"Like that gal, Sally Hayes, getting shot just as you walked into the room?"

Buck gave him a curious look.

"Hell, word gets around. There's always someone slipping into town for one more drink or a last fling with a chippy."

"Who slipped into town?" Buck asked, but Peewee only grinned and Buck didn't push it; he'd slipped into town too many times himself over the years. "What do you know about the new men?"

"Not much. We've all heard stories about Mitch Kroll, and Big Kona's got as good a reputation on the trail as any man I know. The others. . . ." He shrugged. "Little Ed seems all right, but Lang and Mead act touchy as skinned snakes, like they was cut from the same bolt of cloth as O'Rourke."

"How'd Mead hurt his hand?"

Peewee laughed. "Fell off the wood wagon," he said, referring to the buckboard of firewood that Jock sent out to the caravan each night that it was camped outside of Corinne. "Clumsy oaf," he added, still chuckling.

"What about Garth Lang?"

"He didn't fall off anybody's wagon that I know of, but he sure acts like he's sore about something. Ray tried talkin' to him last night, but the man wouldn't hardly converse."

"It's a puzzle," Buck said moodily. "Men get their dander up all the time, but they generally work it out or fight it out. It seems like half this crew is riding on chapped butts, but I'm damned if I know what's chafing 'em."

After a moment's hesitation, Peewee said: "Well, the K's got its ghosts, Buck. I reckon you know that even if we don't talk about it."

"What ghosts?"

Peewee gave him a patient glance.

"The mutiny? Lord, Peewee, that was thirty years ago. I don't know why those damn' rumors haven't died out by now."

"They ain't all rumors," Peewee said, then hastily added: "I know you're close to Jock, and I know you love Dulce, and I know Mase was like a pa to you, but there's . . . well, Jock ain't the same man now that he was thirty years ago. He's still a hard-ass, but he was worse then."

Buck's tone stiffened. "Are you saying Jock killed those men, like the rumors claim?"

Peewee was silent for a long time, then finally shook his head. "I wasn't there, Buck."

"But you believe the stories?"

"A lot of men do."

Buck made a dismissing gesture with his hand and started to walk away. "They're jealous, Peewee, that's all."

"Mase. . . ."

Buck jerked to a stop. "What about Mase?"

Peewee sighed. "Well, he was always kinda protective of you, Buck. He didn't always tell you the whole of a thing."

"First you called Jock a killer, now you're saying Mase was a liar, is that it?"

"If Mase was a liar, it was only because he wanted what was best for you. That's one of the reasons the boys all come to think so highly of him. He done right by you, Buck, near as I've ever been able to tell. He wasn't always like that before you come along."

Buck looked away but didn't speak.

"You was gonna hear it sooner or later," Peewee added almost apologetically. "With Mase gone, folks'll start talkin' more openly. I just didn't want you gettin' in a brawl over something without knowin' the backside of the story."

"What backside?" Buck asked quietly.

But Peewee had said all he intended to on the subject. "I reckon it's enough right now that you know there is a backside. Just . . . don't go jumpin' the gun." He patted the younger man's shoulder with affection. "You're doin' a good job, Buck. Keep on doin' what you're doin' and we'll make it to Montana just fine."

"Ghosts or no ghosts?"

"Yes, sir, ghosts or no ghosts."

They were on the road before sunup the next morning. Peewee kept his mules at a brisk walk until the grade steepened; after that, he let them set their own pace.

The train passed the Devil's Glade relay station late in the morning, then broke for an early midday rest half a mile beyond it. Buck noticed the intense looks both Gwen and Thad gave the station, but he didn't say anything. His anger toward Gwen had cooled overnight, his thoughts occupied with the long climb that lay before them.

While the mules cropped the fresh spring grass, the men lounged in the shade of their wagons or fished for trout in Devil's Creek. Grazing the remuda was the main reason they stopped for a couple of hours each day around noon; with full bellies, the mules were more apt to sleep restfully at night, that way maintaining their strength for the following day's pull.

Buck kept today's break short and had them on the move again in under an hour. The grade grew worse after Devil's Glade, but still wasn't horrible. It was a long, steady pull, though, without any stretches of level ground to give the teams a break.

They reached the summit around 2:00 P.M. and Buck called another halt, although they kept the mules in harness this time. He and Milo rode back along the length of the train to help the drivers lower their drags, then maneuver the cradle-like shoes under the rear wheels of the lead wagons. With the day more than half gone, Buck was feeling pressured to get the outfit off the mountain, and he drove the men hard, sweating and cursing under his breath at every delay. The teamsters gave him a wide berth when they could, but no one seemed to take it personally. Not even Kroll or Mead or Lang.

They were rolling again in less than thirty minutes, with Buck up front to set the pace. Milo brought up the rear. The grade was gentler on this side. Had it not been for the length of the descending slope and a steep, narrow spot maybe half a mile below the crest, they probably wouldn't have lowered their drags at all.

Buck wasn't anticipating any problems as they entered the narrows, which was why the loud pop, followed by the shriek of tearing lumber, gave him such a start that the hairs across the back of his neck seemed to jump up like hackles. He yanked

Zeke around just as Peewee's lead wagon lurched forward off its drag, nearly jack-knifing on the slender thread of road. The breechings on the two big wheel mules drew unmercifully tight as nearly six tons of wagon and freight tried to run up over them.

Buck cursed and drove his heels into Zeke's ribs, racing back the way he'd come. Peewee's wheelers were scrunched low to the ground as they frantically pushed back at the massive weight that continued to gain on them. Peewee was straining on the brake cord with his left hand, attempting to tighten the wooden pads against the iron rims even as he struggled with the jerkline to control his mules with his right. He wasn't having much luck with either. His second wagon was veering toward the sharp drop and his mules were jumping wildly, their brays like damaged trumpets blaring in the narrow cañon.

Forcing Zeke alongside the nigh-leader, Buck grabbed the mule's bridle and yanked the animal's head toward him. "Keep 'em movin!" he bellowed to Peewee. "Don't try to hold 'em back!"

He didn't know if Peewee could hear him or not above the cacophony of wagons and panicking mules, but the teamster suddenly loosened his hold on the jerkline and Buck yelled—*"Hup!"*—into the leader's ear while tugging madly on the headstall. "Come on, dammit, *move!*"

The nigh-leader surged forward with a baleful snort, dragging its mate along via the jockey stick fastened between their bits. The mule's ears were laid flat and its long, yellow teeth snapped viciously at the air above Buck's leg. Only the mule's solid connection to the off-side leader prevented the frenzied animal from peeling the flesh from Buck's thigh.

"Come on, you flop-eared son of Satan," Buck growled, straining on the headstall. Then Peewee shouted a warning and Buck looked over his shoulder just as the whole outfit began rapidly to pick up speed.

"Run 'em into the hill!" Peewee shouted, pointing to the cedar- and boulder-strewn slope at their side. "Run 'em aground before the mules stampede!"

Buck's heart was like a lump of clay lodged in his throat as he hauled roughly on the mule's bridle. The hot, smoky odor of slipping brake pads soured the air as those mules caught between the wagons and the lead team began bunching up in a desperate effort to avoid being crushed. With the leaders turned, Buck twisted in his saddle to shout hoarse encouragement to the rest of the hitch.

The twelves, tens, and eights were already crashing through the scrub pines and sage, but the lower teams were still on the road, the wheelers just inches ahead of the runaway wagons. Then Zeke burst through a screen of chest-high cedars and his front hoofs caught a protruding stone, throwing the leggy black to his knees.

Buck lost his grip on the nigh-leader's headstall and grabbed for Zeke's dusty roach. With Peewee's mules scrambling up the side of the hill behind him, Zeke had to throw himself awkwardly to one side to avoid being trampled. Buck lost both stirrups in the mêlée, but managed to hang onto the saddle horn. Spooked by the close call, Zeke started bucking across the mountain's crazily-tilted slope. By the time Buck got him stopped, he had only one rein left and was tipped halfway out of his saddle. Behind him, shrouded in roiling dust clouds, Peewee's long hitch had come to a jarring halt, a near hopeless tangle of leather and chains and blowing, kicking mules. The leaders, twelves, tens, and eights were standing in the sage on the side of the mountain, their muzzles pointed in half a dozen different directions. The sixes, pointers, and wheelers were at the side of the road, the lead wagon jammed up hard against the steep slope, the trailer pointed toward the gorge.

"Son-of-a-bitch," Buck breathed, slipping free of his saddle and looping Zeke's reins around the branches of a scraggly cedar. He was stumbling back down the mountain even as Nate, Joe, and Lou Kitledge were hurrying forward, their eyes wide as hen's eggs as they scampered up the side of the hill to skirt the wreck. Glancing at the caravan, Buck was relieved to see that the other teams, although high-headed and snorty, were standing firm.

Peewee had dismounted but was keeping a firm grip on his jerkline as he attempted to soothe his nerve-rattled wheelers. When Buck got there, he ordered Nate, Joe, and Lou to help with the rest of the hitch, then continued on to the lead wagon, swearing under his breath when he saw the left front wheel rammed solidly into a boulder. Three of its spokes were destroyed; two others were badly splintered.

At the rear of the lead wagon, Milo and Charlie Bigelow were squatted half under the bed. Charlie rose when Buck came up, his face a mask of rage. Lifting a length of heavy chain for Buck to see, he said: "It's been tampered with, Buck. Some dirty, rotten son-of-a-bitch loosened it right out from under the frame."

Buck gritted his teeth as he accepted the chain from Charlie, but as he examined the eyebolt, he knew the muleskinner was right. The final few threads of bolt had been stripped clean, but the rest of the shaft—nearly four inches of new steel—was undamaged.

"That ain't no accident, by God," Charlie fumed.

"Not by a long shot," Milo agreed, staring at Buck. "Somebody loosened it on purpose . . . ran that nut out until it was barely holding."

"I checked that brake last night," Peewee said, and Buck turned to find the muleskinner standing behind him, his gaze riveted on the end of the chain, his face pale. "That bolt was tight when I went to bed."

"I ain't arguing with you," Buck said wearily.

"Whoever did this knew what was gonna happen." Peewee looked up, meeting Buck's eyes. "They had to."

CHAPTER FOURTEEN

Arlen Fleck was no frontiersman. It was a shortfall of character he would have cheerfully admitted to. He preferred cities, the bigger the better, and saloons that stayed open twenty-four hours a day, seven days a week. Lights and noise and the comforting cloak of humanity where he could fade into the background was his idea of a home range. He didn't even care for horses, although he would have denied his fear of them to anyone, including Nick Kelso, whose fault it was that he was out here now, tramping miserably across the middle of nowhere, as lost as a body was ever likely to be.

No doubt about it, Arlen thought, he'd let Nick down badly by allowing the kid to get away, and Nick was making damned sure he paid for it. Right now, Arlen was somewhere north of the Snake River, so deep into Idaho Territory he might just as well have been on the moon. He was riding with a couple of men he'd never met until the day before yesterday, but who carried themselves with the same go-to-hell confidence that marked Nick's swagger, the same hard-edged glint in their eyes that said they'd as soon kill a man as look at him.

The leader of this duo of bearded savages was Gabe Carville, a lanky, stoop-shouldered man who sat his saddle like a vulture waiting for its next meal. The other *hombre* went by the name of Henry Reese, a shorter, stockier version of his partner, solid as a chunk of seasoned oak, prickly as a cactus pad. Ex-trappers, they wore grease-blackened buckskins and floppy-brimmed hats that looked like they'd been hooked out of a muddy river after having been flushed through a steamboat's privy chute. Their faces were crevassed by long years in the wilderness and their hair hung over their shoulders in stringy locks. They carried heavy-barreled rifles across their saddlebows and wore a brace of pistols each, in addition to huge hunting knives that looked like they could cut a man in half with one swipe.

Arlen's jaw had nearly bounced off the floor when Nick told him to saddle up, that he was going to accompany the two barbarians on a little task he wanted done, then report back to Nick when the mission was completed. It was one of the few times Arlen had argued with Kelso. Afterward, he remembered why he didn't challenge the frost-veined gunman more often.

Arlen and Nick had run across the two old mountain men at a relay station called King's, north of the Malad Divide. Arlen could tell that Nick hadn't expected to run into them there, but that he was glad he did. He'd pulled the two aside almost immediately and, over a bottle of whiskey they passed back and forth without the use of glasses or wiping the bottle's mouth between swigs, they had schemed well into the night. Before dawn, Nick came into the room where Arlen was sleeping and roughly smacked the bottom of his bare feet, telling him what he wanted while Arlen searched for his socks.

That had been two days ago, and except for swimming their horses across the Snake River, somewhere west of the Montana Road, Arlen hadn't a clue where they were now. Not that he didn't already have enough to worry about. Although Carville and Reese were concern aplenty, there were also bears and catamounts in the hills, and rattlesnakes so thick in the sage and rocks that he nearly smothered himself at night, wrapping up in his blankets. He tried to do it on the sly, figuring there would be no end to the hell his companions could cause him if they ever discovered his fear of reptiles. They were hard enough to tolerate as it was, barely acknowledging him through the long, dusty days other than to make fun of the way he rode—his butt cheeks were already so galled he could barely force himself into the saddle in the morning—or his ignorance of the terrain and the fauna that inhabited it.

They worked him like a woman in the evenings, ordering him to collect firewood and tend their suppers like they were lords, which in a way, they were, at least out here where he was such a foreigner.

The only chore they wouldn't let him do was care for the horses. Not even his own, which would have been humiliating had he not been so weighed down with everything else that had happened to him since leaving Ogden.

It was late into their second day since leaving King's, and the afternoon sun was blazing into their eyes when they topped a low rise, woolly with sage and rabbitbrush. Henry said something that Arlen didn't catch and Gabe grunted what might have been agreement. Then Henry said: "Looks like the men be back, too."

"I hope they found buffler," Gabe grumbled. "This child's near starved fer some good hump meat."

Coming up behind the shaggy outcasts, Arlen didn't see anything other than what he'd been looking at for the past two days. "Who's back?" he asked, his voice croaky with dust.

"Let's get on down there, 'fore Runs-His-Ponies thinks we're lookin' fer a fight," Henry said, and Arlen's heart went *thump-thump,* real fast.

"Runs-His-Ponies? That sounds. . . ." He held his right hand palm flat along the narrow brim of his porkpie hat and squinted into the sun, while the rest of what he was going to say stumbled and fell on his tongue. Through the late afternoon light he could just make out a hazy cloud of smoke, hanging above a grove of trees about a mile away. Below it, he could see numerous brown, conical tents, a horse herd grazing not too far beyond them. "Indians," he breathed.

Henry, making a gagging sound that Arlen had come to understand was a chuckle, said to Gabe: "I believe the pilgrim's finally gettin' some mountain smarts about him."

"Are they . . . Sioux?" Arlen asked with an involuntary shudder.

At his question, Henry gave him the same withering look Nick sometimes did, when Arlen said something the gunman considered too ignorant to respond to. Seeing it, Arlen suddenly recalled that the Sioux lived east of the Rocky Mountains, a long way from Idaho. "Blackfoot," he second guessed.

"He ain't soundin' so smart no more," Gabe observed without looking around. "How ya figure he survived this long, Henry?"

The old trapper's remark sparked a flash of resentment in Arlen. "I get along just fine in my own place," he retorted. "Probably in a city like Ogden, you two would be as lost as I am out here."

The grubby frontiersmen laughed, and Gabe added: "I doubts it, boy, I shorely do."

Sadly Arlen figured he was probably right. "What are we going to do?" he asked, changing the subject. He'd hoped they might by-pass the village so that he wouldn't have to deal with this new experience, but it was becoming apparent that the ragged collection of hide tents had been their destination all along.

This time it was Gabe who looked back, gracing him with a yellow-fanged grin that reminded Arlen of the dog that had cornered him in Corinne. "Why, boy, we's gonna start us a little Injun war, and, if ye ain't keerful, it'll be yore scalp we lift first."

Arlen just nodded and said—"Oh."—and let it drop, deciding right then and there that he didn't really want to know what they were going to do here, and that taking care of the fire and the food was just fine.

Chapter Fifteen

They pulled the front wheel off the trailer to replace the broken wheel on Peewee's lead wagon, so that he could drive it another half mile down the mountain to a small cove along the road. Then they returned with the good wheel to bring the trailer down, the rest of the caravan following without incident.

Buck sent Rossy and Manuel up the mountain to cut a suitable pole from the taller pines near the top, while he, Peewee, and Milo pulled the larger right rear wheel off Peewee's trailer and returned it to the front of the lead wagon. When Rossy and Manuel got back, they trimmed the thigh-thick trunk to shape, then rigged it to the trailer's rear axle to create a makeshift skid that held the hub about a foot off the ground. When they'd finished, Buck stepped back to view the result. With its odd-size wheels up front and the drag on the trailer, the whole outfit looked mismatched and slightly ludicrous, but he figured it would hold together long enough to get them to King's.

King's was an old Oliver and Company relay station, sitting just off the Malad's northern foothills, where the Marsh Valley Road from Franklin merged with the Montana Road. The last time Buck had been there, there had been a blacksmith, a wheelwright, and a carpenter on duty. It was the wheelwright Buck was hoping to find today.

He had Paddy O'Rourke bring up his off-leader, a big-boned sorrel with a gentle disposition. While Buck and Peewee lashed the broken wheel to the mule's back, O'Rourke stood off to one side and grumbled about the unfairness of losing half his team to a Box K chore. Buck ignored him and swung into his saddle, telling Milo, loudly enough for rest of the men to hear: "Keep this train moving. You should reach King's by midmorning tomorrow. With any luck, I'll have this wheel fixed by the time you pull in." His gaze swept the crew. "We all know this wasn't an accident," he said bluntly. "From here on, everybody keeps their eyes peeled. Anything suspicious, you come to me, Milo, or Peewee. I don't want something like this happening again."

An uneasy murmuring rippled through the crowd, but Buck was relieved that no one demanded further explanation.

It was still light when Buck reached King's. He reined into the shade of the stable and stepped down just as John King emerged from the building's interior with a welcoming smile.

"Hello, Buck," the station manager said, reaching out to shake the younger man's hand. Nodding to the pack mule with a wry grin, he added: "Lose your wagon?"

"Just about." Buck related the incident that had nearly sent Peewee to the bottom of the Malad gorge. When he finished, neither man was smiling.

"Any ideas who your traitor is?" John asked.

Buck shook his head. "Not a one."

"Word I've heard is that half your crew is new, and that you've got a new ramrod to boot."

Buck's lips twitched in a smile as he turned to the sorrel. "I ain't seen a telegraph line yet that can deliver news faster than a teamster."

"This came from a Gilmer and Salisbury man," John confessed, moving around to the other side of the mule to help Buck lift the awkward load from its back. "They're faster than freighters but generally won't take time for details."

"Is that what you're fishing for, details?"

"No, I got the details from a Salt Lake Freight outfit that

passed through here a couple of days ago. It's the talk of the road, Buck, this race between the Box K and C and L." They wrestled the heavy wheel to the ground, then rolled it over to lean against the stable wall. "Folks are talking about Mase's death, too," John added solemnly. "There's some who wonder if maybe Crowley and Luce aren't behind it."

"I've heard that," Buck said vaguely. "Where is the Crowley and Luce train, anyway?"

"It hasn't come through yet."

Buck nodded but didn't grin, even though he wanted to.

"Lot of the boys, independents especially, are watching this race close. Some of them are saying that if C and L wins, Corinne will be a ghost town by the end of the season."

"I've heard that, too," Buck said, glancing at the twin wagon tracks of the Franklin Road that came in arrow-straight from the southeast.

"Traffic out of Franklin has been slow so far," John said, noticing the direction of Buck's gaze. "Some light farm wagons hauling their own harvests from last fall, but nothing heavier than a half ton. It's that damn' Marsh Valley stretch that's got them stopped, but that should be drying out pretty quick now. Was a prospector through here yesterday saying the Franklin outfits are gearing up for a big push. Said the whole town is getting behind Crowley and Luce. Going to let them have first whack at the road, then stay out of their way until they get a good start." He paused briefly. "If he's right, C and L could be here as early as tomorrow."

And to the Eastern speculators, insulated by twenty-five hundred miles of easy rail and reams of false paperwork from Utah Northern's agents, it probably wouldn't matter a whit that Lew Walker already had a train in Montana, a good two weeks ahead of the earliest Franklin outfit.

"Whatcha got for me?" called a voice from the darkness of

the stable, and Buck turned as King's wheelwright, Les Turner, strode into view.

"I've got some spokes that need replacing," Buck said, shaking the wright's hand. "How have you been, Les?"

"Right pert, other than my feet."

"He's been soaking his feet down at the spring every day since the weather turned warm," John added. "It's gotten so bad the cattle won't drink."

"Them cows'll drink when they get thirsty," Les replied peevishly to the laughter of the two men. " 'Sides, it ain't gonna be long and I'll be humpin' it sunup to sundown keepin' them big rigs rollin'. Come fall, my feet's gonna be so swollen I'll be hobblin' around like some gray-muzzled old ox."

John chuckled and slapped the wheelwright's stomach lightly with the back of his hand. "That won't be because of the work, Les, that'll be because you're already an old, gray-muzzled ox. Haven't you looked in a mirror lately?"

"There ain't nothin' in a mirror I got a hankerin' to see," Les shot back, walking over to examine the wheel. "Yeah, we can fix this," he told Buck after a couple of minutes. "How far back is your wagon?"

"It ought to be here tomorrow morning."

"Sure, we'll be ready by then," Les promised, then started the damaged wheel rolling toward his shop behind the stable.

Gathering Zeke's reins and the pack mule's lead rope, Buck led them to a nearby corral. He piled their tack beside the gate, then made sure they had feed and water. Afterward, he walked over to watch Les repair the wheel, pitching in whenever the wright asked for assistance.

It was no small task to change out the broken spokes. The wheel's iron rim had to be pulled first, then the fellies pried gently apart so that the spokes could be removed and replaced, sort of like an intricate Chinese puzzle. Done wrong and the wheel wouldn't last a hundred miles. Done right and it would last a hundred years—barring any further collisions with mountainside boulders.

By the time the light was starting to fade in the west, the two men were fitting the forge-heated rim back over the wheel, dousing it with buckets of cold water that drew the iron strap tight as a weld.

Jerking his face away from the billowing steam that rose off the hot iron, Buck leaned one of the long-handled tongs he and Les had used to lower the rim over the fellies against the wall. Arching his back against the knot of muscles that had knuckled up along his spine, he said: "I don't know why you're complaining about your feet. My back's so kinked up I don't know if I'll ever walk straight again."

Les laughed as he circled the horizontal wheel, giving the rim a few experimental taps along the way with a steel-headed mallet to satisfy himself that the job had been done right. "You ought to grab yourself something to eat, Buck," he said without looking up. "Cookie'll keep the bar open till bedtime, but he runs a tight kitchen."

"Are you eating?"

The wheelwright looked up, smiling. "Sure, I'm gonna eat with my wife and kids. John'll eat with his brood. You're gonna have to share grub with Cookie and some jasper been hangin' around the last couple days like a snake in a hen house."

News of a stranger piqued Buck's interest. "What jasper is that?" he asked.

Les shrugged as he continued his slow tramp around the wheel, keeping watch for uneven cooling. "He won't give up his name or even the time of day. Just sits there sippin' beer and starin' down the road."

"Which road?"

"The Franklin Road." Les glanced at Buck. "I ain't sure that means anything, you understand?"

"No, but I appreciate the warning."

"Hell, if it's a warning you want, shy away from Cookie's oatmeal. Stick to the venison. It's tough as leather, but it won't ferment in your belly overnight like them oats."

Buck chuckled politely and promised to do just that, but, as he left the wheelwright's shop, his thoughts immediately skipped back to the stranger hanging out at the bar. Standing in the gathering darkness outside, Buck could make out the glow of evening fires at the Box K camp, less than ten miles away. Farther up the mountain, near its summit, was a second small globe of light that he knew was the fire of another freighters' camp, capping the shallow pass like a rising moon. Although the Franklin Road was still dark, Buck knew that would soon change. If what John King's prospector had said was true, in another few days their back trail at night would be lit by a string of distant cook fires from rival firms.

The roadhouse door was propped open to admit the evening breeze, and Buck spotted the stranger as soon as he stepped inside. He nodded once, then made his way to the bar where Cookie was sitting atop the near end, looking as affable and as dirty as ever. He grinned when he saw Buck, revealing an uneven row of tobacco-stained teeth. "Hey, Buck!" he called loudly. "Good to see you, boy."

"How, Cookie?"

Pushing off the bar, Cookie said: "Want a beer?"

"I wouldn't turn one down." Buck glanced at the stranger. "How about you, pard? Can I buy you beer?"

The stranger's brows wriggled uncertainly, as if the question had caught him off guard. He shook his head no.

"You can buy me one," Cookie volunteered, pulling a pair of greasy mugs off the back shelf. "I ain't had hardly a sniff of the stuff since noon."

"Pour it," Buck said, standing so that he could keep his eyes on the stranger.

"That's Jasper," Cookie said, grinning. He had both hands under the bar, where the gurgle of running beer from a hidden tap promised quick relief for Buck's thirst. "Jasper don't talk much but he must like my cookin', 'cause he's still here."

"It's not your cooking I like," the stranger replied, pulling his legs under him and shoving to his feet. "It's the beer."

"I'll be damned," Cookie murmured. "You must have the magic touch, Buck. Ol' Jasper here ain't peeped more'n a dozen words since he rode in several days ago."

Jasper walked over to the bar, taking a position a couple of yards from Buck. "I've been hearing about you, McCready. They say you're the lead mule for the Box K."

"I captain one of its trains," Buck replied, "although I don't remember mentioning my name to you."

A cool smile twitched at the stranger's lips. "You didn't. Cookie mentioned it when you rode in. My name's Nick Kelso."

"Well, I'll be damned for a second time," Cookie said, sounding suddenly wary. "He's got a name, too." He set one of the mugs in front of Buck, thick foam sliding down the outside of the glass. "I swear that's the most he's talked since Carville and Reese rode outta here a couple days ago."

"Gabe Carville and Henry Reese?" Buck asked curiously.

"Uhn-huh."

"Mind your beer, barkeep," Kelso advised, "and don't go mouthing off about affairs that are none of your concern."

"I've heard a lot of bad stories about Carville and Reese," Buck said, eyeing Kelso. "They've been accused more than once of stealing other trappers' furs. Of course, that's just campfire talk. Maybe you know them better than I do."

"No, I'd say that talk was about right," Nick replied. "They've been known to lift a few mules from time to time, too. They're not particular."

"Stealing mules is a good way to get shot," Buck said. "Or hung, if they ain't particular."

"There's some who'd like to, I suppose."

Buck sipped at his beer. He thought it odd that Kelso would speak so openly of Carville's and Reese's nefarious reputations, although he wasn't sure it signified anything. Glancing at the barkeep, he said: "You got any grub left, Cookie?"

"I got some cold oats, and the bread's almost fresh."

"That bread's got hair in it," Nick accused.

Grinning sheepishly, Cookie lifted his well-stained bowler. "I'm gettin' kinda sparse on top, Buck, and I don't wear a hat in the kitchen on account of it's so dang' hot, so you might find a strand or two, although it ain't killed nobody yet that I know of."

It was widely believed that some of the best and worst cooking a man was liable to encounter could be found in Western roadhouses. It was just as true, Buck thought, that Cookie's meals usually ran nearer the latter than the former. "What have you got on your shelves?" he asked.

"I got a heap of elk jerky. In cans I got corned beef, sardines, peaches, tomaters. Outside of cans I got powdered milk, crackers, pickled eggs . . . shoot, just about anything a feller'd want if he's hungry enough."

Buck ordered a can of corned beef, another of peaches, a dozen crackers, and a couple of pickled eggs. While Cookie gathered his supper, Buck laid out change for the food and beers. Keeping his mug in hand, he gathered his purchases in his arm, telling the bartender: "I'm going to bunk outside tonight. I'll bring your mug back in the morning."

"That works," Cookie agreed.

Buck glanced at Nick. "Good to meet you, friend."

Kelso's tight smile remained unchanged, although he did lift his mug in a short farewell salute.

Outside, Buck checked his mules first, then sank down, cross-legged, beside the barn to eat his supper. When he'd finished, he set his empty beer mug on the porch, then took his bedroll across the road and spread it out in the sage. Although he was tired, sleep was elusive. He kept running over everything that had happened since Mase's murder. Some of it, like the shots fired at him and Dulce along the Bear River and the murders of Lotty Beals and Sally Hayes, was already starting to seem like a long time ago. But the terror he'd seen in Peewee's eyes that afternoon when the two big Murphys had almost gone over the edge was still so fresh in his mind he had to force himself to relax.

He must have dozed, because when he opened his eyes next, the moon was already well up. He didn't know what had awakened him until he heard Zeke's nervous whicker. Rolling up on one elbow, he peered through the lower branches of sage, spying a man at the far end of the corral, a saddled horse hitched to one of the rails. The light was too poor to make out any details, but Buck had a good idea who it was. He kicked free of his blankets and pulled on his boots. When he looked again, the man had moved close to the barn, creeping through its shadows like a stalking cat. Even in that murky light, the silhouette of the man's pistol against the pale log wall was unmistakable.

Buck's throat worked convulsively as he slid his own revolver free of its holster and thumbed the hammer to full cock. Although the distance was a good forty yards, the sound traveled clearly in the still night air. The dark figure whirled smartly and fired, the bullet crashing through the sage near Buck's shoulder. A second round probed the brush on his other side, and Buck dropped flat with a startled epithet. At the barn, the man was racing for his horse, swinging smoothly into the saddle and wheeling it on a short rein. Buck scrambled through the sage, hollering for the man to halt, but the lanky stalker laid down two more quick rounds instead, the second one coming close enough for Buck to hear the bullet's sizzle. Then the man was racing out the roadhouse yard, his horse stretched low to the ground as it pounded north along the Montana Road.

"God damn!" Buck roared, breaking free of the sage. He skidded to a stop in the middle of the road but held his fire. The distance was already too great. "Son-of-a-bitch," he breathed.

He hurried across the yard to the corral. Zeke met him at the gate, his long ears perked inquisitively forward, nostrils flaring at the sharp, sulphurous odor of burned gunpowder. Buck patted the john's neck affectionately. He was pretty sure there was one horse missing, a bay, if he remembered correctly.

"What the hell's goin' on out here?" Cookie demanded from the porch, standing there in a flowing nightshirt, a double-barreled shotgun in his hands.

"Over here!" Buck called, shoving the Colt inside the waistband of his trousers. He walked over to where Cookie had stopped at the near end of the porch, his bare toes wiggling over the edge like a troop of stubby worms.

"Buck? That you?"

"It is. Someone took a shot at me."

"The hell you say? Who?"

"I could make a guess. There's a bay horse missing from the corral. I've got two bits says it's Nick Kelso's pony."

"Huh," Cookie said thoughtfully, lowering his shotgun. "Jasper rode in on a bay, all right. Let me check." He disappeared into the roadhouse. When he came back a couple of minutes later, he was still toting the double-barrel. "He's cleared out, all right."

"I was wondering," Buck said softly, "did he own a lever gun, maybe a Forty-Four-Forty?"

"Yeah, he did. How'd you know that? He kept it in his room with the rest of his stuff."

"Just a hunch."

"That's a hell of a hunch," Cookie said doubtfully.

Buck stepped away from the porch to stare north along the Montana Road. "It is, ain't it?"

Chapter Sixteen

Sitting quietly before her evening fire, Gwendolyn Haywood pondered the monumental mistake she had made in pirating her brother's summer position with Bannock Mining. She'd wanted to prove her maturity, to flaunt her independence in the face of her father's disapproval of her lifestyle and the friends who shared it. In the beginning, it had seemed like a grand adventure, little more than a continuation of the game she and her father had embarked on the night of her coming-out ball.

Peewee Trapp's near-fatal wreck that afternoon had crushed that view, and the consequences of what they were attempting, she and these rough-barked men of the Box K, and the repercussions that were sure to follow no matter who won this race to Montana, were only now starting to sink in.

This was no longer a game. This was deadly serious.

A heavily-accented curse startled Gwen, and she raised her eyes from where she had been staring into the low, yellow flames of the campfire. Paddy O'Rourke sat across from her, sucking resentfully on his thumb. A butcher knife lay in the dirt at his feet, its tip glistening with blood. Gwen assumed he'd cut himself while wiping the steel blade clean on a rag, but she didn't inquire. Paddy O'Rourke frightened her, and she was pretty sure he frightened Dulce Kavanaugh, too. She wished Thad hadn't hired him, but Thad had insisted reliable linesmen were hard to find, and that O'Rourke came highly recommended. Perhaps that was true, Gwen thought, but it didn't calm the feelings of dread she felt whenever the swarthy Irishman turned his brooding gaze upon her.

O'Rourke looked up now, and Gwen quickly averted her eyes. She knew he was aware of her slight, angered by it, and a chill skittered down her spine. She stared at the rear boot of the mud wagon, its sloping leather cover dyed the color of the night, and wondered how long she could pretend interest in something she could barely make out. She could feel the jehu's thorny visage still hard upon her and feared he would continue to stare until she was forced to acknowledge him. Then, with a muttered curse, O'Rourke pushed to his feet and stalked away, leaving his knife where it had fallen.

Gwen shuddered and lowered her face. Tears welled in her eyes. She recalled the passion of the linesman's oath, the dark power of his gaze, and knew that this was a thing she had no control over. She had discovered quite a few of those recently. Life was larger out here than anything she had ever imagined, harsher than she would have believed possible. But she wouldn't go back, wouldn't give her father the satisfaction of quitting almost before the journey was begun.

She stood and glanced around the camp, dabbing at her eyes with a small, powder-blue handkerchief. Most of the muleskinners had already retired, and all but her own fire had burned down to coals. With a sigh, she turned toward the tent she shared with Dulce. Its interior was dark, suggesting that the younger woman was already asleep.

Gwen made her way to the tent, where a tin basin filled with cold water sat on top of a wooden stand next to the entrance. She washed her face, then brushed her teeth with baking soda, all the while reflecting upon the private bath in her family's home on Society Hill, the little stove in the corner where water could be heated. She hadn't had a proper bath since leaving Ogden and dreaded to think how she must appear to others. It was a blessing, she'd decided early on, that she had brought along only a small oval hand mirror; anything larger might have shamed her into a long coat and veil.

She changed into her nightgown and quickly slipped under her blankets, shivering from the cold. That a country could be so hot during the day, then turn so abruptly cold at night, was just another reminder of how far out of her element she truly was. In Philadelphia, the heat and humidity during the summer never seemed to let up.

Despite her weariness, Gwen managed only a light sleep, enough to start her down a path filled with familiar faces and illogical conversations. Her friends from home and school were there, as was Buck McCready and Thad Collins. The path led to a ballroom filled with light and laughter, and dancers swirled by on every side. But she sensed there was something wrong, too, and went in search of Buck, riding his mule, Zeke. Only it wasn't Buck she found, but Paddy O'Rourke, still angry over her refusal to recognize the cut on his finger. O'Rourke cursed and began to advance on her, covered in blood from a now severed thumb, his eyes like twin sockets drilled into a misshapen lump of skull. . . .

Gwen awoke with start. The fire outside had died and everything around her was without form. Moving her hand experimentally in front of her face produced only the faintest of shadows. Lying back, she tried to slow the beating of her heart. She could hear the mules grazing on the hillside below the camp and coyotes in the far-off hills and . . . *crack*. . . .

Gwen's eyes flew open. She threw her blankets back and swung her legs off the cot. Her sheepskin-lined slippers rested on the carpet beneath her and she eased her feet into them before rising and pulling a shawl around her shoulders. She debated lighting a lamp or waking Dulce, then decided against it. Gwen already felt like an outsider. She didn't want to risk making a laughingstock of herself by reacting too hastily. This was a wagon train after all, perched on the side of a mountain in the middle of a wilderness. Of course there would be unexplained noises.

Gwen made her way to the canvas door, her fingernails rasping softly on the stiff fabric as she searched for the first of the four cloth ties that held the entrance closed. She freed the one nearest to her face first, then two others below it. Easing the right-hand flap back a couple of inches, she pressed her face to the narrow gap. The darkness outside was intimidating, but not as complete as that within. Moving deliberately so as to make as little noise as possible, she slid through the door. Starlight capped the small cove, illuminating the nearby brush and boulders. Screwing up her courage, she stepped away from the entrance. As she did, movement from the corner of her eye caused her to whirl just as a tall, lean figure slammed into her. She caught the strong odor of teamster, of leather and sweat and mule hide, even as she stumbled backward, falling hard. A calloused hand grabbed her chin and yanked her face around to the dim light of the stars. A knife flashed. Gwen tried to scream but couldn't force the sound past her throat.

"Bitch," a voice growled in her ear.

"What's going on over there?" a second voice demanded from the far side of the tent. It was Thad, curious but not yet alarmed.

The man above her hesitated, then shoved her roughly back and fled. Gwen's head thumped solidly against the rocky ground and she rolled onto her side with a low whimper. She heard footsteps coming toward her, and for a moment she lay there waiting to be rescued, reassured, then returned safely to her bed—as her father had done so many times before.

Stubbornly Gwen pushed to her feet, brushing the dirt and grass from her nightgown, straightening her shawl. Her lips were pinched tightly when Thad rounded the corner of her tent, her anger growing.

"Miss Haywood," Thad said uncertainly. "Is everything all right?"

"No, everything is not all right. I interrupted a prowler."

"A prowler? Where?"

"Here!" She waved a hand over the spot in front of the tent. "Where do you think? He pushed me down and threatened me with a knife."

"Someone pushed you down?"

"Must I repeat everything?" Gwen snapped. "He threatened me with a knife, while you slept blissfully away."

Thad came closer and Gwen saw that he was in his stocking feet, but that his revolver was drawn. He was studying the nearby bushes speculatively. "Did you see who it was?"

She hesitated. He had called her a bitch with more hatred then she had ever heard before, and her face flamed with humiliation. "How dare he?" she whispered.

"What was that?" Thad asked, turning.

"Nothing." She took a deep, quavery breath. "It was probably just one of the mule drivers."

Thad frowned. "Why would one of the drivers threaten you with a knife?"

"How should I know, Thaddeus? Perhaps I reminded him of an old girlfriend." Tears came to her eyes. She blinked them back, grateful for the darkness. "It was nothing," she said then. "An accident."

Thad came closer, sliding the pistol into the waistband of his trousers. "Miss, we can't assume anything after what happened on the mountain today. If someone threatened you, I need to know who it was. If it was a deliberate attack, action needs to be taken."

Gwen shuddered. She hadn't considered the possibility that

there might be a connection between what happened to Peewee Trapp that afternoon and the dark figure tonight. "Very well, you may report the incident to Mister Newton, but . . . don't tell him I was threatened. Just tell him there was a prowler, and that you frightened him away."

Thad hesitated. Gwen could tell he was uncomfortable with those restrictions, but not yet ready to defy her authority. "All right," he said finally, "but I'll tell him now. I want to have a look around before I go back to bed, and Newton can help."

She nodded and turned toward her tent. "I shall await your return in my quarters," she informed him.

"Newton will want to talk to you," Thad reminded her.

"I have no doubt," Gwen replied crossly. Milo would want to talk to her and so would Dulce, when all she wanted right now was to escape into blessed sleep.

Milo brought the train into King's before 9:00 the next morning, and by 9:30 they had the wheels switched and the repairs made. While Peewee and Ray returned jacks and chocks to the mess wagon, Milo pulled Buck aside to relate Gwen's story of a prowler outside the women's tent.

"Is Miss Haywood all right?" Buck asked.

"Scared, but trying not to act like it."

"Did she see who it was?"

"No, but apparently Collins heard something, too, and went to investigate. Gwen says whoever it was ran off when he heard Collins stirring." Milo pulled the makings from his pocket and started a cigarette. "I don't guess it necessarily means anything. On the other hand, maybe it does."

"What time did this happen?"

"About midnight."

"Who else knows about it?"

"Dulce, maybe O'Rourke. I didn't talk to him about it

because he was still in his blankets when I got there. I told Gwen and Dulce and Collins to keep it under their hats until I talked to you. I doubt if O'Rourke would say anything even if he does know about it. He doesn't get along well enough with anyone to start rumors." Milo struck a match to light his cigarette, then shook it out and dropped it in the dust. "Some of the boys are beginning to wonder about what happened back at Hampton's Crossing, too," he added. "No one's asked about it yet, but I figure they will."

"Well, I can't say I'm surprised," Buck admitted. "We won't be able to keep it quiet much longer."

"That could be," Milo concurred, his cigarette bobbing between his lips. "There's one more thing. Lou Kitledge was telling the boys last night that part of his harness might've been tampered with back in Corinne, right before we pulled out. He says a rivet in his off-wheeler's breeching was pulled nearly through, but that he'd checked all his harness earlier and that everything was all right." Milo shrugged. "A rivet's an easy thing to overlook, but with everything else that's been going on, I figured I ought to mention it."

"Did he say anything about it at the time?"

"Nope, just fixed it himself, like I would've done. Like we all would've done. It's interesting, though. A breeching strap on a wheeler would be about the last one you'd want to bust on a downgrade."

Buck nodded agreement, but his attention was distracted by John King's approach. "Get the wagons rolling," he told Milo. "I'll be along in a few minutes."

"Sure," Milo said, stepping into his saddle and pulling his mule around, his cigarette still riding in the corner of his mouth.

"I've been listening to some of your 'skinners," John said, coming up. "They sound pretty jumpy."

"They're spooked after what happened yesterday, but they'll

feel better in a day or two."

"What about you? Cookie told me what happened last night between you and Kelso."

Buck shrugged. He didn't know what to think of Nick Kelso. It could have been connected to the Box K's recent troubles, or it could have been something as simple as a botched robbery attempt.

There was a shout from the forward end of the column, and Peewee's voice filled the still, dusty air: "Get up, Cassie! Pepperjack, Diego, move out!" Similar calls began to echo up and down the line, punctuated by the cracking of bullwhips that shattered the warm air like fragile glass, but disturbed not a hair on a mule's hide. Soon the whole outfit was in motion, a rumbling procession of men and animals easing into a familiar formation. Buck and John stepped clear of the dust and waited for the train to pass. Buck had already written out a check on Jock's account for the repairs to Peewee's wheel. He handed it to John now, accepting a receipt in return that he tucked in his shirt pocket. "We'll see you on the way back," Buck said, swinging astride his black mule. "Maybe things will have settled down by then."

"Good Lord, I hope so," John replied, and Buck smiled and pulled Zeke around, cantering after the train.

Chapter Seventeen

It was obvious to Arlen that the negotiations between Gabe Carville and the Shoshone chief, Runs-His-Ponies, weren't going well. After two days of steady discussions, the two were beginning to look as testy as a couple of jilted bridegrooms. Gabe continued to harangue Runs-His-Ponies for a favor owed him from years past, but the cagey old Indian—Arlen reckoned he had to be on the shady side of fifty—wasn't buying it. Runs-His-Ponies was of the opinion that helping Gabe and Henry attack the Box K mule train would lead to an all-out war with the white-eyes, something he wasn't keen to risk.

"It ain't like ye never stolt nothin' from the white-eyes afore," Gabe repeated at least once every hour, with an ever-growing tone of resentment. "I know damn' well ye didn't buy that needle-gun you're totin'."

Runs-His-Ponies wouldn't deny that he'd filched an item or two over the years, including the trap-door Springfield he carried everywhere with him, but he'd never used the gun on a white man and had no intention of starting now. "No war," was his dogged reply.

It didn't help that there already existed bad blood between the two over a Paiute woman, the details of which had proven too complex for Arlen to follow. Gabe and Runs-His-Ponies were conversing in a polyglot of heavily accented English and an Indian dialect more reminiscent of breaking wind than spoken words, at least to Arlen's untutored ear. The two bridged whatever gap in language that sprang up between them with sign talk.

Now, deep into their second night of talks, it was clear the parley was breaking down. Gabe and Runs-His-Ponies were sitting opposite each other over a small fire in front of Runs-His-Ponies's lodge. Probably twenty or more warriors stood behind the scowling war leader, everyone armed with knives or clubs or tomahawks, and looking as grim as death as Gabe's prattle became increasingly insulting.

Leaning close, Henry whispered: "Get ready, dumb-ass, hell's fixin' to pop."

Arlen's breath escaped like steam from a locomotive as the image of his skull, parting under the blow of a rusty tomahawk, lodged in his mind.

"If shooting starts, ye point your pistol into the thick of things and let fly, hear?" Henry added.

Runs-His-Ponies's eyes were blazing as Gabe wrapped up his speech. The Indians behind him weren't taking it well, either, and Arlen whispered a question to which Henry replied: "Called Runs-His-Ponies a woman and said he didn't have the nerve of a rabbit."

"Well, that ain't good," Arlen said, puzzled by the mountain man's approach. "Won't that just make Runs-His-Ponies madder?"

Henry looked at him and laughed. "Dumb-ass, ye be a wonder."

Runs-His-Ponies took that moment to jump to his feet. Gabe followed, whipping out a long-bladed butcher knife. Runs-His-Ponies as well pulled a knife, and the crowd around the fire scrambled to get out of the way.

Gabe was snarling like a cornered wolf. "I'll cut ye, boy, ye come at me. I'll geld ye quick," he told the husky Indian.

Runs-His-Ponies replied in Shoshone, eliciting quick grunts

of approval from several of the braves behind him.

"Just these two is gonna fight," Henry told Arlen, "though I wouldn't get too relaxed. Things could still blow up in our faces."

Gabe and Runs-His-Ponies moved away from the fire. The crowd closed in around them. Arlen found himself front and center, too fascinated by the unfolding drama to think of escape or his own danger.

The two old veterans circled cautiously, performing a dance as old as first man, each seeking an opening in the other's defense. Runs-His-Ponies feinted. Gabe parried it with the practiced ease of a seasoned brawler. He moved in, feigned left, came back right, then darted forward like a striking rattler, but his knife caught only empty air. Runs-His-Ponies smiled tightly. No stranger to the blade himself, he appeared unintimidated. Gabe made three more attempts to pierce the wily Indian's guard, but Runs-His-Ponies deflected each deadly thrust as if swatting away a fly. Gabe was growing more incensed by the minute, and Arlen could tell Henry was worrying about that.

"Damn' idjit," Henry muttered at one point. "Can't he see what Runs-His-Ponies is tryin' to do?"

If it was to make Gabe careless through anger, Arlen thought it was probably working. The bearded mountaineer was circling faster now, his knife weaving erratically as he spat out curses like watermelon seeds. When Runs-His-Ponies finally drew blood—a long slash inside Gabe's left bicep—Arlen didn't think anyone was surprised. It was Gabe's reaction that caught them all off guard. Without pause, the old trapper rushed in, taking a deliberate cut in his side in order to bring his own blade up in a long, vertical swipe. It came away from Runs-His-Ponies's torso bright with blood, the old warrior staggering backward, eyes wide in disbelief. Gabe didn't give him time to recover. Leaping forward, his knife flashed once more.

There was a cry of rage from the onlookers as Runs-His-Ponies's knife tumbled from his fingers. The Indian's right hand seemed to dangle helplessly from the wrist, the severed tendons gleaming white as bone in the firelight.

"Shit fire," Henry grunted.

Arlen swallowed hard, feeling suddenly queasy.

Runs-His-Ponies tried to back away but Gabe wouldn't let him. He kept crowding the old warrior, while the tip of his knife gouged one small hole after another into the Indian's body.

"Why doesn't . . . ?" Arlen started to say, but Henry jabbed him hard in the ribs and he shut up.

A murmur of angry disapproval rippled through the Shoshone spectators, but no one attempted to interfere. This was between Runs-His-Ponies and Gabe Carville, and to halt it now, with Runs-His-Ponies losing, would only bring disgrace to the old Indian. Even Arlen understood that.

When Runs-His-Ponies finally stopped backing away, Arlen thought surely Gabe would run him through with his long blade. But Gabe stopped, too, as a low, eerie wail bubbled from the Indian's blood-pinkened lips. The crowd fell silent until only Runs-His-Ponies voice could be heard, growing stronger even as his body weakened.

"It's his death song," Henry explained to Arlen. "The old boy knows he's goin' under."

Arlen couldn't move, could hardly breathe. It was as if Runs-His-Ponies's wavering song had cast a spell over everyone. Even Gabe had lowered his dripping knife to stand several feet away, his chest heaving. Runs-His-Ponies lifted his eyes to the twinkling canopy of stars overhead, and, in that instant, a falling star streaked across the night sky, brighter than any Arlen had ever seen. There was a gasp from the Shoshones as the light in the sky quickly faded. Then Runs-His-Ponies fell as if his soul had been sucked out of him, dead before he hit the ground.

At Arlen's side, Henry Reese breathed: "Aw, shit."

Chapter Eighteen

Buck squinted into the blasting glare of sunlight. The land lay flat before him, the road a pale scar winding through the tall sage. His dry lips and parched throat reminded him that he would have to dig his canteen out of the mess wagon tonight and fill it at the Portneuf. Although still only April, the days were growing unseasonably warm.

He turned at the sound of an approaching horse, smiling as Dulce rode up, although her own expression was strained. "Is it all right if I ride with you for a while?" she asked.

"It would be my pleasure. I've been wanting to ask you about last night, anyway."

She gave him a sharp look. "Is that all you wanted?"

"No, I like your company, too."

His reply seemed to appease her somewhat, and her face lost some of its stiffness. "I suppose you're talking about her highness's latest disturbance," she inquired.

"Milo says Gwen scared off a prowler."

"She says she scared off a prowler. For all anyone knows, it could have been one of the men talking a stroll."

"They ran off when Collins got up to investigate," Buck reminded her.

"So you believe her?"

"If someone was sneaking around out there, they likely weren't up to any good."

"Unless Miss Priss was feeling neglected and looking for attention."

Frowning, Buck said: "You think she made it up?"

"I think she's been making up quite a bit of stuff," Dulce replied coolly. "Including her position with Bannock Mining as its representative."

Dulce had a point there, Buck thought. There was something out of kilter about Gwen's presence in Corinne and her claim that she was there at her father's request.

"Do we even know she is Robert Haywood's daughter?" Dulce demanded. "For all we know, she could be a Crowley and Luce agent."

"There's something shady about the way she showed up," Buck acknowledged, "but I'm not ready to brand her a spy just yet. She seems too spoiled for that kind of work."

"Too spoiled, or too attractive?" Dulce broached.

Laughing, Buck said: "Don't let Gwen Haywood get in your craw."

"What makes you think she's in my craw?"

"The way you look at me when I'm talking to her alone. Like you want to skin my hide and peg it to a wall. Besides, I'm thinking she just does it to annoy you. Gwen's the kind of person who likes to smack a hornet's nest with a club, just to see what comes out . . . as long as it's someone else getting stung."

"She can be so sweet at times," Dulce admitted. "Almost like a friend, then. . . ." She made a growling noise in her throat. "Then she'll do something so annoying I'd just like to grab her and give her a good shake."

"Well, this trip isn't over yet," Buck said. "Maybe you'll get your chance."

"Wouldn't that upset her privileged little apple cart?" Dulce replied, but when she looked at Buck, there was concern in her eyes. "You aren't attracted to her, are you?"

"Naw."

"That came out awfully fast. Have you been thinking about it?"

"The only thing I've been thinking about is getting this train to Montana in one piece."

"She's pretty, though, don't you think?"

"Gwen's kind of like a flashy horse, fun to look at but too delicate to ride. She's fickle, too. That'd get old real fast."

Dulce bit her lower lip. "Then what does that make me, if I'm not flashy? Am I an old nag?"

"I'd prefer to think of you as a good, stout Missouri mule," Buck replied solemnly, then reached over to swat what he could of her bottom, planted in the saddle. "Made for the long haul and the big hitch," he added, grinning.

"Buchanan McCready," Dulce scolded, pulling her horse away. Her cheeks were flushed red, but Buck didn't think she minded nearly as much as she let on. "Don't you ever do that again," she said, then lowered her voice, "not in public."

"This ain't all that public," he protested good-naturedly, waving an arm toward the empty horizons. But Dulce was looking behind her now, and, when Buck glanced over his shoulder, he saw that she was staring at Gwen, and that Gwen was staring back.

They pushed on until late, and reached the head of Portneuf Cañon by nightfall. Leading the train to a piece of flat ground bordering the river, below the level of the wide plain they'd spent the day crossing, Buck swung his arm in a circular motion to indicate where he wanted the wagons parked, then got out of the way.

Normally Buck would have cared for Zeke first, then walked the length of the train to check with the crew, but he had something else in mind tonight, and jogged his mule to the southern end of the flat just in time to see Paddy O'Rourke coming in off the road. Reining over to where Ray was already unhitching his leaders, Buck said: "What's going on with O'Rourke?"

"How would I know?" Ray tossed over his shoulder.

"Has he been falling behind again?"

"He's back to his old habits, if that's what you mean. Not that the son-of-a-bitch ever really gave 'em up in the first place. Bastard was a quarter mile behind me the last couple of hours, maybe more."

"I'll talk to him," Buck promised, annoyed that Milo hadn't already taken care of the problem.

"Be quicker to shoot him," Ray opined, turning his leaders loose, then moving on to the next span. "He might listen better if he was dead. Sure as hell couldn't do any worse."

"I'll talk to him," Buck repeated, but reined Zeke in the opposite direction. He rode along the edge of a sprawling thicket of wild plums that were starting to leaf out until he'd put some distance between him and the wagons, then he climbed the steep bench to the south, topping out well east of the Montana Road. There wasn't much light left by now. A few stars were twinkling in the east, but, behind him, along the narrow Portneuf River, there was only shadow against shadow as the men cared for their stock.

Buck rode slowly through the short grass, grateful for the solitude. His destination was a nearby butte of volcanic rock. *Butte,* he supposed, was a bit of a stretch in everything except its classic form—sheer-sided, flat-topped, capped with a thin layer of soil grown over with grama and prickly pear. Barely wide enough to hide one of Ray's big Schuttlers, it nevertheless offered a clear view all the way south to the Malads.

Leaving Zeke ground-tied at the bottom, Buck climbed a

rocky trail along the butte's north wall that he'd used before. On top, he walked to the far end, then stopped to stare back along the pale trace of the road. It was as he'd feared. From here, he could make out the fires of no less than five separate outfits coming up behind them. Two were about where John King's roadhouse would be, at the foot of the Malads. Two more were still on the mountain, little pin pricks of yellow light against the low ridge. The fifth lay to the southeast, along the Franklin Road.

"So you finally made it to the race," Buck said softly.

As if in answer, he heard a low scuff of leather on stone and whirled with his hand darting to his pistol, his pulse quickening. At the head of the rocky footpath, a figure paused uncertainly. "You wanting to be alone, boss?" Milo asked.

Buck let his hand drop away from the Colt. "What's going on?"

"Nothing. I saw you slip away and thought maybe there was trouble. When I saw your mule standing there alone, I wondered what you were looking at. It wasn't until I got up here that it dawned on me that maybe all you wanted was some peace and quiet." He came forward uninvited, his hat brim bobbing toward the distant fires. "They're closing the gap."

"There's only one outfit we need to worry about," Buck said. "I figure that's them off to the left."

"You reckon?"

"We'll know for sure tomorrow. Soon as it's light, I want you to ride back and take a look. If it's not Crowley and Luce, we'll be in good shape. If it is, then they're close and we'll need to worry. A few more delays like the two we've already had and they could overtake us."

"I've been thinking that maybe it's a good thing the boys know that what happened to Peewee yesterday day wasn't an accident. It could help them keep on their toes."

"It might."

After a short silence, Milo said: "The reason I wanted to talk to you is that I've been getting the feeling you're trying to throw a wrench into my romance with Miss Haywood."

"You don't have a romance with Miss Haywood," Buck told him. "Not while you're ramrodding for the Box K."

"Now, I just might have to argue with that, boss. Truth is, I kind of like her, and not just because of those pretty blue eyes, either."

"Her daddy's money wouldn't have anything to do with it, would it?"

Milo chuckled. "Well, that could account for some of it, I suppose, but the fact is, she's got a spark I kind of like in a woman, and money's got nothing to do with that."

"What happens when she goes back to Philadelphia?" Buck asked. "We both know she's going to get tired of all this heat and dust. Sooner or later, she'll want to go home and have her maid draw her a bath. Where do you think you'll fit into her plans then?"

Milo's teeth flashed white in the gloaming. "Why, you never know. I might just talk her into staying. Or better yet, maybe I'll let her talk me into going back East with her. I believe I could get used to a maid drawing my bath. If she's pretty enough, I'd let her scrub my back."

"You might as well try to rope the moon," Buck said, chuckling despite himself.

"Shoot, you've been sparking Dulce too long. You've forgotten the thrill of the chase."

"You just leave Dulce out of this," Buck said curtly, then fixed the ramrod with an accusing eye. "Why is O'Rourke falling behind again?"

Milo's smiled faded. "That Irish bastard's been falling behind a little more each day. I've told you that."

"Dammit, don't tell me, tell O'Rourke. I want him to keep up."

"I say we let the Shoshones have his scalp."

"No," Buck said bluntly. "Not as long as he's part of the Box K."

"All right," Milo conceded. "I'll talk to him tomorrow."

"Talk to him tonight."

The last of the good humor left Milo's face, and his eyes went flat. He started to turn away, then swung back. "I figure you ought to know that some of the independents are starting to wonder if you're going to have what it takes to get this train to Montana. Kroll's saying a kid like you . . . a squirt, is what he's calling you . . . won't be up to the task."

"I know what Mitch Kroll thinks. It's you I'm starting to wonder about."

"You got no cause to wonder about me, although I guess I can understand why you would, what with me being new and all the hard luck that's been dogging us. But you need to know that Kroll's going to challenge you pretty soon."

Buck felt as if another weight had been added to his shoulders. "I'd figured as much," he said finally. "Has he picked a place yet?"

"Not that I've heard. Of course, I'm not privy to everything him and Mead and O'Rourke talk about."

"Where'd you hear this?"

"Little Ed got it from Garth Lang, then told me."

"Kroll, Mead, and O'Rourke?"

"Lang, too. He's a part of that bunch. They'll be a splinter in your butt until you fight one of them, convince them you're more than Jock Kavanaugh's pet wagon boss. I guess you know it'll be Kroll you'll have to fight, too."

"You tell O'Rourke that I want him to keep up with the train. Tell him that if he doesn't, I'll start docking his pay."

Milo shrugged. "I'll tell him," he said, walking away.

Buck tarried a while longer, mulling over the strange connection between Kroll, Mead, O'Rourke, and Lang. Was it just coincidence, or something more? Sighing, he made his way down the rocky trail. Zeke was still at the bottom, having wandered off only a few yards in search of grass. Buck gathered his reins above the black's withers and was stretching his toe for the stirrup when he noticed a solitary figure at the edge of the bench above the plum thicket. At first he thought it was Milo. Then the figure darted away and Buck realized it was too tall and slim for Milo, too slope-shouldered.

"Hey!" Buck shouted, stepping away from his mule. "Come back here!"

The figure dropped over the edge of the bench, disappearing into the shadows.

"Son-of-a-bitch," Buck grated, drawing his Colt and sprinting after the fleeing form. He reached the edge of the bench just as the tall shape ducked into the brush along the river. Buck plunged after him, taking the steep bank in yard-long strides. The wagons were a hundred yards to his left, near the west end of the thicket. Buck approached the tangled growth of wild plums at an angle, hoping to cut off the bolter before he reached the train, but the thorny, loose-barked limbs were too entwined to force a swift passage, and when he finally stopped to listen, only the sounds of the distant camp came to his ears, muted, serene.

Buck backed out the way he'd gone in, emerging scratched and bloodied, his shirt ripped from elbow to wrist along one sleeve from the sharp thorns. He clambered part way up the side of the bench until he could see over the top of the thicket, but there was no movement to give away the tall man's escape, and Buck knew that whoever it was had either made it back to camp undetected or, if he wasn't a part of the crew, had mounted up and ridden in the opposite direction.

Returning the revolver to its holster, Buck tried to recall as much as he could of the fleeing suspect, but the moment had been too brief. Only one thing stood out clearly—that in flight, the tall figure reminded him sharply of the man he had seen running away that night along the Bear River, after taking a shot at him and Dulce.

Buck couldn't match the loping shape to anyone on the train. It could have been Lyle Mead or Garth Lang or even Thad Collins, but then it could have also been Joe Perry or Ray Jones. Even Lou Kitledge bore a slight resemblance to the hazy form locked in Buck's memory.

Returning to Zeke's side, Buck stepped wearily into the saddle. But he didn't rein immediately toward camp. He sat there a while, recalling that evening on the Bear, the yellow flashes of gunfire and the angry, wasp-like sound of bullets passing close. He thought of the two accidents that had already occurred, nearly costing Peewee his life. He recalled Mase's death and the murders of Lotty Beals and Sally Hayes, and the shots fired at him last night by Nick Kelso, and he knew with a sickening certainty that before this was journey was over, before they reached their final destination, someone else would die. It seemed inevitable.

Chapter Nineteen

Arlen flinched and ducked as Gabe Carville's scratchy voice came over the rim of the creekbank like a volley of razor-sharp pieces of flint. He hadn't known the leathery old mountain man was back. Now that he did, a feeling of dread enveloped him. For a long time he had hated the way Gabe and Henry made him feel. Like he was not quite right, not quite human. That had changed drastically after last night.

Runs-His-Ponies's death wasn't the first Arlen had witnessed, but it was surely the most gruesome. Even now, he almost gagged on the image of the Indian's corpse—the scalp lifted, ears severed, legs and arms split to the bone. And the Shoshones had stood by silently, allowing Gabe his ghastly play.

"He's earned it," Henry had spoken into Arlen's ear even as Gabe continued his mutilations. "These ol' boys don't like it"—he'd nodded toward the knot of warriors who hadn't walked away after Runs-His-Ponies's death—"but they know it was an old feud 'twix Gabe and Runs-His-Ponies, and they'll let it happen. Like I would've if Runs-His-Ponies had won."

Squatting now beside the nameless creek to fill a hide bucket with sun-warmed water, Arlen shuddered. Yesterday when he'd performed this task, the creekbank had been alive with women and children going about their own domestic chores. Today it was deserted, the flat above uninhabited save for their own miserable shelter of rank-smelling deer hides draped carelessly over a pole frame.

The Shoshones had pulled out during the night, leaving behind only refuse, stone teepee rings, and the dark, dusty ground where Runs-His-Ponies had bled out.

Gabe had been saddling his horse, threatening to wipe out the whole damned Shoshone nation, when Arlen awoke that morning. "I'll bring back Tall Bear and his boys or know the reason why," Gabe had declared loudly. "By God, them redskins owes me."

"They won't calculate it that way," Henry had drawled. "Not after the way ye gutted Tall Bear's brother last night."

"Then mebbe I'll just gut me a few more fer breakfast," Gabe had replied defiantly, jerking his horse around. "Ye 'n' dumbass get them ponies packed. We're likely gonna haf to pull out quick when I get back." He grinned wolfishly. "I gettin' half froze fer a fight, Henry, by God if I ain't."

"Go on," Henry had said disgustedly. "Git it outta ye system. I got some ponderin' to do."

"Wagh!" Gabe had roared, driving his heels into his mount's ribs. "I'll be back afore midmorning, boys!" he'd yelled as he raced away.

Gabe was going after Tall Bear, whose countenance had nearly drained the blood from Arlen's face the first time he laid eyes on the battle-scarred old warrior. Lord God, but no amount of argument could make him see the logic in that. It was like putting a noose around your neck and jumping out of a hayloft, convinced to your core that the center pole would break at the appropriate moment.

Now Gabe was back, alive but unhappy. "I'll kill that sorry-ass 'coon, next I see 'im," Gabe was ranting. "Should 'a' done it today."

"They'd've killed ye, Gabe, if ye did," Henry replied reasonably. "Runs-His-Ponies was different on account of that Paiute squaw ye 'n' him tussled over, but ye won't walk away from that kind of fight again."

"I ain't seed a redskin yet can best me in a fight, Henry . . . knives, fists, or powder-'n'-ball. Where's dumb-ass?"

Arlen cringed, gave fleeting thought to concealment, then sighed and stood. "Down here," he said. "I was getting water."

"What'n hell's takin' ye so long?" Gabe demanded, then guffawed contemptuously. "Have trouble findin' the creek, did ye?"

"I was waiting for fresh."

Gabe shook his head at the absurdity of such a comment. "Fresh what, ye dolt? The snow's done melted in these hills. Ye want fresh, ye'll haf to ride to the high country fer it." He spat. "Use that water to put out the fire, boy. We's ridin'."

"Where to?" Henry asked.

That savage grin again, like a man not only comfortable with killing, but partial to it. "Something Runs-His-Ponies said yesterday, 'fore he got persnickety. Said Jimmy Bonner 'n' his boys is up on the Little Lost River. We's gonna find 'em, Henry, get 'em to throw in with us."

Henry was silent a moment. "Ye give up on throwin' in with a pack of redskins?" he finally asked. "Kelso made a good point when he said it'd help if folks thought Injuns was behind it."

"After what happened last night, I figure my welcome's plumb wore out amongst the redskins in these parts. 'Sides, we'll git a bigger share this way." A smirk twisted Gabe's features. "Ye ain't goin' yeller on me, are ye, Henry?"

Reese shook his head. "Naw, I ain't turnin' yellow. Hell, no! Go fetch the horses while me 'n' dumb-ass get the packs throwed together."

"*Wagh,*" Gabe grunted with satisfaction, pulling his mount around.

As he rode away, Henry wagged his head. "He's a crazy damn' fool, ye know that, don't ye, dumb-ass?"

"Who?" Arlen asked meekly, not sure if he should speak at

all. "Gabe or Jimmy Bonner?"

"Both, when ye come down on it. Bonner 'cause he's Bonner, and crazy is what he is, and Gabe 'cause he wants to throw in with the bastard." He glanced at Arlen. "I'll tell ye this, too, I ain't lookin' forward to it. You shouldn't, either. Jim Bonner ain't as easy-goin' as me 'n' Gabe. That boy's just pure-devil mean, and likely to get us all killed 'fore this is through."

Chapter Twenty

They made it through Portneuf Cañon in a single day and camped that night within sight of the towering cottonwoods that marked the junction of the Portneuf and Snake Rivers, several miles to the north. Buck ordered the train to camp on top of a rocky flat, then rode off alone as he had the night before. There was a low knob a couple of hundred yards to the east, and he dismounted there and loosened Zeke's cinch so that the mule could graze more comfortably.

Sitting on the knob with his elbows over his knees, Buck watched the caravan settle into its usual formation of two long columns, with a corridor down the middle that could be roped off in case they needed to corral the mules. From here, he considered the six men he thought could fit the shape of the man he'd seen running away last night. There was Lyle Mead, Garth Lang, Thad Collins, Joe Perry, Ray Jones, and Lou Kitledge. They were all tall enough and lean enough to match the fleeing form, but it was difficult to think of any of them as the man who had deliberately disabled Peewee's hitch not once, but twice. They were all good hands, steady with their mules and quick about their evening chores. Even the two most sullen among them, Mead and Lang, had given Buck no cause for suspicion.

He sighed, only half aware that he did. The sun was below the horizon, spiking the western sky with hues of fiery red, cotton-soft gold, and gentle turquoise. Zeke lifted his head and whickered questioningly as Dulce left the wagons and started toward them. She was on foot but wearing her pistol, a little .32 Smith & Wesson, in a holster belted tightly around her waist.

"It's getting kind of late in the day to go bear hunting, isn't it?" Buck asked as she came up.

Dulce smiled. "Papa insisted I bring it, and, with everything that's happened of late, I decided I should start wearing it." She stopped in front of him and he stood and wrapped his arms around her waist. "I've been wondering when you'll come to supper," she murmured in his ear, putting her arms around his neck.

"I know. I guess I don't have much of an excuse."

Her breath was warm on his neck. "You don't need an excuse, Mister McCready, but you do need to make an effort. I've started to think you're avoiding me."

"I've been pretty busy," he said.

"Apparently." She leaned back to peer into his eyes, and he tensed defensively. "What do you think about all the time?" she asked. "Do you still believe a traitor lurks among us?"

"I don't think there's any doubt of that."

Her expression lost some of its gentleness. "Do you have any suspects?"

"Yeah, too many."

She tightened her hold on his neck. "Do you realize this is the first time we've been alone since we left Corinne?"

"I know, I've been. . . ."

"Busy," she finished for him, lowering her arms. "Yes, I believe you've mentioned that."

He studied her as closely as the fading light would allow. He wasn't surprised by the abrupt turn of her mood, having witnessed it so often in the past, but it saddened him tonight, heaped on top of everything else he'd had to deal with lately. "It can't be helped, Dulce," he said patiently. "You knew what it would be like before we started."

"Perhaps the fault lies with your abilities as a wagon master," she suggested acidly. "I wonder, are all captains so overwhelmed by their duties?"

Buck let his hands drop from her waist. He didn't know what had triggered her temper, but past experience told him it could have been anything if she was already feeling tired or put out.

Turning away, she tossed aloofly over her shoulder, "Come to supper sometime, Captain. I assure you, I wouldn't keep you from your all-important responsibilities overly long."

Buck kept his silence as she walked away. He supposed he should go after her. There were rattlers in the sage and cougars prowled the hills, half starved after the long, wet winter, but he decided to let those creatures fend for themselves if they should cross her path in the darkness. As for himself, he was too weary to attempt it.

Milo returned around midnight, guiding his spotted molly between the wagons and dismounting at the first mess. Buck pushed his blankets back and quickly his boots. Peewee met them at the fire, already dressed. "Hungry?" the muleskinner asked.

"Hungry enough to chew the rim off a wagon wheel," Milo confessed, flipping a stirrup over the saddle to loosen the cinch. He nodded cheerfully to Buck. "Howdy, boss."

"Howdy," Buck replied, shrugging into his jacket. "What's news?"

"What you figured it'd be. Crowley and Luce is the third outfit back, maybe twenty miles behind us but looking fresh as daisies. There's a Salt Lake Freight and a Leavitt Brothers train between us and them. Leavitt's is just inside the mouth of Portneuf Cañon, hauling light and making good time. I reckon they'll pass us in another day or so."

"Who's bossing for C and L?"

"Fella named Tim Lomax. Know him?"

"I've heard of him."

"Lomax is an old hand at freightin'," Peewee added. "Used to make that run between Salt Lake City and San Diego all the time. That's a tough haul, but Lomax never lost a cargo."

"Few men do," Buck reminded him gruffly. "Question is, how honest is he?"

"I reckon he wants to win this race as much as any of us," Peewee said mildly. "I don't know that he'd do anything crooked unless Herb Crowley or Anton Luce pushed him to it. Even then, I ain't sure he would."

"There's not much he can do with a BMC rep riding along," Milo said. "Anything shady would have to come from Crowley or Luce personally."

"Like gettin' to one of our drivers?" Peewee asked.

Milo paused, his eyes darting between the two men. "Something happen while I was gone?"

"No," Buck said, "although with C and L so close, it'll likely increase the odds. They'll have to make a move to get around us sooner or later." He glanced at Peewee. "No matter how honest their captain is."

Peewee shrugged and started feeding twigs to the coals of their supper fire. Milo lifted his saddle from the molly's back and dumped it beside the rear wheel of Peewee's wagon. Rolling his shoulders, he said: "Boys, I'm frazzled. That was forty miles I rode today, or close to it."

"Forty miles for your mule, too," Buck reminded him without sympathy. "Go take care of her. We'll have some supper ready when you get back. Tomorrow you can ride in one of the wagons and give that molly a rest."

"Now I wouldn't mind that a bit," Milo said, his features brightening. "Either of you gents seen how Rossy's got his bed laid out in his pa's wagon? Got a little straw-filled mattress in there that's cushioned with buffalo robes. Got a water jug and some biscuits for snacks. It looks mighty comfortable or I wouldn't say so, and big enough to sleep both of us, if Rossy doesn't flop around too much."

"I think I'd rather you ride with Paddy O'Rourke tomorrow. Keep him from falling so far behind."

The ramrod's expression crumbled. "Aw, hell, boss!"

"While you're at it, see if you can pry some information out of him. I'm real curious about what made him leave Arizona for Utah."

"Nobody likes him," Milo said, as if that explained everything. "He looks at you like you're something to scrape off the bottom of his boots."

"You don't have to like him, just get him to talk. Find out where he's from and what he thinks about Jock and the Box K."

Milo shook his head in disgust but led his mule away without further argument.

Peewee chuckled as Buck lowered himself beside the fire. "You took the wind outta that boy's sails real fast."

"Milo's got plenty of wind to spare," Buck observed dryly. He nodded at a skillet sitting beside the fire. "Have we got any grub left over from supper?"

"I'm gonna warm up some beans and pan bread. He'll have to do without coffee unless he wants to grind some beans. I ain't his mama." Peewee turned silent while he fussed with supper. It wasn't until the food was warming that he spoke again. "I know I checked that eyebolt, Buck."

"I believe you."

Peewee nodded. He'd already known as much, but it was good to hear it again. He said: "Mitch Kroll's making a stink about it."

"What kind of stink?"

"What it boils down to is Kroll wants to be the bull of this here outfit. It rubs him wrong that you're a green kid and I'm a runt who couldn't keep a job if Jock didn't take pity on me."

Buck laughed. "Is that what he's saying?"

"More or less. It's a bucket of cow flop and the boys all know it, but Kroll keeps pickin' at it like a scab. Thing is, if these accidents keep happenin', he could stir up some trouble."

"The hell with Mitch Kroll," Buck said dismissingly.

After a moment's silence, Peewee said: "Normally I'd agree with you, but Kroll's got some of the boys sidin' with him now."

"Who?" Buck asked.

"Mead, Lang, and O'Rourke for sure. Maybe Collins, and I ain't completely sure about Little Ed Womack any more." He looked up. "Was a time when I was."

Buck frowned. When he'd talked to Milo last night, Womack and Collins hadn't entered into the equation at all. Was this new, or was Peewee overreacting in the wake of two near-fatal accidents? "You figure we need to start worrying?" he asked.

"No, not yet, but it could come to that."

"You mean a mutiny?"

Peewee nodded. "I've seen crews mutiny, and it gets real messy real fast . . . minutes, not days. Not even hours. It just blows up like a bomb was tossed into the fire."

Buck shifted restlessly. "Well, we won't lower our guard, but I'm not sure we can raise it much, either. A mule train is vulnerable in too many places . . . the stock, the men, the gear, even the cargo. If someone wants to slow us down, there are too many places they can target, and we can't watch them all, no matter how much we try."

He was silent a moment, recalling Tom Ashley's description of the man Mase had tangled with in the International. Big, burly, with long greasy hair and worn-out clothing, not tall and slim and hunch-shouldered like the shadowy figure he'd chased after more than once now. What did it all add up to?

"They's too many loose ends to pull this puzzle together all the way," Peewee said quietly, as if reading his thoughts, "but we can sure as hell say someone wants this train stopped." He met Buck's eyes across the fire. "They want that bad."

Buck nodded soberly. "I believe you."

Chapter Twenty-One

It was past noon when Buck called a halt the next day at the old Hudson's Bay trading post of Fort Hall, on the Snake River. While the muleskinners saw to their teams, Gwen and Dulce jogged their horses to the front of the column in search of Buck. The fort loomed before them like an ancient ruin, its pale adobe walls crumbling in places, weeds growing along its walls. Brown-skinned teepees were scattered around the outside of the post, and a mixed herd of horses and mules grazed on the hills to the south.

At one time, Fort Hall had been a major stop along the Oregon Trail, a bustling trade center that catered to Oregon-bound pioneers, local Indian tribes, and fur trappers who still hunted the surrounding valleys, but the post's influence had waned with the completion of the Transcontinental Railroad. Now only a few independent traders used its spacious rooms, and although emigrants still stopped here on their way to the coast, their numbers were dwindling every year.

Gwen's attention had been drawn to the hide lodges, set up in the post's shadows. "I should like to visit these people," she informed Buck.

He eyed the village thoughtfully. The hard-packed, barren earth surrounding the lodges was littered with dung, discarded bones, fly-blown deer skins, and empty whiskey bottles. The odor was stout but not unfamiliar and the worst of it kept down by the breeze off the river.

"I would consider it a crime if I came this far and didn't explore the lifestyles of our nation's aborigines," Gwen added. "I have some knowledge of anthropology, you know."

"No," Buck replied with scant interest, "I didn't know that. What is it?"

Gwen's expression instantly became that of an indulgent parent. "Anthropology is the study of the lesser classes within their native habitat, similar to Darwin's study of the species on the Galapagos Islands. Only with humans, of course."

"Of course," Dulce returned drolly.

"Maybe later," Buck replied. "I've got some paperwork to catch up on."

"Paperwork?" Gwen looked puzzled.

"Every captain maintains a daily log," Dulce explained irritably.

"Let it go, Dulce," Buck said. "She didn't know."

"She didn't know because she hasn't paid any attention," Dulce fired back. "I would think a student of anthro-whatever would have noticed."

"I don't see any need for worry," Gwen said to Dulce. "Surely I'd be safe with Thad. It is full daylight, after all."

Dulce rolled her eyes but said no more.

"These are blanket Indians, Gwen," Buck explained patiently. "Their people call them Hangs Around The Fort, or Hang Arounds. A lot of them drink pretty heavily and afford it by prostituting their wives and daughters. Not that the women are any better. They just cut out the middle man when they want some booze. They're a crusty lot, hardly an example of their tribe."

"Shoot, they can't be all that crusty," Milo said, riding up and tipping his hat to Gwen. "I reckon I've got enough experience to escort Miss Haywood through this village. Miss Kavanaugh, too, if she's inclined." Noting the darkening of Buck's expression, he hastened to add: "The mules are in the capable hands of young Roscoe Evans and associates, and I'm free as a bird on wing. Besides, this way, I'll be sober when the boys get back from their debauchery."

"I doubt very much that any Box K driver will return debauched," Dulce said coolly, "and as far as joining you and Miss Haywood, I'm afraid I have other matters to attend to."

"Then it'll be just me and Miss Haywood," Milo said, his eyes lighting up at the prospect.

"It'll be you and Gwen and Thad Collins," Buck corrected the ramrod. "Stay close to the fort and don't go down by the river where you can't be seen from the wagons."

Milo grinned amiably. "That'll be just fine. I reckon Miss Haywood . . . Gwen . . . can study a redskin lodge up here as easily as she could from the cottonwoods." He gave her a happy glance. "Shall we go?"

Gwen raised her hand to her forehead, parroting a salute. "With your permission, Captain?"

"Go," Buck said, content to have the conversation ended, the two of them out of his hair for a while.

"You're too indulgent of them," Dulce said, after the pair had ridden away.

"Maybe," Buck said, briefly recalling the many times he'd felt the same way about Dulce. He studied her closely, wondering what had become of her anger. Had it disappeared overnight, or did it lurk just below the surface, like a steel trap ready to snap?

Dulce returned his gaze evenly but he could read nothing from her expression, other than that she expected him to speak first. "Well," he said after a pause, "I do have to catch up on that journal. I haven't touched it since the other side of Malad."

Dulce's lips thinned as she started to rein away.

"Maybe later . . . ," he started to say, but she cut him off.

"Yes, maybe later, when things slow down." She kicked Beau

in the ribs and rode off at a gallop, leaving Buck no doubts about her anger now.

Wearily he loosened the cinch on his saddle. By now, most of the muleskinners had turned their stock over to the swampers, and he wasn't surprised when he spotted the lot of them approaching on foot. After pulling the saddle from Zeke's back, he walked out to meet them. "You've got one hour to do whatever it is you think you need to do inside Fort Hall," he said roughly, before anyone else could speak. "After that, I want everyone back here, sober and ready to roll. No exceptions, and, if anyone comes back drunk, I'll dock them a day's wages."

It was the way Mase had handled it in the past, and it had always seemed fair to Buck, although he could tell that several of the independents—Kroll, O'Rourke, and Mead in particular—didn't care for it. "No exceptions," he repeated for their benefit, then gave the men a curt nod of dismissal and turned away.

Buck kept the Box K's leather-bound journal in the iron-strapped box called the office, bolted inside the mess wagon. Unlocking the lid, he withdrew the journal and a fine-tipped lead pencil from one of the pigeonholes, then made himself comfortable against the front wheel.

Some wagon masters were verbose in their descriptions of the day's activities, but Buck had never cared much for writing. A sentence was enough to record weather and road conditions; another could usually complete his observations of the stock and gear. Today it took a full paragraph to describe what had happened on top of Malad, then a second paragraph to detail his suspicions of a traitor among them, just to get it on record.

By the time he finished, several of the teamsters had already returned from Fort Hall. He saw Peewee and Ray sitting, cross-legged, in the skimpy shade of a wagon, smoking their pipes and chatting quietly. Nate Evans was also contentedly smoking his pipe, while Andy LeMay sat nearby, puffing luxuriously on a nickel cigar he'd purchased at the trading post.

It occurred to Buck that none of the old hands smoked cigarettes, although a number of the new men did. Milo had picked up the habit in Kansas, probably from Texas drovers, and O'Rourke had likely been exposed to it in Arizona, where it was popular throughout the Mexican-Spanish culture. Buck didn't know where Lyle Mead had mastered the art of rolling his own. Cigarettes seemed more like a chore than a pleasure to Buck, who'd smoked a pipe briefly in his teens, then gave even that up as too much trouble. Most men he knew preferred pipes and cigars to the nuisance of fragile cigarette papers that tore easily in the wind and produced only a brief, uneven smoke.

When Buck figured an hour had passed, he walked over to where Peewee and Ray were lounging with an unobstructed view of the fort's entrance. "Do you two know who's still inside?"

Ray scratched his stubbled jaw. "Lemme see, I ain't seen Mitch Kroll or Lyle Mead yet. Who else ain't come back, Peewee?"

"O'Rourke ain't. I don't think Lang's come back, either." He looked up, his brows furrowed. "Do you want some help?" he asked quietly.

"No, you two stay put." Buck's heart was thumping loudly and his mouth felt dry. He'd expected this, yet still felt unprepared. "Keep the others out here, too. Kroll won't consider it settled if this ain't done man to man."

Looking worried, Ray said: "They was all in Kendrick's when I left, pourin' it down pretty heavy. There won't be anything settled if they all jump you at once and we ain't around to even up the odds."

"Kroll's too proud to let that happen," Buck replied, thinking that, if it did come to a knuckle-buster, that would be about the only thing he could count on from the burly muleskinner. He touched Mase's bullwhip, as if for reassurance.

Peewee shoved to his feet, Ray close behind. "You watch yourself, Buck," Peewee said tautly. "Use your knife or pistol if you have to, but don't try to take that bastard down with your fists. He'll fight dirty if you do."

Buck smiled wanly. "I wouldn't expect anything less," he said, heading for the fort.

"Oh," Gwen murmured, coming to a startled stop at the edge of the bank overlooking the Snake. The bulk of the Hang Arounds' village was behind them now, but below them, hard by the river's edge, remained a scattering of sagging hide lodges and brush shelters. Pointing out a brush abode with a gray-haired Indian woman sitting in front, Gwen announced: "I wish to speak with her."

At her shoulder, Milo eyed the shelter doubtfully. "I don't think that would be a very good idea," he said.

"Why ever not?"

"Something about it doesn't look right to me."

"Posh," Gwen said dismissingly. "If you're afraid of an old woman, stay here."

"Gwen," Milo said sharply, but she was already on her way, eager to meet this woman who looked as if she could have known the captains, Lewis and Clark, on their famous journey to the Pacific.

Gwen's stride slowed as she neared the squat structure, perched on the sandy shore like a tangle of storm-shredded twigs caught in the weeds. A nauseating odor of decay seemed to emanate from the interwoven branches, causing Gwen to a halt several yards away. *My Lord,* she thought, wrinkling her nose, *this is horrible.* Then, affecting the brave demeanor of an anthropologist, she took another few steps forward. "Excuse me. I wonder if I might have a word with you."

She thought the old Indian's eyes might have flitted briefly toward her, but she couldn't be sure. Moving even closer, Gwen repeated her question. This time, she was certain the woman heard her.

"Easy, Gwen," Milo cautioned from the top of the bank. "There's something wrong here."

"Nonsense," Gwen replied, but her conviction was wavering. Although only a few feet away now, the old woman refused to look at her.

"Ask her where her husband is!" Milo called.

"Hush," Gwen scolded, but she was feeling suddenly lightheaded from the smell, and wished she'd heeded Milo's advice to keep her distance.

Gwen glanced at the blanket-covered entrance to the brush lodge and wondered what lay behind it, then decided almost immediately that she didn't want to know. Instead, she focused on the woman, sitting so still that she reminded Gwen of a portrait, done in shades of brown and gray. A leather dress *sans* any kind of native decoration clung to her thin frame, and her face had texture similar to that of a walnut's hull. Her jaw was hanging slightly agape in a kind of obscene grin that exposed her rotting gums and the few blackened, corn-kernel stubs of teeth that remained. Her eyes were filmy and pitted, and, when Gwen peered closer, she saw gnats on the tiny, cataract-glazed pupils.

Gwen's hand trembled as she reached out to touch the older woman. It was only when her fingers brushed the parchment-like flesh of the ancient crone's cheek that Gwen confirmed her suspicions.

With a soft cry, Gwen backed away. It was as if the dead woman were communicating with her, laughing at the younger woman's own fragile mortality. Then Milo's hands were on her shoulders, pulling her around, breaking her brief connection between this world and the next.

"Come on," he said gently. "Let's get away from here."

"But . . . who will bury her?" Gwen whispered numbly. "Why is she just sitting there? Doesn't anyone know . . . ?" Her voice broke and she twisted free of Milo's grip, snapping: "Leave me alone."

"Her people will take care of her," Milo said, unruffled by the flash of her temper. "The best thing we can do is stay out of their way, not butt in."

Gwen turned her back on the tiny shelter and its ugly secret. "I've seen enough," she said tautly. "I'm going back to the wagons." Tears blurred her vision as she stumbled up the bank to the main village, the image of the old woman refusing to leave her mind.

She was almost out of the village when Milo caught up. He grabbed her arm, pulling her to a stop. "Gwen . . . ," he started to say, but she whirled and jerked free, her jaw rigid with fury.

"Do not paw at me, Mister Newton," she advised. "I shall have you horsewhipped the next time you do."

Milo stepped back, but there was no fear in his brown eyes; they sparked dangerously, and his voice roughened in a way she'd never heard before. "Miss Haywood, I will kill the son-of-a-bitch who tries to horsewhip me. Man or woman, I don't care how pretty she is or how much money her daddy has."

"Then we understand one another perfectly, don't we?" Gwen replied haughtily, although, in truth, Milo's threat had undermined her self-confidence. She kept forgetting how dangerous the world was outside of her father's house.

"I sorely doubt it," he replied. "Even after what you just saw, I doubt if you understand anything."

Gwen's cheeks reddened. "What I just saw, Mister Newton, was a hideous example of frontier reality, grotesque and appalling, and you may be assured that I shall never again view our nation's aborigines as anything resembling Cooper's stately Mohican. They are heathens, sir, and deserve to be treated as such."

Milo shook his head in disgust. "Twenty minutes ago they were noble and proud. Now they're repulsive?"

"Repulsive is an entirely apt description," she replied coldly.

"Is that what you intend to tell your friends in Philadelphia?"

"It is my intention to enlighten them, yes. I have experience out here. They don't."

"Yeah, you're a regular Kit Carson, aren't you?"

Gwen's voice rose a notch, as did her chin. "I will not tolerate that tone, Mister Newton. I'd suggest you moderate it."

Milo's smile stretched thinly. "All right, how's this?" he said calmly. "You're a damn' fool, Miss Haywood. You don't have any more experience out here than a cat does navigating a ship. You got one warped view of an Indian village and now you think you've got the whole problem figured out. Trouble is, you're so naïve you haven't even seen the problem."

"Right now," Gwen replied in a brittle voice, "my problem is a hired man who has forgotten his place."

"No," Milo countered. "Your problem is that I've finally figured out my place, and it isn't where you want it to be. Ever since I first met you, I thought I wanted to be with you. I guess in looking back, that makes me as big a fool as you are."

Gwen's eyes flashed hotly. "Your presumptuousness is intolerable, Mister Newton. . . ." Her words trailed off and her lips parted in surprise. Milo Newton had turned his back on her and was walking away. "You bastard," she hissed, but she didn't call after him or demand that he return. For a moment, she hated them all—vile, despicable characters, no cleaner or smarter than the beasts they drove. *No better than the Hang*

Arounds, she thought savagely, as tears welled in her eyes once more.

Her fingers were clenched tightly as she made her way toward the mule train, but she slowed and frowned when she saw Thad Collins backing out the far door of the mud wagon. Gwen quickened her pace to intercept the bodyguard. Milo Newton might consider himself above her authority, but dear Thaddeus would soon learn who paid his wages, and whose vehicle he was to guard with his life but never enter. She'd barely covered ten yards when she jerked to a stop, realizing that Collins wasn't alone.

Max Kendrick's place was the first building on the left, just inside Fort Hall's main gate. Kendrick was leaning against the trade counter when Buck walked in.

"Howdy, Buck," he said easily. "What'll you have?"

Buck shook his head. He'd stopped just inside the door to stare at the contract teamsters gathered around a table at the back of the room. A bottle of whiskey sat between them; an empty bottle sat on the floor beside Lyle Mead's boots. "Past time, boys!" Buck called. "Finish what you've got poured and get back to camp."

Kroll, Mead, and O'Rourke returned Buck's gaze insolently. Only Garth Lang looked uncomfortable ignoring the wagon master's command, although he made no effort to get up.

"I reckon we'll stay here a while," Mitch replied lazily, refilling his glass. "We can catch up later."

Buck's anger was already on a set trigger. Crossing the room in half a dozen long strides, he slapped the bottle from the big man's hand. Grabbing the edge of the table, Buck tipped it into Kroll's lap, forcing his chair over backward. Mead and Lang scrambled out of the way, spilling their own drinks in the process. Paddy O'Rourke jumped clear, then sidled out of the way, one hand resting on the large-framed revolver at his hip.

Mitch threw the table off his lap and clambered to his feet. The front of his shirt was dark with spilled whiskey and his eyes blazed. "You're gonna pay for that, McCready," he growled, his thick, stubby fingers curling into fists. He stopped when Buck laughed.

"Not here, Kroll," Buck said. "Outside."

"Outside?" Mitch's eyes narrowed suspiciously. "Who you got waitin' outside?"

"Not a damn' soul."

After a pause, a smile wormed across the burly muleskinner's face. "You sayin' you finally worked up enough backbone to fight me without a crew backing your play?"

"Let's get it done," Buck said curtly. He spun on his heels and walked outside, moving instinctively to the center of the quadrangle. Mitch followed cautiously, his eyes darting left and right as he stepped out of the building.

"Don't be afraid," Buck taunted across the empty space.

"I ain't been afraid of nobody since I beat hell outta my teacher when I was eleven years old," Mitch retorted. "I crammed that damn' ruler down his throat until he puked blood. I'm gonna do the same to you today with my fists."

Buck touched the bullwhip at his waist, his fingers playing lightly over the knot that held it to his belt. "I've got other plans for you today, Kroll." His fingers twitched and the long snake fell free, the butt clutched firmly in his hand. He tossed the braid out behind him, letting it rest in the powdery dust. He was aware of other men appearing out of other buildings to watch the fight, but didn't take his eyes off Kroll.

"You're crazy, McCready. I've handled a blacksnake since I was twelve years old." Mitch moved away from the building, pulling his own long whip free. "I'm gonna skin you raw, bub."

Buck's arm moved swiftly and the long blacksnake darted

forward to crack like a pistol shot in front of Mitch's chest. The big muleskinner flinched, and his cocky attitude wavered. Then he tossed his own braid out to the side, a hefty fourteen footer—a good two feet longer than Buck's whip, equipped with a pair of lead-tipped poppers that looked twice as heavy. *Trust Kroll to carry something a little stouter, a little more deadly than needed,* Buck thought.

Mitch's smile returned. "You won't be the first man to bleed on my whip," he promised.

"I'm going to beat you at your own game, Kroll, and, when I'm through, you're going to go back to your wagons and get ready to roll. Today will be the last time I put up with your bullshit."

"That's mighty big talk, bub, but you ain't whupped me yet."

"Get it started," Buck challenged tersely.

Mitch leaned forward and Buck stepped aside to let Kroll's poppers whistle past his elbow with enough force to shatter bone. It cracked loud enough to hurt his ears, then withdrew like a flickering snake's tongue. Buck sucked in a ragged breath. He'd seen men fight with whips before and knew how lethal a blacksnake could be in the right hands, but he'd never fought that kind of a battle himself. He thought he'd chosen the wisest course of action when he loosened his whip, reasoning that Mitch's size made a bare-knuckle brawl little more than suicide, and that a knife or pistol would be too permanent. Besides, he was a muleskinner, confident in his own abilities with a whip. Now he wasn't so sure.

"I once laid a balky mule's hip open to the bone," Mitch crowed, slithering his whip behind him with a practiced hand. "I've popped the corks outta whiskey bottles and snapped the blooms off cactus pads without disturbin' a thorn."

"How are you with something that snaps back?" Buck asked.

Kroll's whip flashed forward, quick as a rattler's strike. This time, Buck didn't dodge fast enough. He felt the searing bite of the leather-wrapped poppers gouge into his lower thigh, just above his left knee, and for a moment a fluttering blackness closed around him. He almost fell but managed to stagger backward a couple of yards instead, keeping his feet despite the whirling sky overhead.

"Jesus," someone said in awe as blood darkened the fabric of Buck's trousers.

Pain coursed up Buck's leg like a runaway team. His mouth watered and his nose ran and tears stung his eyes.

Mitch laughed boisterously. "First time bit, McCready? I got a dozen of 'em scarrin' my arms and legs. By the time you get as many as me, you won't hardly notice a new one, but them first few is gonna feel like they're tearin' out bone."

Buck wiped his eyes with the back of his hand. "Is that the best you've got?" he asked hoarsely.

The smile on Mitch's face disappeared. "Why, no, sonny, I've got a lot worse than that." He lunged forward, bringing his whip high around his head, then letting it swoop low. Buck raised his boot to deflect the poppers' blow, but the snake wrapped around his ankle with a bulldog's grip and yanked him off his feet. Buck slammed hard to the ground, the breath driven from his lungs. Dimly he heard someone laughing and knew it was Lyle Mead.

Mitch let the whip go slack and Buck wiggled free. He pushed to his feet, lurching drunkenly until he got his balance. His left leg throbbed as if on fire and his hat lay in the dust behind him. Mitch was grinning broadly, sure of himself now, convinced of victory. "You ain't doin' so well, bub," he observed.

Struggling to drag air into his starving lungs, Buck rasped: "It ain't over yet."

Mitch's grin widened. "I'm thinkin' all that's left is for you to fall down. You look pretty damn' close to it already."

Buck eased forward, making a casual swing that Mitch easily side-stepped. Laughing, Mitch brought his own whip back for another strike. Before he could launch it Buck flipped his black-snake up as if lifting it straight from the ground. The twin poppers cracked in front of Mitch's nose like a pistol shot, and the smile vanished from the big man's face.

"You've drawn blood twice now," Buck said huskily. "It won't happen a third time."

"You ain't got nothin' to say about that."

Buck's whip darted forward, cutting into the flesh of Kroll's heavily-muscled gut. Mitch cried out in pain and surprise. Buck cracked his whip again, wrapping the tip around the muleskinner's leg and taking a chunk out of his calf. Mitch's whip curled awkwardly through the air like a slow-moving but extremely sharp knife. Buck dodged it to the right, then let his own whip strike once more, licking deep into Mitch's shoulder.

Kroll howled and stumbled. Buck crowded him, his snake lashing out twice more, popping the air on either side of Mitch's head. Then he stepped back, out of reach. "Let it drop, Kroll," Buck panted. "Give it up before one of us gets hurt."

"I'd rather rot in hell," Mitch snarled, drawing his whip close.

For the second time, Buck seemed to lift his snake off the ground as if it had a life of its own. It was a trick Mase had taught him, something few men ever conquered. His poppers cracked against Mitch's right knee like tiny clubs and the big man screamed and fell, rolling onto his side as he clutched his injured leg with both hands.

Lyle Mead stepped forward, whether to help Kroll or take up the big man's battle, Buck couldn't tell. Before Buck could figure out the lanky muleskinner's intentions, Kendrick appeared with a double-barreled shotgun.

"That's enough!" the trader bellowed, and Mead jerked to a stop.

Mitch climbed laboriously to his feet. He'd lost his hat, too, and his long, greasy hair clung to his forehead with perspiration. He looked pale, and blood was seeping from his nose into his mustache and beard. He glared at Buck. "That was slick, bub, but it ain't gonna be slick enough."

"I don't want to hurt you," Buck said, his chest heaving.

"That ain't likely."

"I said, that's enough, and I meant it," Kendrick said. He came forward, shoving Mead out of his way. "Next one of you sons-a-bitches lifts a whip in this compound gets a belly full of double-ought."

Buck let his arm go slack. Mead, O'Rourke, and Lang looked on blankly. Only Kroll's expression changed, becoming more curious than angry, as if wondering what Buck's next move would be.

"God damn, if you two want to kill yourselves, go somewhere else to do it," Kendrick added.

"He's right," Buck said. "This has gone far enough." He began reeling in his bullwhip, coiling it into its familiar roll.

Warily Mitch pulled in his own whip.

"You three get back to your wagons," Buck ordered Mead, Lang, and O'Rourke. "Mitch and I will be along in another minute."

The three muleskinners returned his stare brazenly, and Buck began to wonder if this battle was truly finished. Then he barked—"Now, goddammit!"—and Garth Lang stepped out reluctantly.

Mead and O'Rourke followed, although slowly, to show that they weren't afraid.

"You got more spine than I figured you for, McCready," Kroll said.

"This train is going through, Mitch. I don't care if I have to fight you every step of the way to do it."

Kroll turned silent for a moment, as if deep in thought, then said: "You won't have to." Glancing at the fort's gate where Lang, Mead, and O'Rourke had halted expectantly, he shouted: "Let's get rollin', boys! The boss wants us on the road . . . *now!*"

When the three were gone, Mitch looked at Buck and nodded. "You'll do," he said quietly.

Chapter Twenty-Two

Both men needed stitches to close the worst of their wounds. Buck's most serious injury was the gouge Mitch had carved in his left leg, above the knee, although his left arm was also badly bruised. Time, he knew, would take care of the ugly mass of blues and purples that covered his bicep, but he would have to watch the wound on his leg for infection. None of Mitch's wounds was as severe as the one on Buck's leg, but the mule-skinner had more of them, scattered over his body like red-bodied leeches.

Buck bit down hard on a strip of harness leather to keep from crying out when Peewee probed the white inner flesh of his leg with a needle and thread. Dulce hovered over Peewee's shoulder, her face puckering with each new stitch. Although Peewee wanted to hold over for a day, an option Dulce heartily seconded, Buck refused.

"We've lost enough time here," he said, pushing to his feet. He limped over to where Milo was finishing up on Kroll. Mitch's swamper, Bigfoot Payne, was watching nearby, wringing his hands and making little sounds of distress in his throat as Milo tied off his last stitch.

"Say the word," Mitch grated. Sweat poured off the big man's forehead and his lips were peeled back as if in a silent snarl, but he hadn't cried out once that Buck had heard.

"Soon as you're ready."

Mitch snapped his fingers and Bigfoot ceased his nervous

whimpering. Speaking softly but firmly, he told his swamper to find their mules and get them hitched. "We'll be ready soon as he gets 'em in harness," he told Buck.

Milo rocked back on his heels, wiping his hands on a bloody rag. "He's done. It ain't a work of art, but he won't leak all over his saddle."

"Get outta my way, flea-brain," Kroll grumbled, pushing Milo aside and struggling to his feet.

Buck grinned. "I notice those stitches didn't do anything to improve his personality."

Milo laughed and Mitch mumbled something unintelligible, hanging onto the front wheel of his trailer like he wanted to puke. Buck motioned Milo aside. "Get the train ready to pull out," he said. "I want this outfit on the road in thirty minutes."

Milo nodded and took off, and Buck went in search of his mule. It took more effort than he would have thought to get Zeke saddled. By the time he was mounted, the caravan was ready to roll. Buck lifted his voice to roll down the length of the caravan. "Streeetch out! Stretch 'em out!"

They made another five miles before sunset, camping in a stand of cottonwoods along the Snake. Buck rode close to the river to dismount behind a screen of red-barked alders. His pain was worse now, and he had to hang onto his saddle horn until he was sure he could stand on his own. He kept to himself that night, letting Milo take care of any chore that wasn't specifically his own. He was still hurting when he went to bed, but that was nothing compared to the way he felt the next morning. He couldn't face breakfast, couldn't even support a coffee cup with his bruised left arm.

Although he was in the saddle by first light, his mind wasn't on the trail and his brow was warm with fever. His temperature rose throughout the day, and, by nightfall he was gimping through his rounds as if in a daze. Sweat was running down his face when he went to bed that night, but he fell asleep almost instantly. Coming awake sometime later was like struggling up out of muddy water. He wasn't even sure where he was until he spied the starlit sky through the trees and heard the Snake's low murmur above the breeze. He tried to sit up, but someone pushed him back.

"Ain't no point fightin' us," Ray said quietly. "You're too damn' wrung out to win."

Buck let his head loll to one side. With the fires all burned down, the darkness under the cottonwoods was nearly complete. It was only against the lighter sky that he could make out the shape of a jug in one of Ray's hands.

Peewee appeared at Buck's shoulder. "You ever feed medicine to a kid that didn't want it, Ray?" he asked.

"Nope, can't say I ever have."

"With someone Buck's size," Peewee said, "one of us'll have to sit on his chest to keep him down. Then we'll grab his nose and pinch it shut until he opens his mouth to breath. That's when we'll shove a spoonful of whiskey down his throat."

"Hell, a spoonful ain't gonna do no good," said Ray. "I got a feedin' tube in my kit that I use when I want to worm one of my mules. Poke that down his gullet and we'll just pour the medicine in."

"Gimme that damn' jug," Buck growled. "I can doctor myself."

Ray chuckled softly. "Man gets to hurtin' bad enough, his bull-headedness just flies out the window, don't it?" He pulled the cork and handed Buck the jug.

Buck winced at the raw odor of trade alcohol but didn't hesitate. He'd learned a long time ago that when the whiskey was bad, the best approach was a full-on gallop.

"Take a couple of snorts," Peewee advised. "Then we'll pull your shirt off and rub some liniment on your shoulders."

"It's my leg that's giving me fits," Buck said, lowering the jug and letting the words come out on the end of a deep belch.

"Well, you're gonna have to pull your own britches down," Ray told him. "There's limits to how much I'll do even for a friend."

Buck smiled and lifted the jug a second time, finding it easier this time to ignore the heady fumes that spilled across his face. "Where'd you get this poison?" he asked, perching the jug on his chest and puffing hard.

"Bought it off Kendrick," Peewee said. "We figured it might come in handy. We just didn't know how soon we'd need it."

"Speakin' of need." Ray plucked the clay vessel from Buck's hands and took a swallow. "Sweet Jesus," he breathed, coughing hoarsely.

"Well, hell, let me try it," Peewee said.

Ray laughed and handed him the jug. "It's the bane of manhood to stick your fingers in a fire just to see if it's as hot as someone else says it is."

Peewee blew lustily as he brought the jug away from his lips, spraying Buck with a fine, fiery mist. "Good Lord," he croaked. "Kendrick ought to pay us to drink this piss, not the other way around."

Buck sputtered laughter and sat up, pulling his shirt over his head and tossing it to one side. With just two swallows under his belt, he already felt loose and comfortable. He slid his pants down to his socks, then pulled the leg of his knee-length underwear up high enough to expose the wound in his lower thigh.

Peewee's good humor faded when he saw the red, swollen flesh above Buck's knee. He set the jug aside and lit a tin bull's-eye lantern, adjusting the tiny aperture to focus a narrow beam of light on the wound.

Leaning close, Ray whistled reverently. "That looks mean,"

he said to no one in particular.

The surrounding tissue was inflamed, but no worse than it had been that morning when Buck looked at it. "It's stiff," he allowed.

"Hot to touch, too," Peewee said, prodding gently at the puffy flesh. "I don't think it's infected, though. That's good."

"Looks irritated," Ray observed.

"It's my pants," Buck explained. "The fabric keeps rubbing on the stitches when I'm in the saddle."

"We'll put some salve on it after we work some liniment into the muscle around it," Peewee said. He leaned back, lowering the lantern. "A fresh bandage'll help, too, but it's gonna leave a hell of a scar."

"Man can't hardly call hisself a muleskinner without a few scars from a bullwhip," Ray said. "He's just lucky he don't have a couple of hoof-shaped dents in his skull, like some I know."

Peewee brought a slim brown bottle of Centaur Liniment into the lantern's beam. "This ought to ease the hurt and take down some of the swelling. Ray, dig that salve out of the box, will you?"

"How'd you two get into the medicine chest?" Buck demanded, struggling now just to concentrate. "It's under lock and key in the office."

"I wouldn't know about that," Ray replied, sliding a small, open-topped box around where Buck could see it. "This is mule medicine," he said. "We considered your personality and decided this was probably the best way to go."

Buck leaned back and closed his eyes. "You're likely right," he agreed.

"Hey, don't go noddin' off on us," Ray scolded, but Peewee made a shushing sound and said: "Let him sleep if he can."

"You just splash some liniment on that leg," Buck ordered the two men distantly, letting the whiskey pull him farther away from the warm flush of his fever. He heard Ray guffaw and Peewee say—"Don't!"—then a spark ignited a bonfire on top of his leg and any thought of sleep vanished like smoke in the wind.

"Lord, God!" Buck hissed through clenched teeth, jackknifing upright to grab his thigh.

"Dammit, Ray," Peewee said, but he was laughing, too. "I reckon we forgot to mention it might burn a little," he added to Buck.

"I ought to box your ears," Buck snapped. He plucked the liniment from Ray's hand and set it on the ground next to the salve. "I appreciate your help, but it's time you two got back to your blankets. Morning'll come early."

Ray leaned back on the balls of his feet, his smile gone.

"Go on," Buck said, shoving the whiskey jug toward Peewee. "Take this with you and hide it where I won't find it, because, if I see it again, I'll bust the damn' thing on a rock."

Pushing to his feet, Ray said: "Damn if he ain't turnin' into the same kind of son-of-a-bitch his old pard was."

Buck looked up, his expression hardening. "Easy, Ray, if you're talking about Mase."

"I don't tread easy for no man," Ray said.

Peewee quickly stood. "Come on, Ray. No whiskey on the train is Jock's rule, not Buck's. Besides, Buck's feelin' poorly. This ain't the time. . . ."

"I'm not feeling that poorly," Buck said, climbing to his feet and pulling up his trousers. "Say what's on your mind, Ray."

"Ray," Peewee warned.

"Aw, I ain't gonna bust the pup's bubble," Ray growled, "but I ain't gonna turn my back on him no more, either." He grabbed the jug from Peewee's hand and stalked off.

When he was gone, Peewee said: "He just riles easy, Buck. You know Ray."

Buck sighed and thumbed the suspender straps over his bare

shoulders. He felt cold again, and his leg was throbbing as sharply as it ever had. "What the hell's everyone got against Mase?" he asked, but Peewee just shook his head. "Well?" Buck demanded.

"Let it go, Buck," Peewee said gently. "Just let it go. You, Ray, everyone, just let it go."

Nate was frying potatoes in a big skillet when Buck came to the breakfast fire the next morning. "Lordy," the black man said, making a face. "I hope you just rubbed that fire on, and didn't drink any."

Buck hesitated, unable to tell if Nate knew about the jug or if he was just making fun of the odor of liniment that fogged the air around him like the stench of a dead skunk. Physically Buck was feeling better, but he was aggravated with himself. He'd been strict in his enforcement of Jock's rules against liquor on a train—most wagon masters were—and it bothered him that he'd ignored them last night, when he was the one needing a drink.

"If I wanted booze," he responded stiffly, "I would have bought a drink at Fort Hall."

There was a derisive snort from behind Peewee's trail wagon and Ray came into view, coiling a length of cotton rope. The look on his face told Buck he'd overhead.

"A little bug juice is what you and Kroll both need," Nate continued, stirring the potatoes with a long-handled fork. "I was watchin' Mitch climb onto his nigh-wheeler yesterday, gruntin' like an old man." He chuckled at the memory.

"Better stove-up than to break one of Jock's precious rules, ain't that right, Bucky?" Ray said.

"Touch of bug juice never hurt no one," Nate countered, still oblivious to the tension between the two men. "Even my Sarah'll take a sip of lightning from time to time. Mix it with honey and lemon, and it works mighty fine on a winter's cough."

"I don't think it's a cough botherin' Buck. Might be his principles, though."

"Back off, Ray," Buck said softly, turning to face the glowering muleskinner.

"Here now!" Nate exclaimed, startled. "What's got into you two all of a sudden?"

"I'd say a promotion and the promise of the boss' daughter," Ray sneered.

"Hey!" Nate cried, standing. "What kind of talk is that? Ray, with everything we're facin', everything Buck's facin', what do you want to push him for? This is Buck, dang it, not some drifter lookin' for a hand-out."

"Stay out of it, Nate," Buck said.

"The devil I will!" Nate looked at Ray. "You go on and help Rossy bring in them mules. Ain't nobody needin' your kind of hazin' this morning."

"Since when did you start giving orders?" Ray asked.

"Since right this here minute, is when." Buck started to speak, but Nate silenced him with a raised hand. "Go on," he said to Ray. "Help Rossy."

"Aw, the hell with both of you," Ray snapped, throwing the coiled line into the dirt at Nate's feet. He stalked off, grumbling about looking for a new job as soon as he got back to Corinne.

Nate grinned and looked at Buck. "That ol' Ray," he said. "Ain't hardly a trip north he don't promise to quit soon as he gets back." He poked Buck amiably in the ribs. "Ain't that right, boss-man?"

"I reckon. It just ain't setting so well this morning."

"That's 'cause you got so much other stuff on your mind, but you got to look at it this way, we're danged near halfway there and still rollin'. Another ten, twelve days'll see us into Virginia City. After that, it becomes someone else's worry."

Buck exhaled slowly. "I guess Ray caught me off guard," he admitted. "I've seen him turn on others like that . . . you, Peewee, even Mase, but it's the first time he's ever turned on me."

"Ray is Ray, Buck. He's been sittin' on fight ever since his wife left him, and that was a good many years ago. Sometimes you got to let him blow off a little steam."

They got off in good order, with Buck taking his usual position about a hundred yards ahead of Peewee's leaders. On his left, the Snake River was flowing powerfully, nearly out of its banks with spring run-off, its wind-ruffled surface littered with débris. The low, rolling hills to his right were green with new grass, and wildflowers bloomed on the south-facing slopes. But the country's beauty was lost on Buck. His thoughts were dominated by darker images—lean, slope-shouldered men, always in shadow, always dangerous.

They came to the Eagle Rock bridge late that afternoon, where the Snake narrowed tumultuously through black stone channels. Buck rode ahead to settle the toll, and by the time Peewee got there the receipt was signed, the gate raised. Buck reined out of the way to watch the long hitches swing into the turn and rattle briskly across the thick ash planks to the north shore.

Milo rode up as Ray was hawing his leaders onto the bridge, his expression flinty. When Buck glanced behind him, his own jaw tightened.

"I already talked to him," Milo said. "I can't put a rope around his neck to make him keep up."

"If you can't handle the job, maybe I ought to put Dulce in charge of it."

Milo grinned in spite of Buck's anger. "She'd probably like that. Gwen, too. They're both afraid of him."

"You rode with him the other day. What did you find out?"

"Nothing. It was like riding beside a keg of gunpowder. He sits up there like he doesn't have a care in the world, but you know he's packed tight enough to blow. That boy's nursing a grudge against somebody or something, but when I tried to talk to him about it, he acted like I wasn't fit to piss on."

"Did he admit to knowing Kroll?"

"He didn't admit to anything. Didn't say more than a dozen words the whole day. I finally started talking to the hind end of his off-wheel mule. I got the same response and didn't have to twist my head so much."

"Dammit," Buck said irritably. "Go tell him to catch up. I'll chew him out later."

There wasn't much of a community at Eagle Rock, but there was a saloon. Not wanting a repeat of what had happened at Fort Hall, Buck kept the train rolling for another hour before he ordered a camp made on a treeless flat along the river. While the rest of the outfit set about their evening chores, Buck jogged to the rear of the train to wait for O'Rourke. By the time the dark-skinned Irishman came in, Buck's anger had reached a boil.

Buck reined into O'Rourke's path, forcing the jehu to haul back on his lines.

"Something is wrong?" O'Rourke asked, black eyes narrowing.

"Milo's told you more than once to keep up. I came back to find out why you haven't been doing it."

"I'm here. There is a problem?"

"You're too far back, in case of trouble."

A thin, mirthless smile wiggled across O'Rourke's face. "I don't have no trouble."

"I ain't gonna argue with you, and I ain't gonna tell you again. Keep up or I'll start docking your pay."

Paddy's smile disappeared. "The lady is who hires me. She

will not dock my pay."

"She'll dock it if I tell her to."

O'Rourke's eyes glittered dangerously. "I think that would not be so smart a thing to do, boss-man."

"Don't threaten me, O'Rourke. You were hired to drive Miss Haywood's coach. Whatever else your problem is, you keep that wagon with the rest of the train."

"Sure," Paddy replied after a lengthy pause. "Sure, after today, Ray Jones is gonna wonder what it is in his hip pocket all the time, and it's gonna be my lead team, you'll see." But there was a look in the Irishman's eyes that chilled Buck's blood. "Now that the order comes from the big man, I know for sure it is for me to do. You see how it works?"

"Just stay close, O'Rourke. This'll be the last time I warn you."

He turned Zeke toward the front of the train, but hauled back when he heard Dulce calling him. She was standing next to one of Joe Perry's wagons, looking worried, and he rode over. "Everything all right?"

"Yes. I saw you talking to O'Rourke."

"I was encouraging him to keep up."

"Why does he do that? His should be the fastest outfit in the train."

"I reckon he's mad about something."

"Gwen?"

That surprised him. "You think so?"

"He resents her horribly, Buck. I see it every time he looks at her. He resents us, too . . . you and I. I can almost feel his hatred whenever he's near."

"Do you think he's a threat to you or Gwen?"

"I don't know. I just know he's angry, but then"—her expression softened—"so are you."

"Hey, how'd I get pulled into this?"

"It's true."

"I'm not angry, I've just got a lot on my mind."

"Do you realize you hardly ever smile like you mean it any more? And that fight between you and Mitchell Kroll." She looked away, blinking rapidly. "You don't come to see me, and that frightens me most of all. Peewee says I should give you room to captain, but. . . ."

He swung down and took her in his arms. "Maybe it was a bad idea, your coming," he said. "It's been a hard trip."

"I thought it would be an adventure, something we could share." She stepped back but wouldn't meet his eyes. "It was silly, I suppose, but I also thought this journey would be a test of our compatibility."

"It's hardly been a fair test," he pointed out.

"No, it hasn't, and it was wrong of me to think you would have time to dine with me every evening, or that we might slip off occasionally to be alone. I was so naïve I even brought along a picnic basket, thinking we might lag behind one day, just the two of us."

"There's nothing wrong with wanting some time together," Buck said.

"No, it was wrong. I grew up in a freighting family and I thought I knew what was involved in captaining a wagon train. Obviously I didn't. This trip has opened my eyes in so many ways. But I wonder if you can see that you don't have to do this alone. You have men you can depend on. Peewee, Joe, Nate. Even Ray, although I know he's upset with you now. And I hope, I really hope, that you know you can depend on me, as well."

"I've never doubted your loyalty, Dulce."

That brought a sob from her throat and she turned away. "I've made mistakes, Buck, but I do want our relationship to survive, for us to have a life together. That is, if that's what you want."

He reached for her but she stepped back. "Buck?" she said softly.

"I want us to survive, too, but we've got a long way to go yet, and I've got a bad feeling that what's happened so far has been just the beginning. We can't lower our guard. I can't lower my guard. Not even a little."

"You didn't answer my question. Do you want the same things I do?"

Now it was Buck's turn to look away. "Right now all I want is to get this train safely to Virginia City, without anyone being killed or maimed. That's all I can think about, Dulce. All I have time to think about."

"Now, ain't that a beautiful sight," Milo said late the next day, after he and Buck had reined their mounts off the road. They were watching the caravan wind its way up through the low hills north of the river. From here, the Snake was mostly hidden behind a wall of leafed-out cottonwoods.

But it wasn't the green valley they were leaving or the new land they were entering that Milo was commenting on. It was Paddy O'Rourke, bouncing along atop the coach, his leaders less than a dozen yards behind the mess wagon's tailgate.

"You figure he was testing your mettle?" Buck asked.

"Now, that'd be downright disappointing if he was," Milo replied. "I'd hate to think I let him buffalo me that way."

"Well, I won't complain as long as he keeps up."

Milo's attention was diverted by a Gilmer and Salisbury express, leaving the trees along the river; its six-horse hitch was loping smoothly. "They keep these roads hot, don't they?"

"They're making hay while the sun shines," Buck agreed. The stage, hugging the west side of the road to pass the Box K caravan on the left, bristled with passengers, including several men perched on top with the luggage. Buck recognized the slim frame and sweat-sheened black face of its driver from two hundred yards away. "That's Hoots," he said to Milo.

"What's a hoots?"

"The jehu, they call him Hoots. I don't know his real name."

Hoots started hauling back on his lines as soon as he spotted Buck and Milo. He guided his rig off the road with his left foot gingerly working the long brake lever that slanted up at his side. "Whoa!" he called to his horses. "Slow down there, jugheads."

"Hoots!" Buck called, jogging his mule toward the still-rocking coach.

"Ho, Buck!" Hoots called, hunching his shoulders to the plume of dust rolling forward over the G&S rig.

Buck knew Hoots from Corinne, but they weren't good friends, and Buck knew he wouldn't have stopped if it wasn't important. "What's up?" he asked.

"Yes," echoed a passenger from within the coach. He poked his head out the window, a dough-cheeked individual in his fifties, with brows like giant woolly worms and a shiny pate that gleamed in the afternoon sun. "Why have we stopped, driver? We've barely left the last station."

"Hold your water, mister," Hoots told his sweating passenger. "I need a word with this man."

"By thunder, you're not paid to converse with strangers," the bald man blustered. "You're paid to drive this coach to Montana as expeditiously as possible."

That gave Hoots pause. He twisted in his seat to stare down at the man hanging out the front window. "You get back inside that coach before I smack your head with the butt-end of my whip," he snapped. "This rig is going to Montana and it'll get there on time, but that sure in hell doesn't mean you have to be on it. Now, git!"

The man's cheeks flamed red as a radish as he struggled for a suitable comeback. Then a feminine hand reached out over his shoulder and pulled him back. Buck could hear the woman's chidings from the shadowy interior of the coach, and he glanced at Hoots and winked.

"What causes you to stop?" Buck asked.

"I got a message for you."

"From Jock?"

Hoots shook his head. "Nope, from Lotty Beals."

Buck's lips thinned. "Lotty's dead, Hoots."

"I know she is, but she had something she wanted you to hear. You recollect a little China gal workin' at the International called Shanghai Lil?"

"I know who she is."

"Well, she and Lotty were friends, and me and Lil. . . ." He let that part of the conversation trail off. "You know life ain't easy out here for a Celestial, Buck, especially the women, but Lotty had a good heart and treated Lil like a sister. I always thought real highly of her for that."

Buck felt a pang of guilt for Lotty's death. "She was a good woman," he concurred.

"As good as they come, I'd say." Hoots lowered his voice confidentially. "Lil wanted me to tell you that it wasn't the big man with the greasy hair who killed Mase Campbell that night. She doesn't know who did do it, but she says it wasn't the card player. I don't know if Lotty knew any more than that, but Lil thinks Sally Hayes might have known something, for whatever good that'd do you now."

"I'll be damned," Buck said softly. "What about the rest of it? What about the small man in the green coat that Tom Ashley mentioned?"

Hoots shrugged. "I couldn't say, although I reckon Lil would've told me if she knew anything else." He leaned forward to release his brake. "I got to get this rig rolling, but I wish you luck and hope you find the bastard. I'd pull the trigger on him myself, if I knew who it was."

"Thanks, Hoots, and tell Lil I appreciate her help."

"I will," the jehu promised. He hollered and shook out his lines, and his six powerful horses surged forward, the stage rocking forcefully on its leather thorough braces as it bounced back onto the road.

Milo edged his mule closer. "What was that about?"

"Just some old business that reminded me of something I've kind of neglected lately."

"What's that?"

"Finding Mase's killer." Buck was staring at the Box K caravan, stretched out like a carpenter's plumb toward the distant line of the Rockies to the north. "Turns out I've been looking for the wrong man in the wrong place."

Milo appeared puzzled. "What do you mean?"

"I mean, I think the son-of-a-bitch who killed Mase is probably the same man who cut the straps on Peewee's load at Hampton's Crossing, then pulled the eye bolt off his brake going over Malad. He's here, Milo. He's somewhere on this train."

Chapter Twenty-Three

It didn't take Arlen long to realize Henry Reese had called it square when he described Jim Bonner as crazy. Crazy mean, anyway.

Bonner was a towering, rail-slim man with long brown hair that fell about his shoulders like an Indian's. Arlen's first impression of the ex-trapper was that he was one of Runs-His-Ponies's kin. Bonner had come at them out of a draw astride a scrawny, thin-maned Appaloosa, waving a rifle above his head and howling like a demon. He'd been hatless save for a bandanna around his forehead, dressed all in fringed, grease-blackened buckskins, and the weathered flesh of his clean-shaven cheeks was nearly the same dark shade as the leather on Arlen's saddle. Only Bonner's eyes had betrayed his white blood, so blue they looked unnatural. Even now, they could send a chill squirreling down Arlen's spine whenever the mountain man looked at him.

There had been some tension between Gabe and Bonner at first. Arlen gathered that the two had had a falling out over a woman some years back. Although Gabe insisted he didn't remember the incident, Bonner clearly did, and Arlen recalled that there had been a similar dispute between Gabe and Runs-His-Ponies over a Paiute woman.

Gabe turned out to be a smooth talker, though, and the promise of nearly two hundred head of Box K mules split evenly among the group—that being Carville, Reese, Bonner, and the six men who rode with him—had helped soothe the last ruffled edges of Bonner's temper.

The split, Arlen'd noticed, hadn't included him, although he hadn't complained. He'd become convinced that if he was going to survive this nightmare, it would have to be by living on the group's fringe and not attracting too much attention to himself.

After that first shaky meeting with Bonner, things had proceeded more smoothly. Arlen found himself once again relegated to the mundane chores of camp life—toting water, gathering wood, preparing meals. He went about them with his eyes down, his mouth shut, fantasizing almost constantly about the numerous ways he could kill Nick Kelso if he ever got the chance.

"*Wagh!*" Gabe barked, causing Arlen to jump. "We be runnin' outta time, Jimmy."

Time was a horse Gabe had been beating on the last several days. He'd originally pushed for striking the Box K along the Snake, then making a dash for the mountains farther east, before swinging south into Utah to sell the stolen mules to the Mormons, but Bonner had scoffed at that proposal.

"Ye're a damn' fool, Gabriel, if ye think the Army won't notice ye sellin' mules to the Saints, and branded mules, to boot. We'll take 'em west to Boise Camp. I know a lad there what'll buy 'em for pack animals, and pay a good price, too."

"We can't ignore that brand," Henry insisted. He'd been leaning toward Bonner's side all along. "The Box K's too well known in these mountains."

"My Boise lad's a master with the runnin' iron," Bonner assured him. "Learned the art down in the Monterey Valley, stealing palominos off the big *rancheros* down there."

"He'd better be good," Henry said. "Jock Kavanaugh's a tough old bird. He won't take this sittin' down."

"My boy won't talk, and we'll leave no witness who might."

A spasm jerked Arlen's bowels when Bonner laid his cold, blue eyes upon him. The men gathered around the small noontime fire laughed, and one of them threw a piece of firewood at Arlen that bounced solidly off his shin. It hurt like hell but he didn't say anything.

Gabe wasn't in the mood for torment, though, and continued to stare at Bonner. "By God, enough of this shit, Jimmy," he said. "If ye be set on Boise Camp, then let's do 'er. Yer boy just damn' well better have the money, or be able to lay his hands on it quick. We's gonna have to cache fer a spell after this. A long spell."

Bonner laughed and slapped his knee. "Now ye're talkin', Gabriel, and about damn' time, too. Don't worry about the money, he'll have it."

Unfurling his lanky form, Bonner threw the dregs from his cup into the fire. Even in moccasins, he seemed to tower over everyone else. "Ye heared the man!" he bellowed. "Saddle up! We've got us a freight caravan to raid."

Chapter Twenty-Four

It was noon before Milo caught up with the outfit. His news was grim. "They're catching up, boss. I don't know how they're doing it, but they aren't more than six hours behind us now."

"Six hours!" Buck echoed in disbelief.

"They haven't been playing by the rules, that's for sure."

"Did you see them doing anything underhanded?"

"No, but I didn't hang around long, once I was sure it was them."

Buck exhaled loudly. He hadn't expected this. When he'd sent Milo back to check on C&L's progress, he'd thought they might have gained an hour or two. Even three or four wouldn't have worried him. But this. . . . "They've got to be driving after dark," he said finally.

"The road's smooth enough for it," Milo agreed. "Solid bed, no ruts or bogs, but they'll wear out their mules if they keep it up."

"Maybe that doesn't matter to them," Buck mused. "It's their first run of the season and their mules are fresh. They could stand being pushed a little harder this trip."

"What about their BMC rep?"

"Reps can be bought off. It wouldn't be the first time."

"Lordy," Milo breathed. "What are we gonna do? If they're cheating, we've got to do the same, don't we?"

"No," Buck answered firmly. "I won't cheat."

"Then what?"

Buck considered his options for a moment, then said: "Get yourself some more grub, then ride back and keep an eye on 'em. Dog 'em every step, and any time you see them break a rule, make a note of it. It'll be something we can challenge them with later, if we have to." He hesitated, remembering Mase and Lotty and Sally, then added: "Watch yourself, too. I've got a feeling things are going to get meaner, the closer we get to Montana."

They camped that night on a windswept plain without a tree in sight. Buck stepped down from his saddle, grunting as his left leg bent sharply in the stirrup, causing the stitches above his knee to pull tight. Although the wound hadn't scabbed over yet, the pain had become bearable with a bandage. His arm felt a lot better, too. The stiffness had lessened considerably, and the deep blues and purples had faded to a pale, ugly yellow. The faint odor of Centaur Liniment lingered however, and the men continued to make fun of it at night around the fire.

When Buck was satisfied that the camp was in order, he tramped back to where Dulce was standing beside the mud wagon, watching O'Rourke kindle a fire from greasewood.

She smiled tentatively when she saw him. "Come on," he said, reaching for her hand. "Let's take a walk."

"Where?"

"Not far." He led her to the mess wagon to dig out a pair of field glasses.

"I'm becoming intrigued," she murmured as Buck draped the flat leather strap over his neck. "Are we going to spy on someone?"

"More or less."

"Mister McCready," she said, feigning shock, "I'm not sure I want to be a party to something so underhanded."

"If you're too busy. . . ." He left the rest unspoken, recognizing the games of courtship they'd played so often in Corinne and finding a kind of comfort in its familiarity. It was enough, for now, to keep them from facing something neither of them were ready to examine too closely.

Buck spotted O'Rourke out of the corner of his eye, squatting beside his fire with a cigarette dangling from his lips. The coachman's low opinion of them was undisguised.

"Don't trifle with me," Dulce was saying. "Tell me where we're going?"

He pointed with his chin toward a knobby outcropping of lava rock, barely visible in the deepening twilight.

"Romantic," Dulce said dryly, the sparkle in her eyes dimming.

"Not much, but it'll give us a good view to the south." He paused. "You don't have to come if you don't want to."

"No, I'll do it."

They left camp while the men were still rummaging for wood for their fires, the designated cooks for each mess rattling their pots and skillets. In the west, a band of lackluster pink lingered on the horizon, but overhead and behind them, the sky was alive with starshine. A gibbous moon was peeking over a shoulder of the distant Tetons like a shy boy with a freshly scrubbed face, illuminating the high desert plain surrounding the wagons.

It was an easy hike to the base of the knob, but the climb up would be more difficult. They circled the sharp-edged black stones, fused together by a heat Buck could barely fathom, until they found a path that seemed to lead toward a small ledge just under the knob's crest, maybe thirty feet above them.

"Over here," Buck said, making for the narrow passage. Feeling his way along, he added: "Be careful. These rocks can cut like flint."

Dulce stopped at his warning. "Buck!" she declared. "What are we doing?"

He glanced over his shoulder. "I want to see how far back the other outfits are. I thought maybe you'd enjoy the view."

"It's dark," she reminded him acidly. "There is no view."

He stepped back down to her side. "You can wait here. It was just an idea, a chance for us to be alone."

"Here?" she asked, spreading her arms wide. "You want me to wait here?"

Swallowing back the ire that rose in his throat, Buck said: "It's an adventure, Dulce."

She was silent a long time, then resolutely squared her shoulders. "All right then, let's climb this mountain. We'll revel in the view no matter how limited it is."

Buck turned away, saying nothing. The summit turned out to be inaccessible, but the ledge he'd spotted from below was wider than it had looked, and they were soon seated upon it side-by-side, their legs dangling over the edge. From here, Buck could make out the evening fires of five separate outfits behind them. The three farthest back didn't concern him. It was the two nearest camps that captured his attention. One of them would be the Crowley and Luce train, the other the same Salt Lake Freight caravan that had been harmlessly trailing them ever since they crossed the Malads. The Leavitt Brothers train, hauling light and moving fast, had passed them several days before.

"Which camp belongs to Crowley and Luce?" Dulce asked.

"One of those, I reckon," Buck said, pointing out the two nearest fires, the closest less than five miles back.

"Why, they're so close. How did they catch up so quickly?"

"I figure they've been cheating," Buck replied. "I sent Milo back to keep an eye on them."

"They should be reported."

"To who?"

"To Gwen! She's our representative to Bannock Mining, not

to mention the daughter of one of the company's vice presidents. She could vouch for what's happening."

"Gwen is BMC's rep, not ours," Buck replied, focusing his glasses on the nearest camp. "Crowley and Luce have their own rep. He'd deny any charges Gwen made against them. Don't forget that Gwen's position is already weak if she's here under false pretenses."

"Which we all know she is." Dulce brought her fist down petulantly against her knee. "These people cannot be allowed to cheat Papa out of what's rightfully his! You have to do something!"

"There's not much I can do right now." Buck lowered the glasses, staring thoughtfully into the distance. "We'll have to wait until Milo gets back and see. . . ." He stopped at the sound of gunfire from the Box K camp. The rose-tinged yellows of muzzle flashes reflected off the wagons' canvas bows even as a scream like that of a terrified woman came to them from the darkness beyond the camp. Buck scrambled to his feet, dragging Dulce with him.

"Come on!" he shouted. "They're attacking the train."

A bullet smacked into the side of the mud wagon and Gwen screamed and jumped, spilling her tea. Her first reaction was anger, thinking that someone had accidentally fired his pistol. Then several more shots raked the night air and she threw herself flat on the ground.

Around her the men of the Box K were scrambling for their weapons. Peewee was shouting orders that Gwen couldn't make out. Someone else, someone outside the double row of wagons, was making a series of eerily high-pitched cries that sent chills down her spine. Someone yelled that they were after the mules, but Gwen had no idea who *they* were.

"There you are!"

She glanced over her shoulder, feeling immediate relief when she spotted Thad running toward her in a crouch.

"What are you doing out here?" he demanded, dropping beside her.

"What's happening?"

"Bandits, after the mules." Thad snapped a shot into the darkness behind Ray Jones's trailer, then quickly chambered a fresh round into his rifle. "You can't stay here," he said. "It's too dangerous."

Gwen eyed the mud wagon fearfully, its dark wood already splintered by bullets. "I won't go in there," she declared.

"Then get inside the tent." He put a hand on her shoulder. "Come along, Miss Haywood, we've got to get you out of sight." Gwen shuddered at the implication. She tried to stand but he pushed her back. "You'll have to crawl," he said tersely. "Come on."

"I can't crawl in skirts!"

"Crawl, goddammit!" he shouted.

"Thad!"

"Move!"

Gwen moved, crying in fear and humiliation. On hands and knees, yanking at her cumbersome skirts every few feet, she made her way to the front of the tent. Thad stayed at her side, firing whenever a target presented itself, urging her to hurry. When she'd crawled inside, he said: "Get down behind your trunks and don't come out until you're sure it's safe."

"Won't you come with me?"

"I can do more good out here, especially if I don't have to worry about you. Now get in there and get down!"

Gwen scurried deeper into the tent's dark interior, huddling down among the stiff leather trunks that had been stacked at the foot of her bed. There was a smaller case under her cot; she reached for it, snapping open the lid. Inside was the shotgun she'd purchased in Corinne for hunting—not nearly as fancy as her birding gun back home, but solid and of larger gauge. Laying the weapon across her lap, she broke open the twin chambers and inserted a pair of brass shells.

A bullet ripped through the tent's sloping roof with an angry *zzzzt,* and she jumped and cried out. The thunder of hoofs grew loud from the north, where the remuda had been grazing, and the ground began to tremble. She could hear Thad shouting and firing his rifle, and in the wildly dancing, dust-hazed light of the mess fires, the distorted shadows of stampeding mules flashed across the canvas walls like a flicker show. She shrank back as the images grew larger. The tent jerked violently as the rear guide rope was ripped from its peg. The mules were racing past on either side, so close she didn't see how she could be kept from being swept away, trampled to death while Thad stood by helplessly and watched.

Then it was past, flowing out the southern end of the caravan's twin columns while the men of the Box K ran after it, firing recklessly at the raiders.

Gwen slumped back against one of her trunks. The tent was twisted in the middle, almost collapsed in back, but it was still standing and she was still alive. Then the canvas door was flung open and Gwen screamed as a dark figure lumbered into the tent, coming toward her with an axe raised terrorizingly above his shoulder.

Buck was still some eighty yards from the nearest wagon when he slowed his mad sprint through the sage. He dropped behind a waist-high boulder, tugging Dulce after him. Her breathing sounded raspy and harsh, and he thought he could hear the frightened pounding of her heart even above his own ragged breath. His eyes swept camp in an effort to make out what was going on, but there wasn't much to see in the poor light. It appeared as if the worst of the attack was over, although there were still several raiders pouring gunfire into the wagons. Buck wasn't aware that he was still grasping Dulce's arm until she wrenched it away from him.

"You're hurting me," she hissed.

He grabbed her again and pulled her deeper into the boulder's shelter. He was on his knees with only his eyes and the low crown of his hat showing above the hump-backed stone.

Dulce drew her Smith & Wesson.

"Put that away," Buck snapped.

"I won't!"

"Dammit, Dulce, that pistol doesn't have the range. It would only draw their attention to you."

"Oh," she said, then sank back. "What are we going to do?"

"I don't know yet."

Her voice calm, Dulce said: "You have to go to them, Buck. You can't hold back because of me."

"I know." He looked at her. "I'm sorry."

"Don't be. I'll be fine. I'll keep my head down and no one will know I'm even out here."

"Stay low and, if they find you, shoot to kill."

"I will. Now go. The men need you."

"I'll be back," he promised, then left the cover of the low rock in a crouching run, making his way toward the rear of the train with his Colt thrust before him.

There was a lot of dust and smoke and a sense of chaos in all the back and forth shouting, but nothing that really told Buck what to expect. He was still forty yards away when a tall man riding a blanket-spotted Appaloosa appeared out of the smoky shadows on his left. Buck jerked to a stop, lifting his Colt and cocking it in one smooth motion. "Hold up!" he shouted.

The raider sawed back on the Appaloosa's reins, his head swiveling. He was dressed in buckskins and had long, dark hair, and, for a minute, Buck thought he was an Indian. Then the raider saw him and swore, and Buck knew that he wasn't.

Driving his heels into the Appaloosa's sides, the raider leveled his rifle alongside the animal's neck and snapped off a round that burrowed into the dirt at Buck's feet. Buck flinched but held his ground. Swallowing back the brassy taste of fear, he lined his Colt on the charging outlaw and squeezed the trigger. Through the powder smoke he saw the man on the Appaloosa jerk hard, nearly dropping his rifle. Then he yanked his horse around and raced off, clutching his saddle horn like a drunkard.

"Buck?"

"Over here," he replied, moving toward the low sound of her voice. He found Dulce creeping through the sage, her S&W clenched tightly in hand.

"I. . . ."

"It's all right," he reassured her. "Come on, let's get inside in case they come back."

They crossed the final distance to the wagons in a crouch. Buck gave a shout when they were close, not wanting to be mistaken for a bandit, and Joe Perry answered, ordering the others to hold their fire until Buck and Dulce came in.

"What the hell's going on?" Buck demanded as soon as he and Dulce were safely inside.

"I'm not sure," Joe said. "It looks like. . . ."

A final shot rang out from the darkness. The bullet slammed into the iron rim of the wagon's tall wheel less than six inches from Dulce's head, then shrilled off into the night. Dulce screamed and clutched her cheek, and Buck grabbed her and threw her to the ground. He lifted his pistol but didn't fire, half sick with the knowledge that this shot had come from inside the twin columns of wagons.

"Who was that?" Joe bellowed from where he'd ducked

behind the wheel. "Who fired that shot?"

Several men were already running in the direction the shot had come from, but Buck knew they wouldn't find anything. He'd chased that elusive form enough times himself. He pushed to his feet, then hauled Dulce to hers. "How bad is it?" he asked, gently prying her fingers away from her face.

"I don't know," she replied hollowly. "Is there blood?"

With his thumb, Buck wiped away a small red smear, dulled by dust. The wound underneath was barely visible—a scratch. "There's some," he told her, "but it isn't deep enough to leave a scar."

Dulce's face was ashen. Her eyes searched his face as if not trusting what she knew had to be true. Buck led her to a nearby cask and made her sit down.

"Someone tried to kill me," she whispered.

"Stay here with Joe," he said. "I'll go take a look."

"I'll watch her," Joe promised, and Buck nodded and turned away.

There was yelling from the east and he moved in that direction, reloading the Colt as he went. He found Peewee and Ray at Nate's lead wagon, peering across the moonlit plain. "What's going on?" he asked.

"Rossy's still out there," Peewee said. "Nate and Chris went out to find him. Lou's getting a lantern."

"Where are the mules?"

Ray spat in disgust. "They got 'em. Took the whole damn' cavvy."

Buck felt a sinking in his breast that was like a hundred pound sack of flour sitting on his chest. Numbly he holstered the Colt.

"I figure that's what they were after all along," Peewee added.

Buck stepped past them without speaking, crossing the gently sloping plain until he met Nate hurrying back to camp with a limp figure cradled in his arms.

They lay Rossy down on a blanket and Buck dropped to his knees opposite Nate, who was hovering over his son like a mourner.

"I'm all right, Pa. I ain't hurt," Rossy said weakly.

"There's blood," Nate said, looking at Buck. He held out his hand, the palm slick, dark.

"It's my leg," Rossy confirmed. "It stings like it's on fire."

"Where's that lantern?" Buck snapped over his shoulder, but Lou was already hurrying toward them with the same bull's-eye lantern Ray had used the night he and Peewee smeared liniment and salve over Buck's wounds.

Ray plucked the light impatiently from Lou's grasp and knelt by Rossy's head, adjusting the small aperture in the door until he had a bright, narrow beam. He turned it on Rossy's legs, quickly locating the wound high on his left thigh. Rossy's trousers were torn and bloody, and he twitched in discomfort when Nate used his knife to cut the fabric away from the wound.

Buck breathed easier when he saw the injury up close. A deep trough had been gouged across the muscle, painful but not serious.

"Damn, boy," Ray said. "You ain't even gonna be limpin' by the time you get home. Shot up in a mule raid and nothin' to show the gals. That's hard luck for sure."

"I feel like I could limp right now," Rossy replied, bringing low, relieved laughter from the men crowded around him.

Buck looked at Nate, still leaning over his son as if the wound had been fatal. Tears glistened like silver streams on the black man's cheeks and his fists were clenched tightly. Pushing to his feet, Buck said: "Let's leave 'em be for a while. We've got mules to round up."

Ray looked up, aggravated. "They ain't no mules, dammit. Raiders got 'em all."

"No, not all of 'em," Peewee said. "I saw quite a few break

away from the main bunch and scatter off to the east. They're still out there, if we can catch 'em. They'll be spooked tonight, though."

"Did you see what happened?" Buck asked.

"Some of it."

Buck glanced at the men gathered around Rossy. "Go see how many mules you can round up. That's the priority right now. Chris, stay here and check around, see if anyone else is hurt. Ray, give Nate a hand dressing Rossy's wound, then go help with the mules. Peewee, come with me."

"They used a cougar's skin," Peewee explained as he and Buck headed for the front of the train. "Fresh-skinned by the smell. I caught a whiff of it myself, just before one of them let out a wail like a cat that made the hair across the back of my neck stand out straight."

"Like a woman's scream," Buck mused, recalling the sound he'd heard back in the lava rocks.

"Sure enough," Peewee asserted. "That's what caused the mules to stampede. We all went humpin' out there, but we was too slow. Them damn' raiders was on top of us before we even knew they was about. Up till then, I reckon I still thought it was a cougar. It all happened so fast, there weren't but a few of us even armed. Soon as we knew what was about, we skedaddled back to the wagons and got our guns, but by then it was too late."

Peewee hesitated, then shook his head. "I'd call it an odd raid, Buck. They could've kept runnin' . . . they had the stock. But five or six of 'em hung back to fight. I can't rightly figure that out unless they was testin' our mettle. Could be that if we'd been slow or cowardly, they'd've stayed to finish the job."

The night hawks—Rossy, Bigfoot Payne, and Manuel Varga—had seen them coming and tried without success to run the mules into camp, Peewee added, but he hadn't seen Bigfoot or

Manuel since the shooting started. Mitch Kroll confirmed the worst a few minutes later when he found Buck and Peewee at the first mess.

"Bigfoot's dead," the muleskinner announced bluntly, his broad shoulders rounded forward as if in anguish. "They shot him in the back while he was runnin' for cover."

"He was a good man," Buck said cautiously.

"The boy had a way with animals," Mitch agreed, all the steel gone from his voice. "It's a trait with simpletons, I've heard." After a pause, he added: "I've never told anyone this, but the boy was kin, my sister's son. I took him on after she died." He looked up. "I want the bastards who did this, McCready, and I want Crowley and Luce, too. We all know they're behind it."

"We ain't making war on Crowley and Luce without proof," Buck responded.

"We don't have to go after 'em that way. I say we win this race, leave those assholes so far behind, Bannock Mining'll have half its mill put up by the time C and L gets there."

"Winning this race is what we've been tryin' to do all along," Peewee reminded him.

"Yeah, but you ain't had full support," Mitch pointed out. "There's been some who've been . . . a little less ambitious, but that's gonna change. We're gonna beat those bastards at their own game if I gotta haul these wagons to Montana myself."

Thad Collins came up before Buck could reply. Gwen was with him, her face a collage of emotions. "A moment, McCready?" the bodyguard asked.

"What is it?"

"Paddy O'Rourke is dead."

"God damn," Buck breathed. "What happened?"

"He attacked Miss Haywood with a camp axe."

Buck's head jerked up. "What!"

Gwen met Buck's gaze. "I . . . killed a man, Buck," she said simply, then looked away.

"I knew from that first day on the trail that O'Rourke didn't like her," Collins admitted. "He didn't like her money or her connections back East or her. . . ."

"No," Gwen said raggedly, "he didn't like me. I . . . I've never experienced that kind of anger before. He came after me with an axe, fully intending to murder me. If I hadn't purchased that shotgun in Corinne to do some birding along the way. . . ."

Her words trailed off, and Buck said: "You did the right thing. Sometimes it comes down just that simple . . . you live or you die."

"It isn't that way in Philadelphia," she said faintly.

"Oh, I reckon it is," he countered. "I reckon it's like that just about everywhere. You just haven't had to deal with it before tonight."

Tears welled in her eyes. "Could you tell me where Dulce is?" she asked almost timidly.

"She's with Joe Perry, over by his wagons."

Gwen looked at Collins, still obviously shaken. "Would you accompany me there, please?"

"Sure," Collins said, taking her arm, "and don't worry, no one else is going to get near you after this."

"Thank you," she said, adding to Buck: "I'll sit with Dulce and . . . she can sit with me." She smiled wanly. "We'll stay out of your way."

Chapter Twenty-Five

So this is how it ends, Arlen thought as Bonner drew his pistol. He flinched as the weapon was cocked, then flinched again when he felt its cold muzzle press into his forehead. He didn't plead for his life or try to run, but he did close his eyes. Death was one thing. Staring into Jim Bonner's cold, blue gaze while waiting for it was another.

"What the hell ya want?" Bonner demanded, and Arlen tentatively opened one eye. The question was startling. He hadn't asked for anything.

"Dumb-ass ain't your'n to kill," Henry Reese said, and Arlen opened his other eye. Henry hadn't been around when Bonner drew his pistol.

"The hell he ain't," Bonner growled, and Arlen felt the muzzle shift as pressure was applied to the trigger. He was nearly deafened by the blast of the gunshot and fell back screaming and kicking, rubbing frantically at his face as if to hold shattered bone together.

"God dammit!" someone roared, and someone else bellowed: "I told ye to back off, ya son-of-a-bitch!"

Arlen took several deep breaths before he could work up the courage to look for himself. He was lying on his back, although he didn't remembering falling. Reese and Bonner stood over him, gesturing madly. Their words were muted by the ringing in his ears, but he didn't think he was dead. If he was, this sure wasn't what he'd expected.

After a couple of minutes, Reese's words started to come together. The mountain man was pointing at Arlen, saying: "If anybody shoots this little runt, it's gonna be me or Gabe. We're the ones been puttin' up with his ignorance."

"Wal, he ain't gettin' no cut outta them mules," Bonner declared. His right hand was still gripping his revolver, his left clamped against his side, where blood had darkened his buckskin shirt in a patch the size of a man's head. Bonner insisted the wound wasn't serious, but Arlen knew that it was. He'd seen it at dawn, all dark and swollen and oozing blood, surrounded by a bruise that seemed to encompass the mountain man's entire torso.

Lifting his pistol to point, rather than aim, at Arlen's nose, Bonner added: "It was yer little runt here what peeled off a good-size bunch of mules last night, bein' where he weren't supposed ta be. I figure twenty head that sawed-off half-wit cost us."

"He's still useful," Henry argued, although without the ardor Arlen might have wished for. "He fetches wood and water right pert. We'll keep him till we're finished with him."

"When the hell's that gonna be?"

"When I say so, but it ain't gonna be today."

Bonner holstered his pistol. "All right, but if ye don't shoot him then, I will. That little sum-bitch cost us money."

Bonner walked away, weaving a little in the loose sand. Kicking Arlen lightly on the hip, Henry said: "Get up, dumb-ass. Ye ain't dead yet."

Chapter Twenty-Six

They buried their dead in the darkness before dawn. Dulce and Gwen cried softly over Bigfoot's grave as the blanket-wrapped body was lowered from sight. They covered the grave with rocks to protect it from scavengers, and, when it was done, Peewee wedged a final stone at its head with Bigfoot's name scratched into it with a nail.

They laid Paddy O'Rourke to rest some distance away, but no one cried over his grave or suggested they protect it from wolves or coyotes.

By dawn, they'd recovered eighteen of their mules, and with that small bunch secured, Buck made his choices from among the Box K teamsters. Ray, Charlie, Joe, Lou, Chris, Mitch, and Little Ed would accompany him after the remuda. The rest would stay behind. With Milo still on their back trail keeping tabs on the Crowley and Luce outfit, Buck put Peewee in charge of the wagons.

Zeke had been one of the first mules recovered, and Buck was glad to have a familiar mount under him. His rifle, a rolling block chambered in .50-70 Government, was already booted under his right stirrup strap, but he carried only a handful of rounds for it in one of his pommel bags. He dug a cartridge belt out of the mess wagon that held an additional forty rounds and snugged it around his waist, above his gun belt. Then he rummaged through his gear for a box of .44 Henry Rimfires for his Colt. Food, a slim bedroll, and a rubber poncho in case of rain, completed his outfit.

Stepping into the saddle, he rode over to where Dulce and Gwen were watching from the shade of the mud wagon. Gwen moved away when Buck came up, leaving him alone with Dulce.

"You'll be all right," he assured her.

"I know. Thad's promised to look after me as he does Gwen."

"Well," Buck shrugged uncertainly, "that's good, I reckon. Thad's a capable man."

"Yes, he was a comfort last night . . . while you were off seeing to everyone else's needs." Her eyes sparked. "Someone shot at me last night, Buck."

"A lot of us were shot at last night," he replied, then shook his head impatiently. Dulce was staring him in the eyes as if willing him to say more, but Buck had nothing more to give, and, wheeling Zeke, he rode off at a trot.

It didn't take long to locate the raiders' trail. Close to a hundred and fifty head of mules, driven through the night at a breakneck run, churned up a path even the poorest tracker could follow. Buck kicked Zeke into a lope and the others quickly fell in behind him. The trail led south for almost a mile before bending to the west, but the remuda's pace never slowed. By noon the teamsters' mules had worked up a good lather, and Buck had the men dismount and loosen their cinches, but they didn't stop. He kept them walking for an hour, then ordered them back into their saddles.

The country turned increasingly rugged as the afternoon wore on. The rolling hills rose into steep-sided ridges, the draws between them sinuous but dry. Slabs of stone jutted from the hillsides like the bones of prehistoric beasts. The raiders weren't making very good time, and, from the sign, Buck knew at least one of them was badly wounded. The bandits were stopping often, and everywhere they did, drops of dried blood spotted the soil.

"They're gonna lose that one if they don't slow down," Ray commented at one point, and Mitch, staring west along the path of trampled grass, added: "He must be a honcho of some kind. Otherwise they would've shot him to keep him quiet and gone on."

They closed the gap steadily, but still hadn't caught up by nightfall. After picketing their weary mules on grass alongside a slow-moving stream, the men suppered on chunks of last night's pan bread and strips of jerky, washed down with canteen water. It was a couple of hours before the moon came up. When it did, Buck, Ray, and Mitch walked to the top of a nearby rise to study the lay of the land to the west.

"Hell," Ray said, after his eyes had adjusted to the dimness. "It ain't that dark."

"We can track by this," Buck agreed. "The mules'll need some more rest, though. We pushed them hard today."

Pointing toward the flanks of a low mountain range about fifteen miles away, Mitch said: "You boys see anything over there?"

At first Buck couldn't make out anything. Then he perked up. "Kind of a glow, but real faint?"

"Yeah, like a campfire'd make if it was reflecting off a big rock or something."

"I don't see anything," Ray grumbled.

"It's there," Mitch replied, lowering his arm. "What do you think, McCready?"

Buck was silent a moment, weighing the pros and cons, then said: "We'll rest here for another hour or so, then head for that light. If it's not our thieves, it's in the right direction."

"It's them," Mitch insisted. "I can feel it in my blood."

Chapter Twenty-Seven

Nick Kelso's throat was dust-dry as he waved the trail-weary mountain men into the mouth of the ravine. He'd ridden hard to get ahead of the fast-moving gang and their cavvy of stolen mules, but, as the grim-faced bunch rode up the gulch toward him, he began to wonder if he'd made the right decision.

Maybe I should have stayed in Utah, he thought briefly, then shoved his doubts aside. He'd come this far in life by not backing down from anyone; he'd be damned if he'd start now.

The sight of Arlen Fleck among the thieves was a surprise. Nick didn't even recognize him at first, mistaking him for one of Carville's and Reese's men. It wasn't until he checked his raw-boned mustang at the edge of the firelight that Nick realized the brown-skinned, slope-shouldered runt was his old partner.

Arlen was dirtier than Nick had ever seen him. His stubble had turned into a beard and his eyes looked red and painful from the sun and dust and wood smoke. Always a slim man, he'd lost even more weight in his travels with Carville and Reese, and his city duds hung from him like rags on a skeleton.

"Who the hell are you?" a towering mountain man in a blood-soaked buckskin shirt demanded. He glared at Nick like a demon eyeing a lost soul.

"He's an acquaintance of ours," Gabe said calmly, reining up beside the bloody scarecrow on the Appaloosa. "How'd ye find us, Kelso?"

"I've been shadowing the Box K for a few days, waiting for you boys to make your play. I was about ready to do something myself when I heard the ruckus last night. I could tell by the sound that you were heading west, so I came out here to get around you." He motioned to the crackling fire behind him. "There's coffee and biscuits and a gallon of Fort Hall whiskey for you boys to share." He glanced at the remuda spreading out on the grass along the creek below camp.

"How many men have you got altogether . . . seven, eight?" He glanced at Fleck with a smirk. "Not counting this one."

"Dumb-ass makes ten," Henry stated flatly, "and he's hung with us ever' step of the way. That's more'n you had the sand to do."

Nick's cocky grin disappeared, his only reaction to Reese's insult. With the exception of Fleck, there wasn't a soft man in the bunch, and he didn't intend to buck the whole gang by himself. "I brought you boys some supplies to keep you riding," he said. "Buck McCready's going to hound you out of the territory to get his mules back."

"We ain't leavin' the territory," scarecrow stated flatly. "I don't give a shit who's followin' us. We don't need your supplies, either, although we's gonna take 'em."

Nick nodded woodenly. For the first time in years he was experiencing an emotion he'd almost forgotten—fear. Glancing at Fleck, Nick said: "Let's go, Arlen. Your work here is done."

"Dumb-ass'll be stayin' with us," Henry intervened, grinning sardonically as he nudged his mount between Arlen's shaggy mustang and Kelso. "Me 'n' Gabe's growed fond of the boy."

"I reckon whether he stays or leaves is his choice," Nick replied tautly.

"Then ye've reckoned wrong," was Gabe's curt response, the muzzle of his rifle swinging around to center on Nick's chest.

Nick's fingers twitched, but he didn't dare make a play for

his revolver. "All right," he said after a moment's calculation. "It's no skin off my hide. I'll leave you boys the food and whiskey and let you go about your business." He walked stiffly to his horse, glad that he'd left it saddled, the cinch snug.

"Kelso!" Reese barked.

Nick flinched in spite of himself and felt an instant's shame. Turning, he said: "What do you want?"

"If we hear our names mentioned in connection with this raid, we's gonna come huntin' ye, boy, and I swear I'll wear ye scalp afore the year's out. Savvy?"

"That's a promise that cuts both ways," Nick replied coolly. He stepped into the saddle and pulled his horse around, riding out of camp with his shoulders rigid, his eyes straight ahead. He was aware of the others coming in, advancing on the fire like scavengers approaching a fresh kill, but he acknowledged no one. He kept his horse to a walk until he was safely around the first bend in the trail, then kicked it into a lope.

Chapter Twenty-Eight

"I'll be damned," Mitch whispered, unable to hide his surprise. "I would've sworn they'd be gone by now."

Buck's eyes probed the distant camp suspiciously. There was no denying that it was the Box K remuda scattered along the creek below them. Nor could he ignore the slumbering camp tucked neatly into a fold in the opposite hillside, the oblong shapes of the raiders' bedrolls circling the dying embers of last night's fire like spokes. But something wasn't right here. Buck could feel it in his bones.

"Let's go get 'em," Mitch growled, pushing away from the low boulder where he and Buck were crouched.

"Hold on," Buck said, lifting his hand. "This is too easy."

"Easy happens sometimes," Mitch replied. "Hell, you ought to know better'n to look a gift horse in the mouth, McCready?"

"I know better than to get within kicking distance of one, too."

Ray crawled over on his hands and knees, dragging his carbine with him. "What're you two jabberin' about? Damnation, we got to move, Buck. They're gonna be stirrin' pretty quick."

"They should be stirring now," Buck reminded them. He and his men were hunkered down among some rocks across from the raiders' camp, maybe two hundred yards away. From here, it was an easy drop to the cañon floor, where all but a handful of mules were bedded down and sleeping. The raiders' horses were picketed in a little side draw close to their camp.

Glancing at Chris Hobson, Buck said: "Take Charlie, Lou, and Little Ed and circle around until you're above the herd, then ease down on it. The mules'll hear you before you get close, but if they don't spook and run, maybe they won't wake those sleeping bastards across the way. With a little luck, you'll have the herd out of here before they even know it's gone."

"What are you going to do?" Chris asked.

"Me, Ray, Joe, and Mitch are going to wiggle down to where we can give you some decent cover, in case it comes to a fight. If it doesn't, we'll wait until you're out of range before we lay into them, but, no matter what, I want that remuda moving. I want those mules back at the wagons before nightfall."

"They'll be there," Chris promised, motioning for Charlie, Lou, and Little Ed to follow him.

Buck turned back to the camp. He could come up with half a dozen reasons why the mule thieves were still in their blankets, but not one that made any sense. The only thing that did soothe his worries was that an ambush didn't seem logical, either. Not if they were just thieves.

Buck took a quick inventory of their weapons. Mitch and Ray were armed with Spencer repeaters and Joe had a single-shot Sharps, not all that different from Buck's Remington. All four firearms packed a hefty wallop, and would do some serious damage in a fight. "Let's crawl a little closer," Buck said, nodding toward a broken shelf of rocks about halfway down the side of the hill where they were crouched. "We can settle in there and still have good cover."

"We gonna fight 'em?" Ray asked.

"They jumped a Box K train, stole Box K stock, killed a Box K man." Buck's face was grim in the pearly light. "Hell, yes, we're gonna fight 'em."

The footing was tricky in the poor light, but not dangerous, and they were soon in place among the shattered boulders. Buck found a low, V-shaped notch above a short, vertical drop and stretched out prone behind it. Fingering half a dozen stubby .50-70 cartridges from his belt, he laid them out within easy reach. The others quickly settled in on either side of him, seeing to their own weapons. It was another ten minutes before Joe spoke quietly. "Here they come."

Buck craned his neck past the edge of the notch. Chris and his men were spread out across the upper end of the cañon, already advancing on the remuda. Several of the stolen mules had pushed to their feet and were staring upcañon, their long ears canted sharply forward. As the riders drew close, Chris raised his hand to signal a trot. As he did, a shot rang out from the opposite wall and Chris was flung from the back of his mount as if swept away by a giant hand.

"Son-of-a-bitch," Buck grated, throwing the Remington to his shoulder and pulling the trigger. Joe's Sharps roared at nearly the same time. Across the cañon, the broken hillside seemed to come alive with zigzagging men seeking better positions. Buck estimated at least eight of them, each one armed with a rifle carried with practiced ease. Buck's gaze flitted briefly to the outlaw camp, where the bedrolls lay undisturbed and knew with a sickening bitterness that he'd led his men into a trap.

Forcing himself to remain calm, Buck found a raider in his sights and fired a second time. The man spun and fell, rolling part way down the side of the hill before stopping himself and scampering for cover. Within seconds, two more outlaws had pitched to the ground—one of them falling to Joe's big Sharps, the other to Ray's Spencer—and the remaining outlaws dropped from sight.

There was a shout from upcañon. Looking in that direction, Buck saw his men, Chris with them, racing their mounts toward the stolen herd. As the men of the Box K swept forward, the loose mules wheeled and bolted downcañon.

"Lay into 'em!" Buck yelled as the remuda thundered past.

The firing from the far side of the cañon intensified, but Buck and his men were pounding the outlaws' position, laying down an unwavering fusillade. As the cavvy pulled out of range, the raiders turned their guns on the remaining Box K men. Lead splatter and tiny stone chips stung Buck's cheeks twice, and a spent round—a ricochet—struck his boot just above his ankle, although it lacked enough energy to do any harm.

Mitch and Ray were slamming round after round into the mule thieves' hiding places, and Joe's Sharps bellowed steadily as he fed it fresh rounds. A third man fell across the way, the fringe on his buckskins flapping like wings as he was knocked off his perch above the cañon floor. There was a shout from the opposite wall, then a lull in the firing. Buck called for his own men to stop shooting, and the four of them waited to see what would happen next.

Without any apparent command, the raiders began backing away, retreating through rocks to the side draw where their horses were tethered. Soon, most of them were scrambling for their mounts, abandoning the fight.

Most, but not all.

Buck's eyes dropped to the cañon floor where a man in buckskins was sprinting toward the trees along the creek. Buck fired at the same time as Ray and the outlaw stumbled, then fell to his knees. He stayed that way for only a moment, before tipping over sideways.

Higher up on the far side of the cañon, the fleeing raiders were making their way toward a low saddle in the ridge above them. When the last man had crossed over, Buck slowly stood. As he did, a man stepped out from behind a boulder across the cañon, his rifle shouldered. Buck knew he'd made a terrible mistake. He wanted to cry out in protest, but there wasn't even time for that. He tensed for the bullet's strike, but, before the raider could pull the trigger, another figure appeared out of the rocks, charging forward like a bull to tackle the first man and drive him to his knees. The rifle roared, its bullet plowing harmlessly into the dirt some twenty yards below where Buck stood.

Rolling onto his back, the first man swung the butt of his rifle around to catch the second man on the jaw. As the second man fell, the first man clambered to his feet, raising his rifle high above his head to cave in the second man's skull. Before he could bring it down, four Box K rifles blazed as one and the first raider was slammed back against the rocks, then crumbled limply to the ground.

Buck approached the scrawny man with the swollen jaw warily, his rifle at the ready. Mitch and Joe were working their way up the far side of the cañon, looking for more survivors, while Ray circled around behind the man in the dirty green coat.

It was the coat that had caught Buck's attention, even from his rocky niche across the cañon. As grimy as the man wearing it, frayed, ripped—but a green plaid, just as Tom Ashley described. A battered brown porkpie was tipped back on the stranger's head, and Buck remembered the International's barkeep's words: *A brown hat with a little bitty brim.*

Earring the Remington's hammer back to full cock, Buck said: "On your feet, and, if you're still carrying a pistol when you get there, I'll blow your god-damn' head off."

The man nodded to a spot several yards away, where a rusty Manhattan revolver lay in the dirt. "It ain't even been fired," he said in a low, mousey voice. "I wasn't a part of that bunch, but they'd 'a' killed me if I tried to slip away."

"You ain't in no better position now," Ray told him, coming up from behind.

The stranger continued to look at Buck and didn't turn around.

"Stand up," Buck ordered. "Ray, search him."

"Be my pleasure," Ray said, switching his rifle to his left hand. "You got a hide-out gun on you somewheres, sonny?"

"I've got a pocket knife in my left trouser pocket that ain't hardly sharp enough to cut anything." He was still watching Buck, waiting patiently for whatever was to come.

Ray stepped back a moment later and tossed a small clasp knife into the weeds. "Piece of junk," he announced. "He wasn't gonna hurt nobody with that."

Buck kept his rifle leveled. "You saved my life, stranger, and I'm beholden to you for that, but I need some answers, and I'll do what I have to do to get them."

"Yeah, you're a Kavanaugh man all right," the scrawny dude said mildly. "I been hearing about that incident down in Chihuahua."

Buck stiffened. "Who told you about that?"

"It was just talk, back in Corinne."

"Talk from who?"

The stranger shrugged. "Hard to say."

"We can hang his sorry hide from a tree limb and beat him with clubs until he looks like raw meat," Ray suggested. "He ain't worth a damn to us if he don't start remembering."

"I already decided I was gonna die," the stranger replied. "It don't much matter any more how it happens."

Buck looked to where Mitch and Joe were working their way down from the side draw where the outlaws had picketed their horses. "By God, we cut hell outta them bastards," Mitch chortled. Coming up beside Ray, he added: "Four dead, including the one that got hisself wounded the other night." He glanced briefly at the stranger. "They took all the horses. Looks like they wasn't too concerned about you."

"No, they wouldn't be," the small man said. "That one you wounded the other night is Jim Bonner. It was his gang that pulled out when he was killed. That one there"—he nodded to the corpse lying nearby, the one he'd tackled—"is Gabe Carville. Henry Reese is the one who tried to get into them trees along the creek. I couldn't say who the fourth man is."

Joe whistled softly. "Damn, that's a rough bunch."

"The only reason you all ain't doorknob dead is because they got hold of some whiskey last night and was still mostly drunk," the stranger said.

Buck jammed the Remington's muzzle into the man's gut. "You're going to be doorknob dead in a minute if you don't start talking. I want answers, dammit. I want to know who you are and what you're doing here, then I want to know who killed Mase Campbell, and why."

The stranger nodded compliantly. "The name's Arlen Fleck. I don't know who killed Campbell, but I was there when it was done and you don't have to get mad about it, 'cause I'm gonna tell you everything I do know, and that's gonna be a heap all by itself."

It was well after dark by the time they got back to the wagons with their prisoner. Coming over the last low ridge and spotting the evening fires of the Box K, the men kicked their mules into a lope. All save Buck, who pulled Zeke to one side to let the others ride ahead. Arlen rode behind Joe, his wrists loosely bound, legs dangling free. Of the four, only he refused to glance curiously at Buck as they cantered past. Arlen kept his gaze fixed on the horizon, as if the train didn't exist.

Dismounting, Buck walked over to the same rock where he and Dulce had crouched during the bandit's raid.

It wasn't Nick Kelso that killed Campbell, Fleck had told them that morning. *It was some stranger I ain't never seen before. A tall feller, kinda skinny. He came outta that alley there beside the International and stopped Campbell for a light for his cigarette, and as soon as Campbell lit it for him, that's when he pulled his pistol and shot him. Hell, Campbell never even seen it comin'. But I didn't get a good look at the fella. It all happened too fast.*

Buck crawled on top of the rock and sat down. He felt sadder than he had since the day of Mase's funeral. His gaze swept the horizon but there was nothing to see, not even the glow of campfires to the south. It was as if the Box K had the road to itself with nothing to stop it, nothing to stand in its way. But a land like this could hide a lot, Buck knew, as a similar country had once hidden more than a hundred Sioux warriors, bent on murder and mayhem. His own family had been the target of their destruction.

They'd been bound for Oregon, the McCreadys of Indiana, although at the time, young Buchanan couldn't have said why. At ten, the growing threat of war between the North and South or the rockiness of his family's hillside farm across the river from Louisville, Kentucky, hadn't made much of an impression. It had to his parents, though, and in the spring of 1860 they'd packed their meager belongings into a prairie schooner pulled by two yokes of oxen and set out for the far Northwest.

Besides his father and mother, there had been two sisters—Kay, older by several years, and Becky, who'd turned eight on the day they crossed the Blue River in Kansas Territory—part of a train bound for the Willamette Valley. All except Buck had died on that fateful day his father allowed the family to fall behind the rest of the party so that Buck's mother could tend a feverish child. Buck had wandered off to explore the Platte River bottoms by himself—they were less than a week out of Fort Laramie by then—while his father hunted the breaks for fresh meat. The Sioux had found his ma and sisters by the wagon, his pa along the river. Buck didn't know a lot beyond that. He'd never asked, although there were folks who could have told him if he had. Those who'd helped bury the dead. Mase had been one of those.

Buck could still remember the first time he'd seen Mase, there on the Powder River far to the north of Fort Laramie and not much more than a stone's throw from the large Sioux village where Buck had been taken. He'd been scared half out of his wits the whole time, and thought maybe that was why he hadn't cried out when he spotted Mase's bearded face taking shape within a screen of buffalo brush growing along the river's edge.

Mase had lifted a finger to his lips to make a shushing sound, his cheeks puffing out comically, eyes wide as silver dollars. With so many Sioux coming and going around the village, it was a wonder Mase had been able to get as close as he had. Buck hadn't known it at the time, but the military had lacked the resources to come after him; if he was going to be freed, it would have to be done by someone else, and quickly, before the Sioux retreated deeper into Indian country.

Buck had been hesitant to follow the crazy-looking white man into the bushes, but too frightened not to. As soon as Buck had slipped from sight, Mase had clamped a hand over his mouth and scooped him into his arms. Buck struggled briefly until Mase snarled for him to quit fighting or he'd leave him behind for the Sioux to scalp. Buck already knew all he wanted to about scalping. He was pretty sure the warrior who'd carried him off had also been in carrying the hair of his oldest sister, Kay, tied to his saddle.

Buck's fear of being scalped had kept him quiet during Mase's awkward sprint downstream to the saddle of a tall sorrel mule hitched to a sapling. Mase had jerked the reins free and stepped into the saddle without even taking time to catch his breath, then reined the animal into the river. When they got around the first bend, putting a ridge between themselves and the village, Mase had kicked the long-limbed brute out of the water and headed south as fast as that mule could carry them.

If there weren't many men who would have attempted what Mase had, fewer still would have done what he did afterward. The commander at Fort Laramie wanted to send Buck to an orphanage in the East, where attempts to locate his extended family could be conducted more efficiently than from an Army post gearing up for war, but Mase had told the officer he would look for the family himself, and the commander hadn't argued.

Buck could vaguely recall an aunt already living in Oregon, his mother's sister, he thought, although he'd never met her and didn't know her name. It had been a lead, though, and Mase had followed up on it. Keeping the youngster with him, giving him simple chores there were never any shortage of around a mule train, Mase had written to newspapers throughout the Northwest, explaining the particulars of Buck's family, their destination and demise. He'd asked for the aunt to respond to the commander's office at Fort Laramie, but no reply ever came. Buck was twelve when Mase finally quit writing. By then, it wouldn't have mattered anyway. Buck had already set his sights on a future that had nothing to do with farming.

Over the years, Mase made an effort to instruct Buck in the fundamentals of writing, reading, and simple arithmetic, often using invoices and freighting contracts as teaching aids. More important, he taught the youngster just about everything there was to know about hauling freight, from the intricacies of front office politics right down to the rough and tumble world of freighters' camps and end-of-trail celebrations that could cost a careless man his life. Buck had stuck it out, even excelled, and by the time he was sixteen, he could handle a rig as well as anyone in the business. Maybe even as well as Mase, although Buck never would have broached the possibility aloud. As far as

Buck was concerned, there wasn't a better man on Earth than Mason Campbell, and the younger man was willing to fight anyone who said differently. On more than one occasion, he had.

Buck stayed with Mase for eight years, but there comes a time in every young man's life when he needs to make his own way. It was no different for Buck. When Mase crossed the Continental Divide to go to work for Jock Kavanaugh, Buck declined an invitation to go along. He went to Colorado, instead, and hauled for Rocky Mountain Freight between Denver and numerous points south—Pueblo, Trinidad, Boggsville, even up into the high country as far as a wagon could get. He stayed with Rocky Mountain for two years, handling a company-owned twelve-mule jerkline hitch, until Mase sent word that a job had opened up in Utah for an assistant. He wanted Buck for the position and was offering top wages if he'd quit his job in Denver and come to Corinne.

Even then, Buck had almost declined. He liked handling his own rig, and wasn't all that sure he wanted the additional responsibilities that went with a ramrod's position. It was only when Mase had written him a second time that he'd accepted the job. He'd arrived in Corinne in the spring of 1870, just after Jock had relocated there from Ogden, and had been working for the Box K ever since. At the time of Mase's death, Buck had known the wagon master for fourteen years—four more than he had his own parents.

Walking over to where Zeke was pulling up clumps of grass, Buck stretched his toe for the stirrup, grimacing as the stitches above his left knee were drawn tight. He swore softly and lowered his leg to flex out the stiffness. As he did, he spotted a woman standing alone by the wagons. The light behind her sharpened her silhouette even as it masked her face, but Buck would have recognized her anywhere—the color of her hair, the firm, compact body. He paused to return her stare for nearly a minute before she abruptly turned away, heading for the mud wagon at the rear of the train. Granite-faced, Buck swung into his saddle and pointed Zeke toward Peewee's outfit at the opposite end of the train.

"Crowley and Luce passed here yesterday," Milo informed Buck, before Buck could dismount. "They were making good time and acted tickled by our bad luck. I followed them a good little ways, but they weren't breaking any of BMC's rules that I could see."

Buck slid from his saddle and nodded gratefully when Manuel came up to lead Zeke away. Turning to the fire, he found himself nearly surrounded by Box K muleskinners, silent but curious about what he would have to say about this latest development.

"Of course, I don't guess they need to break the rules any longer," Milo added glumly, after a moment's pause. "Damn 'em."

Speaking for the first time, his voice raspy with fatigue, Buck said: "How's Chris Hobson? I saw him shot off his mule this morning."

"I'm fine, boss," came a reply from the rear of the crowd. Pushing his way to the front, Chris touched his side where a medium-size butcher knife with a shattered grip resided in a plain leather sheath. "The bullet hit this," he said, touching the exposed, dented tang. "I've got a good-size bruise, but that's all."

Buck smiled with relief. He'd feared the worst all day. "We'll see if we can't get Jock to buy you a new knife when we get back to Corinne."

Several of the old hands guffawed, imagining the look on Jock's face at such a request.

"Hell, that ain't likely," Chris said, but he was grinning, too.

"Peewee," Buck said. "Have you got any coffee left?"

"Sure do. It's fresh, too, and there's ham and beans and bread if you want it."

"I want it," Buck replied simply, heading for the fire. The muleskinners backed out of the way to create a narrow path for him to pass through, then fell in behind like a congregation of sinners. "Any more trouble while we were gone?" Buck asked Peewee.

"Nary a bit."

"What about the mules Chris brought back?"

"They're tired, and a lot of 'em's got small cuts and such, but nothing much worse than what they'd get from one another in a corral."

"Are any of them lame?"

"Nope."

Buck dreaded his next question. "How many did we lose?"

"Not a one." A grin like a tiny banner spread across Peewee's face. "I told these boys, Buck, that the mules them raiders didn't get'd come wanderin' back on their own, and that's exactly what they done. I'd like to see how many horses or oxen'd do that."

Laughter erupted from the crowd like a release valve on a boiler. It made Buck realize how long it had been since he'd heard genuine laughter from the crew, and reminded him that this had been a difficult trip for everyone.

"We gonna try to catch up to 'em, boss?" Charlie Bigelow asked.

"We ain't gonna try, Charlie, we're gonna do it," Buck vowed.

More laughter greeted Buck's reply, and Charlie shouted happily: "By God, boys, don't fold yer hands just yet! This race ain't over, after all."

★ ★ ★ ★ ★

It was a several hours later when Buck was making his way down the column of wagons that a figure stepped from the shadows. He jerked to a stop, his hand dropping instinctively to his revolver.

"Might I have a word with you?" Gwen asked quietly. "It's rather important."

Buck let his hand fall away from his Colt. "It's past midnight, Gwen. We'll be on the move by first light. Is it that important?"

"I think so, yes."

He almost refused anyway, then shrugged and said: "All right, what is it?"

"Not here." She gestured toward the empty desert beyond the wagons. "There, away from large ears."

Buck motioned for her to lead the way. They were silent as they walked through the sage, stopping a dozen yards out. After a pause, Gwen said: "It's occurred to me that I haven't been very fair to either you or Dulce. I fear that she thinks I'm pursuing you, although that couldn't be further from the truth."

"Dulce and I go back a ways," Buck replied simply.

"Yes, I recognized that some time ago, but I suppose I didn't want to accept it. In the beginning, I was curious as to how you would react to the simple flirtations that are so common at home. I must admit I was disappointed by your lack of interest, even as I grew more intrigued by it."

"I'm sorry if I've disappointed you," he said absently. "I've had other things on my mind."

"You misunderstand, Buck, but, then, so does Dulce. I realized after Mister Trapp's near disaster on top of Malad Summit that there is more involved here than my own little adventure. I've tried to convince Dulce of my change of heart, but so far I've been unsuccessful."

"Trust ain't an easy thing to patch once it's been broken."

Gwen's smile faltered. "You Westerners are such a blunt people. That's something I've yet to get used to. You realize, of course, that you can't overtake Crowley and Luce without bending BMC's rules."

Buck's tone hardened. "You said you wanted to talk to me, but so far you haven't said much."

"Then I shall come to the point. Ray Jones informed us of your prisoner's confession this morning, which I consider adequate proof of outside efforts to subvert the Box K's chances of success. Even this Nick Kelso person was apparently hired by others. Based upon that and other events, I've decided to release you from your obligations to Bannock Mining's rules. You are free to do whatever you think is necessary to win this contest, Mister McCready, and I shall stand behind whatever decisions you make."

Buck's expression remained as hard as his voice. "I appreciate the offer, but I already made that decision on the morning we buried Bigfoot Payne. The Box K is going to Montana and it's going to get there ahead of Crowley and Luce . . . and to hell with fair play."

Chapter Twenty-Nine

On the high desert, the wind never seemed to let up, but its temperament could change in a heartbeat. By the time Buck crawled out of his blankets the next morning, the oilcloth coverings on the tall freighters were popping crisply against their arched bows, and gritty sheets of wind-borne dust were swirling through the camp.

It was a warm wind, peeled off the lower regions of southern California and Nevada, where summer had long since settled in, but those who had freighted this country for years cursed it as they went about their chores. They knew a storm was brewing—not in the southwest where the wind came from, but from the northwest, beyond the mountains. Even the mules sensed the coming change and were acting as flighty as green-broke colts as the men struggled to get them into harness.

"This ain't good, Bucky!" Peewee shouted above the wind. He flipped a mule's heavy leather collar off the ground with his toe, caught it expertly in his left hand, then slid it smoothly over the neck of his off-pointer.

Buck was looking north, although there wasn't anything to see except fading stars. "Might be rain," he said.

"Might be snow," Peewee tossed back.

Especially in the high country, Buck fretted, envisioning the route that lay before them. "Well, it ain't storming yet," he said, then started down the line of wagons. He found Rossy helping his father hitch up. Although the younger Evans was still limping from his wound, Buck noticed that he was pulling his share. Motioning him aside, he said: "How's the leg?"

"It ain't bad," Rossy replied self-consciously. "I can work well enough."

"So I noticed. How'd you like a promotion?"

Rossy's head came up cautiously. "What kind of promotion?"

"Paddy O'Rourke's dead. I need a linesman for the mud wagon. Think you can handle the job with a bum leg?"

Rossy's expression brightened, then just as quickly dimmed. He glanced around at his father's approach. "Pa, I . . . Mister McCready offered me a job. That is, if you don't need my help here."

"I heard," Nate replied, staring hard at his son. "Now let me ask you somethin'. Just what makes you think I don't need your help? You think I been draggin' you along all these years 'cause I liked your cookin'?"

Nate looked at Buck, scowling fiercely. "You actually figure this pup can handle that kind of responsibility?"

"I figure he can," Buck replied evenly.

"And you're gonna *pay* him for it?"

"Pay him the same as any other muleskinner, sixty a month and enough work to make an old man out of him before he's thirty."

Nate snorted. "Sixty a month? That's top-hand wages, Buck. Ain't you watched this boy work?"

Rossy's gaze rose to meet his father's, his eyes swimming with confusion.

"Yeah, I've watched him," Buck said. "That's why I offered him the job."

"And you figure the other drivers won't quit when they hear how much you're payin' him?"

Buck grinned. "Naw, I don't think they'll quit. You all right with this, Nate?"

Now it was Nate's turn to smile. He looked at his son with a warmth Buck found oddly disconcerting. Mase had never looked at him that way, not even when he was a peach-cheeked kid learning the ropes. Of course, Mase hadn't been his father.

"What about it, Roscoe?" Nate asked. "You want this job, or do you intend to ride your daddy's coattails the rest of your days?"

"I want the job, if you can get along without me," Rossy said, hope glimmering in his eyes.

Nate clamped a large, work-scarred hand affectionately on his boy's shoulder. "Oh, I reckon I can muddle along. Might have to do what I was doin' before you was hatched, like what everybody else around here does day in and day out without a pup gettin' underfoot every time he turns around."

"Go get that coach hitched," Buck said, laughing when Rossy hobbled off with a boyish yell, his limp barely slowing him.

"No fancy stuff!" Nate hollered after him. "You're a Box K man now, and Box K men's got no need for showin' off." Nate sighed and looked at Buck. "It's kind of discombobulatin' to see your boy runnin' off after his first full-payin' job. Makes a man feel old and creaky."

"I reckon you've got another trip or two left in you," Buck said, slapping the larger man's shoulder fondly before moving away.

Despite their troubles with the wind-skittish mules, the caravan got under way without trouble. It didn't hurt, Buck supposed, that both mules and men were nearly worn out after their long ordeal with the Bonner gang.

It was just past 4:00 A.M. when the train jolted back onto the Montana Road. The wind was at their backs now, but no less annoying. Buck kept the train rolling until noon, then called the midday halt. To the north, the distant peaks of the Rocky Mountains were clearly visible, their flanks dark with pines, their rounded summits capped with snow. From here, the mountains didn't look all that intimidating, but that dull-toothed range was the backbone of the Rockies, the Continental Divide, and the Box K was going straight over the top. A heavy storm of either rain or snow could make the climb grueling—or stop them cold.

Buck had put Arlen Fleck on top of the mud wagon with Rossy, with the promise that he'd kill the scruffy outlaw slowly and painfully if he so much as harbored a thought of harming the boy or escaping.

Arlen had laughed at the seriousness of Buck's tone. "Right now all I want is to live long enough to get back to civilization," he'd assured the wagon master.

Now, while the muleskinners lounged beside their wagons and the remuda spread out to graze under the watchful eyes of several armed guards, Buck tramped back to where Arlen was still perched on top of the mud wagon. The bandit held up his manacled wrists as Buck approached, rattling the short length of chain that secured the cuffs to the seat's low, iron railing. "You boys surprised me!" he called. "I didn't know mule trains carried their own shackles."

Buck stepped up on the front hub to free the chain's padlock. "Get down," he ordered.

Arlen climbed over the side of the box and dropped to the ground. Leading him to the lee of the coach, Buck handed him some bread and bacon and a canteen of water. Arlen studied him curiously as he settled, cross-legged, beside the front wheel. "You ain't gonna hang me, are you? Jones said you would."

"Ray Jones would. I haven't made up my mind yet."

"Maybe we can make us a deal, McCready. I tell you what you want to know and you let me go?"

"How about this? You tell me what I want to know and I won't turn Ray and Mitch loose on you tonight. You've heard of

Mitch Kroll, haven't you?"

"Yeah, I've heard of him. That the big fella that rode in with us?"

"That's him."

"I didn't know he drove for the Box K, but I don't guess it matters. Dead's pretty much dead. It don't much scare me no more."

"One of your bunch killed Mitch's nephew the other night and he wants you to pay for it."

Arlen shrugged as if it didn't matter, but Buck could tell that he was wavering. "I didn't kill anyone," Arlen said quietly, staring at the ground. "I didn't even fire my pistol."

"I doubt if that'd matter to Mitch."

Arlen's shoulders slumped. "All right, what do you want to know? I already told you I didn't see who killed Campbell."

"It ain't Mase I'm asking about," Buck said, squatting on his heels a few feet away. "It's something you said yesterday, about Mexico."

Arlen nodded warily. "The Chihuahua mutiny?"

"Yeah, tell me about that. Tell me everything you know."

They met Lew Walker's returning caravan shortly before noon the next day. The two outfits passed with friendly greetings and good-natured ribbing between the muleskinners, but they didn't stop. In freighting, success was measured in days rather than tonnage, and no train worth its axle grease would stop without good cause.

Lew was a large man with broad shoulders and a horseman's narrow waist and hips. He was in his sixties now, but he was still as quick and tough as a cougar. Breaking away from his caravan, he met Buck in the sage beside the road, his expression sympathetic as he shook the younger man's hand. "I'm sorry as hell about Mase," Lew said. "I reckon he was pretty much a pa to you."

"Pretty much," Buck agreed, although it wasn't Mase who came to mind with Lew's use of the word pa, but the easy interaction between Nate and Rossy.

"It had to be a rotten scoundrel who shot him," Lew opined, his voice roughening. "You ever find the son-of-a-bitch, you let me know and I'll help you kill him."

Buck nodded politely even as he was eyeing Lew's returning wagons. "What have they got for us in Montana?"

"I'm hauling lumber and rough-grade ore. I told Fred Sweeny you'd be along in another week or so, looking for a load to haul south. He said he'd put something together for you."

"What's the road like?"

"She's rough as a cob going over Monida. It was all right northbound, but we pulled a lot of mud on the way back." He glanced behind him at the sky. "I'm thinking it's puckering up to storm. That'll mean snow in the high country, and, cold as it is up there right now, it could dump a heap of it."

It was late April, but Buck had seen it snow in Virginia City in June more than once. "Well, I reckon it'll do what it does," Buck said philosophically. The caravans had passed each other now, leaving the two captains alone with just the blowing wind for company. Pulling Zeke's head out of a clump of grass, Buck added: "Have a safe trip, Lew. I'll see you on the way back."

"Buck. . . ." The older man's nostrils flared above his mustache. "You watch yourself, boy, watch your back. The whole damn' road's heard about the trouble you're having, and whoever's doing it, whoever killed Mase, they won't hesitate to do the same to you. They're running out of time and they know it."

"We're watching," Buck assured him. "All the boys are."

"Good," Lew said gruffly. He thrust out a hand and they

shook farewell, parting without further conversation. It would be like that the next time they met, too—a few shared words, then back to their jobs. They'd do that three or four times a year, before winter shut them down for the season.

Buck loped after his own caravan, swinging wide through the sage to avoid the dust that billowed from the wagons' massive wheels. The dust would have been nearly intolerable if not for the wind that swept it away, although Buck figured most of the crew would have preferred the fine grit of the road to the buffeting zephyrs that had been pummeling them the past couple of days.

Monida Pass lay starkly before them, their last major hurdle. After that, it would all be downhill, five more days into Virginia City—assuming the weather held. As the train entered the broad mouth of Monida Cañon, Buck thought it didn't look very promising. Twisting in his saddle, he motioned Milo up beside him. "Grab some supplies and ride ahead. I want to know how much of a lead Crowley and Luce have on us."

"Hell, they've got a good twenty-four hours on us," Milo said.

"They might've slowed down after they passed us the other day. I want to know exactly where they are."

When Milo was gone, Buck shucked his jacket and laid it across his saddlebows. It was less than half a mile inside the cañon when the walls abruptly narrowed, rising higher and steeper on either side. The road ran alongside a creek, crossing it from time to time, but even in the midst of spring run-off, its waters were neither deep nor threatening. The temperature inside the cañon was pleasant, the winds calm after the high desert tempest they'd left behind, but, after only a couple of hours, the thin, blue band of sky that ran a serpentine path above them began to dull. Clouds the color of dirty laundry water rolled in, and the air turned heavy and moist. It was warm, but Buck knew that wouldn't last. Riding back to Peewee's side, he ordered the muleskinner to pick up the pace. "We're pulling on borrowed time now," he said.

Peewee shot him a worried look, but that was all. As Buck jogged back to his usual spot a hundred yards in front of the train, he heard the muleskinner's whip popping loudly, urging his animals on at a quickened gait.

They were barely halfway up the cañon when night fell. Retrieving a lantern from the mess wagon, Buck took a position just in front of Peewee's leaders, guiding the mules with its light. In the darkness along the cañon floor, no one could make out much, but the muleskinners trusted their mules and the mules followed the trailers in front of them without fear. Buck kept them at it until midnight before he called a halt.

The men cared for their stock, then retreated to their separate messes, already grumbling about the late hour and the early dawn to follow. Buck found Peewee, Ray, Charlie, and Joe at the first mess. "If we can get on top by noon tomorrow, we ought to make Red Rock Creek by dark. The trail will drop pretty quick after that."

"That's a hell of a climb to make by noon," Charlie rebutted, his expression sullen.

"It can be done," Buck said. "The sooner we get over the top, the better our odds of not getting snowed in. Even a few hours can make a difference this time of year."

Peewee cleared his throat hesitantly. "Fact is, some of us been talkin', Buck, and we're thinkin' that pushin' like we're doin' is gonna hurt our teams. You got to remember that most of these mules was run hard by Bonner's men and never was given time to recover from that."

"No one's reporting a lame mule," Buck pointed out.

"It ain't what's happened so far that's worryin' us," Ray said. "It's what's gonna happen if we don't slow the hell down. What we done today would've been too much on level ground, and this sure as shit ain't level. Keep this up and we'll have mules turning gimpy before we ever reach the top."

"I don't think so," Buck replied, struggling to keep his tone nonconfrontational. "The stock can take some pushing."

Peewee and Ray exchanged frustrated glances, and Joe said: "Buck, ain't nobody going to hold our losing this race against you. Hell, we all know what happened. Most outfits would've still been stranded back there, after having their stock run off like we did. You've done everything Mase could've done and more."

Buck's gaze narrowed dangerously above the dancing flames of the fire. "I ain't Mase, Joe," he said evenly, "and I intend to get this train through on schedule. We may not beat Crowley and Luce any more, but I plan to be scraping the mud off their hind wheels when we roll into Virginia City."

An uneasy silence greeted Buck's blunt reply. He didn't think any of the men were expecting it. Before anyone could respond, a gust of wind swept down the cañon, flattening their fire and stirring up a litter of ash. Holding out his hand, Buck felt a drop of rain glance off his thumb. He could hear it behind him, too, pattering lightly against the wagon canvas like mice in the attic. Lowering his hand, he said: "It's raining, gents, and, like as not, it'll be snowing by dawn. I'd suggest you eat your suppers and go to bed. We're going to need all the strength we have before this is over."

Chapter Thirty

Hawley City sat draped across the rocky brow of a low hill like a fallen flag. It was surrounded on three sides by thick forest, and to the west by a timbered mountain range still blanketed in snow. Despite its designation as a "city," Hawley was little more than an overgrown mining camp. Most of its dozen or so businesses were constructed of canvas tenting rather than lumber, and its single street seemed to meander with no more forethought than that of a wandering beetle. Less than twenty yards to the north, the once pristine Pine Creek was lined with piles of earthen rubble, its water thick with silt.

Guiding his horse down the middle of the street, Nick Kelso marveled at the miners swarming over their gravel heaps like frenzied ants, every damned one of them convinced that this would be their last season scraping their knuckles raw in icy streams. And every damned one of them a first-class fool, Nick thought. He knew their luck would never change. Born dumb, they would die the same way, still gullibly believing that one more season would see them rich beyond their wildest dreams.

Nick had given up on such fantasies years ago, knowing that a wise man made his own luck—or took it from others weaker than him.

Swinging down in front of the Nugget Saloon, he wrapped his reins around a crooked pine rail, then unbuttoned his coat to free access to his revolver. The Nugget was constructed of unpeeled logs, its sod roof grown over with grass and weeds that were being whipped about in the wind. There were no windows, but the lamplight that spilled past the propped-open front door looked inviting in the gathering dusk. Nick glanced briefly at the dark, turbulent clouds building up in the northwest and was glad he'd made it in tonight. He hadn't been looking forward to another desolate camp alone on the high desert.

Inside, he ordered a bottle of whiskey, then went in search of a place to drink it. He found a table in back that seemed barely sturdy enough to support the bottle, then sank into a chair that didn't feel much stronger. A hungry gleam came into his eyes as he poured his first shot, and, for a moment, all seemed right. Then the image of Jim Bonner rose in his mind and Nick's mood plummeted. He threw the drink against the back of his throat. "By God," he rasped, glaring at the scarred table top, "I'll kill that son-of-a-bitch the next time I see him."

Arlen Fleck's face swam before his mind's eye, too, and the almost disdainful cast of the runt's weasel-thin face as Nick rode out of the raiders' camp made his blood boil. By God, there was another one he would look forward to killing.

Nick slumped back in his chair, envisioning the look of surprise on Fleck's face when his bullet drilled between the scrawny man's eyes. Nick was still musing on the subject an hour later when a slope-shouldered whore with thin blonde hair approached his table.

"Hidy, honey," she said, pulling out a chair and sitting down. She was skinny as a bean pole and none too pretty, but Nick still might have been interested if she hadn't just come from the side of a curly-haired buck in tattered clothes.

"What's the matter?" he growled. "That dirt-grubbing tin pan too broke to afford you?"

She glanced at the young miner and shrugged. "His charms is lacking," she allowed, "although he promised that, if I let him have a free one tonight, he'd pay me double as soon as his claim started paying off."

That struck Nick as funny and he laughed along with the whore at the curly-haired youth's innocence. The boy looked their way as if he suspected they were talking about him, and Nick raised his whiskey in a taunting salute, causing the kid's face to flush.

"The world is full of idjits," the whore said offhandedly, eyeing Nick's bottle. Its level had dropped noticeably since he'd started drinking. "You wanna share a sip with a lady?" she asked.

"First, you pay," Nick replied, grinning brashly.

The whore's eyes flashed white-hot. "I ain't buyin' no damn' drink when they's plenty around who'd give me one for free."

"It's just business, sweetheart," he said. "Like the business you and I are going to conduct in a couple of minutes."

Her expression softened. "I ain't cheap," she confided, "on account of I'm the prettiest one here."

"The prettiest what here?" Nick asked, toying with her.

That flash in her eyes again, like miniature daggers. "You looking to get my goat, mister?"

"Like I said, it's just business. You're a whore and I'm a man in need, but I'm not desperate. I'll give you two-bits for a roll on whatever you call a mattress in this shithole of a town, providing you take a bath first."

The blonde woman's mouth fell open, but only for a moment. Then it snapped shut and her face turned ugly. "You're a bastard," she hissed. "I wouldn't sleep with you for all the gold in Idaho. I'll bet your. . . ." Her voice caught in her throat and her face paled. She stood up and took a step backward as Nick casually laid a long-bladed clasp knife on the table; its steel blade flicked open with his thumb.

"One thing about a whore," Nick stated matter-of-factly. "No matter how bad she looks, she can always be made to look worse."

The woman lifted her chin defiantly, then spun and stalked back to the bar. Nick wasn't surprised when she walked straight to the curly-haired kid's side and started running her hand up and down his arm. Leaning close, she whispered in the boy's ear. Nick folded his knife and put it away, feeling a keen anticipation for what was to come.

The kid glanced uncertainly over his shoulder and Nick grinned cockily to encourage him. The whore was leaning into him now, her lips moving rapidly against his ear. The boy shook his head and the whore pressed closer, flattening a breast against his arm. He shuddered, then turned to face Nick. Down the bar, a bearded miner said: "Let it go, Curly." But the boy shook his head. "It's too late for that, Dan."

There was a triumphant smile on the whore's face as she sloped back against the bar. Nick noticed a small, brass-framed revolver in the kid's waistband, but nothing intimidating. Curly crossed the room hesitantly, stopping at Nick's table. "Mandy says you insulted her," he announced, loud enough for the whole room to hear.

"What about my insult to Mandy upsets you?" Nick asked in amusement.

That seemed to stump the boy. "Well . . . I think you ought to apologize to her."

"Aw, hell, Curly," said another miner, sitting at a nearby table. "Don't go getting yourself shot over a whore."

"She ain't a whore," Curly flared.

General laughter greeted the youth's outburst; even Mandy snickered, and Curly's face darkened. "Well, I reckon you'd better apologize anyway," he said to Nick.

"I reckon not," Nick replied.

Curly swallowed hard and looked around as if for suggestions. Everyone was watching, fearful of what he'd do. "I ain't afraid of you," he told Nick finally, although there wasn't much conviction in his words. "I just think you should. . . ."

Nick stood abruptly, kicking his chair back, and Curly flinched as if threatened with a whipping.

"Easy, mister," said the miner at the next table. "He's just a kid. He doesn't know any better."

"Maybe he ought to go back home until he does," Nick suggested.

"Likely he should, but it ain't worth spilling blood over."

"It's his call now," Nick returned coldly, staring the kid in the eyes.

"I . . . I got no quarrel with you," Curly choked out, looking more confused than frightened.

"Don't let him buffalo you, Curly!" Mandy called, and several men nearby growled for her to shut up.

"Jesus, mister," Curly said, "I didn't cause you no harm."

The kid was desperate to escape the corner he'd backed himself into, but Nick had no intention of letting him go. His pulse was thundering in his ears and his voice was raw with shame. "I'll tell you what, Bonner, I've about had a gut full of your kind. Maybe it's time I taught you a lesson."

Curly carefully raised his hands. "My name ain't Bonner, mister, and I don't want no trouble. I swear I don't."

Nick shook his head to clear it. "If you didn't want any trouble, you wouldn't be standing there," he snarled, but he was aggravated, too, for having let his feelings toward Bonner get the better of him for a moment. "If you want to leave, it's going to cost you," he added.

"Sure," Curly whispered, looking relieved. "How much?"

"Get down on your belly and crawl out that front door like a snake."

For a moment, the kid didn't seem to understand. Then he slowly shook his head. "I can't do that, mister. I'd rather be dead."

"Lay off the boy," the bearded miner said angrily.

"You want to take his place?" Nick snapped, but continued to stare at Curly. "What about it, boy? Are you going to pull that hogleg or crawl out of here on your . . . ?"

Nick shut up abruptly as Curly started to sway back and forth. He jerked his Colt free but didn't cock it. Curly's face had turned as pale as whey, and his eyes did a slow roll up under his lids. Then his knees buckled and he tipped stiffly backward, hitting the floor flush and sending little puffs of dirt squirting out on either side.

At the bar, Mandy screamed: *"You killed him!"*

"God damn," the bearded miner breathed, wide-eyed. "Curly done had a heart attack."

"He didn't have a heart attack," the miner at the table answered scornfully. "He passed out."

Nick straightened, returning the Colt to its cradle. "Well I'll be damned," he said softly. "I scared the boy witless."

The two miners came forward. One of them said: "We're going to take him back to his claim unless you want to go ahead and shoot him."

"Get him out of here," Nick said, pulling his chair back and sitting down. He looked at Mandy and smiled wickedly, and she turned away with an angry motion.

The two miners didn't return, but the crowd inside the Nugget grew larger and noisier as darkness fell. Nick felt good after his encounter with the kid, whole again, a man to be reckoned with. He figured the wide berth the citizens of Hawley City were giving him was proof enough of that. His exuberance was still running high several hours later when a trio of buckskin-clad men entered the Nugget. Nick didn't know their names, but he recognized all of them. They were members of Bonner's gang, and two of them were sporting bloody bandages.

Nick stood and tugged his hat low over his eyes. Something

must have gone wrong, he thought, otherwise these three would be on their way to Boise Camp with Jim Bonner and the Box K remuda.

"Sons-of-bitches," Nick muttered as he made his roundabout way to the front door. With the three mule thieves entrenched at the bar, Nick thought he was going to make his escape undetected, but he'd barely stepped through the door when he bumped into a tall, heavy-gutted man in leather clothing, smelling of grease and blood.

"You!" the man grunted, clamping a hand firmly on Nick's shoulder. "You double-crossin' bastard, you led 'em straight to our camp."

"I didn't lead anyone anywhere," Nick protested, but the towering mountain man was shaking him like a dog shook a rabbit, and the words came out choppy and hard to understand.

"Let's go," the big man said, shoving Nick toward the door. "The boys'll want. . . ."

The sound of Nick's revolver was muffled against the outlaw's belly. The big man staggered backward, wrapping his arms around his protruding gut, then slumped to his knees with a disbelieving curse. Nick stepped quickly past him and ran to his horse, glad that he'd neglected the animal earlier, that his saddle was still cinched tightly in place. He vaulted astride the horse just as a couple of Bonner's men burst from the saloon, their pistols drawn.

"It's Kelso," the man on the ground groaned. "He's killed me."

Nick slammed two rounds into the saloon's log wall, showering the raiders with splinters and loose bark. Then he gouged his spurs into his mount's sides, racing down the crooked street heading east, the way he'd come in. Between the tall pines flanking the roadway and the gathering storm clouds, the darkness was nearly complete, and the raiders' bullets flew past harmlessly.

Nick knew he'd made a mistake by not putting a second round into the gut-shot outlaw's head. Now he'd been identified, everyone knew his name, and word of what he'd done—even if it had been unintentional—would spread quickly. He would have to leave the mountains for good now, there was no way around that, but before he did, there was one last chore he intended to take care of. It waited for him along the road to Montana, and this time it was personal.

Chapter Thirty-One

No one was surprised when the rain changed to snow overnight. By the time the crew wiggled out of their bedrolls the next morning there were several inches on the ground, and more was falling. Buck could hear it in the inky blackness before dawn, the big, wet flakes striking the snow already on the ground with a gentle hiss. The storm muted the rattle of chains, softened the disgruntled curses of the muleskinners as they dug their harness from under its wintery blanket.

Buck rode down the line of wagons to where Dulce and Gwen were standing close to a lantern that hung off a dead branch on a tree beside the road. Their horses were saddled and waiting, snow already powdering the hard leather seats. Arlen was in place as well, his manacled wrists connected to the seat's railing with a length of chain. He was holding a blanket over his shoulders in lieu of a winter coat, and his porkpie hat was tugged low to cover the tips of his ears. All three looked miserable in the unexpected cold.

Rossy, by contrast, looked comfortable inside a bear-hide coat with the hair still on. Sturdy wool gloves with leather palms protected his hands. He was standing beside the mud wagon's rear boot when Buck rode past and made a motion with his brows that Buck acknowledged with a small nod.

"Buck!" Dulce exclaimed as he walked his mule into the lantern's light. She and Gwen were huddled close to the yellow glow as if it were a roaring blaze of warmth and security. "Can we travel in this weather?" she asked.

"We'll make it," he said, then looked around. "Where's Collins?"

"I assume he's up front somewhere," Gwen said. "He wasn't here when we awoke. Fortunately Mister Evans was kind enough to strike our tent for us this morning."

Buck glanced at Rossy. The youth was staring back with an intensity that spoke loudly in the suddenly charged air. "We're going on," Buck told the women as he reined his mule away from the lantern's light. "There's not enough room in this cañon to turn around even if we wanted to." Riding over to where Rossy waited patiently, Buck mouthed: "What's wrong?"

"Over here," Rossy said quietly. He led Buck to the far side of the mud wagon, where an oblong bundle wrapped in wagon sheeting rested in the snow. Noting the obvious contours, Buck dismounted with a hollow feeling in the pit of his stomach. "Collins?" he asked.

Rossy nodded somberly. "He was stabbed in the throat."

"When?"

The young man shrugged. "I found him this morning. He was already cold and covered with snow, so I figure he's been dead a while. Weren't no tracks I could find, either."

Squatting on the balls of his feet, Buck tugged the canvas back. Collins's face looked nearly as white as the snow surrounding it, the deep puncture in his neck a funnel of raw meat, as if whoever had done it had worked the knife around a bit. There were no signs of a struggle. Letting the canvas fall back over the dead man's face, Buck said: "Who else knows about this?"

"Just Fleck. I had him help me wrap the body."

"Your dad?"

"No, sir."

"Let's keep it that way. We've got a hard day ahead of us,

then some more hard days to come. Another killing won't help us."

"The women'll know," Rossy reminded him. "The crew doesn't come back here very often and might not miss him for a few days, but Miss Kavanaugh and Miss Haywood will know soon as we stop tonight."

"I'll tie Collins's horse behind Peewee's outfit and tell the crew he's got a bad case of the trots. That'll keep them away. I'll tell Dulce and Gwen that I sent him ahead to scout the trail until Milo gets back."

"That's a pretty flimsy lie," Rossy commented.

"I know, but I still think the fewer people who know about this, the better the odds of whoever did it tipping his hand."

Although Rossy nodded dutifully, he didn't look convinced.

"Let's put him in the boot," Buck said. "Cold as it is, we could probably haul him all the way to Virginia City if we had to."

It wasn't hard to slip the body under the black leather cover at the rear of the mud wagon. Only Gwen's wall tent and heavy oriental rug competed for space with the corpse. Buckling the leather cover in place, Buck said: "You got a gun, Rossy?"

"Ain't got a pistol, but I got an old Sharps that shoots paper cartridges."

"Is it loaded?"

"It will be."

Buck handed the younger man Collins's revolver. "Keep this hid but handy, and keep an eye on the women. I don't want any harm coming to them."

"I reckon I'll be keeping a damn' close eye on all three of us," Rossy promised.

It continued to snow heavily as the caravan snaked its way toward the distant summit. Although Buck kept the wagons moving steadily—and they were making excellent time considering the conditions—he couldn't shake the hollow feeling he'd gotten that morning when Rossy showed him Collins's body. There was a killer among them, and he was showing far too much interest in the women. What was their connection to this race between the Box K and Crowley and Luce?

Or was there one?

Sensing his rider's agitation, Zeke began to forge ahead. Soon, the train became lost behind veils of falling snow, leaving man and animal alone in an ever-shrinking world of white. It was several hours later before Buck finally checked the mule's progress. The narrow avenue he followed continued its upward climb, but the familiar landmarks were hidden beneath a mantle of snow, so that he wasn't sure how far he'd come or how far he had yet to go. He was about to turn back when movement on the trail ahead caught his eye. He eased a gloved hand back to the butt of his Colt, then relaxed. It was Milo coming toward him, the spotted molly lifting her hoofs high above the snow.

"Hey, boss!" Milo called as he drew near. He looked half frozen in just his thin buckskin jacket. His nose was red, his fingers white where they gripped the reins.

"Didn't you take along any heavy clothing?"

Milo gave him a peeved look. "Sure, but I loaned it to a frostbit jack rabbit a while back and ain't had time to shop for something new."

Buck smiled and let it drop. "Did you find C and L?"

"I saw them from a distance, already starting down the far side but moving slow in this mess."

"You've been over the top?"

"Uhn-huh, a couple of hours ago." His expression was serious. "It doesn't look good. The snow's already a foot deep on top and still coming down." He glanced at the road behind Buck. "They're probably a mile or so back yet. Damn," he said softly, shaking his head. "That's too far."

"We'll make it," Buck replied, unwilling to contemplate anything less. "Does C and L know we're behind them?"

"I don't think so. They aren't pushing very hard if they do."

Buck's enthusiasm stirred for the first time in days. By God, it was about time *something* went in their favor. He began unbuttoning his heavy coat. "I want you to go back and keep an eye on C and L for as long as you can. We ought to be on top before dark, maybe started down the other side a little way. Take my coat, but, unless something happens, plan on being back at the wagons by nightfall."

"You just keep that coat," Milo said as if insulted. He pulled his molly around and started back along the track he'd made coming down.

"Dang it, take the coat!" Buck called. "Don't be stubborn."

"It's not so much being stubborn," Milo flung back with a grin, "as that I figure any man damn' fool enough to ride out without his coat ought to be damn' fool enough to finish the job that way."

"You're gonna freeze your ears off!" Buck shouted.

Milo's reply was muted by the falling snow. "It's not my ears I'm worrying about. It's not my fingers or my toes, either. It's my. . . ." But his words were lost in a sudden gust of wind, and sheets of snow whipped across the road between them. When it settled, Milo was no longer in sight.

There was still some daylight left when the train reached the top of Monida Pass. The snow had continued falling throughout the afternoon—nearly eighteen inches since midnight, on top of what was still there from last winter—but the wind was calm and they had that to be thankful for. Drifting snow would have put an end to travel for days.

With the wagons on level ground, Buck ordered a halt, then

went back to check on Rossy. He was aware of the dark looks the men gave him as he rode past. They were concerned about the weakening condition of their stock, and Buck couldn't fault them for it. The mules were suffering, their muzzles hanging low, their long ears at half mast.

Rossy was standing beside his nigh-leader when Buck came up. Arlen was still in his seat, his shoulders hunched under a frosted blanket. Gwen and Dulce sat their horses close together in the caravans' snowy wake, several rods behind the coach. Buck averted his eyes from their tired stares. Gwen looked pitiful with the shadowed flesh under her eyes and her chapped lips, but Dulce had the appearance of someone in search of a fresh scalp, and Buck tugged his hat down a little tighter before turning his full attention to Rossy. "Everything all right on this end?" he asked.

"Right as rain."

"How's your prisoner holding up?"

"He's been quiet. I think he's too cold to cause trouble."

Buck studied Arlen thoughtfully. "If we turned you loose, do you reckon you could stay close and not try to escape?"

Arlen shrugged. "Where would I go?"

"If it's anywhere other than where Rossy tells you to go, I'll turn you over to Mitch and Ray."

Arlen smiled faintly but made no reply.

"Take the manacles off him," Buck told Rossy. "Let him help with the chores. He might as well earn his keep."

"He won't be any trouble," Rossy said.

"Don't let him slicker you," Buck cautioned. "If he tries anything shady, shoot him. He ain't worth getting hurt over."

Buck reined around without addressing the women and rode back to the front of the column. He grew puzzled as he passed the teams standing alone in harness, but located their drivers a few minutes later alongside Peewee's rig. Even from several outfits away, Buck could tell there was trouble brewing. His fingers strayed to Mase's fancy bullwhip, fastened to his belt, then he deliberately forced the hand away. This was his train. He would handle whatever problems came up in his own way.

The teamsters fell silent as Buck reined to a halt. "What's going on?" he demanded.

"It ain't what's going on, Buck, it's what ain't going on, and that's us," Andy LeMay said, his jaw thrust stubbornly forward.

"They got a peek at what's in front of us," Peewee added sheepishly, as if it might somehow be his fault the road ahead looked so ominous.

Buck eyed the rugged terrain to the north, falling away in eggshell folds. The road they would follow wound through the lowering mountains like a thin white thread dropped from above, before it disappeared into the foggy distance. A solid gray blanket of clouds hung low over them, and a light snow continued to fall. "What's the trouble?" he asked. "Everyone here's hauled over worse roads than this."

"Not if we didn't have to," Lou Kitledge countered. "And we don't have to do this, Buck. We can sit this storm out right here."

"Like hell we can," Buck replied irritably. "Without graze, the mules'll starve down to hide and bone in a couple of days."

"They'll die in harness if we keep pushing them like we have been," Andy fired back.

"Our mules are in a bad way, Buck," Lou added. "They're cold and footsore, and they need rest." His voice roughened with anger. "God damn, we all do!"

Buck's breath thinned to a cold hiss as a rumble of discontent spread through the teamsters. Was this how it began for Jock, way down on the Chihuahua Trail so many years ago? The stories Buck had heard of that incident had always insisted the weather was crackling hot, worse than anyone could remember, and the water holes had been few and mostly dry. Those that did hold some little moisture had been almost jellied with mud and slime, undrinkable to all but the most desperate.

Cold could work on a man the same way as heat, Buck knew, and they'd been pushing hard this trip. Even more so since Bonner's raid. Bad roads and breakdowns were an expected part of freighting; murder and sabotage weren't.

But that was the hand they'd been dealt, and Buck straightened his shoulders, his eyes flat and hard. "We're going on, and I ain't asking. Milo says Crowley and Luce have slowed down, and that means we stand a chance of catching up. I won't let an opportunity like that pass."

"Catch up!" Lou echoed incredulously. "Buck, we ain't gonna get off this mountain in one piece the way it is." He scooped up a handful of snow and shook it over his head. "Christ, boy, what do you think this stuff is?"

"We've bulled through deeper snow than this," Buck replied.

"It's awfully wet and heavy, though," Peewee said with that same sheepish look on his face. "I ain't one to give up easy, but maybe the boys are right about this. We gave it a hell of a run, but. . . ." He shrugged. "Maybe it's time we quit chasing what we likely ain't never gonna catch."

Buck kept his expression unchanged, but he felt as if he'd been sucker punched. He hadn't expected this from Peewee. Suddenly he felt betrayed, unsure of himself.

"I ain't goin'!" Lou Kitledge stated firmly. "The hell with catching up!"

"I ain't killin' my mules to satisfy Jock Kavanaugh's greed!" Lyle Mead shouted.

"That's what it'd amount to, too!" Garth Lang cried in response. "I'd lose everything I owned if I lost my outfit."

"Nobody's going to lose their outfits!" Nate hollered, but Lyle quickly retaliated. "What would it matter to a Box K driver if he did? It ain't their money invested in stock and harness and wagons."

"Easy, god dammit!" Ray yelled. "You independents shut up now. This is a Box K problem, not yours."

"The hell it ain't," Lyle and Garth shot back in fiery unison, and Mead added: "Ease off your own god-damn' self, Jones, before you get stomped."

"I'd by God like to see you try," Ray snarled, taking a threatening step forward.

"Jesus," Buck breathed. He drew his Colt and pointed it uncertainly skyward but didn't pull the trigger. Almost immediately the shouting tapered off. "God-dammit!" Buck roared. "God-dammit to hell, I ain't gonna let this happen and I ain't gonna argue about it." He leveled his revolver on the crew. "We're going on, and anyone who refuses. . . ." His words trailed off, and he wondered again: *Was this how it had happened with Jock?* The men of the Chihuahua train had mutinied—no one ever denied that—but Buck had always believed that, once the fighting had been quelled, the leaders of the revolt had been given a choice—keep driving or leave the train. It was Arlen Fleck who'd given him the rest of the story, bringing down everything Buck had believed in like a trip lever on a gallows.

"They weren't given no choice a-tall is what I heard," Arlen had told Buck. "They was kicked out. No food, no water, no guns, and they died hard in that Mexican desert. Two of 'em from thirst, but the third one was captured by Apaches and he must've died hardest of all.

"Only it wasn't Jock Kavanaugh who turned 'em loose," Arlen had added almost as an afterthought. "It was Mase Campbell."

Buck had grabbed the smaller man's lapels in a blinding rage, but Arlen had lost his fear with the Bonner gang and nothing Buck threatened fazed him.

"I wasn't there, McCready," Fleck had said when Buck let

him go. He brushed his coat with his hands, straightening the lapels. "I couldn't say what really happened. That's just the story I heard that night in the International after Campbell walked in drunk. It was Campbell who turned them teamsters loose without any way of protecting themselves. Killed 'em same as if he'd hung 'em. Maybe he wasn't that poison-hearted when you knew him, but he must've been a hell-roaring son-of-a-bitch when he was younger."

Buck knew the story was true. For years he'd sensed that there was more to the tale than anyone had been willing to tell him. Now he knew why. It wasn't Jock who turned them loose, it was Mase Campbell.

And now, thirty years later, Buck was facing the same hard choice. Could he kill a man just to keep the Box K rolling? Would he? Milo had said of Mase—*Was never a train Mason Campbell didn't get through, never a cargo he lost.*—but Buck knew he wasn't cut from the same bolt of cloth. He couldn't go that far, not for a wagonload of mining machinery. Quietly he returned the pistol to its holster.

"Buck," Peewee said gently.

"It's all right." Looking at the rest of the crew, he said: "If that's the way everyone feels. . . ."

"Put runners on the wagons."

Buck twisted in his saddle, surprised to find Rossy Evans tramping forward in snow past his knees.

"Runners?" Peewee repeated thoughtfully.

"Turning these wagons into sleds'd take us two days or more," Ray said. "It'd be a fair idea in a different situation, Roscoe, but it won't work here."

"We wouldn't have to put runners on all the wagons," Rossy insisted. "Put them on one or two and let those wagons break trail for the rest."

A short silence followed, then Ray said: "Well, I'll be damned."

"We could put 'em on my two wagons," Peewee volunteered. "That'd be enough to pack the snow down for the rest of the column."

"We could double hitch if we had to," Buck added, warming to the idea. "Switch off teams so that no one bunch has to do all the work."

There was a growing excitement among the men as Rossy's suggestion began to take shape. Buck felt it himself—the thrill of the chase, a contest not yet lost. He straightened in his saddle. "Ray, take a couple of men and cut down four stout pines we can use for runners. Get 'em shucked and slicked down as quick as you can, then get 'em back here. Use a couple of Rossy's mules to drag them in.

"Peewee, pick two men to help you pull the wheels off your wagons. I want both those rigs sitting on jacks when Ray gets back. Nate, take half a dozen men and split them into two groups to look after the mules. Feed 'em what grain we've got left, then let 'em bed down wherever they can. Look after every man's team tonight as if it's your own. This ain't a time to stand on tradition."

"I don't want anyone but me taking care of my mules," Lyle Mead said sullenly.

Buck shrugged indifferently. "All right, steer clear of Lyle's hitch but take care of the others. Lou, Andy, rustle up some firewood. The women'll do the cooking, but you two keep a fire burning for them. Keep it hot for the rest of us, too. It's going to get cold when the sun goes down and we've got a long night ahead of us."

"*Yeeeehaw!*" Ray yelled, startling the men standing closest to him. He yanked his hat off and slapped it against his thigh, his shiny pate gleaming in the weak afternoon light. "By damn, the ol' Box K's gonna make history tomorrow, boys! They's gonna be talkin' about this when we're all old and toothless and the only thing we're skinnin' is rockin' chairs."

Several of the men whooped loudly. Even Big Kona had a large grin plastered across his normally stoic face. Hardly able to believe the sudden turn of events, Buck shouted: "Let's go! We're running out of daylight, and I want those runners in place before the sun sets."

Chapter Thirty-Two

It was a couple of hours after dark before they finished fitting the last adz-shaped trunk into place, but the delay wasn't a concern for Buck. It was enough that, for the first time since leaving Corinne, the crew was working together as a real team.

They ate in shifts around a single, large fire rather than at separate messes, and slept that way, too, wrapping up in their bedrolls in the back of whatever wagon had room for them. It was bitterly cold and no one got much rest, but they managed the best they could and not a man or woman complained.

Only Buck shunned his blankets that night, pushing himself relentlessly as the hours slid past. No one mentioned Thad Collins, but Buck knew Dulce and Gwen were wondering about him. Dulce, in particular, was starting to look concerned, and Buck wondered if she had struck up a friendship with the bodyguard during the long trek north. He supposed it was inevitable that Dulce would be drawn to Gwen's party, no matter what her personal feelings were toward the other woman. Dulce's world had been centered at the rear of the train, the mud wagon its nucleus; Buck's had been up front, a gap measured in more than just mules and wagons.

The snow stopped falling shortly after sundown, and in the west and northwest the clouds began to break apart. Stars appeared in the crevices, and the moon's waxen light bathed the far-off hills. More than twenty inches of fresh powder had fallen that day, but that wasn't going to be enough to stop them. Not with runners on the two lead wagons to pack down the worst of it.

It was after midnight when Peewee rose from his blankets to find Buck squatting on his heels beside the fire, a cup of cold coffee in his hand. "You gonna try to get some sleep tonight?" Peewee asked.

Staring into the lowering flames, Buck said: "You knew about Mase all along, didn't you?"

"What do you mean?"

"That he was the one who turned out those men in Mexico."

Peewee sighed. "Who told you?"

"Arlen Fleck."

"Fleck? What's he know about it?"

"He didn't have anything to gain by lying," Buck pointed out.

"Aw, hell, nobody wanted to lie, Buck, but you just wouldn't listen. Not the first little bit. Someone spoke ill of Mase and you'd jump in with both fists swingin'. Besides, Mase changed after he pulled you outta that Sioux camp. Taking you under his wing kinda mellowed him. He was a better man for it, too, you ask me."

"Fleck said he was a hell-roaring son-of-a-bitch."

"Well, he was that when he was younger." Peewee chuckled in memory. "There won't ever be another like him, that's sure."

"Sally Hayes said he was rough with women, that he liked to. . . ." Buck let the rest of what he was going to say die.

"Yeah, I've heard that, too," Peewee said, lowering his eyes.

"I didn't believe her when she told me. I never believed any of the bad things I heard about Mase over the years. Now I wonder how the hell I could've been so blind."

"He took you in when you was a runt, Buck, and treated you good, too. I'd say that entitles you to a little blindness."

Buck was silent, thinking. Peewee's words seemed honest

enough, but they didn't put Mase back up on the pedestal that truth had toppled him from. Maybe nothing ever would. Mase had been a cold-blooded killer at one time in his life, and even at his death, among women at least, he'd been a brute of the worst sort. Buck couldn't respect any man who would beat a woman, yet how could he turn his back on what Mase had meant to him before he died? The man who had saved his life, who had cared for him as staunchly as any working man ever could? How could he ever meld two such dissimilar personalities into a single, congruent human being?

Slowly Buck tipped his coffee over the flames, raising a cloud of steam that feathered up into the night. "I'm not sure what I think of Mase any more," he admitted. "It's like a part of him was a stranger I never met, yet I worked with him for most of my life."

"Mase was Mase," Peewee said kindly, "and Buck McCready is Buck McCready. You might've partnered with the man for a good many years, but that don't mean you've got any business knowin' everything there was to know about him. In my opinion, it speaks highly of Mase that he didn't tell you everything, you being just a tadpole when the two of you hooked up. Far as what others say, that don't matter, not as long as you remember the good things he done in his life . . . like goin' after a scared little kid he didn't even know who'd got hisself captured by the Sioux."

Peewee's tone softened. "I reckon it'll take some time for you to sort it all out, but I ain't sure that's a bad thing. Leastways you don't have to do it tonight. Stew on it for a spell. It'll settle into harness soon enough."

Buck smiled. "I reckon that's good advice."

"Sure it is. Why don't you go burrow into your blankets and catch some shut-eye? Sun's gonna be up before you know it."

"We're not going to wait for sunup."

Peewee eyed him suspiciously. "Why not?"

"Because we're going to pull out now."

"Now! Shit, Buck, the men ain't had much sleep and the mules ain't, either. That's gonna rankle some of the boys again. . . . Andy and Lyle, for sure."

Buck looked to where the women were sleeping nearby. Milo was stretched out near them, encased in a heavy buffalo-hide coat and gloves of the same bulky skin, his blankets pulled tightly around him, a wool scarf tied under his chin to protect his ears. He'd come in at dusk looking near death but bringing the news that C&L was stopped less than thirty miles ahead, still in the snow and, as far as he could tell, still unaware that the Box K was closing in on them from the rear.

"I reckon Andy and Lyle will have to get over it," Buck told Peewee. "We're pulling out. Go call levee on the men, then help 'em bring in the mules. I want the outfit rolling inside the hour."

Peewee stared morosely into the fire for another moment, then shook his head and with a quick, harsh bark of laughter, said: "Well, hell, if C and L's that close, let's go get the bastards."

Buck called an hour's halt at sunup to rest the stock and bring up Ray's mules to hitch to Peewee's wagons, sending Peewee's team to the rear of the column to pull Ray's outfit. They continued that way the rest of the day, switching teams regularly and taking more breaks than Buck would have preferred, but still making good time. By nightfall, they'd reached the spot where C&L had waited out the storm. Buck's excitement grew large when he spotted the trail of the C&L outfit in the snow. Not only had the Box K gained significantly on them, but now it was C&L that was breaking trail and wearing out their stock.

"Let's get those runners off," Buck told the men that night. "We'll put 'em in Nate's wagon in case we need them again." He glanced at Milo. "Take Thad Collins's bay and ride after

Crowley and Luce. I want to know how far ahead they are, and your molly's nearly wore out."

Milo nodded dully. His eyes were red-rimmed from lack of sleep, his lips and nose chapped, his face slimmed down to the point of gauntness, but he headed for the remuda without protest. He'd gone only a few steps when he stopped and turned with a puzzled expression. "Where the hell is Collins, anyway?"

Buck glanced at the rest of the crew and knew the cat was out of the bag. "Thad's dead," he replied.

There was a murmur of surprise from the men and a quick gasp from Dulce before she hurried away. Gwen remained beside the fire, her face ashen.

"Naw," Peewee said in disbelief.

"What happened?" Charlie Bigelow asked, looking like a man who'd just walked into a wall he hadn't seen.

Buck told them what he knew, including Rossy's and Arlen's participation in the cover-up. "Whoever cut the straps on Peewee's load at Hampton's Crossing, then tampered with his brakes coming over the Malads, is still with us." Buck's eyes shifted deliberately from man to man, but, if Thad's killer was among them, he didn't give himself away.

"I reckon if you knew who it was . . . ," Little Ed began tentatively.

"If I knew who it was, he'd be in chains," Buck stated resolutely. "It's a hell of a note, but there's nothing we can do except keep our eyes open. I've been saying all along that, sooner or later, he'll trip himself up. I still believe that."

"You said Collins was killed outside the women's tent?" Peewee asked.

Buck nodded. "Yeah, and it's the second time we know of that someone was caught sneaking around their sleeping quarters. From here on into Virginia City, the women will sleep beside the fire . . . one fire that we'll all share. It'll be more crowded than separate messes, but I want every man here keeping an eye on Dulce and Gwen as if they were his own sisters. Understand?"

There was a quick chorus of assents that Buck found gratifying, although he watched closely to see if anyone held back.

"Don't you worry about them gals," Ray said emphatically. "Ain't no one gonna get close to 'em after tonight."

Buck nodded with relief. It was a load off his mind, and it came at the right time. He had a heavy feeling in his gut that the days ahead were going to be some of the most dangerous they'd faced yet. Especially when Crowley and Luce learned how swiftly the Box K was overtaking them.

Buck found Dulce standing alone behind Nate's trailer. Tears tracked her wind-roughened cheeks and her nose was red. He approached tentatively, not sure if he should intrude, or if he even wanted to. Her grief for the tall bodyguard baffled him; he might have expected it from Gwen, but not from Jock Kavanaugh's iron-willed daughter. Dulce, he recalled, hadn't even cried at Mase's funeral.

"Are you all right?" he asked, stopping several feet away.

"Oh, Buck," she whispered, moving awkwardly toward him in the heavy snow.

He met her halfway, wrapping his arms around her and pulling her close. "It's all right," he said gently. "We're going to make it."

She buried her face in his shoulder and wept harder. It was several minutes before her sobs began to lessen. "I am so sorry," she said into his chest. "So very, very sorry."

He frowned in confusion. "You don't have anything to be sorry about, Dulce. It wasn't your fault he was killed."

She leaned back, looking at him. "He died saving us, didn't he?"

"It's possible. I don't guess we'll ever know for sure."

"We might if you'd find his assassin, but you won't, will you?" She sighed heavily. "No more than you'll ever discover who killed your friend, Campbell."

Buck dropped his arms.

"It's not your fault," she hastened to add. "I'm not sure Papa could even solve this riddle."

"Just what are you so angry about, Dulce?"

She met his gaze squarely, her voice harsh. "I am angry about this trip that you brought me on, this dreadful journey that will never end."

"I seem to remember you saying you wanted to go to Montana, that you wanted to experience the same kinds of adventures your mother did when she crossed the plains with your father."

"That was a long time ago," Dulce replied. "Another age. Everything has changed."

"What's changed?" he demanded.

"I no longer have an urge to cross a plain, Buck, and Montana sounds as exciting as a toothache. Is that clear enough for you?"

"Yeah," he replied, taking a step backward. "I reckon it is."

"I want to go home. Take me home."

"Is that all you want?"

"For the moment. I don't know how I'll feel when all this is behind me. We can only wait and see."

"We?"

"Don't make this any harder than it has to be." She folded her arms across her chest, like an iron gate being slammed shut.

"All right," Buck said evenly. "Let's go back to the fire. Gwen's going to need your help with supper."

"You go. I want to be alone for a while."

He shook his head. "Uhn-uh, I want you where we can keep an eye on you."

Dulce's eyes flashed, but the moment passed. "Very well, *Captain* McCready, your wish shall remain my command." She wiped her eyes with the heel of her hand and stepped over the short tongue connecting Nate's lead and trail wagons.

Buck waited until she was gone, then waited a while longer, but whatever emotion he might have expected never materialized.

Buck had worried that news of Collins's death might undermine the crew's new enthusiasm, but instead it seemed to sharpen it. The men gathered around the fire that night, ignoring the muddy ground close to the flames, the cold air that nibbled at their backs. The old-timers with the Box K regaled the independents with tales of the days before the coming of the railroad to the Great Basin, when the giant freighters ruled all of the land.

Little Ed spoke of his adventures freighting out of San Diego, and broke them all up with his account of an encounter with a rattlesnake den that had spewed forth diamondbacks like steam from a teakettle. Even Big Kona stepped tentatively into the conversational waters, relating stories of his years on the big island of Hawaii, where the women went topless and snow never fell.

"Lordy," Ray breathed when the Sandwich Islander finished speaking. "Kona, what's the prospects there for a muleskinner? Could a fella like me find work?"

Kona's response was drowned out by the raucous laughter of the other teamsters. Even Gwen chuckled. It was as if nothing had occurred—neither death nor sabotage—and the road before them lay straight and dry.

Buck stood at the rear of the crowd and marveled at the muleskinners' resilience. Collins's name wasn't mentioned. Neither were Herb Crowley's or Anton Luce's, and the only reference to Nick Kelso came at Arlen's expense, causing the shabby outlaw to duck his head in embarrassment. They stood there, talking and laughing late into the night, then were out of their blankets well before dawn, moving out smartly at first light.

Buck started the morning in his usual position in front of Peewee's leaders, but by midday he'd increased his lead to more than a mile. It was shortly after noon when he spotted his ramrod stretched out on a large rock beside the road, lazily smoking a cigarette. The snow close to the rock had already melted back, and what remained in the road was turning to slush. By this time tomorrow, Buck mused, he would be worrying more about run-off and mud than having a wagon slide off into some snow-hidden gully.

"How's the bed?" Buck asked, reining up a few yards away.

"I'd prefer a feather mattress and a pretty woman," was Milo's quick response.

"What about Crowley and Luce?"

Milo sat up with a thoughtful expression, pushing his hat back on his head. "Why, boss, I don't know who they'd like to sleep with. I was only speaking for myself, you understand?" When Buck's demeanor didn't change, Milo quickly added: "They're about a day ahead of us yet but still taking their time."

"Then they don't know we're here?"

"They don't act like it. They probably figure they were the last ones over Monida Pass."

A smile tugged at the corners of Buck's mouth. This was shaping up better than he'd anticipated. "Maybe we ought not be pushing so hard," he said reflectively.

"I'd think we'd need to catch up as quick as we can. Sooner or later they'll send someone back to have a look. They might be surprised when they learn we're here, but they won't stop to ponder how we did it."

"Our mules couldn't stand a flat-out race into Virginia City, they're too wore out," Buck replied. "I want to close the gap, but not by too much. I think I know a way we might be able to get around them and retake the lead . . . provided we can keep from being discovered too soon."

Chapter Thirty-Three

Buck returned to his place at the head of the column. Peewee's mules were pulling strongly, keeping the long fifth chain taut, and with the Crowley and Luce train breaking trail, they were making good time. Buck estimated they were within fifteen miles of the Franklin, Idaho outfit by the time they stopped that night. Close enough, he decided.

With the weather turning warm, Buck decided they needed to bury Collins. They did so beside the creek where they were camped. Afterward, Dulce wrapped a sheet of paper with some personal information about him in a strip of oilcloth and secured it under a stone at the head of the grave. Watching her back away, Buck was struck with a sudden jolt of understanding. He hadn't seen it before, not even in the tears Dulce had shed when she first learned of Collins's death, but he saw it now and wondered if they had been lovers as well, or if the circumstances of the Box K's race to Montana had robbed them of that opportunity.

He looked around at the crew but couldn't tell if any of them had made the connection. Gwen had; he could see that in the way she was looking at him, although he supposed that didn't surprise him. Not nearly so much as his own lack of feelings. Where was the anger, the hurt, the sense of betrayal? The best he could summon was a peculiar numbness, as if what he and Dulce had shared had died somewhere back along the trail. Turning away, he made his way back to the teamsters' camp.

They were three days getting out of the higher elevations. By the time they reached Dolsen's trading post at the head of the Beaverhead Valley, the snow was nearly gone, the road muddy but firm. Buck ordered the wagons to keep rolling while he rode on to the post. He counted eight freight outfits scattered down the valley behind Dolsen's, waiting for the pass to open to the south, and probably two thousand head of mules and oxen grazing on the surrounding hills.

Buck hitched Zeke out front and went inside, making his way to a short bar at the rear of the room.

"Well, as I live and breathe," mocked the lean, bearded trader the post was named after. "What are you doing north of the divide, McCready? Don't you know your outfit's been stranded in Idaho Territory by the Bonner gang?"

"Is that a fact?" Buck replied. "Why don't you pour me a beer and tell me about it? Sounds like an interesting story."

Van Dolsen laughed and reached for a mug. A crowd of teamsters had gathered around them, hungry for details of the Box K's encounter with Bonner's men. Buck didn't resent their queries, although he did feel somewhat put out that no one asked about Mase. It was as if the wagon master's death had become old news. By keeping his answers short, the questions soon petered out.

Dolsen waited until most of the freighters had wandered off, then leaned across the bar and lowered his voice. "I'm thinking you'd like to hear what your ramrod had to say."

Buck looked up curiously. "Milo was here?"

"This morning. He asked me to tell you that everything was flowing smooth as Kentucky bourbon. I assume he meant the Crowley and Luce train doesn't know you're so close. C and L camped north of here last night, and their wagon boss, Lomax, came in to ask about the road. He seemed under the impression that the Box K had been stopped cold."

"Did he mention Jim Bonner by name?"

"He did, although he didn't say how he happened to know that little tidbit of information."

"He shouldn't have known about it at all," Buck replied. "His outfit was already well down the road before we learned who it was."

"Now I consider that informative information and more than a little incriminating, not that it'd stand up in a court of law."

"I don't intend to take it to the law," Buck vowed, sitting his empty mug on the bar and wiping his lips with his sleeve. "Who else knows about Milo?"

"That he works for you? No one. He kept his mouth shut and acted like any other out-of-work saddle tramp."

Buck nodded, relieved that Milo was playing it close to his vest. "What have you heard about the Ruby Cut-Off?"

Van stared at him for a moment, then his eyes slowly widened. "Well, I'll be go to hell. Is that what you're planning?"

"It's just a question."

"Yeah, but it's a hell of a question. I wish I could answer it. No one's used that route this year that I know of. It was never a good road, but it used to be passable if a man was in a hurry. Everyone goes through Twin Bridges now."

"Last you'd heard, could wagons make it over the cut-off?"

"Hell, Buck, I don't know what to tell you. If you wasn't trying to beat C and L into Virginia City, I'd say avoid the Ruby Cut-Off like the plague, but. . . ." He shrugged. "I will tell you this . . . I'd bet every nickel in my cash box that Lomax will know you're here before the sun goes down tonight. You don't have anything to lose by trying the cut-off." His face took on a funny look. "Except your mules and wagons, of course."

Buck nodded and tossed a coin on the bar for his beer. He knew the cut-off was the Box K's only hope of beating C&L. The main Montana Road went north as far as the town of Twin

Bridges before it split—one route going on to Helena and Fort Benton, far out on the plains, the other veering sharply southeast to follow the Ruby River to the many mining camps in that direction, Virginia City being the largest of the towns right now. The main road's advantages were a smooth, solid bed and a pair of bridges over the Ruby and Big Hole Rivers. Good graze and water made a difference, too. It was an extra day's pull to go through Twin Bridges, but everyone considered it worth the effort.

The Ruby Cut-Off swung away from the main road just north of Beaverhead Rock, some miles above Dolsen's trading post, and ran almost due east, skirting the northern tip of the Ruby Mountains before it joined the southeastern fork of the Montana Road at the upper end of the Ruby Valley. It was a rough stretch even in the best of conditions—hard on stock and equipment alike. Buck had never traveled the cut-off himself, but both Mase and Lew Walker had. They'd called it a spine-jolting trip through a corner of hell that neither man wanted to repeat—but they'd still done it. Barring rock slides or high water, Buck intended to do it, too.

As he turned away from the bar, he spotted a short, stocky man in a brushed riding coat and expensive topper get up and walk out the front door. Something about the stranger's manner caught Buck's attention and he went outside to look for him. The man was nowhere to be seen, but there were several men nearby that Buck knew, and he walked over to talk to a couple of Leavitt Brothers muleskinners.

"By jingo, Buck, they're sayin' you busted up that Bonner gang pretty good," a teamster named Boyd said.

"I heard that same story," Buck replied. "I couldn't say how true it was, though."

Boyd chuckled and the second Leavitt man, a woolly-bearded Mormon named Jenkins, added: "Whatever you did, it likely improved the character of the territory. Far as I'm concerned, they should hang the whole bunch of 'em."

"You guys see a short-legged gent in a topper leave here?" Buck asked, changing the subject.

"Sure," Boyd said. "Frenchy. He a friend of yours?"

"Never laid eyes on him before."

"I hadn't either until a couple of days ago. He drinks some, but mostly stays to himself. A Utah Freight driver tried to egg him into a fight last night by making fun of his hat, but Frenchy pulled a pistol from somewhere and that Utah Freight man backed off so fast I thought he was going to go through the wall."

"Speak of the devil," Jenkins murmured, and Buck looked up to see the stubby Frenchman coming out of the stable astride a handsome sorrel. He looked strangely out of place atop his heavy Santa Fe saddle. His cream-colored trousers were stretched tight across muscular thighs and his shoulders looked straight as a carpenter's level beneath the brushed twill of his long coat—a suit more practical for carriage rides in the park than the Montana frontier—but as he rode out of the yard, he gave Buck a look that made the hairs across the back of his neck stand up like a dog's hackles.

"Wonder where he's going," Boyd murmured as Frenchy kicked his horse into a canter.

"Why was you askin' about him, Buck?" Jenkins inquired.

"I couldn't rightly say," Buck confessed. "Something about him bothers me, but I can't put my finger on it."

"I don't trust a Frenchman," Jenkins stated, then spat as if merely uttering the word was distasteful.

Boyd said: "You don't trust nobody that ain't a Mormon or a Leavitt man."

"Ain't no reason I should, either," Jenkins retorted.

Buck walked away before he could be drawn into an argument he had no interest in. Mounting Zeke, he reined after the Frenchman, but he didn't try to catch up. He felt a need to get back to the Box K, and thought maybe he shouldn't wander too far away from it any more.

Gwen guided her chestnut up the gentle southern slope of Beaverhead Rock, then reined east toward the top of the cliff that gave the formation its name. Buck rode in front of her, his black mule picking its way carefully around the low, jutting stones that peeked out from the clumpy new grass.

Gwen had been eager to view the famous landmark ever since she'd learned the caravan would pass within its afternoon shadow. She'd first heard of it from her father's readings, when she and Eddie were still small enough to sit on his lap. In those halcyon days of her youth, Robert Haywood had read to his children nightly—stories by Hans Christian Andersen and Lewis Carroll and Sir Walter Scott. But it was the condensed journals of Captains Lewis and Clark that had captivated Gwen—tales of her own country, of exploration and adventure, giant bears and unknown rivers. And somewhere deep within that land of bewitchment, a huge rock shaped just like the beavers the city kept in its small, riverside menagerie.

Gwen had thought young Roscoe Evans was making sport of her when he'd pointed out the craggy stone wall that morning and told her it was the Beaverhead. "It doesn't look much like a beaver from the south," he'd hastily reassured her, noticing the doubting look on her face, "but you can make it out from the north if you look close."

Gwen had decided then and there to brace herself for another disappointment—one more fallen myth among many. Still, she was curious and had quickly galloped after Buck when she saw him making his way toward the rear of the bluff. Although he'd shrugged indifferently at her request to accompany him to the top of the Beaverhead, she hadn't taken his stony silence personally. She'd seen the look of comprehension that had come over his face when Dulce backed away from Thad Collins's grave. That entitled him to a certain amount of aloofness, she thought.

As they drew rein on the formation's brow, Gwen's breath was sucked away. "It's so beautiful!" she exclaimed, staring at the snow-capped mountains on every side, the lush greenness of the valley, dissected by rushing streams. Although the sun was warm on her shoulders, there was a chill on the breeze that played with her hair and fluttered the collar of her blouse—an icy reminder of what they had only recently left behind.

"There they are," Buck said softly, pointing with his chin toward a line of distant wagons. "Crowley and Luce, maybe five hours ahead of us yet."

"We've made such grand progress," Gwen observed softly, "yet the competition maintains its lead. How will we turn our current position into victory?"

He ignored the question, but Gwen sensed a shift in his thoughts. They were sitting their mounts side-by-side, so close together their stirrups occasionally bumped woodenly against one another. Turning his hard gray eyes on her, he said: "Tell me about the man in the coach, the one that passed us that day south of the Malad Summit."

Gwen was caught off guard by the intensity of Buck's stare, but not by the question. She'd been expecting it ever since they started their climb over Malad. "I suspect the man you're speaking of is my father, nothing more sinister than that."

"Your father!" Buck looked almost stunned by her confession.

"I am fairly certain of it, actually, even though I had only that one quick peek." After a moment's hesitation, she added: "You will recall that later that evening, Thad and I rode ahead to the Gilmer and Salisbury relay station on Devil's Creek. Unfortunately the coach had already departed there, and I wasn't able to learn the truth of the individual's identity." She paused again, picking deliberately at the stitching on her saddle horn in an effort to gather her thoughts, to decide how much she wanted to reveal. "My father is a rather imposing person, Buck. Just this morning I was reminiscing about his many kindnesses when I was a child, recalling some of the stories he used to read to us in the evenings, but his personality changed as we all became older. I suppose his association with Weber, Forsyth, and McGowan had much to do with that. In advancing middle age, Father has become a man of limited patience and fiery disposition. Both my brother and I. . . ."

"You have a brother?"

"Yes, Edward is a year older than I, although rather capricious in his moods. Sadly he is also a devotee of Chinese tar."

"Opium?"

"My family isn't perfect, Mister McCready. It just has more to lose if our façade ever fails." She met his gaze unflinchingly. "I lied to you, you know?"

"About your position with Bannock Mining?"

"Yes. This was to be my brother's responsibility, an effort at shoring up what little character he has left. It was Father's idea, but perhaps the task seemed too daunting to Eddie. He disappeared in Ogden without even a good bye."

"Disappeared? Where?"

"I haven't the vaguest idea, although it's hardly the first time he's done so. I do know that he is currently somewhere ahead of us, traveling with Father." Her fingernail quickened on the linen thread and her voice sounded strained, even to herself. "Robert Edward Haywood, the Third, is my father. My brother is the fourth Robert Edward. We call him Eddie." She glanced at Buck with a grateful smile. "You were concerned for my safety that night, south of Malad. I had returned in a disheveled state and you suspected poor Thaddeus of mischief, but what happened was truly an accident. He and I were on our way back from Devil's Creek Station, and I'm afraid I became a bit too harsh with my steed. Thad's horse and mine collided and we took a tumble. No one was hurt, but on top of everything else that had happened that evening, I'm afraid I became rather combative toward your questioning. I apologize for that. You had only my well-being at heart. To be honest, I wasn't sure what I should do. I was certain Father had recognized me. I can only assume that he'd decided this was a bed I had made for myself and that I should darned well sleep in it. I can assure you, it was rather a shock to realize I was so completely on my own. It was even worse the next day, after Mister Trapp's near accident on top of Malad, when I began to truly realize how the fate of so many others rested, at least in part, upon my decisions. Because of Father's influence, I'd never had that kind of responsibility before, and the reality of it was more than I'd imagined. I wasn't sure I was up to the task and I'm still not certain of it, although I am rather proud of myself for continuing onward." Her expression fell. "Of course, I shall still have to face Father when we reach Virginia City."

Buck remained silent for several minutes as if mulling over everything she'd said. Then he pulled his mule's head out of the grass, saying: "Come on, let's get back to the wagons."

Milo was waiting for them at the Ruby Cut-Off. "Is this the one?" he asked skeptically when Buck rode up. He indicated the rutted tracks behind him, curved away from the main road in a long but shallow arc toward the northern tip of the Ruby Mountains several miles away.

"This is it," Buck confirmed, eyeing the twin paths with the same wariness he would a growling dog. The bare earth in the tracks was smooth and undisturbed save for the prints of Milo's horse. "How bad is it?" he asked.

"I didn't ride it all the way, but it gets worse. There are some pretty deep gullies we'll have to cross."

"Can it be done?"

Laughing, Milo said: "Hell no, it can't be done. But then, there's no way we could have made it over Monida Pass in a blizzard, is there?" He crossed his wrists over his saddle horn. "You know, boss, I'm glad Jock took me on. I wouldn't miss this for all the gold in Montana."

Buck smiled in spite of his worries, then twisted in his saddle to wave Peewee onto the cut-off.

The muleskinner's eyes widened in disbelief. "You ever been this way, Bucky?" he shouted, but Buck ignored the question and waved again, in no mood to debate the issue.

There was a look of surprise on Nate's face, too, but he gee-ed his team into the broad turn after Peewee without comment. Watching the big wagons rumble past, Milo said: "They know we're here."

Buck looked at him. "Are you sure?"

"Lomax sent his ramrod back. He must've recognized me because, when he got close, he all of a sudden whipped that jugheaded mule of his around and cut a fine fog riding back to tell his boss."

Buck's jaw tightened.

"It was only a matter of time," Milo allowed, pulling the makings for a cigarette from his pocket. He stripped a thin sheet from his little bible of smoking papers and shaped it into a trough. "We're lucky they didn't discover us earlier," he added absently, focusing on his smoke. "The question now is, can our mules handle a final sprint into Virginia City?"

Although Buck's expression didn't change, he winced inwardly. He'd been asking himself that same question ever since they'd come down off Monida's snowy northern slope.

The mules' eroding fitness was clearly evident in the gauntness of their flanks and the dulling shine of their eyes. They were worn down nearly to bone and sinew and wouldn't last much longer if they didn't get some good rest soon.

"How much farther is it to Virginia City?" Milo asked, looking up as he sensed his boss' doubt.

"We ought to make it in by tomorrow night if nothing else goes wrong."

A lucifer flared in Milo's cupped hands and the tip of his cigarette glowed cherry red. Shaking out the match, he said: "It's going to be a hell of a race."

"A hell of a finish anyway."

"Assuming we make it over the Ruby Cut-Off."

"Yeah," Buck replied faintly. "Assuming that."

CHAPTER THIRTY-FOUR

By the time Nick Kelso arrived in Virginia City he was chilled to the bone, ravishingly hungry, and ached in every muscle and joint in his body. It wasn't illness that had sucked the strength from his body, but his long, freezing passage over the backbone of the Rockies—a nightmarish journey of falling snow, near starvation, and a soul-penetrating cold that not even the pint of whiskey he'd purchased at Dolsen's had been able to alleviate.

Based on the stories he'd heard in Utah, Nick had entertained high hopes for Virginia City, but his visions of luxury withered with his first full view of the community. Up close, the town's muddy streets and weathered buildings looked even less appealing than Ogden's.

He reined in at the first livery he came to. A slim black man working out front paused with his pitchfork when Nick rode up. "Owner around?" Nick asked, his voice crackling a little from disuse.

"You're lookin' at him." At Nick's scowl, the black man added: "Don't worry, it ain't gonna rub off on your hoss."

Nick swore sourly and dismounted. "You just fetch this horse something to eat. He's had a hard trip, and he's going to have an even harder one in another few days."

"They's a stall at the far end of the entryway only cost you four bits a night."

"I'll find it," Nick said. He led his horse into the livery's murky interior and was making his way down the middle of the aisle when some inner instinct flashed in his mind like a small explosion. He stopped and put a hand on his revolver, but, before he could pull it, a voice from the shadows told him to leave it where it was. Nick cursed again at his carelessness but kept his hand still. "That you, LeBry?"

"You recognized my voice, *mon ami.* I am flattered."

"I smelled that damn' black licorice you always stink of."

Baptiste LeBry chuckled as he stepped clear of the lightless doorway of the tack room. He wore a brushed twill coat and a low topper with a boat-shaped brim. A nickel-plated Colt Peacemaker was clutched familiarly in his right hand, its hammer cocked. "Tell me, you have completed your obligations to my employers?"

"It's done."

"Done?" LeBry smiled sadly, wagging his head. "When I left Dolsen's trading post, the Box K was intact. Behind Crowley and Luce, to be sure, but not so far behind as one might wish."

"They might not be where you wished them to be, but they're not going to win this race. That's what you wanted, isn't it?"

"To an extent, *oui.* You were instructed to slow their progress and you accomplished that, but no one was to die in the process. You recall that stipulation, don't you, old friend?"

"I ain't your friend, LeBry."

"Instead, you present my clients with the embarrassment of sabotage and cold-blooded murder. And that raid." LeBry tsked twice in disapproval. "You would consider such a thing coincidence? The race fair? I think not. Nor will the citizens of Utah."

"What the hell do I care what anybody in Utah thinks? I did what I was hired to do, and Crowley and Luce will win their contract because of it. That ought to make them happy."

LeBry snorted contemptuously. "You think this race between Kavanaugh and Crowley and Luce is about a simple contract, *monsieur?* Surely not even you can be that naïve."

Nick frowned. "You saying Crowley and Luce ain't the ones who hired you?"

"The men who hired me wish to remain anonymous, as such things should be among men of breeding, don't you agree?"

"I figured it was C and L you were working for," Nick said, vaguely bothered that he'd guessed wrong.

"Nicholas, the stakes in this contest are much higher than anything even Bannock Mining could envision. The fate of territories rested in your hands, *mon ami,* and for one brief moment in time you were an important man. How sad you were not aware of it."

Nick flexed the fingers of his right hand. He knew he was going to have to kill LeBry. The stocky little Frenchman had probably been sent here to kill him. But Nick wanted to know who the money men were first. If he had to flee the West after his confrontation with Bonner's men in Hawley City, he would need money, lots of it. The kind of money blackmail could almost certainly guarantee him. "Who hired you, LeBry?"

"The smallness of your inquiries tries my patience, Nicholas. I wonder, how badly did I misjudge your competence? But it is no longer a matter of concern. For the moment, I will be content to know how much information you have in your possession that can be traced to me."

Nick grinned tauntingly. "Kill me today and you'll never know what I left behind, or where."

"Perhaps." The nickeled barrel of LeBry's Colt glinted in the skimpy light from the front door. "However, I would prefer to know now."

Likely he would, Nick thought, but not enough to postpone pulling the trigger. Smiling, he let his hand swing easily to the butt of his revolver. "Let's get this over with, Frenchy," he said.

Killing Kelso should have been simple. LeBry's pistol was

already leveled, already cocked. But popping a cap on a man was never simple when it came down to the final squeeze of the trigger. At the last minute, LeBry hesitated, giving Nick time to make his draw. The roar of the two revolvers was deafening in the dark confines of the livery. Nick's horse tore free, bolting for the front door. Nick let it go. Waving away the clouds of powder smoke, he advanced cautiously. He was leery of a trap but needn't have been. Baptiste LeBry lay sprawled in the straw-littered dirt beside the tack room door. He was dead, and whatever secrets he might have possessed regarding the men who'd hired him were dead, too.

"You stinking little shit," Nick muttered. He knelt at LeBry's side and quickly rifled the man's pockets but found nothing except an empty shoulder holster and a greasy paper bag containing chunks of black licorice. There wasn't even a wallet. Swearing, Nick pushed to his feet. He knew LeBry had to have something somewhere—money, extra clothes, a razor. Maybe within those simple articles he would find the answers he would need to make him rich. . . .

"Don't move!"

"God damn," Nick grated, stiffening.

"Don't turn around and don't move."

"I heard you the first time," he snapped.

"Drop your gun."

Nick kept his hands away from his sides but he didn't drop his pistol. He turned slowly, squinting through the lingering tendrils of drifting powder smoke at a short, stocky man with a badge on his vest, a double-barreled shotgun in both hands. This time when he was told to drop his gun, he did so.

"You're under arrest, Kelso," the lawman said.

"This?" Nick made an innocent gesture toward LeBry's body. "This was self-defense, Sheriff. He tried to rob me."

"I got my doubts about that, not that it matters. I'm arresting you for the kidnapping of Robert Edward Haywood, of Philadelphia, but I'm betting I'll find a lot more than that to charge you with."

"I don't know what you're talking about," Nick said, but he was having trouble breathing all of a sudden and his heart was beating wildly.

"I'm talking about that kid in Ogden you kept doped up on Chinese tar," the lawman said, grinning. "He's here and so is his daddy, and they're wanting you behind bars for a long time. I'm betting they're gonna get their wish, too. What do you think?"

Chapter Thirty-Five

Buck knew something was wrong as soon as he saw Milo racing back to the caravan. Kicking Zeke into a lope, he rode out to meet him.

"We've got some big problems up ahead, boss!" Milo called when he was close, swinging his horse around to fall in at Buck's side. "The road's washed out real bad in at least three different places, and no way to get around them, either."

"How bad?" Buck asked. They had been making good time since leaving the main road, but Milo's news wasn't unexpected. There were reasons no one used this route any more.

"Two, three feet deep, same across. A mule could jump it, but not in harness."

"Go grab a shovel and pick out of the mess wagon," Buck instructed. "Get 'em up here fast as you can."

Milo nodded and cantered off. Buck jogged back to talk to Peewee. "Keep 'em rolling," he said, after filling the muleskinner in on what lay ahead.

"We'll be right behind you," Peewee promised, his voice jolting under the steady trotting of his mules, nearly drowned out by the banging of running gears and the squeak and squeal of ties holding his cargo in place.

Buck rode on without waiting for Milo. He came to the first wash-out within a mile, cutting diagonally across the road like an unhealed wound. The pounding of Milo's bay beat a rapid cadence across the sloping plain as Buck stepped down.

Milo hauled his horse to a high-headed stop and jumped clear. "There's two more wash-outs in the next half mile," he said, tossing Buck the shovel. "I don't know what's beyond that third one."

"We'll worry about that when we get there," Buck said, gouging at the bank with his shovel.

They hacked viciously at the thaw-softened earth, tearing down the walls until they had a shallow crossing for the wagons. They were sweating by the time they finished but didn't take time for a breather. The next wash was similar to the first and they soon had that knocked down as well. The third was even easier, which was good because Buck's muscles were starting to protest.

"Here they come," Milo observed, puffing heavily.

Buck glanced over his shoulder at the mule train, less than two hundred yards away. Wiping sweat from his brow with his sleeve, he said: "Let's keep riding."

They climbed stiffly into their saddles and pushed on. It was another mile to the next big wash, and neither man spoke as they approached it. Dropping resolutely from their mounts, they dug in without complaint. They were slower this time, though, and had barely finished when the caravan rolled up. Buck shouted hoarsely for Peewee to keep his rig moving and he and Milo rode on. When they reached the next steep-sided gully, Milo groaned aloud. "Lord A'mighty," the ramrod blurted, peering into the crevice. "It's no wonder no one uses this damn' road."

"It'd take a heap of work to keep it fit for wagon traffic," Buck agreed. He looked past the wash to the flat plain of the Ruby Valley still several miles away. They were over halfway there by now, and Buck thought that if they could reach the more forgiving ground of the valley's floor before nightfall, they stood a chance.

They weren't quite done when the caravan came up this time, but Buck waved for Peewee to stay with his wagons. It took only a few more minutes to finish the job, then he and Milo creaked back into their saddles. Buck was riding through a fog of pain and fatigue; nothing seemed real any more other than the throbbing of his tortured body.

The next two washes were relatively easy, and as the sun began its descent behind the western mountains, Buck's hopes started to rise. But as they approached the last wash before the land flattened out, a sense of foreboding overcame him. Glancing at Milo, he saw the same expression of dread there, but it wasn't until they reached the edge of the wash that the gravity of this final hurdle became clear to them.

"Aw, no," Milo breathed, his shoulders slumping.

"Son-of-a-bitch," Buck whispered in disbelief, staring mutely into a yawning crevice at least fifteen feet deep and no fewer than twelve across. It might as well have been a cañon.

"I guess this is it," Milo ventured, watching Buck out of the corner of his eye.

Buck nodded dully. It had been a good race, but Milo was right. This finished it.

With the sun down and the train ground to a halt, the mules began to grow fidgety. They wanted to rest. Their bodies craved it, their spirits needed it, but Buck was reluctant to grant it. Squatting on his haunches at the edge of the gulch, he eyed the far bank for probably the hundredth time. Even with everyone working together, he knew it would take all night just to knock the banks down enough to squeeze a buckboard across. To hammer out a path stable enough to bear the weight of a freight outfit hauling up to six tons of cargo. . . . He shook his head in frustration. They'd gambled and it seemed they'd lost. Apparently it was going to be just that simple.

"What now, Buck?" Peewee asked gently.

"I reckon we'll camp here tonight. We can decide tomorrow whether we want to backtrack or take time to carve out a crossing."

"Carve a crossing?" Ray made a sound of disgust. "Hell, we'd need a bridge to get a wagon over this thing, Buck."

"Well, we sure ain't building no bridge," Charlie Bigelow retorted.

"I didn't say we was," Ray snapped, his flaring temper reflecting the disappointment they all felt. But Buck was no longer listening. He was staring at the slopes of the Ruby Range. There were trees up there—tall, straight pines that could easily span this final obstacle. But it would take so long, he mused, recalling how hard it had been just to snake in the logs for their runners.

"Let's get the mules hobbled and fed," Milo said, stepping between Ray and Charlie before their spat could escalate. "We'll run separate messes tonight. . . ."

"We could do it," Buck said, standing. Milo shut up, and the rest of the crew turned to him with questioning looks. "We could do it," he repeated.

"Do what?" Milo asked.

"Build a bridge."

An uneasy silence greeted his declaration. Peewee said: "Sure we could. We can start first thing in the morning if that's what you want to do."

"Naw," Buck said, his voice rising with excitement. "We could do it tonight, in a few hours."

Almost as one, the muleskinners glanced at the darkening slopes of the Ruby Mountains. "They're awfully steep, boss," Milo said tentatively. "It'd be suicide in the dark."

But Buck's gaze was fixed on the gulch, not the mountain. Turning abruptly away from the shadowy chasm, he said: "We've already got the timber, Milo, if Nate is still carrying those runners."

"They're in my trailer," Nate replied dubiously.

"They'd be long enough," Peewee agreed, "but they ain't gonna be wide enough."

"We've got four of them," Buck reminded him. "That'll be enough." Stepping away from the gulch, he said: "Nate, you and Ray run back to the mess wagon and fetch the toolbox. Bring some hammers and nails, too. Charlie, get someone to help you haul those runners up here."

"Gawd dammit, Buck, them runners is too narrow," Ray squawked. "They're too light, too. You ain't gonna get a mule to put one foot down on such a jury-rigged contraption."

"Ray," Buck said coolly, staring into the muleskinner's faded blue eyes, "you go get those tools and do it quick." He looked at others. "Gentlemen, we're going to build a bridge, and I don't want anyone else saying it can't be done. Now let's get rolling."

Constructing a makeshift bridge to span the deep, V-shaped gulch wasn't as complicated as Buck had feared, but it was time-consuming. They paired two runners next to each other with their flat sides up, then secured heavy oak sideboards from Nate's wagons over the top to hold the runners together and in place, and give the wagons a flat, solid surface. They had to use the holes already drilled for wagon bolts for the nails, since the thick, seasoned planks were too hard to drive a nail through.

Rossy and Arlen drove foot-long iron stakes from the women's tent into the ground on all three sides of each end of the runners to keep them from sliding out from under the wagons' massive weight. Two-by-sixes pried from Peewee's lead wagon, where they had been used to hold the smokestack in place on steep grades, were placed under each span for additional support, their lower ends pounded into the sides of the gulch with sledge-hammers. The result, when they were finished, was a pair of footbridges sixteen inches wide reaching from one side to the other. They were springier in the middle than Buck would have preferred, but not enough that he was willing to call off the operation.

While Buck and half the crew labored on the bridge, others lined up Peewee's rig with the crossing, then unhitched his trailer so that the wagons could be hauled over one at a time. Meanwhile, Peewee and several others led a couple of teams above the ravine to the far side. They were an hour making the trip, having to climb well up the side of the mountain before they found a deer trail that would take them through the dark timber. With the arrival of full darkness, Buck ordered every lantern the caravan had brought up for light. Using a second fifth chain to reach the wagons, Peewee backed his hitch up to the brink of the gulch while Buck secured the finger-link between chain and pull-rod.

When they were finished, everyone backed off to view the end project—Peewee's lead wagon on the west side of the ravine, his mules on the east, the two long fifth chains that connected them lying slack in between.

At Buck's instructions, Rossy brought up a pair of heavy iron wagon jack handles with short prongs on one end that fit into the crank box. Buck took one of the jack handles and handed the other to Milo. "We'll walk across just in front of the wagons," he told the ramrod, "and use these to keep the tongue from whipping back and forth."

Milo's face paled when Buck's words sank in.

"Hell's bells, Buck, this ain't worth risking anyone's life over," Peewee interjected. "If one of those planks break or a wheel slips off the edge, the whole damn' outfit'd drop straight to the bottom. You'd both be killed."

"If any kind of slack develops in that chain and your mules

take it up too fast, that tongue's going to whip back and forth like a snake's head," Buck countered. "That'd put a wagon over the side for sure, but a man on each plank might be able to prevent that from happening."

"Or he might not," Joe added. "Hell, what we're doing is dangerous enough, Buck. There's no sense in putting a man out there."

Buck looked at Milo. "I won't force you to do this. I could use someone on that other plank but I can handle it myself if I need to."

Milo's color was still wan, but he nodded gamely. Before he could speak, Mitch Kroll stepped forward, snatching the jack handle from the ramrod's hands. Grinning wickedly in the yellow light, Mitch said: "Ol' Kansas here is too scrawny for that kind of work, McCready. What you want on the other side of that tongue is someone tough enough to make it mind its manners. I reckon that's me." He lifted the handle shoulder-high, like a lance. "This god-damn' thing is gonna break in two before that tongue swings my way."

"You're not a Box K man . . . ," Buck began, but Mitch cut him off.

"I am this trip. Besides, I intend to be waiting for Crowley and Luce when they pull into Virginia City. I still aim to make someone answer for what happened to Bigfoot."

Buck shrugged, but he was too tired to argue. "Take the uphill side," he said. "I'll take downhill."

"Uhn-uh, I'm stronger than you are. I'll take the downhill side. If that tongue wags, it's gonna wag that way first."

"All right," Buck conceded, then lifted his voice so that everyone could hear. "Let's get this done. Peewee, get in your saddle. I want Nate, Rossy, Ray, and Charlie up front to help Peewee with his mules. The rest of you get the hell out of the way . . . just in case."

Those men not assigned to a specific chore seemed to take Buck's warning literally and quickly backed off. Only Gwen lingered a moment longer than necessary, staring at Buck with concern in her deep-blue eyes. Buck searched for Dulce and found her standing with the others, well back from the edge of the gulch. Their gazes met but nothing passed between them; it was like exchanging glances with a stranger on the street.

Buck's mouth was dry as he approached the uphill plank. Beneath him, the shadowy gulch looked bottomless. Glancing across the empty space at Mitch, he saw fear in the big man's eyes, making him feel better about his own rapidly beating heart.

Returning his look, Mitch said: "Long way down, ain't it?"

"It won't seem so far if this bridge collapses."

"No," Mitch returned soberly. "I expect not."

"Ready, Buck?" Peewee called from the saddle of his nigh-wheeler.

Buck glanced at Mitch, who nodded tautly. "Stretch 'em out, Peewee!" Buck hollered. "Slow and easy, but keep 'em moving unless I tell you to stop."

Peewee yelled at his mules and Buck's attention was quickly drawn to the big Murphy wagon that seemed to loom over them in the distorting light of half a dozen lanterns. At his feet, the fifth chain stirred. He could hear Ray cursing steadily under his breath in lieu of prayer, and Nate praying openly.

"Easy!" Buck called as the chain slipped off the plank toward the shrouded floor of the ravine. It crept slowly back into view, swinging gently as the slack was removed. "A foot!" Buck shouted for Peewee's benefit, then: "Six inches! Easy now!"

The chain rose as if by magic until it was level with Buck's knees, then seemed to stretch languidly. The wagon's running gear groaned and its wheels jerked abruptly forward, then stopped just as quickly; the chain seemed to hum as slack was given, then taken away.

"Easy, gawdammit!" Ray nearly screamed, all but drowning out Peewee's muted: "Sorry."

Buck swallowed hard and glanced at Kroll, but the burly muleskinner's gaze was locked on the Murphy's front wheels, creeping steadily toward the planks. The wagon's tongue extended over the lip of the gulch like the probing appendage it was named after, its tip quivering as Peewee's mules leaned into their collars.

"Here she comes," Mitch breathed, reaching out with the pronged end of his jack handle to poke tentatively at the iron hardware bolted to the tip. Buck followed his lead, pushing on the weathered oak behind the wear plate. He figured they could control a small jump of the wagon's tongue, but too much would likely send one or both of them plunging backward off the planks, leaving the wagon's guidance to fate.

Despite the iron stakes on every side, the narrow bridges slid forward several inches as the front wheels nudged up against them. Peewee's whip popped above the backs of his mules and the chain drew tighter. Then the wagon lurched unexpectedly and the front wheels rolled onto the planks.

Buck and Mitch stayed even with the front of the tongue, their iron prongs pressed solidly into the wood. The long planks sagged as the wagon's massive weight reached the center of the bridge, and for a brief, sickening moment, Buck feared he'd underestimated the strength of the seasoned oak. Something cracked sharply below them and the bridge trembled. Buck cried out softly under his breath, then raised his eyes to Mitch, who was returning his stare across the abyss.

"You all right, boss-man?"

"Yeah," Buck croaked. "Must've been something I ate."

Mitch grinned weakly. Sweat sheened his broad, fist-scarred face. "I must've ate outta the same kettle," he confessed. "I'm feelin' kind of queasy myself."

Side-stepping carefully, they were almost across when the wagon's rear wheels struck the two planks like the blow of a hammer mill. Buck's weak leg, the one Mitch had cut so deeply with his bullwhip, seemed to give at the knee and he swayed dangerously.

"Look out!" Nate shouted as Ray's stream of obscenities crackled shrilly. Then Buck regained his balance and he and Mitch leaned even harder into the tongue. With all four wheels on the narrow timbers, the wagon began to roll more smoothly and in no time it bounced off the far end.

Buck stepped out of the way as soon as he had solid ground behind him. His pulse was thumping loudly and his palms were clammy. He drew a dirty sleeve across his parched lips and watched the lead wagon disappear into the darkness beyond the lantern light.

"I'll be damned," Mitch said quietly from several feet away. "I didn't think we'd make it." He was looking at Buck with new respect. "By God, McCready, you'll do to ride the river with, and I'll kick the ass of any man who says otherwise."

"Don't heap it on too thick," Buck replied as chains rattled in the darkness and men prepared the next wagon for crossing. "We've still got twenty-seven more wagons to drag across this son-of-a-bitch."

They fell into a rhythm after a while, although they didn't let their guard down, not even when they hauled Rossy's light coach over a couple of hours before dawn.

With the caravan parked safely on the east side of the ravine, Buck walked away from the lantern light to drop, cross-legged, on the ground. He was still there twenty minutes later when Gwen came up with his coat and a cup of coffee.

"There are some beans and side pork at the fire," she said, handing him his coat first. She let her fingers rest lightly on his shoulders, then pulled them away as he shrugged into the heavy wool garment. "You were brave, Buck," she said softly. "I am in awe of what you accomplished tonight, what you've accomplish this entire trip."

"It ain't that much," he replied dismissingly, then quickly changed the subject. "Anyone take Mitch some coffee?"

"Mister Kroll came to the fire," she informed him. "You didn't." She sank down beside him, her shoulder brushing his. "It's almost three o'clock. How long do you intend to remain here?"

"Not long. We'll let everyone grab a bite to eat, then be on our way." He could tell by the sounds that several of the mule-skinners were already harnessing their teams, preparing to pull out. "We lost a lot of time tonight," he said, almost to himself.

"Have we lost too much?"

"Maybe." He took a sip of coffee, grimacing at its unexpected taste. "What did you put in here?"

"Bourbon from my own stock. I thought a bit of warmth might help combat the mountain chill." She eyed him quizzically. "Are you not a drinking man?"

"Jock's got a rule against drinking on the trail." He hesitated, recalling the raw taste of the whiskey Peewee and Ray had given him back at Fort Hall, then regretfully returned the cup. "It's tempting, but I reckon I'd better pass. I do appreciate the thought."

"You are a difficult man to fathom, Mister McCready," Gwen said, pouring the laced coffee deliberately onto the ground. "I would say that your sense of duty is skewed. However, as you are still the captain, I shall honor your wishes . . . whether I agree with them or not. Tell me, is supper within the realm of possibility or have you decided to abstain from food as well?"

"I reckon I can eat," Buck said, pushing to his feet. He took Gwen's hand and pulled her up toward him. She came forward too fast and stumbled against his chest. Her lips were only inches from his and stray strands of her hair touched his cheeks.

"Buck," she breathed, leaning more firmly into him. He felt her lips on his and responded hungrily, his hands running up and down her spine. Then he tore his face away from hers, sliding his hands around to her stomach to push her back.

"Why?" she demanded almost angrily. "Because of Dulce?"

"No."

"My virtue then? Because if it is. . . ."

"It's not your virtue," he interrupted roughly. "It's your position with Bannock Mining, plus my own with Kavanaugh Freight."

She looked at him in disbelief, then lowered her arms from around his neck. "Don't tell me your sense of ethics precludes even a kiss."

"It does," he replied raggedly, taking a step back.

"But Dulce is different?"

He nodded. "Something like that."

"Very well, then I hope my rash behavior didn't jeopardize . . . what exactly is it that you fear, Buck? Your standing with the crew? With me?"

He took a deep breath. "Neither," he said. "To tell you the truth, I kind of like your boldness. It's just not a good time right now. Maybe later, when we aren't so hobbled by our jobs."

Gwen shook her head incredulously, but there was no rancor in her reply. "I still maintain that your sense of duty is skewed, even abnormal, but my respect for it hasn't diminished one whit." She slipped her arm through his. "I shall look forward to the day of your . . . unhobbling. In the meantime, I suggest supper. The kitchen will be closing shortly, and I understand the cooks are rather impatient with late arrivals."

Zeke expelled a great, gusty breath of disapproval as Buck hauled himself wearily into his saddle. He leaned forward to pat the mule's neck in apology. "One more day, boy, that's all we'll need." Straightening, he looked back down the line of wagons and hollered: "Streeetch out! Come on, boys, let's go to Virginia City!"

No one cheered in the approaching dawn of this final day on the road, but there was an immediate jangling of chains, the creak of harness leather and running gears as the long caravan got under way. After sending Milo ahead on his spotted molly—Collins's bay was tied behind the mud wagon at the rear of the train, a fitting position for a horse, Milo had declared as he switched his saddle to the Box K mule—Buck took his usual place at the head of the column. They were still some distance from the Virginia City road when Milo came back, reining in beside Zeke. "They're going to beat us, boss," he announced glumly. "I spotted them down the road and, dammit, they're going to beat us."

"By how much?"

"No more than an hour and maybe closer to half that, but they've got a good, solid road and they're using it to their advantage."

They caught sight of the Crowley and Luce outfit while crossing the Ruby. As Peewee's wheelers came splashing up out of the icy waters, the muleskinner shouted and pointed toward the road. Buck waved in recognition. He'd already spotted the tail end of the C&L caravan rounding a bend half a mile ahead.

"We're closer than I thought we'd be," Milo admitted.

"We're going to get even closer," Buck vowed.

"They won't let us pass."

"When the time comes, I don't intend to ask for permission," Buck replied grimly. He twisted in his saddle and shouted for Peewee to pick up the pace. The muleskinner shot him a surly look, then unfurled his bullwhip and cracked it loudly above the backs of his flagging sixes, goading them into a shuffling jog. Soon the entire train was rattling along the Virginia City road at a good clip, the massive wheels throwing up rooster tails of gritty, half-baked mud. Buck and Milo loped ahead until, rounding a bend, they came in sight of Crowley's and Luce's wagon boss, Tim Lomax, sitting his mule alone in the middle of the road. The Box K riders pulled up a couple of hundred yards away but otherwise made no acknowledgement of the C&L captain.

"That bastard knows he cheated," Milo muttered, returning Lomax's stare.

"Sure he knows," Buck said. "He knows that we know it, too, but he'll deny everything when we get into Virginia City. Their Bannock rep will back him up and there won't be a damn' thing we can do about it. But maybe we won't have to. We've got one more chance, something that didn't even occur to me until this morning. There's a place up the road where we might be able to slip around C and L, and, if we play it right, they won't even know it until it's too late." He glanced at Milo. "We're gonna have to be ready to jump when we get there, though, and at the same time we can't let Lomax know we're even thinking about jumping."

"That sounds kind of chancy," Milo said.

"Chancy as hell and it could lead to gunfire, but we're still going to try it. Ride back and tell Peewee to move up quick as he can. Tell him I want him hugging C and L's ass when we reach the bend where Lew Walker broke his leg a couple of years ago. He'll know the place, and he'll figure out why I want him there when he thinks about it."

Milo nodded and took off, and Buck leaned back to rest his hand on his saddle's skirting. He returned Lomax's stare without malice, letting his thoughts skip ahead to the spot where Lew's mule had slipped in the mud on the last run of the 1872 season, snapping Lew's right leg cleanly just below the knee. The road there ran up over the brow of a hill, but there was a wide spot along the river where teamsters sometimes stopped for the night. A narrow, pot-holed trail wound through the trees connecting the campsite to the road at both ends. The flat was maybe three quarters of a mile long and wouldn't normally be any faster than staying on the main road—unless Peewee really laid into his mules, forcing them into a run.

It would be reckless as hell, Buck knew, a risk to animals and cargo alike, but, if they were successful, they could force C&L to a standstill while the Box K took the lead.

Buck smiled lazily as he pictured it. The look on Lomax's face, the catcalls of the Box K teamsters as they rolled past, the livid expressions of the C&L drivers—images as sweet as sugared strawberries. He and Milo would have to stand by with their rifles, of course. There was no telling how Lomax or his men would react if they didn't, but Buck knew a cocked weapon could cool even the hottest temper, usually without a shot being fired. As long as he and Milo remained alert, he didn't anticipate any trouble.

The Crowley and Luce train, along with Lomax, was long out of sight by the time Peewee got up to where Buck was waiting but it was still several hours to the place where he intended to make his move. There would be plenty of time.

Buck kept the train rolling steadily. The morning air grew warm as the sun climbed higher, the hottest it had been since they'd left the Snake. C&L didn't break for its customary mid-day stop and neither did the Box K. The grade began to climb as they pushed on into the afternoon, and the cedar- and sage-covered hills began to pinch down on each side. The long meadow lay only a few miles ahead now, and Buck slowed Zeke to allow Peewee to come up even with him.

Milo was riding alongside Peewee's leaders but reined in

silently at Buck's side. Sweat streaked the ramrod's face and the stubble on his cheeks had turned reddish-gray from the grime of last night's digging. Although Milo looked exhausted, it was the leaders and those mules immediately following them that caught Buck's attention like a slap to the face. His jaw tightened with anger as he took in their debilitated condition. Jutting his chin toward the near number eight, its lower left leg pasted with dirt and blood, he said: "What the hell happened?"

"Stumbled and fell a few miles back. Two of Little Ed's hitch have gone down, too, and one of Charlie's mules is lame."

"Why haven't they been pulled out of harness?"

Milo fixed him with a steely gaze. "Because there hasn't been time, Buck. Not if you want us on C and L's ass when we reach that meadow."

Buck's nostrils flared and he quickly looked away rather than meet Peewee's accusing look as the muleskinner rolled past. Nate's hitch didn't appear to be in any better shape, and Buck sucked in a deep breath as if in pain. His eyes traveled to the tall mountains rising in the east. Virginia City lay at their western base, so close now he thought he could make out the faint haze of chimney smoke above the nearest hills. The long meadow where Lew had broken his leg was less than a mile away. Victory could be theirs yet, and, with it, the Bannock Mining contract. Then he exhaled and said: "Slow 'em down."

Milo stared at him as if he wasn't sure he'd heard correctly. "Huh?"

"I said to slow 'em down, we're going to stop. There's a meadow up ahead. . . ."

"Where Lew Walker broke his leg?"

"Yeah. We'll pull in there for the night, then go on into Virginia City tomorrow afternoon."

Milo continued to stare as if still trying to figure out what Buck really meant. Finally he said: "Lord A'mighty, Buck, we can't give up now!"

"The hell we can't," Buck replied softly. "I'll be damned if I'll cripple a mule for a dollar bill . . . not for Jock or any man." *Not even for a dead man,* he thought sadly, remembering the promise he'd made at Mase's graveside. He looked at Milo and nodded, his decision made. "Slow 'em down."

Chapter Thirty-Six

Buck wasn't sure what kind of reception to expect when they pulled into Virginia City late the next day, but he wasn't surprised when the town's citizens acted as if they hadn't even heard of the five-hundred-mile race between the Box K and Crowley and Luce. Or if they had, they didn't care. Virginia City wasn't built on freighting the way Corinne was, the way Franklin wanted to be. It's heart beat for gold rather than goods, and Buck doubted if anyone gave a damn one way or another where their supplies came from as long as they were there when needed.

He led the caravan to Fred Sweeny's wagon yard, sprawled across the knob of a hill high above a town built on hills. Fred was standing on the loading dock as the long Box K hitches rolled through his gates. Peewee continued on to the rear of the big lot where there would be enough room to park their outfits while Buck rode over to talk to Sweeny.

"Made it, I see," Fred said by way of greeting. He was a tall man with a full head of wavy gray hair and a hawk-like nose. His eyes were hooded beneath bushy brows and a neatly trimmed mustache shaded his upper lip. He watched critically as the wagons rumbled past, then glanced at Buck. He didn't say anything, but Buck could tell he wasn't happy.

"Something on your mind, Fred?"

"No, I guess not. There's a gent named Haywood waiting for you in town. He's with the company Jock was hoping to contract with. Of course, that's just wishful thinking now for all of us, isn't it?"

"Where can I find him?" Buck asked, ignoring the receiving agent's scorn.

"He's staying at the Parker Hotel, but I understand he's been doing business out of the old Wallace building on Main."

Buck nodded. He knew the place. Riding into the wagon yard, he found Milo supervising the parking of the big rigs, lining them up at angles so that Sweeny's yardmen could pick and choose which one they wanted to unload first. "Reckon you can handle things here?"

"Sure." Milo gave him a questioning look. "Trouble?"

"No, just some loose ends to tie up. When you've got everything lined out, take the boys to Carlson's for a drink. Tell the bartender to keep pouring until he's emptied twenty dollars' worth of booze. I'll be along later to settle the bill." He glanced at the mud wagon where Rossy was unhitching. "Where's Gwen and Dulce?"

"They left us on Main Street." Milo grinned crookedly. "It seems Miss Haywood's father is in town. Did you know that?"

"Gwen mentioned the possibility."

"She must've spotted him from the street. Last I saw of her, she looked like she was on her way to her own hanging. Dulce went along to read her the last rites."

Buck cocked his head. "And you didn't gallop to her rescue?"

"I gave up on Miss Haywood some time ago," Milo admitted. "She's pretty as a picture but more interested in the lead mule than someone from the middle of the hitch."

"I'd say you made a wise decision," Buck concurred, reining away. He went to the mud wagon where Arlen was coiling the slim leather drive lines for Rossy. "You ready?" he asked.

"You could change your mind," Arlen suggested, without looking up.

"That ain't likely."

"He's not a bad fella," Rossy said tentatively, coming over with a collar over one shoulder, three more in his hands. "He could've escaped more than once if he'd wanted to. He's had enough chances."

"He's got to go back to Corinne, Rossy. He was there the night Mase was murdered. He saw it happen."

"But he didn't kill him."

"Maybe, but he was a part it, or was planning to be. I won't turn my back on that."

Rossy looked at Arlen and shook his hand. "I'm sorry," he said.

Buck scowled at Rossy's defense of the scruffy outlaw, irritated and a little surprised that he would side with anyone involved in the death of a Box K man.

"It ain't your fault," Arlen told him. "Hell, I appreciate you speaking up. I didn't expect it."

"Go help your dad," Buck told Rossy gruffly.

"Go on," Arlen said, winking. "I'll take care of this." His smile disappeared when Rossy was gone. "Come on, McCready, let's get this over with."

They walked down the hill to the sheriff's office, Arlen on foot, Buck astride Zeke. Arlen waited on the boardwalk while Buck hitched his mule to a slim pine rail out front, then led the way inside. The sheriff was a short, stocky man with a no-nonsense cast to his face. He was sitting behind his desk when Buck and Arlen entered but quickly stood and pulled his pistol around on his belt where it would be easy to grab. "This Fleck?" he asked after Buck had shut the door.

"How'd you know that?" Buck asked.

"Word travels fast along the trail, Mister McCready." He shook Buck's hand. "I'm Elmer Poindexter. I knew Mase Campbell well. He was a good man."

"Yeah, he was," Buck said by rote, then tipped his head toward Arlen to change the subject. He spoke tersely, outlining the outlaw's part in the mule raid first, then adding what he knew of Arlen's involvement in Mase's murder. When he finished, he added: "I was ready to hang him when I first got my hands on him, but. . . ." He shrugged. "I reckon I've changed my mind. He ain't all bad, just easy to manipulate."

Arlen gave him a amazed look, Poindexter seemed confused. "What are you saying, McCready?" the sheriff demanded.

"I'm saying I ain't as mad about Mase's death as I was right after it happened," Buck replied, as vexed with his own admission as he was with the lawman for asking for it.

"Well, fortunately, the law doesn't care how you feel about it," Poindexter said. He took Fleck by the arm and spun him around and, after a quick but thorough search for weapons, pushed him toward a single cell at the rear of the room. To Buck, he added: "I've got some things to take care of this afternoon, but I want you back here bright and early tomorrow morning to fill out some paperwork I'll have ready for you."

"I'll be here," Buck promised. He started to turn away but stopped abruptly when Poindexter swung the cell door open. A figure emerged from the shadows at the rear of the iron-strapped compartment and Buck grunted with recognition, turning for the cell with murder in his eyes.

"Uhn-uh," Poindexter said, putting a hand on Buck's chest to stop him. "You leave him be. He's in my charge."

"I want to talk him," Buck growled.

"I figured you would, but it won't do any good. He isn't co-operating."

"I'm willing to beat the information I want out of him, if that's what it takes."

Poindexter glanced over his shoulder, barking: "Get away from the door, Kelso!"

"Hello, McCready," Nick Kelso sang out mockingly. "So you finally made it in. Too bad you didn't get here yesterday, you might've collected that BMC contract for Kavanaugh and made a name for yourself. Way it stands now you're just another jackass working with jackasses."

"What's he doing here?" Buck demanded, brushing the lawman's hand off his chest.

"He's been charged with kidnapping for openers, but we're going to slap a murder charge on him, too, for gunning down a sawed-off little Frenchman in one of our liveries. Anything you can add to that will just make my day brighter."

"I want to know who hired him," Buck said in smoldering tones. "I want to know who was behind Mase's murder."

"He doesn't know, McCready," Poindexter said gently. "I've already used everything but a pair of pliers to drag a name out of him, but he keeps insisting the man he killed the other day was the only contact he had. Says he shot him in self-defense, and as much as I hate to admit it, because I'd really like to see this bastard hang, his story has a ring of truth to it. It'd make sense that whoever fronted the money for Kelso's shenanigans would want to eliminate any connection that could lead back to them. Now, and I'm just guessing, mind you, I'd say whoever ordered Baptiste LeBry to hire Kelso had more than a passing interest in the outcome of this competition between the Box K and Crowley and Luce."

Buck tore his eyes away from the killer, puzzled by the lawman's remarks. "Hell, I know that."

"I don't think you do. I'm saying Herb Crowley and Anton Luce are small potatoes in this kettle of mischief. I'm not suggesting they're squeaky clean, but I'm guessing it was someone higher up the flagpole that made the decision to murder Mase in order to stop the Box K."

"Someone from outside their firm?"

"More than likely someone outside of muleskinning altogether, at least far enough out that you won't ever see any mule shit on their shoes. Might be someone connected with the Utah Northern Railroad or the transfer station in Ogden, or maybe some corporate man back East with ties to Utah you'd never guess existed. I just don't think we're ever going to know for sure."

"I'll guarantee you one thing, McCready," Kelso piped up from his cell. "If I knew who it was that hired LeBry to bushwhack me, I'd use that information to buy myself a ticket out of this hole."

"Son-of-a-bitch," Buck said quietly.

Nick was at the bars again, and now his attention turned to Fleck. "Hello, dumb-ass," he taunted.

"I told you to get back!" Poindexter yelled. He shoved Fleck into the cell, then swung the door closed with a bang. "You two get along," he added, turning the key in its lock.

Buck's business with the sheriff was finished, but he lingered curiously as Arlen edged deeper into the cell. Arlen looked almost shocked by the appearance of his old partner and nemesis, and, with the iron door closed, Nick wasted little time in making his move. Coming up on Arlen's left side, he leaned close to whisper into the smaller man's ear. There was a smirk on his face when he stepped back.

Arlen didn't immediately respond. He turned to Nick and smiled, then, stepping back for leverage, Arlen threw a punch into Nick Kelso's face that looked powerful enough to cave in a wagon bed. Nick flew back with a strangled cry and slammed into the wall. His knees buckled and he slid to the floor and sat there. Blood streamed across his lips and chin from a broken nose and his eyes rolled without focus. Before he could regain his senses, Arlen came to stand above him.

"Those days are over, Nick," he stated flatly. "If you ever talk to me like that again, I'll break your neck."

Poindexter guffawed. "By God, I believe he means it, Kelso. I'd give that boy plenty of room, was I you."

Nick's mouth hung open like a beached fish's but he didn't reply.

"Fleck!" Buck called, and Arlen looked his way. "Find out what you can from him."

Arlen grinned and nodded, and the sheriff's good humor disappeared. "No, you don't. I won't abide that kind of behavior in my jail, Fleck. That goes for you, too, McCready." He blustered suddenly: "I mean it, by damn. Neither one of you wants to get on the bad side of me."

"All I want is to know who hired Kelso to kill Mase," Buck replied calmly. "Maybe Fleck can find out what you couldn't."

"You do not tell me my business, mister," Poindexter said, but he had to lift his voice to be heard. Buck had already left the building.

It was less than a block from the jail to the old Wallace building. Buck walked, leading Zeke, and tied the leggy black to the rail alongside Gwen's chestnut and Dulce's claybank.

At one time the Wallace building had furnished both home and office to an attorney specializing in mining claims, according to the peeling gilt script across the front window, but whatever dreams lawyer Wallace might have entertained for a future in Virginia City must have withered a long time ago. What remained was a frame structure of weathered gray planking and dusty windows, its sills littered with dead flies, hinges squeaking from disuse. That the old building was about to be reborn was evident in the half dozen or so sweating laborers who scurried about the premises with hammers, saws, and plumb lines. The smell of cleaning ammonia was stout in the front room.

A bald clerk with sleeve garters and ink-stained fingers met Buck at the front door and ushered him into a large, side-room office cluttered with unpacked boxes and wooden crates. A desk and filing cabinet had been wedged into one corner to accommodate BMC's immediate business needs. The smell of ammonia was strong in here, too, but not unbearable with the window open.

There were five others in the room when Buck arrived. A large man with bushy muttonchops whiskers sat behind the desk. Tim Lomax leaned casually against the rear wall next to the window overlooking the Ruby River gulch. Gwen and Dulce sat together on a small bench opposite Lomax, their expressions contrite. A third man stood at Gwen's side, his face pale, his build more gaunt than slim, and his hands subtly trembling. The resemblance between him and Gwen was slight but noticeable, and Buck thought this must be the brother she'd mentioned.

There was even less resemblance between the Haywood siblings and the man behind the desk, a cigar clamped between his jaws like a leg off some kind of prey. He was of average height but stoutly built. Sitting down, his resemblance to a bulldog was astounding. When he said—"You're Buchanan McCready."—in his deep, resonant voice, Buck wasn't sure he would've argued with him even if his name had been something else.

"You're Robert Haywood?"

"I am." He took the cigar from his mouth. "Senior vice-president with Weber, Forsyth, and McGowan, of Philadelphia, and currently in charge of their Montana project." He leaned back in his chair, regarding Buck inquisitively. "Mister Lomax tells me you gave C and L quite a run for its money."

"We did what we could."

"Couldn't hang onto that lead, though?"

Buck's face turned warm, but he didn't rise to Haywood's bait. "That's what I've been hearing," he replied evenly.

"I know what you've been hearing, Mister McCready. I've been hearing the same thing myself for the past several days. What I want to know is . . . why? You had C and L beat handily at the Malad Range. You'd proved your point, or more accurately, Jock Kavanaugh's point, which is that the Franklin route will never be a viable option as long as wagons have to negotiate Marsh Valley. Once the Utah Northern lays tracks north of there, Corinne will be finished, but I don't see that happening for a long time. It might not have happened at all if you hadn't failed so miserably."

"Father, you're not being fair," Gwen said, but the elder Haywood held up his hand and his daughter fell dutifully silent.

"What is your reply, Mister McCready?" Robert Haywood persisted.

"We had a run of bad luck. It happens sometimes."

"Bad luck?" Haywood's brows rose like miniature arbors. "I'd hardly characterize what my daughter so briefly reported as 'bad luck,' sir. One constant string of disasters would be a more valid description."

"Good luck or bad, it washes the same," Buck replied, his pulse starting to throb in his temples.

"You don't seem particularly concerned that you came in second," Haywood observed.

Buck's voice hardened. "We ran a good race. There aren't many outfits that could've done what we did, and I'm damn' proud of what we accomplished. It might look like second place to you, but I'll lift my drink to every man in my crew tonight and mean every word of congratulations that I give them."

Haywood seemed unmoved by Buck's response. "You stopped, sir. Yesterday, in the middle of the afternoon, you ordered your caravan stopped and your mules unharnessed. You didn't even come in yourself to protest C and L's victory. I call that odd behavior."

"Our mules were played out. Pushing them any harder would have jeopardized their health. A caravan doesn't get very far with crippled stock."

"You were afraid to push them . . . mere miles from your destination . . . because you were concerned for their welfare? You do realize that with what Bannock Mining was offering, you could have replaced your entire herd with new stock?"

"I reckon that's true," Buck replied, hooking his thumbs in his gun belt and wondering how much longer this would go on.

"You reckon that's true?" Haywood seemed to mock. He leaned back in his chair and looked at Lomax, still propped against the wall beside the window. "But you did want that contract, didn't you, sir?"

"You bet we did," Lomax replied enthusiastically. "Crowley and Luce delivered as promised, Mister Haywood. The Box K didn't. It's as simple as that."

"Tell me, Mister Lomax, what is your knowledge of the obstacles thrown into the Box K's path? Sabotage and mule raids are hardly the norm, are they?"

Lomax stirred uncomfortably. "Well, I wouldn't know about that. *We* didn't have anything to do with it, if that's what you're wondering about. Everybody has bad luck from time to time. I reckon this was just the Box K's turn. But C and L delivered the goods. We said we'd be here first and we were. That's what matters."

"*Hmmm*, you'd think so, wouldn't you?" Haywood mused.

"What's that mean?" Lomax asked.

Haywood stared thoughtfully into space for a moment, then leaned forward and stubbed his half-finished cigar out in an ashtray. "I don't know what went on out there, Mister Lomax, nor do I particularly care. That's a matter for Mister Kavanaugh and his attorneys to pursue if they so wish. But I do know that I like a man with the courage to do what's right even in the face of certain criticism."

He glanced at Buck with a faint look of admiration. "And especially when BMC equipment is at stake."

A panicked look came into Lomax's eyes. "You promised that contract to the firm that got here first, Mister Haywood. That's Crowley and Luce, not the Box K."

"Actually Bannock Mining was careful to promise only *consideration* for the freighting company that delivered our goods in advance of the competition," Haywood corrected the C&L wagon boss. "Award of the contract was implied, not guaranteed."

"Jesus," Lomax breathed, looking stunned. "You're double-crossing us."

The mien of predator that Buck had seen on the older man's face earlier suddenly returned. "If you'd be so accommodating as to leave us, Mister Lomax, I'll speak with your supervisors upon my return to Utah Territory. Meanwhile, consider the contract awarded to Kavanaugh Freight."

Dulce jumped to her feet with a cry of joy and Gwen's eyes sparkled with delight. Robert Haywood's words tumbled slowly in Buck's brain, as if he needed to examine each one separately to be sure he hadn't misunderstood. Lomax stormed out of the office, leaving the door ajar. The clerk who had escorted Buck in earlier peeked inside to make sure everything was all right, then quietly closed the door.

Haywood looked at Buck. "I owe you a debt of gratitude, sir."

"For what?"

"For the care you gave my daughter on the trail. I learned of her little ploy from a detective I hired in Ogden. It was he who traced her to Corinne. Mister Kavanaugh confirmed my worst fears well after you were on your way. My initial inclination was to immediately set off after her and drag her back to civilization, but I had a change of heart as my son and I made our own way north. I'd already spoken with people who knew you and Miss Kavanaugh, and I began to believe that Gwen would be in safe hands in your company. I was certain this could be a learning experience for her, as I'd hoped it would be for. . . ." His gaze traveled to his son, who lowered his eyes submissively. "At any rate, I would have changed my mind instantly if I'd known what was in store for the Box K, but, fortunately, it all worked out for the best."

He glanced at Gwen and Dulce. "I'll have one of my men escort these young ladies to the Parker Hotel, where I've already secured rooms for them in anticipation of their arrival. I'll be leaving Montana in two days with both of my children, but . . . ," he spoke to Dulce, "you would certainly be welcome to accompany us, Miss Kavanaugh. Perhaps I could afford you the same protection southbound that Mister McCready provided for your northward journey."

Dulce glanced at Buck, then away. "Thank you, Mister Haywood," she replied. "That would be most kind. I would like to return to Utah with you and Gwen, the sooner the better."

"Good, then it's settled." Haywood stood and Buck crossed the room to shake his hand above the desk. "We shall talk later, Mister McCready," Haywood said. "We have the off-loading of equipment to arrange and I'm sure my daughter will want a final good bye, but, for the moment, I have much to accomplish and very little time left."

Buck nodded, recognizing the dismissal and frankly glad to have it. As he turned to leave, Gwen smiled and promised to send word as to where they could meet. "Perhaps for supper tonight," she suggested.

Buck assured her he wouldn't be hard to find. He looked at

Dulce but she pretended to be busy searching for something in the small cloth purse she was carrying, and that was all right, too, he decided.

Chapter Thirty-Seven

Only Nate, Rossy, and Manuel were at the corrals when Buck returned to Sweeny's, although Milo was on the loading dock smoking a cigarette and talking with one of Sweeny's warehousemen. He came over when Buck rode up. "Everything taken care of, boss?"

"More or less. How are the mules?"

"Most of them are already on pasture. We put the lame animals in a separate corral where we can keep an eye on them, but I think they'll be fine with some rest."

Buck was relieved. It was the same conclusion they'd come to last night after examining the stock along the Ruby River, but it was good to know that none of the animals had worsened on the final trek into town. "Where is everyone?" he asked.

Milo grinned. "You serious? I'd say they're right where you told them to go . . . Carlson's. They might scatter later, but right now everyone wants a share of that twenty dollars' worth of booze you promised them."

"But not you?" Buck asked curiously.

"Aw, hell, someone has to stay sober, and I didn't know what your plans were."

Buck laughed. "Maybe we'd both better stay sober for a while. We've still got one more loose end to tie up."

Buck dug his valise out of the mess wagon, then rode back into town. A stall for Zeke cost him 50¢ for the night. After caring for the mule, he treated himself to a haircut and a fresh shave, then spent thirty minutes soaking off the grime of five hundred miles in a bathhouse next door to the barbershop. Leaving his trail clothes to be laundered and picked up later, he skinned into the blue suit he'd purchased for Mase's funeral and stepped outside.

Haywood's clerk, the one with the ink-stained fingers and sleeve garters, was waiting for him on the boardwalk with a note from the BMC executive, inviting Buck to dine with him and his daughter that evening at the Parker Hotel's small restaurant.

"In about an hour," the clerk instructed.

"Tell him I'll be there," Buck said, shoving the note into a jacket pocket. He waited until the clerk had hurried off, then continued down the street to a doctor's office. A small brass bell jingled above the door when he walked in, signaling the physician from a rear room. He eyed Buck silently for a moment, then said: "Gun shot, knife cut, or horse kick?"

Most of the wounds Buck had received from Mitch's bullwhip back at Fort Hall had already scabbed over and were nearly healed; only the deepest, the one in his left thigh, continued to weep. "I reckon cut would be closest," he replied.

"In here," the doctor said, holding open the door to the back room.

Buck limped out of the doctor's office forty-five minutes later, his leg considerably sorer than it had been when he walked in but freshly cleaned and bandaged. In addition to a tin of salve, he carried with him the doctor's conviction that, considering the original severity of the wound, it would probably heal just fine.

"You won't listen," the doctor had said as he accepted the silver dollar Buck handed him for payment, "but stay off that leg for a few days. A week would be better."

Buck began an excuse that the physician quickly shushed. "It ain't my limb," he said grumpily, "and it won't fall off if you don't listen to what I say. It'll just take longer to heal. Go on now, I'm late for my supper."

The sun had set while Buck was having his old stitches pulled, and the mountain air was turning cool as he made his way to the Parker Hotel. Dulce wasn't seated at the quiet corner table Robert Haywood had already procured; she'd begged off with the excuse of a headache. Eddie wasn't there, either, which didn't surprise Buck nearly as much as Dulce's absence.

The conversation between Buck and Gwen seemed strained under the imposing presence of her father, but that was just as well, Buck reflected afterward. The memory of her hand slipping from his seemed to fade as quickly as the echo of her final, whispered good bye. If there had ever been any promise of a future between them, Buck had never detected it.

He waited outside the hotel for half an hour, then went back in and climbed the stairs to the second floor. He had no enthusiasm for what he was about to do but was determined to see it through. Gwen had confided to him that Dulce's room was across the hall from hers, facing the street. Buck could feel a lump forming in his throat when he stopped in front of her door. Before he could knock, a soft voice beckoned from the open door to the balcony. He followed it into the darkness.

"I expected you earlier."

He nodded, then shrugged, the words he'd wanted to say deserting him like a band of cowards. "I've been. . . ."

"Busy," Dulce finished for him. She stood hatless in the shadows close to the wall, wearing a plain blue dress and a shawl over her shoulders. A breeze toyed with her red curls, lifting them off her shoulders, then letting them bounce back. She looked beautiful in the filtered moonlight, but there was no welcome on her face, no warmth in her voice.

"There's been a lot to do," Buck said, annoyed that she'd bring up such an old source of contention. Dulce didn't reply, and, after a moment's awkward silence, Buck said: "I came to say good bye. You'll be leaving with the Haywoods day after tomorrow, and I wasn't sure if I'd see you before you left."

"How gallant," she replied cynically.

"I'm a muleskinner, Dulce," Buck said. "It's not just what I do, it's what I am. I reckon I just wasn't cut out to marry the boss' daughter."

Dulce's head came up sharply, her eyes wide with surprise, and Buck realized she hadn't expected this, that she'd thought he would come crawling back. She'd wanted the decision to part to be hers, not his.

"Do you have everything you need?" he asked.

"I will someday."

"I mean for the return trip."

"I didn't."

Buck sighed and moved to the railing. From here, he could see the northern tip of the Ruby range in the west, its flanks dark with pines all the way up to the snow line. "I always liked Montana," he said absently.

"I hate it. I want to go home. Do you even know what a home is? Have you ever had one?"

"I had one, a long time ago."

"With your parents?"

"Uhn-huh."

"But none since?"

"Just what me and Mase made for ourselves," he said, but the words were forced, spoken more out of habit than belief. He still hadn't sorted out his feelings about Mase's involvement in the Chihuahua massacre or his reputation among the women of the International.

"Mase," Dulce snorted derisively. "Has anyone told you the truth about him yet, about what he did to those poor men in Mexico?"

"I've heard," Buck said, turning, frowning. "I didn't know you had, though."

"Everyone has. You're the only one who didn't know because no one wanted to tell you. No one wanted to shatter starry-eyed Buchanan McCready's image of the great Mason Campbell. I swear, you looked up to him like he was some kind of hero."

"I reckon he was to me," Buck replied softly. "Wasn't anyone else coming after me when the Sioux killed my family."

"So you created a hero out of a murderer?"

He stared at her as he would a stranger, unable to comprehend the viciousness of her attack. Then he recognized the intent behind her words and knew it shouldn't have surprised him after all. He'd seen her this way before, with people she despised. Buck turned away sadly. He hadn't wanted it to come to this. His affections for Dulce had always been genuine. Their differences had torn them apart, not circumstance; circumstance had only hastened the inevitable. Keeping his voice low, he repeated: "Do you have everything you need?"

"Yes, *everything.*"

He nodded, satisfied. He'd done what Jock had asked him to do. From here on, Dulce's safety would reside in Robert Haywood's hands, and Buck had no doubt that she would be well looked after. As he started to walk away, a discarded cigarette arched into the street from a dark alley across from the hotel. Its shower of tiny sparks briefly illuminated a tall, lean figure standing just inside the alley's mouth. Reacting instinctively, Buck slammed into Dulce's side, knocking her out of the way just as the sound of a gunshot cleaved the still night.

Dulce cried out loudly as she and Buck tumbled to the floor. Her fall was partially cushioned by Buck's body but he quickly pushed off, scrambling to the balcony's edge just in time to see the tall figure across the street turn tail and run. Palming his Colt, Buck sent two quick rounds after the fleeing bushwhacker, but he knew even before the smoke cleared that he'd missed.

He went back to Dulce's side and knelt beside her. The look of terror in her eyes was only partially veiled by the coppery curls that fell across her face. Buck grabbed her shoulder, squeezing. "Are you hurt? Dulce, are you all right?"

"Let me go!" she screamed, scooting away from him.

"Dammit, Dulce, are you hurt?"

A lamp's pale light appeared behind them and a pistol's muzzle was pressed into the back of Buck's skull. "Get away from her, you brute!"

Buck glanced over his shoulder. Robert Haywood stood above them, a chunky Webley revolver clutched firmly in his right hand, the lamp held high in his left.

"McCready! What in thunder are you doing?"

Buck got to his feet. "Someone took a shot at Dulce. I don't think she's been hit, but she's scared. Look after her, will you?"

"Someone took a shot at her?" Haywood looked stupefied. "Who?"

Buck didn't answer right away. He returned to the edge of the balcony to stare across the street. Then he said: "I'll be damned, I think I might know."

There was no point in exploring the alley where the tall man had lain in wait. Whoever had taken the shot at Dulce—and Buck was convinced now that it was she, not he, who had been the intended target all along—would be gone by now.

Pausing in front of the hotel, he punched the empties from his .44, then fed it fresh rounds. Returning the Colt to its holster, he started up the street in swift, determined strides.

Elmer Poindexter wasn't around when Buck entered the jail, but figures stirring in the deeper gloom of the single cell confirmed that the prisoners were still behind bars. Even in the poor light of a lamp turned low, Buck could see that Fleck and Kelso had been at it again. Both men were bruised and bloodied, and Nick's eyes were nearly swollen shut from his broken nose. Arlen struggled to his feet when Buck approached, draping his arms through the strap-iron door. He grinned expectantly, then made a face and gingerly touched his split lip.

"What happened?" Buck asked.

Arlen's smile returned; this time he ignored the pain. "I don't think Nick is convinced yet that things have changed between us, but he's learning."

"What did you find out?"

"Nothin'. That lawdog's right. If Kelso knew anything, he'd be bragging about it."

Buck gripped the bars. "Tell me that story again, Fleck, about the night Mase was killed."

"Hell, I've already told you that. . . ."

"Tell it again."

Arlen shrugged. "I was standin' outside the Central Pacific depot waitin' for Campbell to come out. . . ."

"But you'd seen him earlier, right? In the International?"

"Yeah, that's where I heard about the Chihuahua massacre."

"After his argument with the big guy who threatened to cut off his ears?"

"No, before that."

Buck's fingers tightened, his knuckles like pale, knobby globes on the strap-iron. "Who was talking about it before the fight?"

"Some fellas at a table behind me. I couldn't see 'em, but I could hear 'em. Thing is, I was keepin' my eye on Campbell and wishin' like hell I wasn't there." He shrugged as if embarrassed. "I reckon I've never been too keen on that kind of work, but I needed the money. . . ."

"Mase," Buck interrupted tersely. "Why were they talking about Mase?"

"Hell, I don't know."

"Was it the same guy who shot him?"

"I told you, McCready, I don't know who shot him. I was keyed up that night like I was gonna bust. I just plain damn didn't pay any attention to who was doin' all the talkin'."

Buck took a deep breath and lowered his hands from the bars. "All right, tell me what happened."

Arlen left out nothing, not the cold desert wind or the briny stink of the Great Salt Lake or the yellow-eyed dog with its matted coat. He described Mase's exit from the saloon and the stranger's unexpected appearance—a tall, lean, unidentifiable presence—materializing from the darkness of the alley like an apparition. Arlen hadn't been able to make out the stranger's features when Mase paused to light his cigarette and then, when the shot rang out and Mase had staggered and fallen, Arlen had fled down the road like a frightened rabbit. . . .

He stopped there and his eyes widened. "What? McCready, what?"

Buck's heart was thumping like a drum as he stalked away from the cell. He'd known the answer was here, just waiting for him to open his eyes and see it.

"Dammit, what is it?" Arlen called, but Buck didn't reply. He didn't even pull the front door closed when he left the jail. Loosening the Colt in its holster, he started down Main toward Carlson's Saloon.

Chapter Thirty-Eight

Buck paused in front of the saloon to remove his jacket. He felt strangely calm as he loosened his Colt in its holster, then pushed through the batwing doors. Carlson's was a long, narrow building with a high ceiling and a plain bar that ran down the left side of the room. Most of the tables near the front were filled with Box K teamsters; most of those in back were unoccupied.

"Buck!" several of the drivers hollered, while others chimed in with cheerful invitations to join them. The long trip was behind them now, and for a while the hard, dangerous work was done. Tonight they could relax and drink and laugh about what only a few days before had nearly beaten them down.

"C'mon and have a drink!" Ray shouted from one of the tables, waving for Buck to join him and Peewee and Joe Perry.

"Have two!" Charlie Bigelow roared from the bar. "Hell, you're payin' for 'em."

The rest of the men laughed at Charlie's joke, but their humor soon died. Buck tossed his jacket on a nearby table, then made his way down the length of the room.

"What's going on, Bucky?" Peewee asked in a hushed voice.

The rear of the saloon, where the light was poorer, the air thicker, was occupied by a solitary individual, slouched over the bar as if trying to avoid attention. He looked up at Buck's approach, a scowl flashing across his face. There was a glass of whiskey on the bar in front of him and he'd just finished rolling a cigarette that he hadn't yet struck a match to. "What do you want, McCready?" he growled.

Buck wrapped his hand around the Colt's grip. "I'm wanting you."

Lyle Mead's eyes narrowed suspiciously. "What for?"

"For killing Mase Campbell and Thad Collins."

There was a murmur of surprise from behind Buck, then a deathly silence. Lyle guffawed. "You getting desperate now that the trip is over?"

"It took me a while to figure it out," Buck admitted. "It was Arlen Fleck who helped me put it together."

"Arlen Fleck doesn't know his ass from a feedbag," Lyle replied scornfully. "Besides, that skinny bastard'd tell you anything you wanted to hear if he thought it'd get him out of jail quicker."

"He heard you talking about Chihuahua in the International earlier that night, then he saw you stop Mase in the street to ask for a light for your cigarette," Buck continued purposefully. "That was the kicker, the thing that's bothered me ever since the first time I talked with Fleck. I just couldn't put my finger on it until he told me the story again tonight. Maybe you've noticed, but there aren't a lot of men out here who smoke cigarettes. Oh, they will. I hear it's a growing fad down in Arizona and New Mexico, and Milo picked up the habit in Kansas from Texas drovers, but right now, along the Montana Road, just about everybody I know who uses tobacco either smokes a pipe or cigar, or chews it. Only you, Milo, and Paddy O'Rourke smoke cigarettes. Paddy's dead and Milo doesn't fit the description of the man who killed Mase. He's not tall enough or skinny enough. But you are. You fit the description perfectly."

"Christ," Ray Jones grunted, his chair scraping roughly across the wooden floor.

"Stay where you are, Ray," Buck snapped without taking his

eyes off Mead. "This is between us."

"Is he the one, Buck?" Charlie asked in an awestruck tone, as if he was looking at a two-headed calf rather than a common killer.

"Yeah, he's the one," Buck said flatly. "You're the one who took a shot at Dulce tonight, too, aren't you?" Buck pressed. "Just like you did the night of the bandit's raid and that night along the Bear River." His eyes dropped to the heels of Lyle's drover's boots, the same kind that had left the print in the soft soil of the Bear. It was all coming together except for one great big hole right in the middle. Why?

Lyle's eyes darted to the rear door, less than half a dozen long strides away. Escape lay just beyond those thin pine planks, but he didn't make a run for it. Like everyone else in the room, he knew he'd never make it.

"You didn't hurt your hand falling off the wood wagon, either," Buck said. "You hurt it that night in the International when the upstairs piano player blew the door apart in your face, after you gunned down Sally Hayes. It was you I saw in the dark above Portneuf Cañon, too, then chased into the thicket."

"You're full of shit, McCready," Lyle said shakily.

"Am I?" Buck replied. "I saw you in the alley tonight. I know it was you who took that shot at Dulce. I saw you toss your cigarette away before you fired. But you missed her, Mead. You failed to kill her the same way you failed to kill Peewee or stop the Box K." He smiled contemptuously. "I'm thinking whoever hired you will be wanting their money back."

A tic jumped in Lyle's cheek and his head snapped back as if he'd been slapped, and in that same instant the wildness fled his eyes and his desire to flee, so evident only moments before, vanished. "Nobody hired me, McCready. I'm an independent, remember? I work for myself."

Lyle's response caught Buck off guard. "Then what did you

have against Mase that you'd kill him for, and what do you have against Dulce Kavanaugh?"

Lyle sneered, beyond feigning innocence now, beyond caring. "I ain't got a damn' thing against that spoiled little bitch. It's her daddy I wanted."

"Jock! You'd kill a woman just to hurt her father?"

Lyle's fingers drifted to the butt of his revolver, sticking out from under his jacket in a cross-draw holster. "You don't have any idea who I am, do you?"

Buck could hear the Box K teamsters shuffling out of the line of fire, bunching up against the far wall, but no one left and no one spoke.

Shaking his head, Buck said: "No, I never heard of you before a month ago."

"Thirty years ago, Mase Campbell and Jock Kavanaugh killed three men in the Chihuahua desert. You've heard of that, haven't you?"

"That was before you or I were even born, Mead."

"Not by much it wasn't," Lyle replied thickly. He eased away from the bar, his fingers closing around his revolver. "Five, maybe six months, but no more than that. Do you know their names, McCready . . . the names of those three men Campbell and Kavanaugh turned loose to their deaths? Don't answer that, goddammit, don't you dare answer it because now you do. Now every son-of-a-bitch in this room knows who they were." Lyle's voice lowered a notch. "It was my father and his brother, my uncle, that they killed. I don't know who the third man was, but he was somebody's son and maybe somebody's father. Not that it would've mattered to Campbell and Kavanaugh. Not with their more-precious-than-God cargo at stake.

"It took me thirty years to find out what happened to my father. The only clue I had was that he'd accepted a job freighting out West somewhere. That's not much for an Ohio boy to go on, but I kept looking, and eventually I learned what'd happened . . . the whole story, McCready, not those fables Campbell and Kavanaugh wanted the world to believe." His laugh was like a plank being ripped in half. "The truth prevails, McCready!" he shouted. "Sooner or later, it always comes back to bite you square on the ass."

"Good, God," Buck breathed. "You killed Mase for a thirty-year-old mistake?"

"I killed Mase because when I told him who I was, then asked if he remembered Samuel Mead . . . do you know what he said? Do you know what that worthless bastard said?"

Buck shook his head, mesmerized by the power of Lyle's story.

"He said . . . 'Who?' Lyle drew in a ragged breath. "That was his response . . . Who? He killed my father and uncle and took away my mother's life, caused her to die of old age before she was thirty-five, and that son-of-a-bitch couldn't even remember their names." Lyle laughed again, not loud or crazy, but like a man trying to expunge something darkly smothering within himself, to make room for air to breathe, for his heart to pump. "Yeah, I killed Mason Campbell," he said softly. "But death was too easy for him, and I swore it wouldn't be that easy for Jock Kavanaugh. I swore I'd cut a hole in his soul as big as the one he put in my mother's."

"Lordy," someone breathed, but Buck didn't look around to see who it was. He couldn't tear his gaze away from the anguish and anger on Lyle's face.

"Kavanaugh's already lost his wife, and his hip is shattered, his health failing, but he's still got a daughter, the apple of his eye, and he's still got what he worked a lifetime to build on the sweat and blood of others . . . the Box K. I'd have settled for destroying either one as long as Kavanaugh eventually knew why I took it away from him, but maybe this'll work just as well . . . kill the son-in-law before he even gets a chance to enjoy the honeymoon."

He was wrong on that account, Buck knew, but Lyle Mead had passed the point of reason. His rage at an injustice that had occurred before his birth, that he'd witnessed in his mother's face every day of his youth, had created a monster logic could never slay.

Lyle's thumb stretched for the hammer on his pistol but Buck had one more question. "Why Sally Hayes? What did she have to do with it?"

Lyle hesitated, momentarily distracted by the direction of Buck inquiry. Frowning, he said: "She saw me, she knew my face."

It made sense. One of the few things that did. Buck didn't have all the answers he wanted, but he knew now that he probably never would. It was clear that Lyle was finished talking. "You won't escape, Mead," Buck said. "Even if you kill me, you won't escape."

"What the hell do I care?" Lyle said distantly, starting his draw.

Buck's fingers tightened on the Colt's walnut grip, but time seemed abruptly to slow down and his limbs moved as if weighted with lead. He pulled desperately at his revolver but Lyle's old cap-and-ball Remington was already sliding free of its holster, its muzzle coming up like a cannon's bore. Buck was sure he was going to die. He saw no way around it. Then the Colt bucked hard in his hand and powder smoke reached out to envelop Lyle's features just as Lyle's revolver belched its own smoke and thunder.

The two thick, gray-white clouds merged even as the sound of nearly identical blasts smacked Buck sharply in the face. The percussion from the shots extinguished several nearby lamps, plunging the rear of the saloon into even deeper shadow. Buck saw Lyle stagger backward, then drop to his knees. His mouth opened as if to voice a protest but no words came. Then he tipped forward like a felled tree, the Remington clattering across the floor.

Buck sucked in a deep breath and nearly choked on the sulphurous fumes of spent gunpowder. Coughing hoarsely, he backed out of the slowly spinning cloud. The Colt hung limply in his right hand and his chest heaved.

"Buck!" Hands grabbed him, pulled him around. *"Buck!"*

He blinked and saw Peewee standing in front of him. Ray and Joe and Milo were behind him. "Are you all right?" Peewee asked. "Are you hit, boy?"

Buck shook his head as if to clear it, then shrugged free of Peewee's grasp. He holstered his sidearm and headed for the batwing doors, but Peewee caught him and guided him to the bar.

"Come on, Buck," Peewee said gently. "Let's have a drink while we wait for the sheriff."

Buck nodded wearily. "I could use a drink," he said.

It was chilly enough the next morning that Buck could see his breath as he crawled out of the back of the mess wagon. Even so, he knew the day would be a warm one; the air already had that feel to it. By the time the big Box K freighters were unloaded that afternoon, the men would be sweating and tired, most of them thinking only of the cool refreshments waiting for them at Carlson's.

Buck was strapping his bedroll behind the cantle of Zeke's saddle when he saw Milo saunter down from the warehouse. Milo's shirt tail was out and he was hatless, his wavy brown hair tousled from sleep. He eyed the bulky saddlebags and the weather-stained canvas war bag behind the saddle, the heavy coat strapped over the pommel where it would be easy to reach in case of bad weather, and the Remington rifle that poked up from its off-side scabbard like a dead branch. Mase's bullwhip was tucked under the coat, nearly hidden from view. "Taking a ride?" Milo asked.

Buck reached inside the Studebaker to retrieve a leather folder that he handed to the ramrod. "There's a key inside that opens the office. That's that box inside the mess wagon where we keep records and the journal. . . ."

"I know what an office is."

"Yeah, I reckon you do. I'm making you wagon boss, Milo, if you want the job."

"What are you going to do?"

Buck shrugged and looked away. "I'm not going back to Corinne, at least not for a while. A long time ago, I had family in Oregon, my mother's sister. Finding her will be a long shot, but I think I'll try."

Milo didn't question Buck's reasoning. An orphan himself, he understood the importance of family, the sense of identity that came with that kind of connection. Buck had lost that feeling of kinship with Mase; it only made sense that he'd want to reëstablish it elsewhere. "I wish you luck," Milo said with genuine friendship. "Does anyone else know?"

"Not yet. Tell 'em for me, will you?"

"Dulce, too?"

Buck pulled his reins loose from the mess wagon's rear wheel and climbed into the saddle. "I reckon Dulce and I have said everything we need to say. Tell the boys I'll be back someday."

"They'll want to know when."

"I wouldn't know what to tell them," he said, evening his reins along Zeke's neck. "Jock can take payment for this mule out of whatever wages I have coming," he added. "I'll let him know where he can forward what's left by mail. There's a letter of recommendation in that folder for Jock, too. I'm suggesting he keep you on full time as captain. I also asked him to help Arlen Fleck as much as he can." He smiled fleetingly, picturing the look on Jock's face when he read that. "I reckon you can figure out the rest by yourself."

Milo stepped forward and they shook hands. "Watch yourself, boss . . . Buck, and thanks for taking a chance on a Kansas boy."

"You keep those long hitches rolling," Buck replied, smiling as he tapped Zeke's ribs with his heels.

The sun was just coming up as Buck rode out of Virginia City. He was heading west toward Twin Bridges, where he intended to pick up the Deer Lodge Road that would eventually take him to Oregon.

As the warming rays of the sun touched his shoulders, he lifted the mule to an easy lope. It felt good to be on his own again, free of the town and the Box K. Free, too, of a past he no longer felt a part of. The future lay wide open before him. He was eager to see what it held.

ABOUT THE AUTHOR

Michael Zimmer grew up on a small Colorado horse ranch, and began to break and train horses for spending money while still in high school. An American history enthusiast from a very early age, he has done extensive research on the Old West. His personal library contains over 2,000 volumes covering that area west of the Mississippi from the late 1700s to the early decades of the 20th Century. In addition to perusing first-hand accounts from the period, Zimmer is also a firm believer in field interpretation. He's made it a point to master many of the skills used by our forefathers, and can start a campfire with flint and steel, gather, prepare, and survive on natural foods found in the wilderness, and has built and slept in shelters as diverse as bark lodges and snow caves. He owns and shoots a number of Old West firearms, and has done horseback treks using 19th Century tack, gear, and guidelines. Zimmer's Western novels have been praised by *Library Journal* and *Booklist,* as well as other Western writers. Jory Sherman, author of *Grass Kingdom,* writes: "He [Zimmer] takes you back in time to an exciting era in U.S. history so vividly that the reader will feel as if he has been over the old trails, trapped the shining streams, and gazed in wonder at the awesome grandeur of the Rocky Mountains. Here is a writer to welcome into the ranks of the very best novelists of today or anytime in the history of literature." And Richard Wheeler, author of *Goldfield,* has said of Zimmer's fourth novel, *Fandango* (1996): "One of the best mountain man novels ever written."

Zimmer lives in Utah with his wife, Vanessa, and two dogs. His website is www.michael-zimmer.com. His next Five Star Western will be *City of Rocks*.